ITALIAN LESSONS

Italian Lessons
Copyright © 2021 by Isabetta Andolini

Printed in the United States of America

Luminare Press
442 Charnelton St.
Eugene, OR 97401
www.luminarepress.com

LCCN: 2021910520
ISBN: 978-1-64388-675-6

ITALIAN LESSONS

A novel

Isabetta Andolini

LUMINARE PRESS
WWW.LUMINAREPRESS.COM

To my mamma, for introducing me to Auntie Mame. 'Live, live, live.' And to my papa bear, whose love notes follow me to every new address, always encouraging me to go for the gusto.

*"Quando ci sentiamo affranti e deboli,
tutto ciò che dobbiamo fare è aspettare. La primavera
torna, le nevi dell'inverno si sciolgono e la loro
acqua ci infonde nuova energia."*

—PAOLO COELHO

LOMBARDIA

Lago di Como

Erbusco

Milano

LIGURIA

Camogli

Santa Margherita Ligure

Paraggi

LAZIO

Roma

ITALIA

1 - VALLE D'AOSTA   11 - MARCHE
2 - PIEMONTE   12 - LAZIO
3 - LOMBARDIA   13 - ABRUZZO
4 - TRENTINO ALTO ADIGE   14 - MOLISE
5 - FRIULI VENEZIA GIULIA   15 - CAMPANIA
6 - VENETO   16 - BASILICATA
7 - EMILIA-ROMAGNA   17 - PUGLIA
8 - LIGURIA   18 - CALABRIA
9 - TOSCANA   19 - SICILIA
10 - UMBRIA   20 - SARDEGNA

MILANO

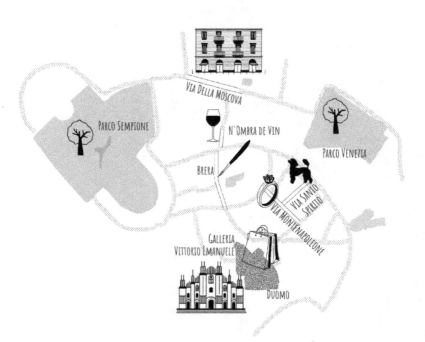

Via Della Moscova

Parco Sempione

N'Ombra de Vin

Parco Venezia

Brera

Via Santo Spirito

Via Montenapoleone

Galleria
Vittorio Emanuele

Duomo

NEW YORK

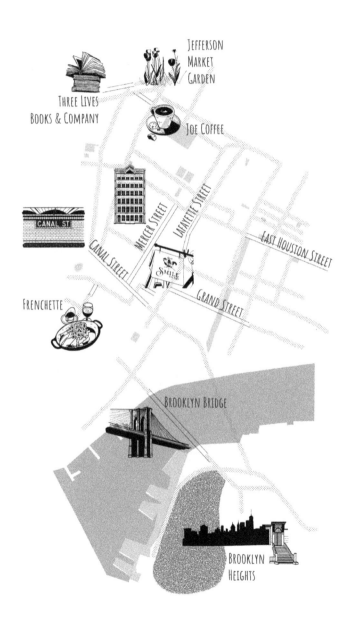

Three Lives
Books & Company

Jefferson
Market
Garden

Joe Coffee

Mercer Street

Lafayette Street

Canal St

Canal Street

East Houston Street

Grand Street

SMILE

Frenchette

Brooklyn Bridge

Brooklyn
Heights

Prologue

NEW YORK, NEW YORK

2019

I don't know why, but you are stuck in my head. You got stuck there when we met, when I heard your voice, your accent, I think. And you looked me in the eye, diagonally from across the high-top table, and I knew that I needed to talk to you before you left but I didn't know how, without seeming strange. You had finished your chicken. There was nothing but remains in front of you, and you had already forgotten that it was ever there to begin with.

Maybe it's that you were, and always have been, a mystery. I don't know you at all- that's how you want it; I assume. I don't know how you are, what you act like with other people, in certain situations, what you've been through, who you've been through. Maybe that's all it is. Chemistry + Nothing to tang it up= Chemistry.

So here I am—knotted up in something. It's unknown territory for me, and I don't know how it happened. I feel submerged, and I am frustrated. I don't know how to act, because I don't know you, and I don't know what you're up to, what your angle is, and you never say what you mean, in classic English fashion, you imply things but never say them, and I am left guessing at your vagueness. I don't know what you think of me or of this or if you feel anything at all, because you've never actually said. So I am tangled up and I can't get out, and I so badly wish you had finished your chicken sooner, and that you had already been done and gone, and that I wouldn't have had to hear your voice and meet your penetrating eyes, looking at me diagonally across the high top table.

But, strangely enough, if you had asked me again, what do I want to feel... Well, I would have said this— this strange, foreign feeling that shakes me upside down. You see, the truth is, I actually love this feeling. And if you had asked me again, what do I want...I would have said... you. Because, in this moment of bravery, I might as well come out with it—I find myself...oh crap. Nicky—...

She stopped typing and thought about that chat. She had read his question so many times, it was practically imprinted in her peripheral vision.

Nick: What do you want to feel?

Margherita: It doesn't matter.

Nick: It does. What do you want to feel?
Nick: What do you want?
Nick: Selfishly.

Margherita: It doesn't matter what I want.

Nick: You have more interest in being aloof than in leveling with me. You won't level with me.

What am I doing, she thought. She closed her iPad and got back into bed.

2016

MARGHERITA HAD BEEN trotting behind Elisio all day, from one development meeting to another. She was growing accustomed to her new boss's unfathomably high energy, his moments of quiet reflection, his sudden changes of plan, his momentous decisions and doses of professional wisdom—even the unexpected tests of her knowledge. She was still in the newbie phase, but she knew that Elisio liked her to interject to underline something he had said—but not too much—and provide just enough additional input to prove her presence worthy.

It started to rain; a sudden summer storm, and they ducked into Pasticceria Marchesi for an afternoon green juice. They seated themselves at a table in the back, just next to the swinging door that led to the gorgeous, sleek bathrooms—the kind that always left people dumbfounded as to how to turn on the sink, but design trumped function in Milan. Margherita ordered her juice with no fruit (the Italians were still very green on the green juice front), and Elisio copied her.

Together they aimed to incorporate several American cultural habits into a new hotel property for the Leonetti

Hotel Group. The property was located within a centuries-old seminary, the piazza of which hadn't been touched in at least one hundred years, and the plan was nothing less than a total "re-imagination" of the space. The ground floor would have a Michelin Star restaurant, a caffè, a bistro, three or four retail shops, an upscale flower market, a spa, and a world class fitness center. The space itself would be booked year round with events, including exhibits during the Salone del Mobile—the city's most prominent furniture and design fair—fashion shows, piano and opera performances, and private affairs as well. Margherita had organized a meeting with the CEO of Seed, the most high-end fitness company in the U.S. (and now the UK as well). That evening, Margherita would meet the two most highly-regarded interior designers in Italy.

"Do not-" Elisio wagged a finger at her, laughing nonsensically as he often did, "do not fall in love with Paolo. Everyone does," he said, in his heavy northern Italian accent, which was tinged with something Germanic.

She rolled her eyes. How soft and cliché did he think she was? She never fell in love with anyone. How silly. Infatuation, yes. Love? How absurd. Even her parents had joked about it for years. Once in a while she would call them after meeting someone dreamy, enraptured in a crush, and tell them she had found her husband. "Which one?" they would ask and laugh.

Anyway, Paolo sounded like a total sleaze ball.

"I think of you as my daughter, kind of." Elisio giggled a little, as was his way, fluctuating between lightness and seriousness. "And I need you to listen to me." He pointed his finger for emphasis, suddenly serious again.

She nodded to appease him but thought—

How ridiculous. I am not a cliché Americana,
But then there was Paolo.
Oh good lord, there was Paolo.

LIGURIA

2016

SUMMER IN ITALY was synonymous with the sea. Romans headed to Sperlonga, la Costiera Amalfitana, or Ponza. Florentines popped up at Tuscan coastal towns such as Forte dei Marmi, Pietrasanta, or perhaps Punta Ala and Castiglione della Pescaia. The Milanese shot off to their houses in Liguria or Capalbio. Criss-crossing occurred occasionally, depending on the family lineage.

The days of inland explorations were over, shutters remained closed throughout the day to keep out the sun, and everyone made a mad dash for the sea. In those first weeks of July, when summer was fresh and there was everything to look forward to, when the heat received a warm welcome and the flowers were not yet dry, the beaches not yet filled and the traffic not yet exasperating, Margherita steered a rented convertible toward a pastel colored beach town just south of Portofino. The weekdays proved much more idyllic, with no pressure to secure a beach spot in the early morning sun and no reservation necessary at the still shiny Langosteria Paraggi.

The winding, single-lane highway was a breeze on a Monday morning, and she felt like the only person en route to one of the Italian Riviera's most legendary ports—for yachts, not cargo, that is. She was looking forward to seeing Benjamin, her half-brother, who was visiting from London. For some reason, he had decided to devote a few days of his precious vacation to see the sister with whom she barely attempted to stay in touch. It shocked Margherita that he even remembered she was living in Milan.

Benjamin, who was incredibly successful in investment banking, had reserved his sister a room at a lovely, if not aged, hotel in Camogli. He chose it for its ideal location at the tip of the seaside town, which was gifted with a sense of seclusion and peace above the Ligurian sea. With a private rock beach and a horizon-wide sea view, her plans to freshen up and head out for a sunset aperitivo were met with summer laze and rightly challenged by the beckoning views. And so, within moments of arrival, she found herself in an evening sun haze, glued to the chaise lounges and the glittering sea, dozing in and out as the waves lapped, the last windsurfer made his way home, and the sky morphed from an azure blue to shades of pastel pink.

Her phone pinged.

She opened her eyes to the sound of a squawking black bird overhead and grappled for her phone in her bag.

Benjamin: Have to jump on a call. I'll meet you there.

Classic Benjamin, to text her at the last minute. How many times had she arranged to meet him for lunch or dinner when he visited New York, and as soon as she arrived at the restaurant, he would text to say he could no longer make it? She could not keep track. He was several years older, and grew up mostly with his father, in Athens. Whenever he visited, it was clear that he was there to spend time with their mother, Francine; he hardly gave Margherita any notice at all. Francine and Benjamin would talk finance, or happenings in London, where their mother kept an apartment, and Margherita would be sidelined. She thought of her brother like a Greek God—charming when he wanted to be, yet also arbitrary, and distant—and had always idolized him accordingly.

He made a reservation at a tiny restaurant at the top of the hill overlooking Santa Margherita Ligure. There were no streetlights on the narrow road heading up, and Margherita drove carefully, aware of the precipice. She had to parallel park on the cliff, and in classic Italian fashion, there were no safety barriers to mark the ragged edge.

Inside, the restaurant was cozy and quiet; the owners gruff and uninviting, the decor tchotchke and floral. She sat on the screened porch overlooking the thousand lights below, reminiscent of the hills of Los Angeles, until Benjamin arrived, his olive green skin always in contrast to her fairness, his liquid gold eyes a perfect replicate of their mother's, his tall, muscular figure resembling his father's Greek stature. A small plate of focaccia and farinata was placed on the table upon being seated, followed by short wine glasses, and a glass bottle of water from which to help themselves. They ordered an antipasto del marinaio, stuffed moscardini, trofie with Ligurian pesto, and asked sweetly for more of the divine focaccia.

"Your dad would love this," Benjamin said, looking around at the little room, as the Italians around them quietly enjoyed a mid-week dinner out. Benjamin had spent his first twelve years living with Margherita's parents, Francine and Tommaso. Although there was an unacknowledged barrier between Benjamin and Tommaso, there was also mutual love and affection. "He'd be 'baking' every day if he were here this week."

Margherita nodded. *Baking was* her father's word for taking in the sun. When asked if he was wearing SPF, he would take a little in his finger like a scared child and dab it on his face as if it were something highly dubious. She wished he would visit her. They could visit Zoagli, the village where his grandmother Rosa was from, relax at the beach and enjoy the food he grew up eating. He would buy himself a few beautiful cashmere sweaters and maybe (most definitely) flirt with the Italian women. Tommaso was too focused on Francine to make the trip, but Margherita often tempted him with photos of all of the above.

"I spoke to him last week. He never complains about any of it. He just goes to work every day as if nothing is abnormal," Benjamin said as the restaurant owner finally arrived with the glass of vermentino she had ordered.

Margherita smiled at the owner, a plump woman with a vast bosom who seemed to be in her 60s. Exactly the type who disliked stupidly smiling Americans.

"I think he's almost relieved that you're here. But then mum complains about it nonstop. Poor guy. She's spent too much time away from work this year. She needs to get back into it."

"I know. I wish she would. I can't speak to her without her going down the long list of Italy complaints."

"Well, just don't marry an Italian. She'll flip. And your dad would be heartbroken," Benjamin said, as he took a bite of focaccia. "Mm, that's lovely."

Margherita raised her eyebrows and nodded knowingly. "Not to worry."

"How's the dating, by the way? Met anyone *interessante?*"

Margherita's entire demeanor changed. Suddenly she was straight-backed and fresh. "Ohhh!" Her eyes grew wide. She looked at the ceiling. "I have. Very charming. Too sexy."

"How old is he?" Benjamin asked with his mouth full of focaccia.

Margherita dismissed him with a flick of her hand. "Oh, shush."

Benjamin nodded knowingly.

"By the way, I ran into Sander a few weeks ago. He works at a company we're buying and was in the due diligence meeting. He recognized me—I had no idea who he was."

Margherita stiffened at the mention of Sander.

"Oh?" She said, looking around the restaurant.

"Apparently he's engaged. A girl he met at LSE. Seems to be getting along quite well."

Margherita felt a pin in her chest. She tried not to visibly react.

"I don't even want to know. I don't care anymore. I haven't thought about him in ages."

"Okay. Shall put him in the bin, then. Besides, he was a total pompous ass. You dodged a bullet."

"Yup, I know."

The next morning, Margherita woke early to go for a sunrise run. Camogli was quiet, save for a few construction workers and fishermen on the docks. The pasticceria *bakery* had not yet opened, and the sun began to warm up the pastel-colored buildings as she ran the length of the tiny village. She stopped for a caffe as soon as she spied an open door and heard the unmistakable sound of an espresso cup on a saucer plate.

"Un caffe, per favore," she asked the man behind the bar.

"Stai correndo? *You're running?* Brava," he said, placing her espresso on a saucer. She nodded. Americans had a reputation for constant and excessive exercising.

Margherita quietly sipped her hot espresso from the scalding hot cup as a gentleman entered and greeted the man behind the bar. The barman handed the man a plain focaccia along with his espresso. In a tiny Ligurian beach town, the day began with a focaccia, perhaps with rosemary, olives, or onions, but usually just a simple oil-coated one with the first caffe. It was customary to pack a few for the beach, and Margherita reminded herself to return to the bread baker after breakfast; she did not want Benjamin to miss the charming traditions of their little Ligurian adventure. She was so proud of her Italy, of its traditions and its people and its daily life. She would never grow out of trying to impress her big brother.

That afternoon, they took the ferry to San Fruttuoso, reachable only by boat (row or speed, though the latter was faster). She wanted to visit one of her favorite trattorias hidden behind the humble pebbled beach, already dotted with colorful ombrellone *beach umbrellas* by mid morning. Babbo, the owner, sat on the deck, debearding mussels in a bucket, while his son set up the lunch tables on the simple, shaded veranda. It was shaped like a narrow rhombus, overlooking the entrance to the ancient abbey.

Bombolone-high children ran around the piazza a few feet below them while Babbo's son brought out the still-steaming pan of spaghetti al mare, and placed it on the table next to Margherita, along with a wooden spoon. There was just the sound of a buzzing bee, the children, and the sauce being encouraged from the pan to the plate.

"So you never told me about the man...?" Benjamin asked.

Margherita shrugged.

"How old is he exactly?" Benjamin asked, as they made room for the plates Babbo's son passed to them, adorned with spaghetti and the scent of the sea.

"Older. Ahhh.... che buono!" She inhaled the dish's scent with its lemony, parsley-inflected, octopus-filled splendor.

"Older than your dad?"

Margherita rolled her eyes and smiled kindly at Babbo's son.

2016

MARGHERITA HAD BEEN late to the business dinner. Elisio had asked her to experience each of the five-star hotels in Milan for research, and her friend Camilla, with her PR prowess, had comped her a gorgeous room with a swanky black marbled bathroom in Via Andegari. Just as the reservation was set to begin and the second summer storm of the day cracked the sky, she left the hotel and got into a cab. She made it to the restaurant twenty-five minutes late.

Paolo sat facing the entrance, and he looked up right away when she entered. His eyes were so blue, they were almost translucent. He stood, all six feet three inches of him, and greeted her with two kisses on the cheeks and a god-like baritone voice that was soft, low, and almost hard to hear. He pulled her chair out for her. He wore a white button-down shirt with the first few buttons undone, and his sun-blonde wavy hair was long enough to run fingers through. He calmly, discreetly oozed something chemical and addictive without meaning to; he was walking danger. When he looked at her, she felt hot. His sea-blue eyes seemed to have no peripheral vision, and he held her gaze in a way she had rarely experienced, without distraction.

He showed kindness and patience when she tripped on an Italian word, and he made suggestions to her from the menu, reading her his favorites. He was inquisitive, but not overly so, and they shared innocent conversation between the two of them. They discovered they both liked to run for an hour each morning, and they talked about the lack of upscale fitness centers in Milan, in Italy in general. While the group discussed the new property, Paolo admired the beautiful photos she had taken that day during the site visit. He held her phone in his large, tan hand, scrolling through her shots of the interior courtyard from the second-floor balcony.

"You have a brilliant eye," he said.

Paolo draped his long arm over the back of her chair, leaning in slightly and at an angle while listening to the men across the table. To her, their unspoken intimacy felt fluorescent in the dark restaurant. He picked up her shawl when it fell to the floor.

"La scialle." He raised it, searching her face for her eyes. He draped the shawl on the back of her chair with care, as if he were tenderly brushing her hair from one shoulder to behind her back. He watched her as she got up to go to the ladies' room, his eyes following her every step until she was out of sight.

He told her about his favorite restaurant, the same one that she had been dying to visit. He insinuated that they would go the following week, and nonchalantly offered to secure her a room at one of the hotels he had designed. It was indeed one on Elisio's list for her to experience. Oh, it was no big deal at all. His pleasure, he said, in Italian, as he did not speak English.

The subject of the upcoming weekend arose. Elisio

mentioned going north to Ortisei, where his family owned a mountain house. Margherita learned Paolo went to the beach or the mountains on the weekends; he had a home in each.

"Magic July," the three gentlemen had chorused. Magic July, Margherita learned, was when the wives took the kids away for the month, and during the five workdays each week, the men enjoyed blissfully quiet days at home to themselves.

"Quando il gatto non c'è i topi ballano," Elisio said with a childish grin.

Margherita rolled her eyes at the men.

"How many kids do you have?" she asked Paolo.

"Four," he said with a loving smile, and he showed her a few photos of his eldest daughter, twin boys, and youngest son. He was smitten with his kids, but he loved his quiet July days at home. No one wanted anything from him for a whole month. He was free.

The next morning, walking down the stairs from the office on Via Santo Spirito to the site, Elisio congratulated Margherita on passing one of his tests.

"Paolo and Matteo were very impressed. Brava. You made me proud."

"Oh, that's good," Margherita said with a slight internal eye roll.

"Paolo asked if we were an item. I said NO, I am happily married, thank you very much," Elisio added with amusement. He looked at Margherita with an upturned mouth and active eyes. She did not know what to say. She assumed Elisio was joking, but she'd noticed that Italians had a different view on what was considered work-appropriate conversation, especially between superior and subordinate.

That afternoon, she received a WhatsApp from a new number with a very sexy, handsome man in the profile photo.

> **Paolo:** Ciao Margherita. È stato un piacere ieri sera. Fammi sapere quando ti va per Langosteria. Anche l'albergo. Organizzo tutto io. Bacio. *It was a pleasure to meet you last night. Let me know when you feel like going to Langosteria. And the hotel too. I'll organize everything. Kiss.*

When had she given him her number? He must have found it on her phone when he was looking at her photos.

Was he flirting? Or just being polite in Italian form? Was there a difference?

> **Margherita:** Grazie Paolo- un piacere anche per me. Si certo- ti faccio sapere! *Thanks Paolo, it was a pleasure, and yes of course, I'll let you know.*

She would not give in too easily. She would give it a few days, but that was as much patience as she could muster.

MILANO, LOMBARDIA

2016

PAOLO: A CHE ora arrivi? *What time do you get here?* Sono qui per un meeting. Forse ci incrociamo :) *I am here for a meeting. Maybe we will cross paths.*

> **Margherita:** I'm walking in now.
>
> **Paolo:** Come up to the roof

Margherita checked into the elaborately glitzy hotel and rolled her suitcase toward the elevator, which was located at the end of a long hallway lined with mirrors. It made her feel like she was being watched, although the only person watching her was her own reflection. The thought of Paolo being in the same building as her at that moment sent her heart into uncontrollable palpitations. It had been one week since their dinner at Langosteria in the Galleria. Ever since, her thoughts had been inundated with Paolo's low, soft voice, his Joaquin Phoenix eyes, his tall, athletic figure.

So far, she hadn't said a word to anyone about her new friend, and the secret was about to explode inside of her, bubbling up from her tummy to the irises in her eyes. As much as it stirred the nerves in her belly, Margherita liked the secrecy. It was a sensation she knew all too well. The fantasies were flowing already, and she daydreamed to the point of distraction at work. Even as a girl of eight or nine or ten, she loved drama, secrecy, and passion. She had always been a voracious reader and loved a good romance the most. She flew through two or three books at a time and could always count on receiving a stack more from her mother.

She loved the recollections of real-life romance too, and never forgot the stories she heard from her grandfather about his mother Rosa. At age fourteen, Rosa was married off to a thirty-nine-year-old man. The next year, at fifteen, Rosa met Margherita's great-grandfather and fell in love with him; they had to keep their love a secret until Rosa and Giovanni left together for New York, to start a new life. To Margherita, nothing sounded more exciting than a story like this, dotted with risk and adventure.

Paolo picked her up on his moto after soccer practice, and when they arrived at the restaurant, she learned he had invited two friends. In her eyes, this was risky behavior, since Taddeo and Carlo knew Paolo's wife; they had all been best friends since they were young. She questioned Paolo's intentions; was she simply a friend?

She and Paolo sat on the same side of a beautiful, velvet banquette—typically stylish for Milano—and she carried on flawlessly in Italian with Taddeo and Carlo. She had observed that lifelong friendships like this were typical among Italians. To her mind, Americans were transient in their friendships, so unreliable, constantly replacing one another. Her life was undeniably void of a friendship as meaningful as the ones she made in Italy.

Paolo told Taddeo and Carlo how impressed he had been with her when they met, how infrequently Elisio invited a protégée into his inner circle, how ambitious she was, and how much she was going to contribute to the new Hotel Leon Milan. They discussed business in New York compared to major European cities (Carlo ran a fashion brand that was in stores all over the world) and American hospitals versus Italian hospitals (Taddeo was an orthopedic surgeon). They talked about everyone's August plans. Carlo and his family had rented a house on the southern coast of Portugal. Taddeo planned to go to the small Ligurian town where he spent summers as a child, the same one that Paolo and Carlo also went to.

Margherita had no plans. The friends she had made in Italy in the past few months were wonderful, but their Augusts were already booked. Camilla and her husband would spend half of their vacation in the Caribbean and half in New York, where Camilla grew up, coincidentally, only a few blocks away from Margherita. Chiara, a university professor at NYU's campus outside Florence, was also going to New York for a few weeks. Sandra was mostly staying in Rome except for one week on the Aeolian Islands (by herself; she didn't like to travel with friends). Lucas was going to Greece with his current boyfriend. Margherita had not realized until the start of the summer how much Milan, Florence, and Rome emptied during that eighth month.

"Go to Alassio with Taddeo. He would love the company," Carlo said to her. She felt put on the spot and imagined how Taddeo must have felt. He was the only unmarried one out of the three. He seemed like a great guy, a little nostalgic, still very handsome for his forty-eight years, and maybe just a little bored and lonely. He already had a full head of white hair and kind eyes.

"Si, certo. Per me sarebbe un piacere," Taddeo said. *Of course. It would be a pleasure.*

"Honestly, it would be nice. Don't feel uncomfortable. We have friends visit us in Alassio all the time," Paolo said to her, just to her, into her ear from his seat next to her, where their legs touched underneath the table.

"But your parents, they will not visit you in August?" Carlo asked. All three men waited for an answer.

The question of her parents was a popular one with the Italians. It was not a very commonplace event for a young, single American woman to move to their country, so far from her parents, with no family nearby. La famiglia was their core, their center point around which their entire world tightly turned.

"No, they'll come another time," she put the subject to rest with a plausible, uncontroversial white lie. She had been asking her parents to visit; she wasn't sure they ever would.

By the end of the dinner, everyone clearly adored her, and she was proud of herself for her advanced, witty Italian conversation. As she wondered where the rest of the evening with Paolo might lead, she could feel each one of her thousands of nerve-endings.

After rooftop drinks at Ceresio 7, Paolo took her back to her hotel on his moto. The city was quiet, the breeze delicious in the July evening. They sat outside talking, delaying something…what, she was not sure.

"I feel like I spend more time in hotels lately than in my apartment," she joked, looking up at the facade of the building.

"You will like this one," he said warmly.

"How's the breakfast? That's the best part."

"I've never tried it. You know Italians don't care about breakfast."

"Ohhh…I dream of it," she said, her eyes widening, her face alight. "I *love* breakfast."

He smiled at her. "How is it possible that you are single?"

She rolled her eyes. "Italians love to be in relationships. After three dates, suddenly it's a relationship."

His eyes floated all over her face. She looked away and focused her attention on her hands, turning her grandmother's serpent ring on her middle finger round and round.

He gently placed his forefinger on the serpent's head when it faced the night sky.

"And you don't? Love relationships?" He asked, in a quiet, tender voice, as he studied her ring.

She shrugged. "I don't know. I guess I just don't *need* one. I'm not desperate for company. If I want to go to Rome for the day, I will go by myself. If I want to have a lovely little Saturday, I can figure out how to do that on my own."

He smiled and nodded. "You intimidate men. You are beautiful and smart and unafraid to be alone. It probably scares them away," he said with a playful smile.

She waved her hand in the air, dismissively. "Maybe I like a little bit of freedom."

"You haven't found the one you want to share it with," he said in a low voice.

"Does that really happen?" she asked, as she spun the ring around again.

There was a silence, a beat unfilled. She leaned into the bench and threw her head back to look at the sky.

"I'm not tired," she blurted. It was two a.m. "I feel like watching a movie. I haven't watched a movie in so long."

He regarded her with pursed lips and wicked blue eyes. In her mind, it was a little daydream momentarily come to life.

"Allora, andiamo a casa mia?" *So, let's go to my place?* He breathed. He was hesitant, but she felt he knew exactly what he was doing. His house would be empty; his wife and kids were in the mountains. He had practice; he was seasoned.

She agreed with a growing pitter-patter of excitement in her chest, like an ignition slowly starting with loud, rapid bursts of fire. Had she known all along that this would happen, or had she been merely hoping? She craved the excitement; she had contemplated no other element of it—not the infidelity, his family, her reputation, her own feelings about all of it... She lived only in the unfolding plot, with its drama and the tingling of her nerves.

She had so much energy inside of her, it was like a fire. This feeling was the same one she had felt since moving to Italy; that she was finally going to *live*. No more nights in a tiny Greenwich Village apartment, alternating between reading and looking forlornly out the window at the fire escape. No more nights in San Francisco watching Antonioni films and feeling exhausted by her mother's illness. She had always felt alone, never able to find her people, her niche, until now. In Italy she finally had found her place. Italy agreed with her; it seemed to match her personality. She felt attached to it as one feels attached to a person. She and Italy were entwined. Italy was the relationship she had always observed from afar, that she had never experienced firsthand—the friend that she had always wanted; the lover she had never had.

They got back on the moto, and the breeze she felt grazing her bare legs was visceral. She smoothed one hand along the top of her thigh, the other hand held Paolo's chest right below his ribs. He had placed it there, his large hand over hers. When they arrived, he was eager to show her his terrace with what seemed a jungle of plants, flowers, vegetables, and fruit trees. She shared his affection for his precious plants; gardening was a pastime she had enjoyed with her green-thumbed father. In that moment, her fantasy gave legs to another fantasy, likely encouraged by the evening's alcohol…she felt that maybe Paolo was to be her great love. She let the fantasy sit in the room with them, swirling around her already-spinning head.

They put on a movie, but within ten minutes, Paolo had fallen asleep with his mouth open. She looked around the room; there were framed photos of his children, along with a photo of him and his pretty wife slicing into their cake on their wedding day. It was clear he had married her years after the birth of their twins. Margherita wondered why.

Eventually at three a.m., with great effort, they rose from the sofa and made their way upstairs.

"Where should I sleep?" she asked. Nothing had actually *happened* yet, and she did not want to assume that it would. She had not yet crossed a physical line, and she could feel the drumbeat increasing in strength inside herself.

"No, dai, dormi con me," *No, come, sleep here with me.* He said nonchalantly. Everything so nonchalant. He gave her a t-shirt, and they climbed into his bed, each on a side. Hers, she assumed, belonged to his wife. There was something very not right about that moment—lying where his wife lay every night—but she was too outside of herself to put a stop to it.

He leaned over to give her a kiss goodnight. "Buonanotte."

"Buonanotte." She wondered if that was it, that was really it. He gave her a second kiss, an innocent kiss not even on the lips, but to the side of her mouth. She lingered, moved a centimeter closer. The end of it. The beginning of it. He swooped, she dived, and there they went.

The next morning, when Margherita returned to her apartment, she realized one of her earrings was missing.

"Damn," she said to herself, wondering if it might have fallen out on his wife's side of the bed.

As the day went on, and her hangover, empty stomach, and lack of sleep began to mess with her emotions, she felt the guilt creep in. She had always tested the boundaries, had played a game or two just for the rush, but she had never acted on it quite so blatantly. She thought about her earring on the floor beneath Paolo's wife's pillow. There was no way anyone could trace it back to her, but in her own mind, she felt it gave her away entirely.

She paced the office's internal courtyard.

Margherita: Thank you again for dinner last night
Margherita: Can you do me a favor and see if I dropped my earring in your bedroom?

Paolo: you're sweet
Paolo: nooo…you left it?

Margherita: I think so :/

Paolo: uh oh. I'll look later.

He clearly wasn't too concerned. Maybe she shouldn't be either.

MILANO, LOMBARDIA

2016

MARGHERITA HADN'T EATEN in days. Her heart beat faster at the thought of him. She felt a rush between her legs, and in her chest; it was a growing sense of wanting, an excitement building. The flutter beneath her skirt intensified when she imagined kissing him. She was secretly consumed.

The elevator doors were about to close when she received a text.

Paolo: Sono dietro di te. *I am behind you.*

She was confused. More nerves. Was he walking behind her? She wasn't ready to see him. She was wearing flats.

The elevator doors nearly closed as she contemplated a reply. A large, tan hand came between them, and the doors opened again.

She barely registered his six-foot-three-inch frame as he lifted her into the air; his body was so capable. She wrapped her legs around his torso and squeezed. She felt his muscular body against her thighs, wrapped underneath her calf muscles. A ten-second kiss unfolded in slow motion with craving leaking from her every pore.

When the doors opened again, he put her down. She fluffed out her white skirt and stepped into the hallway like nothing had happened.

Only it had.

"Ci vediamo dopo," *I'll see you later,* he said with a mischievous grin, flattening out his t-shirt. She walked to her hotel room, shaky, her heart racing.

ERBUSCO, LOMBARDIA

2016

DELICATE CLATTER. THE sounds of espresso cups placed on saucers. Hushed background voices. A whistle in the vineyard that stretched before them.

"Desiderate qualcos'altro?" *Would you like anything else?* The dark-haired owner's daughter appeared and cast her polite smile and her cocoa eyes first on Aldo, then on Margherita. Aldo had been resting with his eyes open, taking in the green vista before them, the swell of the hot day finally releasing in the shade of the veranda. His empty espresso cup was pushed forward a few inches on the table, along with the remains of his crostata di pesche. Margherita looked at him, at his weightless white hair, and his forehead skin thin and tan from decades of Italian sun.

He regarded the owner's daughter with his friendly eyes; they were really quite beautiful eyes; blue, strikingly blue, like the Sicilian sea. They were the first thing Margherita had noticed about him when she saw him a few weeks before in the garden section of a classy restaurant off Corso Magenta in Milano.

_____

She was having a 'working' lunch with Camilla—they used the excuse once in a while to go somewhere chic and take a longer ora di pranzo *lunch hour*. Aldo was on a business lunch, in a crisp navy suit, surrounded by other crisp navy suits. They had exchanged a few glances, and when his group got up to leave, he stopped at her table and said to her:

"You are the most elegant woman in the room."

She looked up at him and smiled.

"Dici?" *You think?*

He left her his business card and she sent him a text message later that evening. He took her to two fabulous restaurants in the same week, and at the weekend, with the heat descending on the city, he invited her on a weekend away.

"He's a little old, even for you," Camilla said, after he left.

"Oh, fooey—he was so chic!" Margherita slipped Aldo's card into her purse.

"You are ridiculous," Camilla said as she waved the waiter down for their check.

"Penso di no, grazie." *No, thank you.* Aldo said politely to the owner's daughter.

She ached to check her phone, which had no service outside of their room at the lovely inn, even when she had brought it upstairs to the restaurant bathroom and stood with her arm outstretched outside the window. Aldo shifted himself toward her, his bony, long fingers covering her milk white hand.

"Cosa dici? È così tranquillo, no?" *What do you say? It's so peaceful, isn't it?*

Margherita nodded, catching the sideways glance of the couple at the table next to them, no doubt wondering what their story was. This man in his late fifties, this young woman in her twenties. How could she move this day along without seeming rude or ungrateful for such a beautiful weekend in the vineyards near Lago d'Iseo? She wanted to get back to Milan, to start the week, a new week, one in which she might see Paolo.

When they returned to their suite, Aldo humming, Margherita lingered in the walk-in closet.

> **Margherita:** Come va il tuo weekend *how is your weekend*
>
> **Paolo:** Marghe ciao! tutto bene, sono in montagna. stupendo. dove sei? *It's good, I'm in the mountains. Gorgeous. Where are you?*
>
> **Margherita:** (photo)
>
> **Paolo:** bello!! Sei in erbusco? *Beautiful! You're in Erbusco?*
>
> **Margherita:** Si
>
> **Paolo:** Ci vediamo questa settimana? *Are we going to get together this week?*
>
> **Margherita:** Forse :) *Maybe*
>
> **Paolo:** (kiss emoji)

How she wished she could have maintained the discipline and not have texted him first. She wondered if his wife ever checked his phone. Did he delete their chats every time? Did he care? Did she? All she knew was that she didn't care to think rationally. She only embraced the butterflies.

Aldo, who seemed to age before her eyes, hummed nearly the whole two hours back to the city along with Mina's deep, bellowing voice on his Spotify. While "Tintarella di Luna" played, he cloyingly squeezed Margherita's hand and told her she was the girl in the song, she with her fair skin and her wide-brimmed hats.

"Your father is Italian, no? How the pale skin?" He asked in his broken English.

"My mother is British. She was born and raised in London."

"Davvero?" *Really?* "Why did she live in New York, allora?"

Margherita looked out the window at the flat fields on either side of the autostrada. "Because investment bankers make more money in New York."

"Your mamma works in banking?"

"Very much so."

"And you? Don't?"

"No, it appears I do not," she said, stating, what was in her mind, the obvious.

She pursed her lips many times. *Be polite*, she reminded herself. *Be gracious, be thankful.* He had brought her on many lovely getaways, taken her to many beautiful meals at her favourite restaurants, introduced her to a few truly exceptional places where she had been able to discover magnificent architecture. Isola Bella on Lago Maggiore was a highlight, a small island with a not so small villa. Visiting Villa Borromeo was an experience that left Margherita's jaw on the bottom of the lake floor. It was a self-proclaimed "Baroque chest of wonders floating on water,"- lined with

Neoclassical stucco, silk and gold tapestries, a precious art collection, an incredible full-floor grotto, and ceilings that made her head spin. She imagined arriving for a dinner party and pulling up to the tiered garden in a boat. What did guests bring in the villa's day in the sun? Surely a bouquet of ranunculus from the flower stand in Stresa did not quite impress. They had docked at the miniature Isola Pescatori, where no more than fifty inhabitants lived, for lunch on a wrap-around veranda overlooking the lake. After a fresh catch of orata under the umbrella shade, they strolled along the atmospheric shore and counted the fish drying on the long balconies.

He had been begging her—*such an unattractive thing, to beg,* she had thought—to join him on a tiny Sicilian island, Favignana, for his August vacation. The thought of being isolated with Aldo on a secluded island was too much to bear; it outweighed the prospect of a gorgeous Italian holiday.

She didn't understand how anyone married for money, with no other form of love or desire. If she wasn't enamored, if she didn't lose her appetite, if her heart didn't beat *forte forte forte* the entire day before she was supposed to see him, what good was any of it?

"Daisies are truer than wildflowers," her mom always said. To deaf ears.

Back in her apartment she opened all four sets of French doors overlooking the quiet piazza below. The sun was setting and the sky over the church was as violet as the frozen grapes they had slowly eaten after lunch. She lingered on her tiny terrazza, soaking it up, turning her head left, then right, then left again, trying to decide which pastel version of the sky was more captivating. How she loved her little terrazza, where she dried her laundry, and nestled hydrangeas and lavender that never lived longer than a month, and herbs that her colleagues told her not to eat, on account of the smog in Milan. She loved to watch the goings-on on the uneven stones below; a lackadaisical woman, walking from one side to the other in a long skirt, sitting on a bench and lowering her gaze to her leather sandals…an older gentleman in a beige suit, hands clasped behind his back in classic Italian gentleman form, his eyes cast far, far down the sidewalk…What was he thinking about? What memories were stirring for him at that moment? She stood there enjoying the quiet end of a Sunday, as the sky turned a midnight blue. A few motos whizzed by, the sound of two young teenagers whirring in the night.

She fell asleep waiting for Paolo to respond to a text, checking her phone every twenty minutes or so, even though the ringer was on.

MILANO, LOMBARDIA

2016

As Margherita drank her hot water with lemon and crushed ginger, her phone rang. It was her landlady.

"Ciao Roberta!" She said in her sweet voice which she saved for the over sixty-five age group.

"Margherita, senti, sono qui in zona. Ho una pianta di lavanda per te. Posso salire?" *Listen, I am in your neighborhood. I have a lavender plant for you. Can I come up?* She always got straight to the point; Margherita was thankful for this, as sometimes Italians could be particularly long-winded.

"Ma si certo!" *Yes of course.*

Margherita left the apartment door open and in came Roberta, who must have already been in the lobby when she called.

"Guarda, mettila qui, all'interno della tua camera da letto. Fa bene per il sonno. Non mettere le altre piante all'interno, okay?" *Look, put it here, just inside your bedroom. It is good for sleeping. Don't put any other plants inside, okay?* Roberta looked out at the terrace and Margherita's hydrangeas. "Stai pulendo il calcio dal soffione della doccia?" *Are you cleaning the calcium deposits off the shower head?*

she politely demanded to know, and she proceeded into Margherita's bathroom just opposite the terrace to inspect the shower head.

Roberta was quite bossy, but she took care of Margherita like a granddaughter and Margherita loved her for it.

"Vai al mercatino dell'artigianato in chiesa il prossimo fine settimana?" *Are you going to the craft market at the church next weekend?* she asked, as she put her sunglasses on to leave the apartment. "Ahhh l'acqua con limone e zenzero, fai bene." *Ah, water with lemon and ginger, good.*

ALASSIO, LIGURIA

2016

MARGHERITA WALKED DOWN to the beach; the town was still quiet, save for the sound of music near their assigned beach chairs. Taddeo and his family had reserved the same spot at their beach club for decades. What began with one weekend quickly led to an unbroken string of long weekends in the little seaside town, and Margherita's muscle memory brought her right to the blue canvas chairs, the blue and white striped umbrella. Margherita was one of the few people on the beach so early in the morning, having already gone for a sunrise run and a quick stop at the organic fruit market for a few perfectly ripe peaches and apricots. Morning saw the most movimento at the fruttivendolo *produce stand*; there was a consistent line of grandmothers buying vegetables for the family dinner, gossiping as they awaited their turn.

"*La luce del mattino, l'abbraccio di un amico, il viso di un bambino, meraviglioso.*" She smiled to herself. She was in heaven; it was such a perfect day. There were moments when she felt so vividly the joy in the simple things—a blue sky, a smile and a buongiorno to a young lifeguard, a few small children with ringlets running past her to get to camp on time, their mother trailing closely behind. Summer wanted for nothing but bathing suits and spirit. For gioventù *youth*, summer meant boundless energy and never-ending days, afternoon ice-pops, and a floating island for diving from morning until sunset, all underneath a sky as unmarred and infinite as youth itself.

Margherita felt that, in Italy, adults also saw the beauty in these moments, more easily than their American counterparts could. For Italians, life wasn't clouded in stress and senseless complaining and deadened hope. In her experience, an Italian adult appeared more content than the average adult New Yorker; she tried not to generalize further than that.

La spiaggia. *The beach.* Il mare. *The sea.* Il sole. *The sun.* Add to that la famiglia and gli amici, maybe a little amore, and the Italian summer was complete. In a country nearly entirely surrounded by water, there were countless beaches to choose from for the August exodus, the month that quasi tutti *basically everyone* made their grand escape to the sea. There were beaches where everyone knew each other's names, and there were beaches where the sand was made for dancing. The former, the type of beach that an Italian would go to on repeat from infancy to old age, was the type that celebrated the culture's devotion to tradition. While in certain connotations such traditions could be considered complacency, in summer it represented charm and nostalgia. It was the kind of nostalgia wherein youth is so tangible, one can almost feel the sticky cocomero *watermelon* between one's fingers.

This beach town, Alassio, on the Ligurian Riviera's western stretch, was a simple town whose charms unfolded gradually. Those who took the time to discover the route to the top of the mountain where the blackberry shrubs bloomed, the Bagno *beach club* cafeteria with the best lemon ice bar, or the best spot on the promenade for a four-euro glass of Vermentino at sundown were richly repaid. Margherita even knew the time of day that nine-year-old Dante ate his focaccia in the sand—(eleven).

There was a time and a place for a stylish bathing suit shop, an upscale hotel, or a chic restaurant, but in the thick of summer, Margherita wanted nothing more than a demonstration of genuine life, of the simple, stripped-down pleasures of summer, like the ones she had loved as a child. The only thing that mattered was that there was sand between her toes…well, that was almost the only thing that mattered.

There were moments when she felt slightly uncomfortable being in Alassio, in the town where Paolo and his best friends had spent every summer since they were born. It was likely that their parents had also passed each summer there, throughout their lives. True to tradition, it was important to Paolo that his kids would grow up to be best friends with his best friends' kids. Not only were the families together during the school year, but they all vacationed nearby in the summer too. Margherita had no choice but to pass under Paolo's house to get her morning caffè, and some mornings she could hear his wife yelling at the kids to get dressed. Once, she saw his youngest son on the terrace, naked and waving to passers-by.

Alassio felt like *his* town, then. She hadn't exactly fol-lowed him there, since it was Taddeo who had invited her, and she was staying in a hotel on the sea. She and Taddeo whiled the time away together at the beach club, listening to music and chatting with people on their way to the lunch counter. To their friends, she was Taddeo's young summer fling or perhaps his young companion. No one questioned her presence; no one asked them how they met or where this young Americana came from. No one cared; they just accepted her, point-blank, though she herself was hyper-aware of the secret lurking in the sand between Taddeo's beach club and Paolo's next door.

Taddeo, who had never married, possessed a silly sense of humor that drove Margherita to tears. He was generous as one could possibly be, always taking care of her and treating her to meals, even though neither had expressed any obvious romantic interest in the other. She felt one helping of guilt for harboring the secret of her affair with Paolo, and a second helping because she might be unknowingly leading Taddeo on, although honestly she could not tell if he was interested in her, or if he simply liked having the company.

The guilt caught up with her at least once a day, and she would nearly blurt out the whole story to Taddeo—that she was actually having an affair with his best friend, that her mind constantly raced with thoughts of Paolo, that her nerves were a bouncy house, and that her appetite had gone down to zilch. She had lost weight; for proof, the built-in bra in her exercise top barely fit the way it should. As she sat on the beach, her conscience felt so heavy, in complete contrast to the featherweight mood that the seaside weekends should have inspired.

She was there for the *chance* that she might see Paolo again, spend an hour or two in his presence, that he might pick her up in his strong swimmer arms, that she might wrap her legs around his torso, and maybe, *just maybe*, he might throw her down onto her single sized mattress in her bare bones 1960s shabby hotel room overlooking the sea. Each time they saw each other, she felt it was worth the nerves, the rapid heartbeat, the loss of sleep every time she woke to check her phone. She was torturously smitten. Though she hoped this high would have no end, she worried that he would grow bored at some point.

On Taddeo's forty-ninth birthday, Margherita decided to go for an evening run and watch the sun set over the beach clubs. Afterwards she ate grilled calamari out of a plastic take-away container, with a plastic fork and a napkin that kept blowing away. Families passed by on their evening walks, eyeing her gently and somewhat pathetically, she felt, clearly wondering why she was alone on the promenade eating out of a take-away. She didn't let it bother her. There was a beautiful sunset in front of her.

Taddeo texted her later in the evening, and asked her to join him and his parents for a slice of birthday cake. When she arrived, it was clear Taddeo was a bit drunk; he was very flirtatious and touchy with her. His mother rolled her eyes on her behalf, and his father, who had been smitten with the little Americana since the first weekend, was just as flirtatious as his son. Margherita didn't have any cake, claiming to be very full. Taddeo explained how careful she was with her diet, while his mother gesticulated at her already petite figure.

After dinner, Taddeo took Margherita's hand and led her toward the closed beach club, shushing her.

"There is a door this way," he said half to himself, guiding her a few steps this way, then a few steps that way, along the path that connected the village to the beach underneath the promenade. He managed to find the spot he was looking for, a gate-style door with an opening on each side large enough for a skinny body to fit through sideways. They each squeezed through, sucking in their bellies, and emerged onto an empty beach, where the chaise lounges and chairs were stacked for the night.

"Vieni, vieni," *Come, come.* Taddeo kept saying, walking closer to the sea. He sat down in the sand and Margherita sat down next to him. He began to play "Meraviglioso" by Domenico Modugno on Spotify, as loud as his phone would play.

"Ma come non ti accorgi, di quanto il mondo sia, meraviglioso!" he sang, loudly.

He played it again so that Margherita could memorize the lyrics, and they played it over and over and over, to the sound of the waves crashing and the silent midnight sky overhead. Margherita didn't have anything to drink, but she could never remember leaving the beach that night. She only ever remembered the feeling. *Meraviglioso.*

MILANO, LOMBARDIA

2016

THE EVENING BEFORE Fashion Week began, Margherita sat down with Taddeo at Latteria San Marco for a late bite to eat. They were both tired; he was slightly agitated at having to wait for a table in the small room, and more-so when he learned that the restaurant did not accept credit cards. Margherita was agitated for reasons she could not say out loud. She wished she could compartmentalize. She was very aware of how quickly and easily she let other people affect her state of mind, and it bothered her that she couldn't seem to control it. She couldn't shut them out.

She was trying desperately to remain calm in Taddeo's presence, to foil his tiredness and trivial annoyance with sweetness and lightness. This was a different Taddeo than the one she knew over the summer, the sun-lazy, laughing, easygoing, Taddeo.

She thought back to laying next to him on the beach; he liked to become exponentially more tan in the sun, while she preserved her Ava Gardner complexion under the umbrella. He had showed her where he waited as a young boy, above the village's train tracks, for his father's car to arrive from Milan each Friday evening. He had driven her to and from the train in the next town as she came and went from work in Milan during the week.

They had ended the summer with a beautiful, peaceful weekend in Engadin, where they stayed in a friend's cabin overlooking the mountains. They went for glorious hikes every day, just the two of them, to catch views of the lake on the mountain top, and hoped not to get shot by stray hunting bullets. They entertained themselves at night with silly things like dancing to 80s music or creating life size drawings of each other on the floor. They cooked a few truly mediocre dinners, when they forgot to buy olive oil at the giant supermarket in town and felt too lazy to go back. Taddeo even convinced Margherita to go to a nude day spa, and afterwards they sat outside at a wine bar overlooking the Eastern Alps, drinking pinot noir and covering themselves with quilted blankets underneath the Swiss August sun. It had been her favorite summer ever, and she had such strong end-of-summer melancholy that she even found herself crying once or twice upon September's arrival, when everyone returned to the city, to their lives, to their busy schedules, to agitation and aggravation.

She had not, through it all, said a word about Paolo. How much easier it would have been if she felt romantically towards Taddeo! He made her laugh, he took good care of her, he was a genuinely kind and giving human being; she loved Taddeo as a friend; rarely had she ever made such a wonderful friend, but she was not interested beyond that. She did not feel the za-za, the whirl in the pit of her stomach. She thought only of Paolo. Paolo who seemed to not care at all that Margherita had suddenly become hip-to-hip with his best friend.

Sitting across from Taddeo at Latteria San Marco, in the harsher light of the old-fashioned restaurant, without any of the Ligurian sun to shine a glow, he looked older, more creased, more weathered. Suddenly Margherita felt what others might be wondering to themselves: what was a young woman like herself doing with this nearly fifty-year-old man who seemed so tired, compared to her youth? Italians had taught her that age was just a number; Paolo had more energy and a more raucous social life than she ever had, but there were moments when Margherita dreamt of dating a thirty-something guy...someone who was ripe now, like she was...who might want to grow older together.

For some reason she never seemed to attract this demographic. She had always felt different, that she was not the typical young woman that most guys her age wanted. In the States she had never felt very American, had never shared the stereotypical habits of her peers. While her high school friends were constantly drunk, she drank just enough to not be left out, and while they bragged about the drugs they did and the pills they took, she never once participated. Sander's behavior was enough to turn her off toward every drug imaginable, and she secretly worried that she might have Francine's same illness buried inside her; drugs might bring it to the surface. Besides which, Tommaso had enough to worry about with her mother, who sometimes took on the role of out-of-control child in their house.

As a senior in high school, the year after Sander went to college, she weathered incessant bullying by girls who used to be her friends, often going home in tears and feeling quite alone. Her closest allies became the two older women with whom she worked part-time in a clothing store on upper Madison Avenue. She spent her weekends watching old films and reading books her mom would recommend—Somerset Maugham and Herman Wouk— growing accustomed to being alone. Margherita sometimes went so far as to wish her mother would have another episode, which would in turn force her into a stronger medication routine for a few weeks and might keep her at home, where Margherita could spend time with her. She felt horribly guilty wishing ill of her mother, but the alternatives were either risking unforeseen events in Francine's manic states, or never seeing her at all, due to her mother's work hours and travel schedule between New York, London, and elsewhere.

She looked up at Taddeo's white hair and thinning lips. She had been looking forward to seeing him, hoping it would quell some of her post-summer sadness, but it only drove it home. The season was over.

"Have you seen Paolo and Carlo?" she asked.

"No. I haven't seen them since Alassio. Everyone's busy now. School started…work…Paolo is always at events, in giro *out and about*, at night," he drifted off. He seemed a little blue as well. Lonely. She hoped she wouldn't end up like Taddeo: melancholy, left out, alone, always thinking about his youth, recalling beautiful memories as if they would suddenly re-enact themselves.

Margherita looked down at her phone. Nothing from Paolo. She had told him that she was having dinner with

Taddeo, hoping that would encourage him to meet up with them afterwards.

Margherita: Andiamo a bere qualcosa dopocena.
Let's get a drink after dinner.

Paolo: Magari. Vado a calcio poi lavoro. E sono morto. *I wish. I have soccer then back to work. And I'm dead tired.*

Margherita: Dai…*Come on…*

Paolo: Ho un sacco di eventi per la moda. Sei in giro questa settimana? *I have a ton of events for fashion week. Will you be out this week?*

Margherita: Solo domani. Poi viene mia mamma. *Just tomorrow. My mom is coming.*

Paolo: Ah carina. Ci vediamo domani. Bacio. *Oh nice. I'll see you tomorrow. Kiss.*

Pang. Disappointment. Pang, pang.

The next evening at the annual September Fashion Week party at the Palazzo Gioia Hotel, Camilla pulled Margherita to the front of the line and put her down as a guest of the PR company that was sponsoring the evening. Camilla's husband Vito was there as well, a rare occurrence. Margherita had never particularly liked Vito. She found that Camilla completely changed in his presence; she went from fun, direct, borderline bossy to wayward, submissive, and people-pleasing. He didn't like for her to have friends over, so Margherita could only visit Camilla's home when Vito was still at the office. Margherita never forgot Camilla's response one June day when she had asked her friend if she wanted to do a girls' weekend at the beach.

"No! Who will make Vito's lunch? I can't abandon him!"

"Are you serious?" Margherita assumed she was joking.

"You'll see, Marghe. When you're married. You can't just leave them alone on the weekend. That's not right."

Margherita was speechless.

She scoured the party for someone cute to flirt with, to bide the time. She spotted someone at the other end of the gently curved bar. He appeared young, in his early thirties, and well dressed in a way that suggested he'd come directly from a law office. She waved him over. He waved her over. She stayed firmly put. So did he.

They eventually met in the middle. They flirted. He told her about a recent trip to Jordan. She didn't even know him and yet she felt left out when he showed her a few photos from the trip, each photo with at least six friends. She dismissed the possibility of him based on the assumption that she would never fit in with this group, but they had fun and ended up kissing in the middle of the party while "Physical" by Olivia Newton John played in the background. The Italians were always playing retro American music. She wasn't interested in the slightest, not past those moments. She was waiting to hear from Paolo.

Paolo: Dove sei amore? *Where are you, love?*

Margherita contemplated the meaning of the text. Either there was a small window in which she could see him, or he was simply drunk and bored and entertaining himself via text, not intending to meet up with her at all.

Margherita: Alla Gioia

Paolo: Ahh bello! Sono al rooftop al Nicosia. *Nice, I'm at the rooftop at the Nicosia.*

Margherita: Bello :)

Paolo: Voglio fare l'amore. *I want to make love.*

Margherita: Vieni qua. *Come here*

Paolo: No, non riesco. Sono qui con un cliente. Vieni qui. *No, I can't. I'm with a client. Come here.*

Of course, she grabbed her jacket and headed over to the hotel. Meeting in a hotel room had become their thing. Sometimes, if she had time to kill on a train, she made a mental list of all of the hotels and hotel rooms in which she had had sex with Paolo. There was something alluring and heightened and dramatic about it, as though they were in a movie.

If one were to ask her what she was doing, having a clandestine affair with a married man twenty years older than her, she would make some sort of snap remark about her age, how she was only twenty-six, as if that somehow explained it. What it defended her against, in her head, was the argument that some girls her age were in serious relationships or were interested in finding one, in cultivating a life with someone, starting a family. She struggled with the contrasting desires. On one hand, the thought of marriage, of a serious relationship even, gave her great anxiety. On the other hand, she often desired salvation from fleeting feelings of loneliness. She feared, however, in an inexplicable way, the banality of relationships, the inevitable mundaneness of them. She was more interested in concocting romantic, thrilling stories about herself and a potential lover, inclusive of dramatic fights. She assumed herself to be very strange for this reason, and was not sure how to 'fix' it.

She told herself that with Paolo, she was following the beat of her chemical drum, and she referenced the many affairs that happened in the world, telling herself there was nothing inherently *wrong* with her actions. Where was the fun in going through the motions like everyone else? What was life without a little risky business?

She had also learned from speaking with friends and listening to gossip, that affairs were often an inherent element of Italian life. While affairs seemed to cause divorces left and right in the States, in Italy, divorce was far less common, though affairs were widely acknowledged, but not discussed. The men never left their wives because the wives were the mothers of their children.

Her friend Sandra, a painter living in Rome, single in her mid forties, had offered a very frank and unapologetic perspective on the matter.

"His wife has a nice life. She has her kids, she has a very good-looking, successful husband who hopefully is a good dad, she has a house at the beach and in the mountains. She has her friends. Why mess with it? To be alone? To complicate everything? Why not just accept that there is no perfect marriage and learn to be content."

Margherita wondered if she could do the same, once she was married…if she ever did marry. Would she be able to look the other way? And would *she* have affairs? It worried her, the idea that she would not be able to avoid infidelity, that she would not be able to say no, that she might even go looking for it. If she was honest with herself, she liked the risk and the drama. The drama let her carry a storyline in her head.

Besides which, she felt it was only wise to think pragmatically, to recognize and reconcile the fact that most people were not faithful. She believed, even in her mid twenties, that this was something to be accepted point blank, and in doing so, one had a greater chance of avoiding unnecessary heartbreak.

The only long-term relationship she had ever known, with Sander, had been permanently stained after she found out he had been cheating on her for more than a year with one of the girls who had bullied her the most. She had not forgiven him, but carried on with him anyways; Sander was her best friend (or so she thought), and he somehow made her feel that she had deserved it. At such a young age, when everything was a first, she didn't realize that she had the choice to walk away. She knew only that she loved him, and she convinced herself that eventually he would be good to her again because he loved her too.

At the Nicosia Hotel, Margherita found Paolo in the lobby. He had come down from the roof to make a reservation for a room. She was a walking tower of nerves, even with a few drinks in her. There was that tickle between her legs, that rapid heartbeat, that patter in the pit of her stomach. He put her on edge, every single time.

He gave her a smile, greeted her with a laugh, put his big hand on the top of her head and pulled her in for a kiss on the cheek. He oscillated between looking at her like she was a little doll and eyeing her with such arousal that she thought he might strip her down right then right there, wherever they happened to be.

"Vieni, Marghe." *Come, Marghe.* He strode toward the elevators, ahead of her, always one foot ahead of her. They had never walked side by side, ever. He wore tan pants, beautiful leather shoes with no socks, a crisp white t-shirt that showed off his remaining tan. His hair was still blonde from the summer sun. He was her Adonis, the most attractive Greek god, but she felt less like his lover Aphrodite and more like her handmaiden, the seductive temptress, Peitho. It was a role she was enjoying.

Just as the elevator doors were about to close, a man joined them.

"Ah, Luca, come stai?" *Luca, how are you?* Paolo greeted the man.

"Cazzo, Paolo, è stato un anno. Come stai?" *Shit, Paolo, it's been a year. How are you?* The two men chatted briefly. Margherita remained toward the back of the elevator car. At the fourteenth floor, Paolo said goodbye to his friend and he and Margherita exited. She wondered what the man was thinking, then, as there could be only one conclusion to draw.

In the hotel room, Paolo didn't waste much time. He asked her about the party at Palazzo Gioia. He asked her about Taddeo and if Margherita found him to be a little sad lately. And that was it, really, no other exchange. Once upon a time, there were a few evenings when they actually conversed, but not anymore.

It reminded her of one night in Alassio.

They had been sitting at an outdoor bar in the little village with Taddeo and a few of their childhood friends enjoying some late night music and wine. Paolo had been the last to join, having gone to dinner with his family. He had had a lot to drink, she could tell. They exchanged a few glances across the low table between them, but nothing more. Taddeo had had a lot to drink as well and was resting his head in Margherita's lap, stretched out on an outdoor sofa.

Paolo: Facciamo l'amore. *Let's make love.*

She had checked the message right over Taddeo's head. She immediately tucked her phone under her leg. Paolo's face gave nothing away.

When finally, *finally*, everyone got up to go to bed, Margherita walked the fifty feet back to her motel room. Taddeo walked with her. When he was gone, she texted Paolo.

Paolo: Taddeo è andato? *Taddeo left?*

Paolo followed her up the three flights of stairs, stopping her on the second floor landing and kissing her passionately, foolishly, recklessly.

"Aspetta," *Wait*, she had teased, and they continued up one more flight. In her small motel room, he bent her over with her dress still on. There was no room for the two of them on the single bed.

Afterwards, he went to the bathroom to wash his hands and rinse his face. He gargled with a little toothpaste. When he came back to the bed to retrieve his t-shirt from the floor, she tried to give him a kiss but he shook her off.

"Scusa, sono un po' neurotico. La mia moglie è cinquanta metri da qua," *Sorry, I'm a little neurotic. My wife is fifty meters from here*, he had said, breathy and nervous.

After he left, she rinsed herself in the shower and worried for the first time that they had never used a condom. She was being careless. She had spent the whole evening waiting for those ten minutes. Then they were done. The aftereffects were rotten.

Inside their room at the Nicosia, after piddly small talk, Margherita knocked her shoes off and stood atop the bed's fluffy white bedspread. Paolo stood in front of her. He was so tall, she was barely a head above him even standing on the bed.

He held his hands on her waist, lifted her in the air, and threw her backwards onto the bed. He yanked off his t-shirt and unbuttoned his pants. Everything fell to the floor. He leaned over Margherita with his long, tan form; muscles extended.

He brushed the hair out of her face and kissed her lips. He looked into her eyes. His eyes, like the Ligurian sea, were bewitching.

Those were the tender moments that caught her off guard, but she knew she was being foolish. She didn't want anything from him except his attention once in a while. She didn't want him to leave his wife or tell anyone about their affair. In fact, she enjoyed the secret. It heightened the rush. The sneaking around—it was mischievous and dangerous and exciting. She was content with the undulations, the excitement, and a few tender moments. The intervals between were torturous, and it was the torture that fed her addiction.

He rolled onto his back, which was almost as long as one of her legs, and pulled her on top of him. He ravaged her for twenty minutes before he realized the time.

"Devo svegliami tra un paio di ore. Porto i bimbi a scuola," *I have to wake up in a few hours. I take the kids to school*, he said. She pursed her lips in resignation.

"Come sta andando con Elisio? Avete trovato qualcuno per il ristorante?" *How is it going with Elisio? Have you found someone for the restaurant?* He asked as he stepped one leg and then the other into his pants.

Sitting naked on the bed, leaning on her hands behind her, she regarded him quietly and apprehensively. She shook her head.

He left her there, on the bed they hadn't even undone. She found her dress and her shoes, her handbag. She took a look at the bathroom, at the amenities of the room, for work research. Then she closed the door behind her, got into the elevator with a bunch of drunk Fashion Week party-goers who were leaving the rooftop bar, and walked home to her empty apartment.

That was what she hoped for each time: twenty minutes. She was starting to feel empty. Cheap.

It was like a drug. There was the wanting of it, the needing it, the agitation at not having it. Then there was the having it, the quick, barely there intake. Then there was the low, the come-down, that desperately lonely feeling that she tried to fill by flirting with other guys, with an extra-long run, with a day wandering around peaceful Lake Como. Yet she could never fully rid her mind of him, of that achy feeling. It crept back, the wanting. She told herself she was in control; that she knew the game, that she was an equal participant. But then why did she feel so hollowed by it?

It wasn't a self-respect thing. It wasn't an "I deserve better" thing like Chiara made it out to be. It was simply that she wanted what she wanted, and she did not have the ability to say no. Her lack of discipline led to her feeling alone and cheap. It made men think she didn't care, that it was as meaningless to her as it was to them, only she wasn't so sure if that was true.

The next day she tried to sleep an hour or two later, foregoing a run, and stopped by Marchesi for a later-than-normal espresso and brioche before getting on the train to the airport. She was going to meet her mom, who had gone to London for a few weeks for work, and they would go to the lake for a few days.

LAGO DI COMO, LOMBARDIA

2016

Walking through Bellagio's Giardini di Villa Melzi with its Neoclassical villa, Margherita tried to engage her mom's appreciation for the beauty of the setting, but Francine seemed tuned-out, nearly numb to the exquisite avenue of plane trees and seemingly limitless azaleas. Her mother was instead focused on a few trades that had gone badly that morning, and she concentrated on her phone.

Margherita pointed out the exotic plants, the camellia hedges, and the statues amidst the flower beds, but the only time Francine looked up from her phone, she seemed to be lost in her head.

In her own head, Margherita could not stop thinking about Paolo. Her joyless mother made her antsy, and not even the glittering lake, which looked like a chartered-boat-load of diamonds had just fallen from the crest of the mountains, could pacify her jumpy nerves.

"So, you liked Benjamin's new girlfriend?" Margherita tried to find a topic Francine would respond to.

"Yes...she seems nice. Has a good job. Benjamin seems happy," her mother adjusted her hat.

"What does she do?"

"She works for a big private equity firm. Very smart. Very pretty. Grew up in Hampstead. I think she wants a family," her mother rattled off. "Has he spoken to you about her?"

"No. Just that he's dating someone named Alice."

"Such a private person, your brother. And you, the total opposite. You can't keep anything to yourself!"

"Hmm," Margherita swallowed a reply.

"He said you are dating someone too old for you."

"Oh, thanks Benjamin."

"I hope you are not repeating the same mistakes, Margherita," Francine said, stopping in the path to type something out on her phone.

Margherita was used to receiving less than fifty percent of her mother's attention. It rarely ceased to frustrate her, however.

"Hi, mom, should I go to lunch without you?"

"Don't be cute," Francine quipped.

"He is older. Twenty years older to be precise. And he's married. With four children. And he's gorgeous and really fun," Margherita said, spitefully, assuming her mom was not listening as she continued to type on her phone.

Instead, Francine looked up into her daughter's eyes. "You are kidding."

Margherita turned on her heels and continued along the path. "The restaurant is this way."

"I have to call Benedikt. This day is awful. I'll be right there," Francine said, as she turned toward the lake to dial her assistant in London. Francine had a desk in the firm's New York office as well as London, and her two assistants worked all time zones.

Underneath the vine-covered pergola at the lapping lake's edge, Francine rubbed her forehead.

"Margherita, I can't believe you could be so foolish. He'll never leave his wife, you know that," Francine said as the waiter poured her a glass of white wine.

"I know! I didn't say I wanted him to. Should you be drinking?"

Her mother studied her and rolled her eyes. "Don't mother me. Is that why you're here? To flounce around with a married man? I think you should come home. Quit the silly job that barely pays and come home and get a real job. Be a grown-up. This is ridiculous. Your brother is talking about marriage, and here you are, playing games with someone else's."

"That is so unfair. I am a grown-up. I did not mean to get myself in this situation. It just happened. And I have a real job. I am sick of you putting my work down. I'm happy here. It's no stress."

"What is stressful at home?"

Margherita rolled her eyes to herself and focused on her fingers on her lap, twisting her ring around her finger.

Francine leaned in toward her. "Do you honestly think you're the only one? You don't think he's got more than one of you?"

"I'm not stupid."

"I sure hope not."

"Whatever. I'm sorry I said anything."

"Let me tell you something. You think it's cute and funny to be like this now. Fine. Flit around as you like. Make yourself easy. But it's not so cute in ten years. In twenty years."

"Okay! I get it."

"Just don't get pregnant." Francine took a big swig from her wine glass and motioned to the waiter for a refill already.

That evening, as Margherita came back from the hotel fitness center, she heard Francine on the phone to Tommaso.

"Don't you dare give her any money. If this job doesn't pay enough, and she wants to stay here, she can ask her married man for money. Absurd. Totally absurd. As if I don't have enough stress. As if I don't have enough to worry about."

Margherita remained paused outside the door.

"Give me a break Tommaso. Yes. Yes. I am taking them. For fuck's sake. That nutcase at Bellevue has called me seven times this trip. How can I possibly work like that? My numbers have been rubbish this month. All of you. Bugger off," Francine said.

Margherita entered the room and Francine eyed her with what seemed like venom. She wasn't sure if it was because of the affair or because Margherita was 'keeping Francine' from her work. She wished her mother was the kind who was excited to visit her only daughter in Italy, who was proud of her for being courageous and putting a life together in another country, for working for a prominent brand doing a job she enjoyed. Instead, whether it was because of Francine's current meds or Margherita living in Italy, Francine seemed to have grown icy toward her, just like one of the bullies from high school. One day she was on her side, and the next, she wasn't.

MILANO, LOMBARDIA

2016

AFTER A WEEK with Francine, Margherita had never looked forward to a work meeting more in her life. She could not wait to have an afternoon to return to the confident and independent Margherita that she had come to know and love in Milan. The meeting was a site visit with the head of Store Development for the Leonetti brand. Obviously there would be a Leonetti flagship within the new hotel space; it was their family name after all.

After she left the property, she jumped in an Uber to Paolo's office on the other side of Parco Venezia. She was meant to give him updated architect's plans for the future rooftop restaurant and bar so that he could begin soft furnishing scheming. She volunteered to bring the plans herself—a credible excuse to see him.

She said hello to Ginevra, the young woman with dry, straight hair at reception who looked straight out of the year 1999, with low jeans and too much eyeliner. She quietly walked into Paolo's stylish office with its vintage leather sofas and stacks of design magazines. Paolo was on a phone call, playfully feigning annoyance that the person on the other line was taking so long. She waited patiently in a leather chair, pretending to read a Taschen coffee table book, and trying discreetly to keep her skirt in place. It had a diagonal slit in the front, and any time she sat down it very nearly separated completely, certainly inviting ones eyes to the lack of material covering her upper thighs. His partner Matteo entered the office, offered her a harried hello and jumped on a call at his desk, opposite Paolo's. Matteo was Paolo's opposite in almost every way—short, unattractive, awkward, and direct. Paolo—tall Paolo, smooth, charming, irresistible Paolo—winked at her playfully.

When he hung up the phone, he came and sat kitty-corner to her. Matteo remained on the phone, irritated by whoever was on the other end. He was either unaware of or outright ignoring the sexual tension in the room, of which there was a great deal.

"Ma, sei nuda," *You're naked*. Paolo said with irony, glancing down at her legs. She smiled and shrugged .

"Did you read my email?" she asked, playing the part of a work related mission more important than merely dropping off plans.

Paolo began to look through his emails.

"I have 5,329 unread emails."

Leave, Matteo, she thought.

"Facciamo l'amore?" *Let's make love?* Paolo mouthed to her, with an innocent, pleading face. He had a sense of humour, an insane body with a never-ending tan, hair she wanted to run her hands through, and a deep, quiet voice that was perfect for making love. She felt the fun would never end...

Only she knew it had to.

She was delaying the inevitable hole she would feel, and even if she knew their actions to be shallow, even if she knew their relationship to be a fling, there was an empty feeling—a sadness, awaiting her at the end of the fun.

"Margherita, vieni qui," he said, jumping up and leaving the office. She felt like a young plaything to him, as if he were a boy with a toy. Who was it that once said to her, when pontificating about dating older men, "When they are twenty-five they are five, and when they're thirty-five they are five, and when they're fifty, they are five."

She thought about his back as she followed him across the hall into another office. His wide shoulders. Lust was a contagion not worth fighting.

"Vieni. Marco. Cosa fai? Margherita, conosci Marco? La Margherita è Americana," *Come. Marco, what are you doing? Margherita do you know Marco?* Paolo said, sitting down on the sofa in Marco's office. Margherita felt like he was showing her off, like his newest play-thing. Yes, she was the play-thing. The young, American play-thing he was having a whirl with.

She looked at her phone. Her mom would be waiting for her at the hotel. She should go.

He walked her out and squeezed into the elevator with her. "Stai uscendo?" *Are you going out?* she asked.

"No, ma così posso baciarti," *No, but this way I can kiss you,* he said, and he leaned down and kissed her. He pulled her up the length of his body, not an easy feat in the small elevator.

The doors opened and they were careful again. Paolo was always careful. He liked to test the limits, but in the open air, there was no kissing or touching. She pulled him into the corner of the stairwell, pulled his face towards her. He kissed her and lifted her into the air, oh it was such a high when he did that, when he lifted her up like a bouncy ball and she wrapped her legs around his solid torso. His shoulders were so wide, his back was so expansive. She could literally feel the flurry rise from her belly to her chest.

"Voglio fare l'amore," *I want to make love,* she whispered.

"Qui? Adesso?" *Here? Now?*

"Ma, si...." she looked around the stairwell, aching for him and his body and him inside of her. She had felt jumpy all day, all week. She needed him to settle her nerves. She all but stomped her foot.

"Ci vediamo dopo amore. Stasera." *I'll see you later, love. Tonight.* He dropped her back down on her feet.

"Non ti credo." *I don't believe you.*

"Vado a calcio, poi ti chiamo." *I have soccer, then I'll call you.*

She knew what that meant.

When she entered her mother's hotel room, she found Francine pacing around the bed while on the phone with her boss.

"I told him to execute it when it dropped to twenty-two." Francine glanced at Margherita and held up her hand as if to curtail any noise her daughter might make.

Margherita took off her heels and washed her hands in the bathroom. She stared at herself in the mirror and breathed in and out heavily. From the bathroom door frame, she watched her mother speak in a language Margherita only half-understood, the language she spoke with Benjamin.

"Fine. Fine. Let's see what Asia does in the morning. I'll be back in New York tomorrow so I can deal with this myself," Francine said, shaking her head, obviously annoyed about something that had taken place that day.

When she hung up, Margherita sat on the bed and waited for her mother to re-focus her attention.

"Disaster. Disaster. I cannot be away from that desk," Francine said, opening her laptop.

"Have you been in this room the whole afternoon?" Margherita asked.

"Of course I have. I have a real job to do."

"Right. So you must be excited to go home," Margherita said quietly.

Francine looked up at her, over the top of her eyeglasses. "Marghe." She sighed heavily and moved from the desk to sit down next to her daughter on the edge of the bed. She pushed a wisp of hair out of Margherita's eyes and tucked it behind her daughter's ear. "I know I'm not the mother you want sometimes but—..."

"Ugh, I hate when you say things like that. You put words in my mouth."

Francine patted Margherita's head and returned to the desk. "Why don't you go downstairs for a snack? I"ll be down soon. I just want to see what happens in after-hours."

Margherita walked downstairs to the hotel lobby feeling deflated.

Margherita: she has sent me away to get a 'snack.' Like a child.

Tommaso: where is she?

Margherita: Where else? On her computer.

Tommaso: Okay. She is very tightly wound this week. I'm sorry Marghe.

Margherita: Why visit me at all

Tommaso: To spend time with you

Margherita: Oh? Is that what she is doing now? It's like one big inconvenience to her. Worse than the dentist

Tommaso: That's not true. She misses you.

Margherita: Doubtful

Tommaso: She was out for a week last month... she feels she needs to catch up. She always thinks she has to prove herself all over again. Just go easy on her.

Margherita: Yup.

Margherita stayed in the hotel room with Francine that night, in order to spend more time with her mother. She hoped she could eke out at least a few less stressed moments from Francine, who had kept one eye on her work the entire week. They woke early, and it could not have been clearer to Margherita that Francine could not wait to leave, that she considered Margherita's life in Italy to be a fantasy. Margherita had the feeling that her mother did not like her very much lately, that she did not like the woman she had become in Milan. Wasn't that strange, because it was the first time in Margherita's life that she felt content, that she felt energized and proud of herself. Besides the omnipresent nerves from the affair with Paolo, she felt she was smooth sailing. Why didn't her mother like this version of her?

Francine raced out of the door after her early wake-up call, taking a few pastries with her, and Margherita tried to go back to sleep.

Margherita: I have an empty hotel room until noon…

Paolo: Bello!

Margherita: It could be…

Paolo: I can't, my love. I have to take the kids to school. I'll see you later.

Only she knew they wouldn't see each other later. She sat in the unmade bed, in the empty hotel room, staring at her phone as if he would suddenly change his mind. She felt immensely alone. She didn't want to have sex with Paolo. She wanted to lie next to him. She wanted him to brush the hair from her face. She wanted to feel his warmth.

She wondered if her mom would ever visit her again.

MILANO, LOMBARDIA

2016

THAT EVENING, SHE went out for drinks with Lucas. It was late, a weekday, and the outdoor tables at N'Ombra de Vin were full. People stood and smoked, snacked on patatine and drank glasses of red wine.

"You'd think she would understand my wanting to work in design. After all, she married my father. I swear, though, if I worked in banking, it would be one constant competition between Benjamin and I. She'd be comparing our numbers all day."

"I feel you. Family can be tough," Lucas said. He was eyeing a petite boy to the left of Margherita. She was always amazed at how quickly gay guys picked each other up, with so few words.

"She just hates my living in Italy. She thinks I will never move back and she refuses to see the beautiful positives to life here. She questions everything. Judges everything. Compares everything to New York or London," Margherita said, taking a sip from her second glass of pinot noir. "We're not in New York or London!" she shook an imaginary shape in the air out of frustration.

"Maybe with time…she'll come around," Lucas said, but she could tell he wasn't really listening.

"You think he's gay?" Margherita discreetly tipped her head toward the young boy. "You like 'em young, don't you."

"Yeaaah," Lucas said, drawing it out, staring at the young man.

"I swear I'm never moving back. Why would I? I am perfectly happy here. I have never been happier," she said, decisively.

A pang of guilt ran through her.

"No one is going to tell you where you have to live or where you have to be happy. If Milan works for you, there is nothing wrong with that."

She hadn't told Lucas about her mom's illness—nothing about her ups and downs, nor about the hospitalizations in recent years. Only Chiara and Camilla knew, and Camilla never missed a chance to make her feel guilty.

"Your mom has been through a lot," Camilla reasoned. But Margherita saw it as two separate things: her mother's health, and her mother's relationship with her daughter, both deteriorating.

Margherita thought about the vacation she and Francine had taken to Italy a few years prior. They had planned it for months, looked forward to it together. They had been so impressed with Milan, with its beauty, its sophistication, its effervescent people, and of course its shopping. They passed a few gorgeous days on the Eolian Islands after Francine introduced herself to a skipper who toured them around on a sailboat, Francine taking the first dives into the sea and egging Margherita on. They shopped in Siracusa and spent their final nights in Rome, where Francine was constantly making a new Italian friend and acting as the unpredictable, vivacious older sister, while Margherita laughed along and tried to keep up. They ate and they walked and they soaked up every minute, and it was one of the best weeks in Margherita's memory bank. It was before Francine's suicide attempt. It was before that unforgettable, horrible phone call Margherita had received one Sunday morning in San Francisco. It was before the doctors put Francine on a different regimen, which left her angrier, more irritable than she had ever been. She wished she could bring that Francine back.

After they finished their drinks and Lucas exchanged information with the cute young man, they decided to call it a night. Lucas was meant to present the portfolio's brand guidelines the next morning. He called an Uber and she waited with him; the bar was only a few blocks from her apartment.

"I feel like no one else takes Ubers here. Everyone judges me when I call one," Margherita said. They stood on the sidewalk in Via San Marco. Lucas towered over her, all six feet two inches of him.

"I know. Everyone says they're expensive. But there aren't any cabs. You hear expensive, I hear convenient."

She laughed. She felt so happy to have friends to have glasses of wine with, and to laugh with. It was so simple, but had seemed so out of her grasp for so many years. Now she had it, and she wouldn't give it up for the world.

Lucas got into his Uber and Margherita turned the corner onto Via Montebello, where a few cigarette-smoking, wine-drinking patrons sat and stood on the corner outside Fioraio Bianchi. She walked slowly toward Corso di Porta Nuova, taking in the night, the clinking of plates, and the rustle in the trees.

MILANO, LOMBARDIA

2016

IN MILANO, MARGHERITA had learned the rules of dress. She wore heels everywhere she went, unless she was running or taking a walk on the weekends, and she often got her hair blown out professionally—a much more affordable treat than it was in New York. One did not leave the house in gym clothes or yoga pants in the world's most fashionable city, and one certainly did not wear exercise sneakers with street clothes in order to walk comfortably from Stazione Centrale to via Montenapoleone. While in New York, she often spent entire weekends in yoga clothes, in Milan she made sure to always be ready for a chance encounter. Margherita also quickly learned that one always put makeup on, even if it was to run downstairs to the tabacchi to buy a newspaper, (or the time she couldn't open a glass tuna jar and she brought it down to the rivista stand where the rough-and-tumble man who sold her overpriced American Vogue opened it for her, the olive oil spilling on his hand). From head to toe, from the moment the Milanese's bespoke shoe stepped into their palazzo's interior courtyard, to the evening's last glass of wine on Via San Marco, there was not one accessory forgotten, not one hair out of place, not one minor brutta figura to forever be remembered by everyone at the Marchesi counter on Via Montenapoleone.

How many times had Margherita walked along that exquisite street, past the superlative window displays which could only be described as art, past the finely dressed Milanese men having one of dozens of daily cigarettes, leaning nonchalantly into a limestone wall as they checked an email, or perhaps a message from their mistress. How many espresso cups had she heard being put down and picked up, put down and picked up, that recognisable clatter that gave her such a sense of place; the first sound she could remember from her first time in Rome as a child.

It was at the counter of one of those cafés one morning, Marchesi on via Montenapoleone, the candy-colored, velvet swathed, literal gem designed by Miuccia Prada herself, where she had stood elbow to elbow with one of the most magnetic, effortlessly elegant Milanese men she had met. He was sporting two days of stubble, and under his wavy chestnut hair, his lapis eyes focused either on Davide behind the bar or on his macchiato and cornetto before him. He offered a polite smile and hand shake to the man next to him. He was not extravagant in his gestures, he was not overly social, just charming and pleasant enough, with a quietude about him.

Margherita stole a few sideways glances, but he didn't register her presence until Davide offered his usual chatter—a gruff hello that turned into a genuine smile and a chocolate not so suavely passed into the palm of her hand. He held her hand for an extra beat, closed around the chocolate, as he always did, their little routine. Davide looked around over her head at the clients who came and went. The men were chic in their suits; the women were chic in everything—the latest handbag, hair perfectly blown out, their make-up just so. They all politely vied for a spot at the bar where they would eat their brioche con marmellata and drink their morning cappuccino. They would chat about a weekend in Mombaruzzo or the hills of Alto Monferatto, laughing, smiling—always smiling—while dusted sugar fell to their fancy footwear. There were, of course, the few that arrived at the gold-piped glass counter and remained perfectly erect and straight-lipped; they were there for breakfast and nothing else—a tradition that held strong in rain and snow, from youth to old age.

The elegant man looked toward her then, having received confirmation, from her chatter with Davide, that she was one of them.

"Uno ogni giorno, penso sia solo per le donne," *One every day. I think only for the women.* She nodded towards the chocolate. She noticed his full lips.

"Non sei Italiana." *You're not Italian.*

"No, sono Americana," she affirmed. He nodded, satisfied, as if this admission explained eighty-five percent of her entire being. His remaining questions, as to the other fifteen percent, could be explained by her reasons for being in Italy. He quizzed her, to complete the picture.

"Amore?" *Love?*

"No."

"Stai studiando?" *You're studying?*

"No."

Looks of confusion, dubiousness. "Allora perché? Di dove?" *So why? Where are you from?* he asked.

"New York." She inched closer toward him to make room for a woman to her right.

"Preferisce Milano. Pazza, questa," *Prefers Milan. Crazy, this one.* Davide interrupted as he wiped a glass dry. The mysterious, elegant man smiled again, and looked her in the eyes.

"Sembri Spagnola, il tuo viso, la tua pelle chiara," *You look Spanish, your face, your fair skin,* he said.

"No, in realtà sono Italiana. Mio papà è nato in Liguria." *No, actually I'm Italian. My father was born in Liguria.*

"Ah. Ma perché preferisce l'Italia?" *Why do you prefer Italy?* he asked.

"Ah, è una storia lunga. *A long story.* The people, the travel, the beauty, the life…the life is better here. It just is. New York is a fantastic city, but it is hard. I don't know. I just feel good here," she said. It was a question she had answered dozens of times before. The Italians could never understand why someone would leave New York for Italy.

This man seemed to understand. He nodded.

"Hai ragione. *You are right.* Cristiano, piacere," he held out his hand in the little space they had left between them.

"Ah, you don't know each other?" Davide asked.

"Margherita," she said. They both looked at Davide, smiling shyly, a little on the spot.

"Cristiano is like the mayor. He owns Romanelli, next door," Davide said. Romanelli was a storied clothing manufacturer and one of the last family run premiere clothing brands, not having been sold to one of the conglomerates like LVMH or Kering. Cristiano watched Davide talk about him with indifference. He had that Italian sprezzatura in spades—that nonchalance, that effortless charm.

"Vieni un giorno. Facciamo un giro. Tu, cosa fai qui a Milano?" *Stop by one day. I'll give you the tour. And you, what are you doing in Milan?*

"Lavoro nel settore dell'ospitalità per la famiglia Leonetti. Stiamo per creare un nuovo albergo qui in zona." *I work in hospitality with the Leonetti family. We are opening a new hotel in the neighborhood.*

"Ah, si. Lo conosco bene il progetto. Allora, fammi sapere quando vuoi venire. Devo scappare. Scusami. Piacere." *Ah yes, I know the project. Okay, so let me know when you want to stop by. I have to run. Excuse me. Nice to meet you.*

He said his goodbyes to Davide and the crew, politely excused himself from his space at the bar, and exited the café. She watched him light a cigarette as soon as his leather shoe hit the sidewalk. She had heard about him, of course, the playboy that he was, heir to the Romanelli company. In the flesh he was even sexier. She would see him again, most certainly.

MILANO, LOMBARDIA

2016

"He has two kids. You would never know," Camilla said, as she slowly walked her bike down Corso Venezia with Margherita.

"Where do they live?"

"With their mom. In Sweden, I think. Or is it Denmark. I don't remember. One of those countries where everyone is tall and blonde and beautiful."

"What kind of father sees their children so infrequently?" Margherita asked as she eyed the pedal of Camilla's bike, trying not to trip on it. Then she immediately thought of Francine, who would see Benjamin once every six weeks, and then over the summer of course. Was she being too hard on Cristiano?

"I don't know. He strikes me as very sad. Gorgeous. But sad," Camilla said. "Oh—see that Sicilian bakery? Can we go in? I've had a craving for weeks."

They crossed at the crosswalk, and Margherita waited outside the bakery with Camilla's bike while her friend, after much consideration, picked out a frutta martorana.

"Oh my god. I am so happy right now. I pass by this place every day and I never let myself go in," Camilla said, taking a bite. "There was a Sicilian bakery next to my school on Seventy-fourth street and I'd beg my nanny to take me every day. Do you eat sugar, like ever?"

"I eat dark chocolate every day."

"God. I wish I could have your discipline."

"Ha!" Margherita guffawed, and they continued toward the park.

NEW YORK, NEW YORK

2013

Jack: And how are the architectural assessments coming along?

SHE HAD BEEN working on a design drawing; eager to show her new boss her Yale education had been a worthwhile investment. When her phone vibrated, her eyes darted toward the lit-up screen and her mouth formed a smile, her eyes ablaze in delight and mischief, her emotions painted over her face with fat brush strokes. She leaned over the screen so no one could peep over her shoulder.

Margherita: Rather slow. Am afraid one cannot match the full steam of your output. Analysis is not my cup of tea.

Jack: My output is total repugnant crap lately. This new client is detestable. Shall we get an actual tea?

Margherita: Will meet you on the corner.

Jack: Who walks out first?

Margherita: Ladies first obviously.

Jack: Oh obviously. See you in a sec :)

Margherita didn't have time to go to the bathroom to check her reflection. She huddled over her compact, smoothed her under-eye concealer, applied lipstick, and quietly rose from her desk, leaving her coat behind to make it look like she was still in the building in case her boss returned. She passed Noah's desk. He followed her with his eyes, raised his eyebrows, and gave her a knowing glance. She smiled at him with indulgent innocence.

On the corner, Jack and Margherita exchanged glances brimming with mischief. They walked a few blocks to a coffee shop they knew none of their colleagues frequented.

"How is the Brooklyn house hunt?" she asked, as his puppy dog eyes stared a hole into her.

"Dismal. Oh the things money can't buy in New York. Or Brooklyn, rather," he said, scanning the café. They sat on stools at a high-top counter, their knees grazing below the surface of the table.

"Missing London?"

"Hmm. I don't think the young'uns were quite happy to have been yanked from school."

"Oh, they're young. They'll make new friends." She waved her hand in the air.

"What about you? Do you have lots of friends in the city? You went to school here. You must have loads of friends," he said, looking at her with those sympathetic Hugh Grant eyes.

She shrugged nonchalantly. "Not really."

"No?"

"It's hard to make girlfriends. *Like? Like, like, like? And, um, I mean like literally!???*" she mimicked.

"Oh. Please stop. That's horrid," he said, his face in a twist.

He was looking at her, looking without saying anything. "What?" She cocked her head to the side.

His face was straight and inexpressive. "Do you have any idea how gob smackingly beautiful you are?"

Margherita shook her head, playfully dismissive, and looked down at her empty espresso cup. Jack grazed his hand over her leg under the table. She gave him raised eyebrows. He raised his back.

"Fuck." He took his hand away and cupped his tea. "When are we going to go for a proper drink?"

"I am not convinced that's a wise idea," she said. She was drawing out the inevitable, playing with something that felt dangerous, enraptured in the attention of this very handsome, six-foot-two-inch, witty, intelligent, nostalgic Brit. Somehow she found herself engaged in a mostly innocent office affair, blurring the lines between reality and daydream.

Well, she did in fact know how it had started. She started it, somewhat forwardly and directly.

One morning, her mother had called her as she was on her way home from a run. She was sweaty, despite the morning's low temperatures, and getting a chill, so she had tried to get her mother off the phone without seeming to rush her. Francine had been in a very touchy mood at the time and could cross from nosey to spiteful in seconds.

"I just watched the most handsome man being interviewed on CNBC. A Brit. He was just hired by Merrill Bates Lee to design a new park on the East River. The city is investing a crazy amount. Apparently he is moving to New York. Incredibly handsome. You should introduce yourself.

He's a few years older than you (twelve to be precise, she learned later with a Google search) but go over there. Say `hello'! You are colleagues now!"

Margherita had rolled her eyes and hung up the phone. Her mother for some reason thought her daughter should be married with babies before thirty. She constantly pressured her in some way. Margherita assumed that either her mother didn't have much confidence in her career prospects, or Francine wanted to see Margherita taken care of. In her lowest states, Francine constantly made references to her life as if it were a ticking clock.

Margherita did, however, watch the CNBC clip. He *was* handsome, in fact, and his crisp English accent and quiet dry humor was precisely the combination that piqued her interest. She strode over to the more senior side of the office and scanned the heads. No tall, brown-haired, fair-skinned man with long arms.

"Can I help you?" one of the partner's assistants asked.

"Oh, I was just looking for Jack Garnet?"

"He starts Monday." The assistant turned back toward his computer screen.

Monday came around and she purposefully let it go by, knowing he wouldn't want to be bothered upon touchdown. On that Thursday, she strode over to the forbidden side of the floor again. There was a tall man who fit the Google photos sitting against the wall, very focused on something on his screen, a form of some sort. Maybe he was updating his HR records. What a pain.

"Jack?" She inquired, head tilted, slight smile. She was aware of her tight blouse, cut low, and her chic wool skirt.

He looked at her, his eyebrows still furrowed at his screen. His posture was very good, she noticed right away, and his skin was fair against his dark brown hair.

"Yes? I mean, hi. Sorry. Bloody insurance. You Americans. Sorry. Can I help you?"

"I don't mean to interrupt. My name is Margherita," she said, putting her hand to her chest, as if to say 'I come in peace.' At that point all of their surrounding colleagues had focused their attention on the awkward introduction. She ignored them completely and carried on.

"I heard you were being transferred here. I can imagine you are very busy, of course, but I wonder if you might have time for a coffee? You worked in Cambodia with my mentor at Yale, Professor Herold…I did a study on your project during my second year. I would love to show it to you, just to hear your thoughts."

"Okay," he said, flatly. "I mean, yes, sure, sounds great." His hands held the flattop of the desk as if it might float away as he stared at her expectantly.

"Okay. Great. Thank you! I'll send you an email?"

"Yes. Good. Here," and he found a piece of loose leaf paper in a stack in front of him and scribbled it down.

"Perfect. Good luck- with the insurance. It's very good— at least, in case anything goes awry." She spun on her heels to return to her side of the floor.

MILANO, LOMBARDIA

2016

MARGHERITA AND CAMILLA met for a quick weekday lunch at Centro Botanico in Brera, their preferred lunch spot for its clean, healthy vegetarian food. It was also where Margherita often spent too many euros on fancy little seed crackers and buckwheat chocolate treats. She scanned the other patrons' plates to see what looked good.

"Cristiano was at the agency this morning for a breakfast meeting. He is so gorgeous but so cocky. He still treats me like the assistant," Camilla said. "I overheard him telling Maurizio he's fighting with his girlfriend. She went back to her parents house in Switzerland for the long weekend."

Camilla loved a bit of gossip. It was fitting, as she worked in PR.

"They have a tumultuous relationship it sounds like," Margherita said, pouring olive oil onto her plate to dip a piece of rye bread as they waited for their food.

"I think he just needs attention. Such a weirdo. He seems so lonely," Camilla said, eyeing the bread. "Excuse me?" she asked the waitress as she walked by. "I asked for gluten-free crackers a few minutes ago…"

With Camilla, Margherita always assumed the role of younger sister or flighty friend. Camilla was bossy and took after her demanding and diva-like Milanese mother, who was appalled at Camilla when she once walked the six blocks between their apartments without makeup.

"I saw Paolo last night," Margherita confessed, awaiting her friend's judgment.

Camilla shook her head. "Ugh. Why."

"It's just too good!" Margherita gushed. "It's so…intense. There just is No. Sexier. Man."

"You're ridiculous," Camilla said, as her gluten free crackers arrived. "Finally! Listen, you need to meet a guy your own age. I wish I knew more straight guys."

"Blah I never meet any guys my own age. And how could I possibly give up this man?" Margherita pulled up Paolo's WhatsApp profile photo once again.

"Do you think Taddeo knows yet?" Camilla asked.

"No…"

"God what a bad friend Paolo is," Camilla said, and their plates of three different veggies arrived: farinata, cicoria, e barbietola for Margherita; miglio, carote con erbe, e zucca for Camilla.

SAN FRANCISCO, CALIFORNIA

2014

MARGHERITA HAD BEEN living in San Francisco for three months when Noah texted her from Los Angeles, letting her know he would be in town. His departure from Merrill Bates Lee a few months prior to her own was one of the catalysts for her leaving; he was one of the only friends she had made since graduating college and without him in the office every day she had felt especially lackluster. He and his girlfriend had packed up their Hester Street apartment and moved to Los Feliz, where they could be artsy LA people while enjoying good weather.

She was counting down the days until their lunch at Cotegna. Slowly but surely she was making her way through San Francisco's most talked-about restaurants, ordering mostly raw fish and not allowing herself to eat anything else during the day. It gave her something to do. So far in her adopted city she had taken about a dozen hikes in both the North and South Bays, gone on a dozen mediocre dates, and eaten her fair share of Acme bread (a supreme indulgence) and farmers market cherries. She was growing a little antsy. Although she had found a job at a start-up, she felt out of place there, in fact, she had felt out of place upon arrival.

Noah: So you make dry, vegan, quinoa bowls, have people order them through a keyhole on an iPad, and serve them in a cube-shaped garage.

Margherita: Well, I don't actually make them. But that is the gist of the company, yes.

Noah: This sounds so San Francisco it makes me sick.

After they ordered grilled sardines and a roasted chicken for two, Noah moved on to the hard questions.

"So what are you doing here." He said it matter-of-factly, not in the form of a question, but rather a "spit-it-out" type of approach.

"Hiking!" she exclaimed. He had been following along on her Instagram, of course, commenting on the photos she had posted of Mt. Tam and the like, poking fun at her newfound nature-loving persona.

"Do you sew your own shoes now? Are they vegan too? Do people even wear shoes here?"

She looked down at her sandals. Miu Miu.

Noah rolled his eyes. "Hiking. Okay. Then what? How's work?"

"It's fine. I'm not sure exactly what I'm supposed to be doing most of the time. I try to look busy. Each of their locations will be designed pretty much exactly the same. Stark. Boring. Sans creativity."

"Riveting. Not exactly drafting multi-level Cartier boutiques, are we?" he asked.

She shrugged and clasped her hands, resting her chin on her knuckles. Noah fixed his eyes on her from across the table.

"Do you like it here?"

She shrugged. "I think so. It's beautiful. Outside the city, at least."

"But you're not a techie."

"No. But…I don't know. It's okay for now," she moved her elbows out of the way as their sardines arrived. Noah let her take the first one.

"Too bad you didn't get that job in Milan. Italy would have been a lot more interesting to visit."

She nodded slowly in exaggerated agreement.

"How's your mum?" he asked as he delicately placed a sardine on his plate.

"Um, she's okay," she answered, uncertainly.

"Have you seen her?" he asked, forking small bones out.

"No. I haven't been back."

"Are you going?"

"No, I don't have any plans. I don't know. We'll see."

He looked up. She was playing with a few tiny bones on her plate, rubbing the fork over them.

"Is she back at work?" he asked, his fork in mid-air.

Margherita nodded. "She's in London for a few weeks."

"Oh wow. That was quick. What does your dad say?"

Margherita shrugged. "Nothing. No one can control Francine." She pulled at her ear lobe continuously and inhaled deeply.

Noah watched her, taking in her fair skin, her cream eyelids. He stabbed a kumquat onto his fork.

"What is this thing?" He asked, offended by its appearance.

She looked up to see his contorted face. She missed his English sarcasm.

"I think it's a kumquat."

"A kum what? You have spent too much time here. Too many farmers markets. Get yourself back to a proper metropolis."

"You live in LA," she said, emphasis on the LA.

"And it is legitimate. This place is *weird*," he concluded, and he plopped the kumquat into his mouth. His face warped in distaste for the acidity.

"I hear Jack went back to London," he went on, pouring himself another glass of wine.

"Oh?"

"His wife writes for *Porter Magazine* now. And he is working on a huge commission in Battersea."

"Right. Good for them."

"It wasn't quite An Affair to Remember, anyway, was it? You need someone more up. Less mopey. More..."

"Cary Grant?"

"Yes! No. He was gay, wasn't he?"

MILANO, LOMBARDIA

2016

MOST MORNINGS MARGHERITA went for a run. She woke early, before seven, and forced herself to get going without an espresso. She didn't have an espresso machine in her apartment; she preferred to go to a caffè and chat, to people-watch and be a part of the day with other Milanese. But there was no caffè in her neighborhood that was open at this hour, so she learned to get her blood pumping with a few extra jumping jacks.

Via Solferino was always quiet at that time, save for the fruttivendolo boys setting up for the day. She glided past the one with curly hair whose name she never remembered; he greeted her with a boisterous 'Ciao' and a big wave, the same call as every morning. She took a right on the mostly pedestrianized Via dei Cavalieri del Santo Sepolcro, past the leaf covered apartment building on the left, the secret garden she adored, past the mini Carrefour and toward Parco Sempione. There were only a handful of runners in the park by seven, which would already be considered late for Manhattan. She ran along the periphery and exited at the Arco della Pace, where she stretched her legs. There was the light, she loved to take in the light at the beginning of the day, with the peace and energy it brought.

On the other side, she ran along the stately curve of Arco Della Pace, past the Triennale, and zig zagged in and out of the elegant blocks in Zona Magenta, admiring the beautiful buildings in Via Leopardi and Via Giuseppe Revere before making her way back toward Montenapoleone. A quick stop was made for an espresso at Marchesi. She was one of the only patrons who dared enter Marchesi in sweaty exercise clothes, but it was early and there was hardly anyone there.

Afterwards, she darted back down Via Santo Spirito, past the future hotel, down along Via Mozart toward one of her favorite piazzas, Piazza Eleonora Duse. She cut back toward Parco Venezia and did a lap around the dusty, charming park, past the little pond and the merry-go-round, and back out toward via Della Moscova.

In her apartment, she smiled in the shower as she looked through the glass door, beyond the French doors of her terrazza, and out onto the treetops across the street. She loved to see the treetops from inside her shower. She loved her apartment. Her home.

She left twenty minutes earlier than usual to buffer her time at the dry cleaner. If there was just one person in front of her, it would take no less than twenty-five minutes. If she was the only one there, it might be at least fifteen. It was one of the fancy dry cleaners that also sold fancy household cleaning things and shower items, like expensive combs and scented soaps.

"Good morning, Signorina," the older man said, as he took out his old fashioned binder where he recorded each transaction. He reminded her of Mr. Bean. There were days when she found him charming, like a caricature, and she appreciated him deeply for the painfully slow and polite Italian that he was. Other days, her New York impatience crept through, like the time at the shop when she all but shouted at the manicured woman in front of her, *The loofahs are all the same! The light pink one does not clean you any better than the white one!* And shoved one in her Fendi.

> **Lucas:** Might have had sex with a cute boy I met on the tram last night.

She was just signing her ticket when she received the text. Her phone was set on voice reading from when she was running, so the message was heard out loud. The Mr. Bean man went red in the face.

"Mi scusi. Grazie, buona giornata!" Margherita said, innocently, and dashed out of the tiny space, the door chiming behind her.

> **Margherita:** So you met him on the tram, and what? Went for a drink?
>
> **Lucas:** No. He got off at my stop. We went to my apartment. No drink.
>
> **Margherita:** Move over, Meg Ryan.
>
> **Margherita:** Leaving the fancy dry cleaner. Be there in 10. Want anything from the San Marco market?
>
> **Lucas:** No grazie!

She walked through the block-long outdoor market, starting at the flower stalls, and stopped at her fruit man.

"Marghe, come stai?" Riccardo asked, his tummy protruding over his dirty jeans.

"Ciao! Sono in ritardo; c'è una mela molto dura?" *I am running late. Do you have an apple, really crisp?* She asked, her eyes scouring the autumn apples.

Riccardo stood with her and touched about a dozen apples before he handed her the perfect one. He was proud of his find. He weighed it.

"Trenta centisimi," *Thirty cents,* he said, watching her, smiling. "Hai fatto la tua corsa stamattina?" *You went for a run this morning?*

"Si, si, l'ho fatta. Ecco," *Yes, I did. Here,* she handed him the change. "Grazie. Devo scappare. Buona giornata!" *Thank you, I have to run. Have a nice day.* She yelled over her shoulder with a smile and a wave. She weaved through the people in the rest of the market and headed left on Via Pontaccio, a perfectly crisp apple from Trentino in her purse.

After a few hours in the office reviewing potential spa layouts, Margherita exited onto the streets of the Quadrilatero D'Oro toward Cristiano's Jacques Grange designed boutique. He cascaded down the carpeted stairs in a wine-colored jacket and pants, spoke a few words to an employee in hushed, deep tones, and suavely greeted Margherita's liquid green eyes with his electric lapis ones. His gaze was penetrating; it made her nervous. She had dug for intel about him since they last met and had learned, for example, that he dined with the prime minister, Renzi, once a week and often flew a private jet to Rome for afternoons of meetings with God-knows-who.

"Feel this," he said, lifting the arm of a double-breasted, handmade cashmere chinchilla and silk coat. He gestured to the shoulder seam of a jacket and asked if she knew the difference between a Milanese cut and a Neapolitan cut. She feigned an education on the intricacies of fine Italian tailoring and suddenly felt glaringly American. They ascended to the women's shop, their footsteps silent as they wound their way up the carpeted stairs. The room was dreamlike; light and airy colors effused femininity as if it were being misted out of the light pink velvet walls. Display cases offered a taste of the Romanelli woman's world: exquisite perfume atomisers, furs, pony-skin baguettes, bespoke jewellery boxes made from ficus sycamore wood, and of course, the stylish women's collection. There was a piece for every occasion, every turning point in the day, as if one had opened a wardrobe inside a first class cabin on the Titanic. She wondered if Cristiano's current girlfriend dressed like this, although Camilla had told her that she was one of those rich daddy's girls who wore scraps of clothing—seven inches of vintage Dior to cover her eight-foot long legs.

On the lower level, Cristiano stood next to Margherita as she ooh-ed and ahh-ed over handmade pieces from a male's treasure chest, a room filled with one-of-a-kind toiletries, shaving kits, smoking and desk accessories, and hand-made knives. There was a faint, humble smile on his face, almost hidden by two days of stubble. He told her how, one hundred years earlier, gentlemen used to carry their own knives to restaurants. He seemed to know an appropriate anecdote for every piece, and she felt like a little girl being shown around the factory by a sexy Willy Wonka.

"Lunch?" he asked, as she finished a loop around the glass case.

They nestled into a garden table at one of his go-to spots down the street, a family-run restaurant for the fashionable set known for their handmade pasta. Cristiano chose one without looking at the menu, Margherita ordered fish ("You ordered fish at a pasta restaurant?!" Camilla later grimaced), and they settled into a decanted bottle of chianti, their heads leaned in toward each other beneath the heat lamp.

The purpose of the lunch was to learn more about his business—a plausible supposition, as she was researching possible retail partners for the new property; perhaps he could be convinced to relocate the flagship. There were rumours he was behind in paying his staff, that his boutique was not profitable, that he sank a fortune into the collections and seasonal photoshoots (the latest in the Arabian desert). He did, however, have very strong connections in the city; whatever the state of his actual finances, one did not cross him.

He was a rich boy in his early forties, though he looked more like fifty-three than forty-three, likely due to drinking, drugs, lack of sleep, and the Italian nonchalance over SPF. He was a ringer for a Milanese Steve McQueen— more elegantly dressed, but with the same roughness, "I don't give a damn" attitude, and undeniable sex appeal. He possessed a mysterious quietude which made Margherita all the more aware of her every word and her every move.

He knew everyone around them at the restaurant, and she wondered if he was concerned about lunching with a young twenty-something girl who was not his girlfriend. Then again, it was Milan, the land of sex and feigned discretion. "So, tell me about what you are doing with Elisio," he said in his unmistakable baritone voice as he topped off her glass. "You know I sail with the Leonettis every summer? In Sardinia. I have been friends with Beck since I was very young." She wondered when he had time to see his children.

She watched him roll a cigarette on the table as she told him how she had come to know Elisio and what she was doing for the new property. As she relayed her vision for the project with vigor, he seemed entranced, a slight smile on his face. Cristiano's blue eyes were set on Margherita's green eyes, on her cheeks, on her hands as they emulated her thoughts. He stopped rolling the cigarette on the white tablecloth and was momentarily caught off-guard when his plate of pasta puttanesca arrived.

They talked about opening new businesses in Milan—the bureaucracy of it all, the insurmountable red tape and politics. He became a bit heated when he described a bill he was supporting about tax breaks for charitable education donations from entrepreneurs and private companies, in order to improve the level of education in the country. He talked about intricacies of some of the government's new agreements with the EU, the permits and licenses required in the neighbourhood, all things that would affect the new property. She was surprised at his breadth of knowledge. He was more than a superbly dressed international sex icon and model for chic shoes in *Esquire*. His sharpness, speed and slight hot headedness made him even sexier.

His phone vibrated at least five times on the table—alerts for upcoming meetings booked every fifteen minutes for the remainder of the day, but he ignored them entirely. She felt she had successfully intrigued him. She was not sure why she had the goal of winning him over, but she was confident that she had.

"I am most excited about the spa design. And the F&B designs. And the guest bathrooms," she gushed as they finished their mains and the waiter appeared to clear the table. "And the retail designs of course, but these could potentially be left to the retail partners to build out independently. We're working with Paolo Lido and Matteo Vasconti on the interiors. Do you know them?

Cristiano nodded. "Ah, si, certo."

"Have you ever worked with them?"

"Io? No. But I have known them both a long time. Paolo and I used to be friends when we were young," he said, his mind tracing back a few decades.

"Are you still friends?"

"Nooo, no. Not really. I see him around. He is still out every night. I think he will be forever, until he is a hundred," Cristiano said with a smile.

Yes, that sounded like Paolo. Having a good time and combing through young unassuming girls until his very last day. Cristiano seemed more private. More discreet. More discerning.

He ordered an espresso and she coquettishly asked the waiter if there might be just a tiny piece of dark chocolate lingering in the kitchen? The waiter in his white jacket nodded conspiratorially, as if he received this innocent request daily and handled it staidly. He returned moments later with a thick wood cutting board, weighed down with a slab of dark chocolate as large as Cristiano's head, and a serrated knife. Cristiano smiled in her direction. Only in Milan.

Cristiano did the carving, and they both ate nibbles. He told her about "his" Milano with admiration and nostalgia; he was so proud of his city. He recounted stories about the oldest palazzi, open air concerts in the park, classic films that were shot on the outskirts of the center. He smiled at the idea of stringing the Christmas lights in the neighbourhood in about a month's time.

"Montenapoleone organises a very beautiful Christmas experience. Not to be missed," he said, looking her in the eye as if it were a command.

His assistant called, and he grazed through his calendar with furrowed brows.

"Devo andare, mi dispiace," *I have to run, I'm sorry,* he said, and he paid the bill and said goodbye to the waiters who knew him so well. He also stopped to say goodbye to a woman who had been sitting two tables over from them, dressed in Valentino head to toe. "My aunt," he said, as Margherita looked at him inquisitively. He placed his large hand ever so gently on her back and guided her out to the street. On the sidewalk of Via Montenapoleone, they said a businesslike goodbye, two kisses on the cheeks and planned to arrange a visit to the new property in the coming week or so, when he was back from London. Then he strode off, on his phone within a millisecond, a cigarette in his mouth.

Interesting. She felt quite accomplished in that moment, quite on top of her game.

Margherita: Just had great lunch with Cristiano Romanelli. He might be interested in moving his Milan boutique inside the hotel. Can we show it to him next week?

Elisio: Brava. I am in Paris next week. You can show it by yourself, no?

She had of course known Elisio was in Paris the following week. She smiled, felt immense satisfaction, and opened up a new chat.

Margherita: Conosci Cristiano Romanelli? *Do you know Cristiano Romanelli?*

Paolo: Amore come stai. *Love, how are you?*

Paolo: Certo. L'hai conosciuto? *Of course. Did you meet him?*

Margherita: Si si, siamo appena andati al pranzo. Cerco di includerlo nel progetto. Cosa dici- sarebbe un buon'idea? *Yes, we just went to lunch. I am trying to include him in the project. What do you think- good idea?*

Paolo: Si, è un nome grande, importante. Di persona e' un po' complesso. *Yes, he is a big name. Important. As a person he's a little complicated.*

Margherita: in che senso? *How?*

Paolo: Non so come a spiegare. *I don't know how to explain.*

Margherita: Boh. Sembrava simpaticissimo con me. *Well, he seemed really nice with me.*

Paolo: Guarda a te…chi non sarebbe simpatico, affascinante, etc? *Look at you, who wouldn't be nice, charming?*
Dove sei? *Where are you?*
Facciamo l'amore? *Let's make love?*

She smiled. Pot stirred. She dropped her phone into her bag and began her walk back to the office.

MILANO, LOMBARDIA

2016

MARGHERITA GOT HOME from work, took a shower, and blow dried her hair. She slipped on a short silk dress with long fluttering sleeves and a v-neck cut. She never wore anything that came up past her collarbone. Francine had often said that a woman's collarbone was one of her most alluring, feminine features, and that Margherita should always dress to display it. She was content with the image that stared back at her in the mirror. She smiled to herself, grabbed her evening bag, and set off towards her own aperitivo.

It was one of her favorite things to do: Get dressed up and see where the evening might lead, whom it might involve, how it could alter her path and lead to new adventures. It was something she learned from her mother. Francine had been fiercely independent in her twenties and thirties; she always had a boyfriend, though she didn't seem to care as much about them as she did about her career on Wall Street.

When Margherita was twenty, traveling through Italy by herself, her mother often encouraged her, "Get dolled up and go sit at a beautiful restaurant bar. Meet someone."

Her intention hadn't been for her daughter to meet married men; she had simply meant for her to go sit out in the world, amongst others, and perhaps have an interesting conversation, whether it be with a man, a couple, or a group of friends. Francine taught her daughter how to be her own company, an advantage and a curse. Even though she sometimes wished she had someone next to her, Margherita was always capable of sitting at a bar by herself, or a table or a sidewalk caffè, whatever it may be. She knew there were girls who wouldn't do this unless they were accompanied by a friend or a date, and she couldn't quite understand the fear.

"Meglio solo che male accompagnato," was a saying she had often repeated to others, by way of explanation.

She entered the Mandarin Oriental from the back entrance on Via Giardini, said hello to the hostess, and took a seat at the horseshoe-shaped bar. She loved the amber glow in the evening, the intimacy of the black marble, large enough for six fabulous people on each side. There was always a fashionable flower arrangement at the center, behind the bartenders, and that evening it was autumnal and equal parts sexy and seasonal. This was perhaps the sexiest bar in Milan, and she enjoyed it mostly in the cooler months, when it was no longer light after a certain hour, as it lacked windows.

She ordered a glass of pinot noir and was given an exquisite aperitivo to snack on, a gourmet work of art. She knew the five-star hotels competed with one another on the bellezza of their aperitivo. She decided to go ahead and order something for dinner, as she had no food at home and was already hungry (it was approaching 7:30, early for Milan but she had no plans later).

Across the bar sat two men in suits having an aperitivo.

One—bearded and tan with strong Roman features— was fixed right on her. He spoke to his colleague but his gaze was fixed straight ahead, his eyes on her as she sipped her pinot noir and took small bites. She thought it was odd, but maybe his gaze simply fell on her from where he was sitting, maybe he hadn't realized he was staring at her.

Seated next to her was another strong-featured man: tan, brown wavy hair, a few extra pounds around his belly, elbows on the bar, picking from a small bowl of fancy almonds and drinking something dark in a tumbler. He was looking at something on his phone. She found it interesting that he had not tried to say a word to her, even though he had stolen a handful of glances. She decided to ignore him, for once, to not be the woman who *started* the conversation, which she often was.

She ate in silence and texted Paolo a few times, hoping to convince him to meet her for a drink. He had been stringing her along all evening, no surprise there.

Paolo: I'm still in the office. We have a presentation in Rome tomorrow.

Margherita: Until?

Paolo: Non lo so amore. *I don't know, love.*

Margherita: Non vuoi venire a bere qualcosa? Poi torni? *You don't want to come have a drink? Then go back?*

Paolo: Mi piacerebbe. Anzi, preferisco ad essere con te che in ufficio. Ti chiamo quando esco. *I'd love to. I'd rather be with you than here. I'll call you when I leave.*

She was used to it. She tried not to let it ruin her evening.

The man across from her who had been drilling a hole in her head paid his bill. His eye contact had been incessant and it had, for a change, made her uncomfortable. Still, he couldn't have been interested in her, if he was leaving, walking out toward the lobby. He had simply not realized he was staring.

She was about to order a second glass of pinot noir when a man appeared at her left, his hand on her wrist.

"Ciao. Devo vederti stasera. Come ti chiami?" *Hello. I have to see you tonight. What's your name?* It was the Staring Man, who she thought had left. He was good-looking—handsome features, dark hair, and fit. He was a little wider around the shoulders, a little under six feet, not very Milanese looking. He was also, apparently, very blunt.

She was taken aback by his approach.

"Sono Giancarlo. Allora, io devo tornare in ufficio. Ma tu cosa fai?" *My name is Giancarlo. I'm heading back to the office, but you, what are you doing?*

"Cosa faccio?" *What am I doing?* she repeated. The people around her were watching. He was not suave in the slightest.

"Si, perché devo tornare a lavorare qualche ora. Ma devo vederti dopo. Cosa fai dopo?" *Yes, because I need to go back to the office for a few hours, but I have to see you later. What are you doing later?*

She was confused. He had a ridiculously large Goyard gym bag on his shoulder. She had never seen a Goyard gym bag before. She judged him hugely for it.

"Dopo? Vado a letto," *Later? I'm going to bed,* She said, almost laughing at his gusto. "Sola!" *Alone!* she added.

The nuts-eating man next to her coughed back a laugh.

"No, devo vederti. Ecco, questo è il mio biglietto di visita. Ma come ti chiami?" *No, I have to see you. Here is my card. What's your name?* Pushy Goyard Roman-Looking Man was almost annoyed with her, as if she was holding him back from a meeting.

"Margherita," she said, only to quiet him.

"E cosa fai a Milano, Margherita?" *What are you doing in Milan?* Suddenly he wanted to get to know her? With his Goyard gym bag weighing down one of his Roman shoulders?

"Uhh…lavoro con gli alberghi." *I work with hotels.*

"Okay. Brava. Devo scappare. Ma, chiamami. Ci vediamo dopo." *Okay. Great. I have to run. But call me. I'll see you later.* He pushed his business card before her and shot off toward the lobby where his friend was waiting.

The entire bar had gone silent. She looked into her wine glass as if it would help her regain her composure.

"Aggressivo," *Aggressive.* The man next to her mumbled as he stared at his phone. Oh, thank goodness for him.

"Veramente." *Really.* She put the back of her hands to her face. Her cheeks were warm and surely red.

"Do you think everyone heard?" she asked the man.

He looked up again, bored, and glanced around the horseshoe bar at the men and women returning to their conversations.

"Yes, definitely."

"Do you think he thinks I'm a hooker?"

He was looking down at his phone again. "Yes, definitely."

Hmm, she said to herself. *That was a first. Hopefully.* She began to reflect on her recent bar encounters.

"You said you work with hotels?"

"Yes, I work with the Leonetti family."

His face altered, he put his phone down. "Ah, interesting. What do you do with them?"

"Development. Interior architecture," she said, vaguely. "What about you?"

"I own hotels." he said, vaguely.

"Oh, which ones?"

"In Rome. I own two in Rome. Palazzo Lutetita and Petite Lutetia."

"Ma certo! I've read so much about both of them. I've never stayed there though," she said.

"Let me know next time you are in Rome. You can be my guest. Mi chiamo Dario."

"Margherita, piacere. So you live in Rome?"

"Yes, oh god yes, I could never live in Milan." He waved away the idea. "I'm here on business. I am opening a small property here, just next door. I'm staying with a friend but I got locked out of his place."

He told her about his desire to open a small hotel on the Amalfi coast in Anacapri, where he went every summer. It would be a good excuse to pass as much time on the coast as possible.

"I love islands. The concept of being separate; to me that is the best way to escape," he said, taking a few salted almonds between his thumb and forefinger and bringing them to his mouth. "Have you been to le isole Tremite? Or the Li Galli islands?"

"No, non ancora." *No, not yet.*

"Go also to the Eolie and Egadi islands, to Favignana, Pantelleria, Isola di Lampedusa…the food in Southern Italy has no comparison. There is nothing like the flavors of fish caught that morning in the Tyrrhenian Sea, or the juicy tomatoes, fresh herbs, the southern citrus fruits…"

"I wish I could fly away tonight!" Margherita said.

Dario smiled, knowingly. "You Americans never find these places. Venice, Rome, blah blah blah.

Growing up I spent summers in the Greek islands: the Cyclades, Paros, Mykonos, Santorini…and in the Ionic. I met my ex-wife in Antipaxos." He stopped abruptly. "So I haven't been back to those islands in a while," he laughed, a small but deep laugh, and took a sip of his wine. "But that's another story."

"Have you been to the Philippines?" He went on, his attention re-focused, as if he had just plugged himself in to a power charge. He shifted himself on his seat, facing her fully. "Boracai. You must go. There isn't even a harbor. It's truly like going off the radar. And the Indonesian islands. Java…. the temples in Java. Extraordinary. There is a hotel you must visit if you go. Especially if you love hotels. The Amanjiwo. They take you to the Borobudur Buddhist temple at four a.m. to see the sunrise from its top. That is the largest Buddha monument in the world, and with hundreds and hundreds of reliefs." He gesticulated, looking up into the air above him. "This is something that stays with you forever," he said, decidedly, and looked at her, nodded his head, took a sip of wine.

"I have so much to see. I feel a little behind," she said.

"Oh, no. You have time. You are young. But don't be too American in life. There is a difference between work and life, between the office and the dinner table. Time spent behind your iPhone and time spent exploring a minuscule archipelago in Vietnam. You understand?"

She nodded in agreement.

"What are you doing now? I am meeting a friend for dinner at Langosteria. Come," he said, now facing her, swatting his hand at her knee in a friendly way. "Or someone else might think you're a hooker." He looked around the bar suspiciously.

"Funny!" She acquiesced, knowing she would not see Paolo.

"Allora, andiamo." *So, let's go.*

And so they went to Langosteria. They sat at the middle chef's bar with Dario's Roman friend who managed the PR for a leading shoe brand. He had just returned to Milan after ten years in London. He was fabulous and worldly and knew everyone worth knowing in the industry. They shared highlights from both of their worlds—stories of parties and old friends, of Mayfair supper clubs and Roman birthday parties. His friend was not stumped in the slightest as to why Dario had invited a complete stranger to their dinner, a feast of oysters and fresh fish, langoustines and lobster spaghetti. That was life in Italy: make a new friend, take them with you. The party got larger.

After dinner, Dario walked her back through the center, back toward Via Montenapoleone. He held her hand as an older gentleman friend might. There was no pressure in it. They discussed the possibility of her consulting for his new property in Milan. She reflected on her work connections in Italy; they had been made and decided within minutes. The Italians made decisions based on feeling. They were emotional beings, and whether that led to success or not; they would simply find out, wouldn't they?

They walked past Loro Piana and Brunello Cucinelli. Dario stopped them in front of the window to admire the display. The street was empty at that late hour.

"I only shop at these stores. Look at that scarf. That's beautiful."

They landed at the Armani Hotel, where they took the elevator up to the bar. They would have a drink and wait for Dario's friend—the friend with whom he was staying, whose apartment he had locked himself out of—to finish his business dinner.

Upstairs, Dario and Margherita found a space at the bar and ordered more drinks. Margherita couldn't keep up with her new friend; she nursed a negroni while Dario asked her questions about the Via Santo Spirito project.

"Ah- there's my friend," Dario said, looking beyond Margherita. A tall man in a wine colored suit appeared at her side. She recognized that suit.

"Eccolo," Dario said and nodded towards Cristiano. Cristiano looked down at Margherita on her bar stool.

"Ma cosa fai qui? Siete amici?" *But what are you doing here? Are you guys friends?*

Margherita was equally surprised. "*This* is who we've been waiting for all night?"

Dario's face was a mixture of confusion and tequila. "Cosa?" *What?*

"We had lunch together today," Cristiano said.

Cristiano gave Margherita two kisses on the cheeks and she recounted the story of the evening.

"You should have seen the figlio di puttana *bastard* trying to pick up Margherita like a prostitute," Dario said. "I think it was her first time being propositioned."

"You told him off I presume," Cristiano said.

"Do I look like a prostitute?"

"Cazzo no," *Fuck no,* Cristiano said.

After another drink, Cristiano suggested that he was ready to go home.

"Dove vivi?" he asked Margherita.

"Around the corner. Via della Moscova."

"Ah, we are neighbors. I'll drive you."

They descended onto Via Manzoni, and she followed one step behind the men as they lit up cigarettes and crossed the street toward a white Porsche Cayenne, fully decked out. Margherita climbed in the back.

"No photos. No social media, okay?" Dario said, half-jokingly.

"I wasn't taking any photos back here by myself in the dark backseat, but okay. Why, though?"

Cristiano became serious in his buzzed state. "Jealous girlfriends. Italian girls are very jealous."

Ah. So I am the secret Americana friend, she thought. *Would it be so bad to be friends with me, and to be public about it?*

The next day, after meeting with a potential spa partner in Geneva, she dropped her bag off at her apartment and headed right back out for a stroll and to call her father. The sky was beginning to soften. It would be lunchtime for Tommaso back home.

Home. It was a strange word. She automatically used the word to describe where she came from, but it didn't feel accurate. Home to her was Italy. Home was also Tommaso, and her mother, in a way, but her life in its most content state, its most comfortable and genuinely happy state, was Italy.

"Hello," Margherita said in a deliberately silly voice.

"Oh, hello," Tommaso said back, in a strange, humorous tone. Theirs was a continuously silly relationship- something like an SNL skit come to life permanently.

"Come stai?" she asked.

"Oh, Como Stu," her father replied. He was Italian, but did not speak it at all.

"How's it going over there?" she asked more clearly.

"Oh, it's going. Busy day. I took your mother to her appointment yesterday, you know, so I am just catching up on a lot. Have to send out revised plans for the hotel in DC, have a call with the builder in Georgetown in an hour, have to look over that again. Have to take care of a few bills."

"Mmhmm. Have you heard back about the Lolato boutique in the city?"

Tommaso sighed into the phone. "No. I haven't. I am on pins and needles about it," he said.

"Nothing you can do but wait to hear, I guess." She bent down to pet a sweet little poodle at the entrance to Parco Venezia.

"Marghe, your mother says she hasn't heard from you all week," Tommaso said.

"Because every time I call her the conversation somehow goes to my not contributing to Social Security and my being an American-slash-English girl and my not meeting her idea of potential husbands," Margherita said with impatience. "That I should at least be living in London where Benjamin can look after me. Oh—the latest was that she could get me into a management program in The Hague. Because I don't have the stamina for an Oxford or Columbia MBA. And then suddenly she has to 'dash' before I can tell her about anything going on in my life. I don't need a babysitter. She needs a babysitter. And I don't want to go back to school. I am never going to work in banking. Why can't she get that through her head!?"

"Don't start."

"She's never around anymore anyways, what difference does it make to her where I am? "

"Marghe you are her best friend. She wants you close."

"Ha! Best friend! Sounds like Benjamin's new girlfriend is her best friend."

"Let's just be thankful she is at work every day without problems," Tommaso said.

"I know. Anyway. What are you all doing for Thanksgiving?"

"Well, your mother asked Benjamin and his girlfriend to stay a night or two."

"Right."

"It's not too late for you to book a ticket…"

"No. I don't want to miss days here. Italy doesn't celebrate Thanksgiving. I'd have to take time off work."

They talked about the progress of the Via Santo Spirito property. Margherita shared the latest updates on the architectural design for the new spa. She shared her excitement for the project and her enthusiasm for her work in general. Tommaso gave her apt advice and asked many questions, interested as always and so happy for his daughter that she had finally found something to sink her teeth into after a string of uninspiring jobs.

The sun had fully set by the time she meandered back toward Via della Moscova.

"It's such a pretty time of year here- so cozy and autumnal. I've been eating so much zucca. I wish you were here- we could do a cozy road trip through Tuscany or Umbria," she said, as the conversation began to wind down.

"Ohhh I would love that. The smell of wood burning fireplaces and all that tagliatelle with porcini mushrooms.

Crackling leaves. Ah, the country," Tommaso said, relishing the thought.

Margherita was so desperate to share her Italy days with her parents, sometimes she brought herself to tears, simply wishing they were there with her—there and appreciating it. There was so much joy to be found in the simple beauty, the character, the architecture, the people, the food…Unfortunately her parents were too consumed to be free to enjoy these pleasures. Francine had been going through a period of constantly changing medications, moods, and doctors. She often found fault with her current doctor on account of his or her medication regimen, and Francine would then stubbornly decide to go off her meds for a while until 'an episode' forced her to find a new doctor and begin a new regimen. Margherita felt simultaneously relieved to not be around and guilty for the same reason. Her brother, conveniently, only surfaced when Francine was steady.

"Oh—that's your mother calling. I'll talk to you later, okay babe?" Tommaso said.

"Fine. Ciao," Margherita said, disappointed. Francine always came first, in a just-in-case sort of way.

MILANO, LOMBARDIA

2017

"Let's go in here," Camilla said, pulling Margherita's jacketed arm toward the busy café on the tip of the U-shaped piazza. It was a neighborhood they did not often frequent, endlessly frenetic and filled with students and younger people who gathered in groups and smoked without pause. Camilla was on her way to a dinner with her family and it was the only time slot that she had free before Margherita flew to New York for the holidays.

"So you don't cook at all? Not even a Christmas lunch?" Camilla asked, once they navigated their confusing way to a seat, having snagged a small bowl of stale chips and a cheap glass of wine.

Margherita did not drink anything, as she was already feeling edgy. "No. My mom orders hamburgers from The Monkey Bar and drinks a bottle of champagne," she said crisply.

"Well, I'm sure she's excited to see you. She'll plan something for you two to do," Camilla said, more placating than usual.

"Hmm. She's certainly excited to see Alice," Margherita said, emphasis on Alice.

"She's excited to see you too."

"Not so sure. I think I've been replaced. Alice will probably get my burger."

"Don't be silly. Besides, who are you kidding- do you even eat burgers?"

"I eat the meat. If there's no bread crumbs or dairy. Yes."

"So basically just meat."

Margherita shook her foot, the one that was crossed over her other leg, and looked around at the festive decor and the young people all excited to get to their ski vacations in the mountains.

"Here," Camilla said, digging through her purse and retrieving a small bottle. "Take a few of these. Not at once," she laughed, "but one a day. They always calm me down."

Margherita regarded the pills in her palm. She dropped them into a napkin and placed it carefully in her bag. She never told her friends about Francine's medicine cabinet at home, about the amount of pills cleverly hidden in Altoid tins in her Bottega Veneta purses lest someone at her office spot an orange bottle. Francine was a walking treasure chest of uppers, downers, and everything in-between.

NEW YORK

2013

MARGHERITA AND JACK sat at the rooftop table atop the Soho office building for a mid-morning vent. They had become each other's office confidantes. They flirted, sent messages from one monitor to another across the floor, went for coffee, and talked about why neither was happy to be living in New York, each trying to talk the other back into loving the city and failing miserably.

"But you are young," Jack said. Margherita was looking towards the Hudson River. She pursed her lips, considering the unarguable fact.

"Yes, yes I am. Which means New York will always be here. And I should go, do, live, while I am young and unattached."

"So where will you go? Besides Italy," he said.

"Well, Italy," she said, decidedly.

"What if you don't get this job, the one you've been Skype interviewing for, in Milan? What then?"

"Ugh. I don't know. You're not helping, Sir Jack," she whined.

"Okay. But you're only- what, twenty-five? Have you given New York a chance?"

"I've been living here my whole life. I'm itching for a change of scenery. You did it. You bopped around." She did not say a word about her mother, about her family, about her anxieties and fears.

"Yes, yes, I've bopped. Boppity-bop. Though there is much to be desired when your clients are essentially politicians who wouldn't know a park from a train track, a theater from a brothel. Why is your city so dirty and so noisy, can you explain?" he said stoically, looking towards Soho. "Where are all the refined people? Where did *you* come from?"

"A Spence Education proves its worth, I suppose." Margherita felt sorry for Jack. She was at least free, unencumbered with a partner or children. Bopping was easier for her.

"So," he picked his head up and tapped her on the knee. "Where shall you go, missy?"

"I don't know. Maybe San Francisco. Everyone seems to love it. I can avoid the winter."

"Ah, but a San Francisco summer. Have you ever? Brutal," he said, his eyes wide.

SAN FRANCISCO, CALIFORNIA

2014

SHE HAD BEEN walking for hours; her feet were tired and the wind was building up. The stubborn fog, so thick that she could barely see the Golden Gate Bridge, had not broken. She stood at the edge of a path that overlooked the water below. Tall grasses blew in the incessant wind and a bicyclist a few feet away from her was taking in the view, the culmination of his ride. She felt a bit like Rebecca on the moors, only there was no great love story waiting for her at home, no Heathcliff, only a stingy roommate who refused to buy furniture, even though her Top Six consulting firm salary put her in a far better position to do so than Margherita's meager start-up paycheck. She thought about the week she had spent with her mom in Carmel before they drove up to San Francisco. She had found the apartment on Craigslist just days before moving in.

"It has no furniture!" Francine had argued. "How can you live with no furniture? What kind of adult lives with no furniture?"

They had been resting after a short walk around the village. Francine's energy was low and she couldn't handle much exertion on the medication she had been given.

"I want to live here one day," Francine had said, looking out to the ocean. Margherita had known what thought next crossed her mother's mind—one Margherita made her promise to stop voicing. She had tried to ignore the occasional signs Francine gave. Francine's depression was due to her medication, Margherita told herself, and soon she would get used to the new regimen, or they would change it, but nothing horribly morbid would ever happen. That was at least what Margherita told herself.

She was so tired of the fog, of the longest, coldest summer she had ever experienced, of the solo walks she took around the city and its environs. If she heard one more tech bro talk about his app, she would scream, and if she passed one more group of twenty-somethings on their way to a lousy bottomless brunch where they would day-drink and pig out on mini hamburgers she would have some sort of emotional breakdown, she was sure of it. Her desire to socialize had shrunk to zero since her mother's overdose attempt back in New York. She had traded dating for watching melancholy films on Netflix, and she had all but given up on maintaining a stylish wardrobe. Nobody else in San Francisco did, so why should she bother?

What if I jumped, she thought, standing at the edge of the cliff, a tall grass rubbing against her leg. There were mornings when she could barely get out of bed; so it was a true wonder that she was able to walk so many miles. When her alarm went off for work, she found herself lying there, physically unable to rise, unable to sit up. Oftentimes she felt tears form in her eyes and drip down her temples, gravity bringing them down onto her pillow. She would turn on her side and bury one eye into the bed, and when she finally sat up, it was wet, and she wasn't sure what to do next.

"You stay there. No reason for you to move back. Focus on you. The new job. Don't worry. Your mother will be fine. Don't worry," Tommaso had pleaded when Margherita repeatedly suggested moving home.

One foot on the ground, then the other. It was a real thing, to be depressed. *I am depressed*, she thought. *What do I do. How do I fix it.* She would bring herself to her bathroom, crying, and brush her teeth, crying, and all she could think about was her mom.

What if I meet someone who I fall in love with and she's not here? They won't ever have known her. How can I be with someone who has never met my mom?

ROMA, LAZIO

2017

MARGHERITA SAT ON an iron chair in the interior garden at the Hotel de Russie. She glanced upwards at the salmon-colored hotel; the last time she had been there was with Francine. They had stayed in a lovely corner room overlooking Piazza del Popolo, and all night long they had been kept awake by the sound of raucous teenagers in the piazza. They had enjoyed the hotel, however fraught their sleep, and she remembered vividly how they discussed the shade of peach sorbet it was painted. Her mother had said it seemed Floridian; it reminded Margherita of Bermuda. Everything that Francine had touched, Margherita remembered. Bits and pieces of their memories together were strewn everywhere. She suddenly missed her mom, but she knew if she called her, she would regret it. Francine was in a state of obsession with her work and hated to be distracted.

She listened passively to Elisio as he described the Via Santo Spirito Hotel's restaurant potential to Everett Ratett, who was visiting from New York. Margherita had learned of his visit from his assistant, whom she had befriended with an agenda (the New Yorker in her), and Elisio and Margherita had zipped down to Rome for an hour's conversation. Elisio would return directly to Florence while Margherita would spend the night and have dinner with Sandra. Cristiano was also in Rome for the evening, and when he learned of their overlapping schedule, he had casually offered his guest room at his Via Giulia pied-à-terre.

She met Sandra at a modern wine-bar/restaurant in Via della Stelleta. Margherita, never one to turn down octopus of any kind, had the calamaretti, while Sandra had tortelli with broccoli romanesco and acciughe. They talked and laughed for hours, and Margherita began her walk to Via Giulia through the narrow winding streets with a full heart and an upturned mouth.

As she meandered her way through the charming Rione Ponte, past the Chiostro del Bramante, she received a frantic call from Cristiano.

"My girlfriend found out that you are staying here. I told you not to tell anyone," he said, with an embarrassing amount of panic for a grown man of forty-six years.

"I didn't tell anyone…"

"Well she knows. And she called me, molto arrabbiata. *Very angry.* You can't sleep here tonight."

Margherita stopped in the middle of Via del Governo Vecchio, as a group of four American tourists drunkenly and noisily exited a restaurant. She backtracked onto the dead-end Vicolo Cieco to placate Cristiano, the man-baby.

"I'm sleeping in a guest room. My things are already there. What is the problem with you having a guest?"

"She is really pissed," he said, breathlessly, as if he were walking quickly.

"Well, why can't you just explain that I am a friend staying in the guest room, e niente?" *And that's all?*

"Okay. Okay. I will tell her Elisio asked you to stay there. I will think of something. But you have to leave in the morning."

"No problem." She was annoyed at his cowardice, but she also felt frustrated at how she was some sort of secret. Why was it not okay for her to be a man's friend? Why did men always relegate her to being a secret?

She went to sleep that night feeling uncomfortable and lonely. She wondered when she would ever meet someone who would want to brag about her, who would want to be with her openly and truthfully.

MILANO, LOMBARDIA

2017

MARGHERITA DID NOT want Paolo to pass the reception desk in order to be let upstairs, so she waited for him in the lobby. He was late. She had left her coat in the room and with the door constantly opening and closing, she was cold. She wore a short leather skirt and short-sleeve-sweater top, with her arms folded to thwart the gusts of winter air, and she slowly paced behind two giant pillars. When he arrived he of course immediately ran into someone he knew and stopped, helmet in hand, to say hello to them. He knew Margherita was waiting, and when he strode towards her, he had that irresistible smile on his face, a *'What?! I didn't do anything!'* expression. He mimicked her folded arms and outpaced her into the elevator.

After their rendezvous, as Paolo put back on his many layers of clothing, Margherita sent a text to Camilla who was already at the restaurant in Brera where they had a dinner reservation with Camilla's mother.

"Sono molto in ritardo. Ma non è troppo lontano, potrei camminare, si? Alla Trattoria Fioraio?" *I am so late. It's too far to walk, right?* She asked Paolo innocently, as she rolled her tights back up her legs and climbed onto an ottoman to stand at the same level as him.

"Amore, no, fa freddissimo e c'e tanto vento. Si muore."
Love, no, it's so cold and there is so much wind. You would die.

"Mi puoi portare?" *Can you take me?* she asked, a hand on each of his wide shoulders.

"Lo farei, ma non ho un altro casco…Dai ti prenderemo un taxi. Dai vieni," *I would, but I don't have another helmet. Come, we'll get you a taxi. Come on,* he said, as he helped her get down from the ottoman. She slid on her boots and they went downstairs together.

He asked the doorman to call a taxi for la signorina and waited for it to arrive before he left on his moto.

At the little trattoria, Camilla and her mother sat on one side of the four-top table and Margherita sat on the other. Camilla's mother held her mini poodle in her lap and ordered an artichoke salad and lasagne while Camilla decided on baccalà alla livornese. Margherita ordered a plate of spinach.

"That's it!?" Camilla's mother's eyes leapt at her from across the table. She did not have much of an appetite after the adrenaline rush with Paolo.

"That's all this one eats. Spinach. And berries," Camilla said, shaking her head.

"No wonder she is so thin," Camilla's mother said, gesticulating with her hands at Margherita.

"I eat a lot of dark chocolate," she replied.

After a few hours of gossip and dermatology chit-chat, the three ladies squeezed into the back of a cab. Camilla's mother had had a few glasses of wine and joked around with the cab driver, making both girls laugh so hard they could barely take a breath.

"Seriously now. Cami, do you want to sleep at home? You can come with me to yoga in the morning," her friend's mother asked as the taxi arrived at Margherita's palazzo. She said goodbye to them and climbed the stairs to her apartment. She always had fun with Camilla and her mom, but lately she felt something like jealousy at their relationship.

FIRENZE, TOSCANA

2017

MARGHERITA WAS A few paces behind Chiara as they walked up the steep hill to the trattoria. "Oh my good lord. Your butt, lady. No wonder," Margherita said, out of breath.

"Aw! I've been doing this walk every day. So good for the tush," Chiara said, turning around to allow her friend to catch up.

It was a perfect day in the hills of San Domenico outside Florence, and Margherita thanked the weather gods for giving them sun and warmth to spend the majority of the weekend outside. They sat at a round, metal table outside of the fattoria, which was one part olive oil mill and one part small trattoria. Chiara ordered a winter risotto and Margherita chose two small plates of fagioli and those dreamy, overcooked greens Italian did so well. When their plates arrived, Margherita let the scent of the white beans drizzled with olive oil and dusted with black pepper waft into her face. Tuscan heaven.

"I can't believe you are still seeing him. Why!?" Chiara demanded, after Margherita had told her about her most recent activities with Paolo.

"Ugh. I need to replace him. It's the only way. But how!"

"Who pays for the hotels?"

Margherita pursed her lips, obvious guilt layered on her face.

"You do!?" Chiara exclaimed.

"Most of the time…it's usually my idea so…?"

"You should send him an invoice!"

"That's actually a very good idea. Brava."

"Humph!" Chiara said, as she ordered a glass of wine.

MILANO, LOMBARDIA

2017

Margherita: I'm in the mood for a glass of wine. What are you up to?

Cristiano: Sono a casa. Vieni pure. *I'm at home. Come on over.*

IT WAS PRECISELY the response she was hoping for. Cristiano seemed the lonely type; he was the unofficial mayor of fashionable Milano, and everyone wanted to be on his good side, or do a deal with him, or otherwise rub shoulders with him, but she imagined he passed many evenings at home by himself.

She walked the four blocks to Cristiano's, around the small church at the corner of Via della Moscova and Via del Giardino, past the refined apartment buildings where some of the most chic Milanese lived and along the edge of the small park. She entered his elegant palazzo and checked her reflection in the elevator mirror. She felt confident, happy, content to have a few people in her neighborhood upon whom she could call for a little company—people she knew and who knew her, familiar faces with whom she could pass a few hours, even if her sporadic, platonic evenings with Cristiano in his penthouse apartment were clandestine. Nevertheless, she had cured a persistent loneliness since moving to Italy; she felt like a new person.

Cristiano's apartment encompassed the entire top floor of the palazzo, complete with a wrap around terrace. It was decorated in jewel tones and sumptuous fabrics. Framed photos of his children sat on a table in the foyer— perhaps the only evidence in his entire existence that he was a father. There was a giant, naked blow-up doll on his living room terrace, and a beautiful vintage motorcycle separated two sections of the main seating area. He sat on the velvet sofa rolling a cigarette, a glass of something dark on a tray before him. He retrieved a glass of wine for her and she settled onto the other sofa, her bare feet tucked beneath her.

"How is Elisio?" he asked in his deep voice, licking the cigarette paper. He wore a sleek, velvet robe in a dark ruby red color, and his feet were bare. She could see his tan chest.

"Oh, you know. Nervous energy knows no heights," she said.

He guffawed, the cigarette scrolled between his lips as he sealed it with his saliva. "He is *veramente* the energy bunny," he said, with an accent and slightly broken English, which he didn't think he possessed.

"Are you going to Sweden any time soon?"

"To see my kids?"

"Si."

"No. My schedule is crazy. They are coming here next weekend. I'm taking them to Nizza."

"With your girlfriend?"

"No. We are fighting a lot," he announced.

"Oh? I'm sorry. What about? If you don't mind my asking?"

"She is a great girl. But she wants marriage and kids and all that. She is twenty-eight; you know—she wants the things any twenty-eight-year-old woman wants. I've been there, done that. I don't want that at this point in my life. I want to be selfish."

Haven't you always? she thought.

"She's my age. I don't want that."

"Well, you are different," he said, looking up at her.

"Didn't she know this about you when you first met?"

"Yes, yes, of course," he said, impatiently. "But she is very intense, you know. She is a very passionate person. We fell in love, and she did not want to let that go. It's one of the reasons she is so fantastic. She becomes very passionate about each thing."

Margherita reflected on her own drive. She highly doubted anyone would describe her in that way. What was she passionate about? She felt there was nothing in particular.

"How is your friend?" he asked with a raised eyebrow and a half smile.

"My friend?"

"You know. Paolo."

"Ah. Oh, I don't know. We see each other once in a while. He is a hard habit to break." She took a sip of wine and rolled her eyes at her own lackadaisical attitude toward it all.

"Lust is more powerful than we give it credit for. Once it is unleashed, it is impossible to control." He rose and walked toward the kitchen. "Do you want anything else? Are you hungry?"

"No, I'm fine, grazie."

He returned with a tin Krumiri Rossi box, the famous Milanese shortbread cookies shaped like half moons. They were very expensive. She had them once in a while when she was visiting Camilla at the PR offices.

"Physical outweighs mental," he said, as he took a bite. "You want? These are like crack."

She gave in and took one from the box.

He smiled. "Hai visto? *You see?* You cannot resist."

NEW YORK, NEW YORK

2018

WINTER HAD COMETH early, with great explosion and unwelcome frigidity. It was the kind of day that made legs go numb and eyes burn, making it even more challenging for her to approach New York with a positive mindset. Certainly in Italy, full-on winter coats had not come down from storage yet. She was missing a beautiful Italian autumn and wanted to cry about it to someone, but she knew this would be frivolous and childish and that she needed to get on with it. At least she had an excuse to wear one of her gorgeous Italian scarves and her colorful Missoni turban. Francine loved Missoni.

She was quite proud with her Self-Wrapping that day, considering how many layers she had on, and let Yulia know that she was heading out for lunch. Every day she thanked the commercial real estate god that the Lolato New York office was in Soho and not midtown. She headed south on Lafayette toward one of her favorite cafés that she used to go to when she worked at Merrill Bates Lee, passing half a dozen duos en route to pick up lunch. She hadn't yet made an office friend, and she suddenly felt a pang of homesickness for her work crew in Milan. It had been the first time she had ever made friends at work and had felt that office camaraderie that she always heard about.

You will meet new friends here, she thought. *You will meet a guy. You will make a little life for yourself here and it will feel like home. You will feel connected. You will feel connected.* She repeated this over and over every day. It was what Francine always used to say when Margherita complained of feeling lonely or blue: "You need to be connected, somehow." It was typical Francine to constantly remind her daughter of what *needed* to be, or what *should* be, but what Margherita always found so challenging to bring to fruition.

At the café, she waited in the line that strung out the door. She felt like the only person who had turned up to grab lunch by herself; everyone around her was chatting with someone. Inside, pushed together with the other thirty-somethings who had the good fortune of working downtown, mostly at start-ups and art-inclined companies, she ordered a plate of the kale salad, roasted carrots with turmeric and pistachios, and the quinoa/lentil parsley mix. She looked back at the two high-top tables as she was waiting to pay, eyeing who would be next to rise and leave. It was always a challenge to time one's visit so that a stool was available. In summertime, everyone brought their veggies outside and sat on the sidewalks along Howard and Crosby Streets, but certainly no one was doing that in thirty-degree weather.

Someone was putting their scarf and jacket on as she took her credit card out. She jumped on the opening with New York vigor.

"Just saving my seat," she said to the young guy and girl who would be her table mates. He was cute, she noted, but in his early thirties—young for her taste. This wasn't really the place to meet a mysterious, sexy, forty-something Milanese man. How she wished she could find those encounters again. *No, no more of those. Time to meet a boyfri*end, she thought.

She sat down with her lunch, her scarf carefully put away in her bag, her turban resting on top. She grazed through Instagram and started a WhatsApp conversation with Noah. She could always count on him for tales of stereotypical LA Life: personal training sessions in the middle of the afternoon, picking kale from his vegetable garden in Los Feliz, elimination diets, cat babysitters, and house parties in Silver Lake. Through it all, thank God, he was still the same sarcastic, dry humored Noah who had made fun of her winter hat collection and plainly told her that her hair looked flat when she showed up to his going-away party at a January's end.

"So, Max's parents own a few properties in Hong Kong and he always wanted to do his own thing in New York. The idea is to take off here and open in LA, Chicago, and maybe DC. But New York is our focus for the next few years..."

Margherita listened to the neighboring conversation, more intrigued after hearing the charming British accent. The speaker was apparently explaining his (and Max's) hotel-meets-workspace company to a pretty young doe, who Margherita couldn't help but notice with quick sideway glances, seemed a bit too smiley and wide-eyed to be giving her full attention to the work-related aspects of the conversation. Margherita continued to assess: young British guy, perfectly symmetrical face, beautiful white teeth, gorgeous dirty blonde hair the shade of a walnut's crevices (the head of hair guys dream about, surely). He punctuated everything with his animated hands, and the more he spoke, the more intelligent he sounded to Margherita. He also possessed a wicked talent for barely-detectable comedic timing.

She had a soft spot for the British, no doubt about it. To name just a few, there was Jack at the architecture firm; and then there was Noah, also at Merrill Bates Lee, who hadn't swept her off her feet but had certainly found a permanent spot for himself in her small circle of favorite people.

Then there was Wilfred (Wilfie), an Oxfordshire guy who she had, until a few days ago, been casually dating for about three weeks. Francine would have been impressed—she had made it to the three-date mark before feeling unbearably antsy and dismissing him politely.

He was funny enough, sharp-witted enough, well-educated, knew how to hold both fork and knife—and extraordinarily incapable of emoting truthfully and honestly. She knew it couldn't last long when he offered to cook dinner at his apartment on Bowery, and she immediately thought, *Well that's no fun. How will I socialize?* To Margherita, the most alluring attribute of dating in New York was getting dressed up, going to a fabulous restaurant, sitting at the bar, and flirting and laughing in sexy dimmed lighting, surrounded by interesting people having a good time. She liked to look around, to survey the scene, and she loved to play the part. To go to someone's apartment, where it was just the two of them, with no external stimuli…that was an intimacy she simply had no interest in. At least not with Wilfred. Plus, she couldn't imagine saying the name *Wilfred* in the heat of the moment.

At the lunch table, she tried to listen in more, enjoying eavesdropping on the cute/young/smart Brit. She noticed him stealing glances at her, and every twenty seconds or so they locked eyes. He had made a bit of a mess with his roasted chicken; the carcass lay in front of him in the recyclable cardboard container, a napkin carelessly thrown over it.

In the line to order, a foot away from their table, was a shout of recognition. "Nicholas! What are you doing here?"

Cute, young, perfectly symmetrical, naturally witty Nicholas turned his attention to a young woman in line. The café was small; now almost everyone was tuned into the commotion. Margherita's interest level increased.

"What is new with you? It's been for-EVER!" the young woman exclaimed with over-the-top dramatics. Nicholas matched her animation.

"I have news!" he declared, his hands framing the air as if he were holding a poster. This was the kind of annoyingly secretive announcement that blatantly wants attention.

"Tell me!" The young woman demanded.

"I'll tell you later," Nicholas said. They said their good-byes and Nicholas returned his attention to the young woman across from him.

"You can't just say you have news and then retract it. We are all dying to know now," Margherita said to the side of his face, motioning to the rest of the café. He looked at her. She gave him a daring smirk and a raised eyebrow. He took the bait.

"Oh, I bet. That was a bit loud, wasn't it? Bit misleading, too, I'm afraid."

She sighed with feigned anticlimax. "That's disappointing. You had Thursday lunch goers throughout Soho at the *very* edges of their seats." She looked back down at her phone.

Nicholas looked at her energetically. She had been hesitant to say anything—wanting to, but unsure how it would be received. Maybe he had been waiting for an opportunity of his own. Well, she thought, *Why hadn't he made one himself?* Typical. It was one of her main complaints about the age group—they didn't have the balls to start a conversation. A forty-something man always started a conversation with her. A thirty-something man glanced at her half a dozen times as she stood next to him in the Whole Foods aisle, paid for his groceries, and left the store.

"I know. Hugely disappointing. What can we rummage together by end of day?" he asked.

"Oh, I get the feeling you don't need any help from me," and she mimicked his animated hands in the air, framing an invisible sign, eyes ablaze. He guffawed, his blue eyes electric. He was too cute. More than cute. He was gorgeous, and his blatant attention made her feel something strange, a very unfamiliar sensation. Was she…nervous? She felt herself fidgeting under the table. Crossed her legs and uncrossed them unknowingly.

Margherita looked at the young woman next to them. "I'm sorry—didn't mean to interrupt. Please, go on about the five-year plan. How many spaces do you plan to launch by 2025? I think I missed a bit," she cocked her head, her face in a mock expression of serious interest, directed at Nicholas again. The young girl next to her was smiling, glancing back and forth, not sure whose volley it was next. Nicholas laughed, nodding.

"Sorry, for real this time. It's tight quarters. Wasn't purposefully listening. Please ignore me," she said, finding a bit of composure and grace at long last and waving her hand through the air as if to erase her presence.

"No, no, it's obviously going to happen. If you hadn't been listening, I would have been massively impressed by your zone-out capabilities. I'm Nicholas, by the way, and this is Lissa. Lissa works at Gloss next door."

Margherita turned toward Lissa. Lissa from Gloss. That seemed to fit. She wondered when Lissa ever stopped smiling.

"Oh, I love the design firm who did your offices." Margherita said to Lissa, intending to steer the attention away from smart, funny, witty, gorgeous Nicholas, in an attempt to show him that she wasn't as interested as she might appear.

"Yes- Yarrow. They did the headquarters last year," Lissa said.

"It's a sublime space. My father bid on that project."

"What do you do?" Nicholas interrupted.

"I work for Lolato. Store design and development."

"Oh, wow. We should talk, actually, because we are researching potential architecture firms. I'd love to hear your thoughts. Do you have a card?" Nicholas asked.

"Yes, I do." She dug in her bag for her wallet, the silence thick as he waited, watching her.

"Margherita Ricatti," he read the card with a perfect Italian accent. He was a bit of a performer, she sensed.

"That's me."

He held the card between his two forefingers. She noticed his nails were perfect, not in a groomed way, just naturally. He looked at her with eyebrows slightly raised, his electric blue eyes bearing into hers, a slight smile on his face. His teeth were so white, and he had a most perfect smile. The first big tooth slightly overlapped the second big tooth. It was endearing. His stare, though—it made her nervous.

"Are you Italian?"

"Si."

"From Italy?"

"I was born here. But I lived in Milan for a few years up until...two? Months ago."

"Fascinating." He was nodding. He glanced at Lissa with a start, as if he suddenly remembered her presence.

"Well, it's really lovely to meet you." He held out his hand across the table, over his chicken carcass. Nicholas, whoever this guy was, stared right into her like an oar settling into its groove, for what felt like the thousandth time over the past fifteen to twenty minutes, with such impact, such decisiveness and intrigue that Margherita found herself squeezing her hand between her legs under the table, gripping the thigh underneath so hard she was surely leaving marks. *Who was this guy?* she wondered. Maybe he was like this with everyone. Maybe he was just naturally excitable.

"Enjoy the rest of your lunch. Fingers crossed the next conversation is more captivating than ours." He threw his jacket on and left, Lissa in tow. Margherita tried to swallow her smile.

Later, she looked him up on LinkedIn. She was surprised, pleasantly so, at his superlative education. She had not been expecting Cambridge and a Berkeley MBA; he seemed so young, and glaringly not-academic in his denim and hoodie, and his Canal street office address.

Hunched over her keyboard at the office, she felt daring. She sent him a LinkedIn message.

Margherita: From Cambridge to Silicon Valley. Is that the new stereotype?

Nick: From Spence to Canal Street...now I'm intrigued.

Margherita: And I live in Brooklyn. How many Carnegie Hill kids can say that?

Nick: I'd say 4 or 5. You clearly are one of them.

Margherita: Don't judge. Where do you live?

Nick: East Village, actually.

Margherita: Really? I so badly wanted to peg you for Brooklyn.

Nick: You mean yet another hooded Williamsburg MBA grad with an Equinox membership and a sweetgreen punchcard? Maybe a black backpack?

Margherita: Snooze.

Nick: Agreed. Just moved actually.

Nick: There were too many of us black hooded backpack wearing SF dudes at Whole Foods every day. Couldn't take it anymore.

Nick: So are you a regular on Howard street?

Margherita: A bit of one, yes. Since they opened. The buckwheat banana bread. Took me years to master that recipe.

Nick: Ah a true loyalist. I could tell.. you navigate the seating with dogged confidence.

Margherita: Yes am quite a pro at that game.

Nick: Any other games?

Margherita: A few. Parcheesi. Bumper cars. Solitaire. You know, the usual.

Nick: Parcheesi! Played with my nephew a few weeks ago.

Margherita: Really you know it? People usually think I'm making it up.

Nick: NO I would never joke about Parcheesi.

Margherita: Your turn. Games of choice.

Nick: Mine are less tangible perhaps.

Margherita: Ah. I'm also quite good at Guessing Games.

Nick: Yeah? You want to take a stab?

Margherita: Well first, are these of the LinkedIn Appropriate category or the not so kosher inappropriate category?

Nick: Ha. We have left the Parcheesi arena rather quickly.

Margherita: Right?! Feels a little wrong even typing the word inappropriate on what is supposedly a professional medium. Send me a whatsapp...much more chat-acceptable. 917-695-5011. Appropriate or otherwise :)

The exchange bolstered Margherita's mood by leaps and bounds. She felt energized, excited. Could she have possibly met a new crush? She felt like jumping.

The flip side of the reaction was how fleeting it would be. She scared herself sometimes, in how easily her emotions could sway so fluidly, either upward or downward. Francine's condition was never a distant thought.

She detected an attraction, though, and innuendo was her style. Her forwardness set the tone, and sometimes backfired on her. Alexandre had once shared his opinion: "You are attracted to someone who can provide you with a set partner, someone to challenge you. Confidence, true confidence, for a man at least, comes with age and experience. You seek someone who keeps you on your toes," he had said. "A younger guy will go down in flames under your intensity."

NEW YORK, NEW YORK

2018

NICK GRABBED HIS notebook and laptop for the Forward Strategy meeting in the conference room. He felt distracted by the unforeseen lunch encounter, and again by her suggestive messages on his LinkedIn. Clearly she was interested; how many girls would take it upon themselves to track someone down on LinkedIn, and send them flirtatious messages? She had guile. She was also witty, intelligent, and curiously elegant in her speech, with not an *um* or *like* to be heard. There was something decidedly temptress-like about Margherita. She was categorically high-risk.

He sat down at the round table with Max, their CEO, Nevin, another co-founder who oversaw the branding and marketing aspects, and Rajan, one of Nick's buddies from Berkeley who headed up finance. The four of them had been straddling the responsibilities of launching and growing the business for the past year, since Max had approached them about his venture. It had been a nonstop sprint with no foreseeable let-up, a constant source of adrenaline and stress, of excitement and apprehension. Nick had no interest in putting on a suit or a button-down every day, or of being anyone's bitch after spending a hundred and fifty thousand dollars on a post-grad education.

He wanted to create something big and noteworthy, that would garner attention and impress his schoolmates, and something that would, within a short time frame, give him the freedom to do something for which he felt true passion.

He had allowed himself very few distractions over the past year and a half. He always had the ability to focus, to work hard, and to keep his nose to the ground. They had started with less than ten people; within a year they reached a headcount of seventy-three. Seventy-three people on a company insurance plan, taking home a paycheck that was stamped with the name of the company that they had originated. It was surreal, and the payroll thought alone was enough to re-stimulate him when he felt burn-out encroaching.

The only distraction, if he could call it that, had been Callie. What a mess that had been. It took a lot of guts to engage one of your buddies' girlfriends in a fling, but Nick hadn't been able to quiet his desires.

He had sent her a message over Instagram after a very drunken and flirtatious birthday party. They met for lunch one afternoon, during the week. They started to sneak around a few times late at night—meeting for a drink here and there, for a walk in Dumbo, where she lived. He never asked about her relationship, and she never offered any information. He wanted her so intensely, it flash-blinded any guilt he felt regarding his friend, a chap he had stayed friends with from his MBA program.

After a month, when she had come to his apartment for the fifth or sixth time, she lay in bed next to him, her hand on his chest, his hand on her hand, and told him that she had broken up with her boyfriend.

He had been a little surprised. She had announced it as if it were the plan all along, as if they were on a team and they had won, together. In truth, he hadn't thought much about where it might go—he had simply been enjoying the excitement while it lasted. He felt that somehow, somewhere along the way, she had conned him. To him, it felt very much out of nowhere.

Immediately he attempted to retract his doubts. He reminded himself how crazy he was about Callie, how much he wanted her when she wasn't near him, how great the sex was, how easy it was to be with her, how she maintained her schedule and he maintained his. Was she a bit shallow, yes. A bit of the predictable rich girl from Melbourne, yes. A bit less interested in culture and nature and the things with which he was raised, yes. But no one was perfect, right? He had to remind himself that she was great. She was a great girl.

He kissed her on the mouth at her announcement, and they had sex. She smiled and read this act of intimacy as an approval of her decision.

The relationship moved on, past the initial phase. Certainly that moment had been the turning point of a new chapter, a less intoxicating one. They revealed their relationship, including to Nick's friend, Callie's ex. Nick apologized, but he knew it was fruitless. He was completely in the wrong, but to himself he ceded that his friend's relationship with Callie wasn't so great to begin with, and it was bound to end at some point.

Most of his friends already knew her and accepted their relationship with few questions asked. He didn't love her friends, but they weren't totally rotten human beings and he managed to pass some time with them.

He spent an occasional night at her apartment that she shared with her sister, who he did not especially like, and he quickly discovered the feeling was mutual. He and Callie got along *at the moment*, in the life they were living in that moment in New York, and he supposed that was all that counted.

She had proven herself to be more giving and helpful than he had expected, or perhaps it was so meaningless and ubiquitous to her, a constant stream of money, that she had simply wanted to put an end to Nick's work stress so that he could focus more on her. When the partners needed a substantial investment in the company, it had been Callie who had set up a handful of meetings with valuable investors. They had been dating just a few months at the time, but she seemed to trust him and the business concept enough to introduce him to personal friends and business contacts of her father's.

He felt indebted to her ever since. Would he have been able to maneuver it on his own, if she hadn't nonchalantly pushed a few powerful contacts his way? The thought kept him up at night. Did she pity him? Was she disappointed? Embarrassed? He couldn't help but feel slightly enfeebled in her eyes.

On that random November day, he encountered a new distraction, in the form of a self-assured, refined woman with composure, charm, and subtle humor. Even her name was suggestive of something profuse, a colorful and robust burst of something. Margherita. He found himself picturing her in her apartment, wearing something incredibly sexy to bed, hair in tumbles as it had been in the café, green eyes inviting…

There they were again—those feelings in his chest. They had lain dormant for some time, since the beginning with Callie, and they were once again incontestably rousing.

NEW YORK, NEW YORK

2018

MARGHERITA WENT ABOUT her weekend trying not to think about how she hadn't heard from Nick. *Girl gives you her phone number, you do something with it,* she thought. She wondered if he had since checked his LinkedIn to see the message. She figured, however, that if he were interested, he definitely would have; therefore, he must not be interested. She had been trying to date as much as possible. It got her out of her apartment where she thought too much of her mother. Dating in New York was so different from her experiences in Italy, where admittedly she never really *dated*, not in the traditional way.

She rarely accepted a date with an American who had never lived abroad, since she felt they would have very little to talk about, though she had a strong interest in men from other countries. Saturday night she had gone to dinner with Eddie, a Colombian guy she had met through one of the dating apps.

Eddie was tall, with long, wavy, dirty blonde hair that he could easily tuck behind his ears and that fell into his eyes when they kissed. He was sensitive, a little too much, and a little shy, but he was sweet and fun and liked to dance and appreciated good food. They had been out four times; she had always chosen the restaurant (better safe than sorry), and he was always impressed with her decisions. He was constantly flattering her, running his fingertips along her neck, over the shape of her lips, looking into her eyes. She would shrug or make a funny face and change the subject.

One night, after dinner at a Portuguese restaurant on East Houston, he convinced her to go to a dive bar, the kind of place she never set foot in. They danced to classic 80s songs and invited a few of his friends to join. She tried to minimize the awkwardness she felt throughout the evening: Margherita recognized that it should have been a very average evening. There they were, out drinking together with his friends, dancing, talking about how someone's new wife was considering a move to Seoul. They acted like a couple for a few hours in the presence of other couples; she spoke to another woman about him, as if they had been together for a long time, as he was standing right next to her, his giant hand on the back of her neck, thumb on one side. The feeling was strange, as if she were playing a part. And yet, as much as she tried to settle into it, she knew she was forcing it. She looked at Eddie, who was very good looking. But something was missing.

She kept trying anyway, because there was nothing particularly 'wrong' with him, and she knew it had to be her who was slightly nuts. She showed him where to find her favorite gluten free peanut butter cookie. He convinced her to join him in Williamsburg one night for a movie. He asked her about going away one weekend, maybe to the Berkshires. She deflected and sent him an article on Mexico City.

"Weekend rendezvous, Mexican-style?" she suggested, knowing full well that they would never go. He took it to mean something.

She poked fun at his sweetness, his softness. He retreated into it. With every date she found herself less and less interested. And he became, at least in her eyes, more and more wilty, like a flower in humidity. Wilt.

Margherita: He is incredibly sweet. So freaken good looking. So handsome. And smart and cultured and is interested in the arts and movies and he sends me new music that I like and he can dance and he loves food, and he's wonderful. And I just…don't care. What is wrong with me?

Chiara: Aw cara, you can't force it. Give him one more chance maybe? And then if you still don't feel anything, let it go. There's nothing wrong with you. You just don't feel the magic.

Margherita: But am I being totally naïve? Is there such a thing as magic in a grown-up relationship?

Chiara: I like to hope so! I haven't found it yet. But I remain hopeful.

She couldn't do it. A few weeks was her limit. She couldn't muster that heartsick-can't-eat-can't-wait-to-see-him-again feeling. She needed that manic elation in order to remain connected, to remain interested. Margherita wondered if that was precisely the reason Francine had wanted her daughter to settle down with someone 'nice and responsible.' Maybe Francine was fearful of Margherita's preference for some kind of manic feeling.

She had felt something like that—like vim, at the café with Nick. She had felt it in their chat. There had been some kind of undercurrent. She had been certain he had felt it too. So, what gives? Why hadn't she heard from him?

Sunday night rolled around and she was getting ready to go to dinner with someone new, a banker from Madrid. His English wasn't perfect and he had missed a few of her sarcastic jokes but she didn't have any other plans, and she was in the mood for the polpo grigliata at Il Buco. In the midst of her final mirror check, she received a WhatsApp message from a new number. The photo was of a cheeky, mischievous five-year-old boy who looked uncannily like Nick.

Nick: You follow Sara Blakely on Instagram. I do too. Something else in common.

A-ha. There he was. She felt a hit of something lithium-like. So he had found her on Instagram. He had gone digging. He was curious.

Margherita: She is a wonder. Made an empire from nothing and is now worth 1 billion dollars. 4 kids under the age of 8. Always laughing. How can you not want to be like her?

Nick: Yes, those are admirable statistics. Did you see the lot of them carving pumpkins over Halloween? That was a lot of pumpkins. 4 kids- at least 2 pumpkins each.

Margherita: I wouldn't be surprised if her kids made the Spanx at home around the dinner table.

Nick: Solely domestic based production line. Yes.

She stood there in her apartment, about to put her heels on to head out the door, biting her thumb nail and smiling. She would have foregone the evening with the Madridleno if Nick had asked her for a last-minute drink. She had to get going though, if she was going to keep the date.

Nick: So what does a Sunday night look like for Margherita?

Margherita: I am heading to dinner actually. What about you?

Nick: Mum is visiting with one of my sisters. Think we are staying put and ordering in.

Margherita: That's sweet. Does she visit often?

Nick: No, not really.

Margherita: Are you very close to her?

Nick: Rattling through the hot topics already. Pumpkin carving.
My mother.
No, not very close. Close, but not.

Margherita: Aw well then enjoy the evening :)

She wasn't sure how to elevate the conversation, how to decipher if he was actually interested or not.

Nick: Yes you too.

And that was it? She was confused. He had inputted her number, had bothered to send the message, had looked up her Instagram…and…nothing. She was distracted and confused all the way to dinner.

NEW YORK, NEW YORK

2018

IN LOLATO's COLD, modern offices on Grand Street, Margherita sat at the large glass table in the glass conference room overlooking Lafayette Street, reviewing a revised plan for the Geneva boutique—or trying to, at least. She had not been able to put Nick out of her head but had remained prideful enough—just enough—to not send him another message. She had not heard a peep from him. She wondered if he were gay, or had a girlfriend, or had been just bored enough to get in touch, but not interested in anything more.

Suddenly her phone pinged.

Nick: I just visited my friend at work. He's a hedge fund guy. Shockingly quiet office.

Margherita: Why shockingly?

Nick: I like to think everyone in banking is like Michael Douglas in the 80s. Lots of commotion. Dunkin Donuts boxes half eaten.

Margherita: Ah, yes. Low ceilings, phones on cords, suspenders...that sort of thing.

Nick: I take you for the kind of girl who gets a rush out of finance guys driving the numbers.

Margherita: And yelling.
Making really offensive remarks amongst themselves.

Nick: One phone wedged between the shoulder and ear.

Nick: Just yelling at themselves.

Margherita: Likely talking smack about each other's wives.

Nick: Just a load of smack.

Margherita: Interestingly I am not super impressed by the above. Much prefer a suave European gentleman, very well dressed, well mannered, lots of charm, maybe an accent. Could also be British. I do like the dry wit. Maybe Welsh. But probably not Irish. I have a hard time understanding them.

Nick: Hold on, writing this down.

Margherita: So who is your next interview at the caffè? Or is this your dating style?

Nick: Interviews. For Life Partner.

Did that imply he was single? she wondered.

Margherita: Ah convenient.

Nick: Ha. I am trying to build out a team. Have been mining contacts for intel.

Margherita: Gotcha. Well good luck with Thursday's batch :)

She was growing frustrated. What was he after, if anything at all? The heightened mood she had felt days ago had nearly deflated, and she suddenly felt very alone again. He was clearly a person who had someone to have lunch with, made plans with friends after work, probably had plans every weekend. Here was someone she knew she could at least be friends with. What were the chances that he would ever include her in any of the above? She just wanted to feel a part of something. Margherita turned her phone face-down and stared emptily at the architectural plan before her.

MILANO, LOMBARDIA

2017

AT DINNER THAT evening with Taddeo and his friend Valerio at a family-run restaurant near the Navigli, Margherita's ears perked up at the mention of her lover's name.

Valerio was telling them about his new girlfriend, a woman who had once dated Paolo twenty years prior.

"It really is a small world here. A bit incestuous," Margherita said.

Taddeo laughed. "È solo che Paolo ha frequentato quasi tutti a Milano ad un certo punto." *Paolo has dated basically everyone in Milan at a certain point.*

"Sta ancora vedendo quella ragazza nel suo ufficio?" *Is he still seeing that young girl in his office?* Valerio asked.

Margherita felt her heart skip a beat. "Ma cosa!" She exclaimed, pretending to be surprised at Paolo's infidelity when really the news shocked her for other reasons.

Taddeo pushed his hands downwards to suggest the hush-hush-ness of the subject. "Ginevra. Non lo so." *I don't know.*

"Cosa successo con Ginevra?" *What happened with Ginevra?* Margherita asked.

"She was in love with him, poor thing. She's a very sweet

girl, actually. But I think they ended it. It had been going on for years," Taddeo said as he took another piece of bread from the basket.

Margherita could hear her heart inside her chest. She suddenly lost her appetite for the fennel and orange salad sitting in front of her. How many young twenty-somethings were there in Paolo's routine? She was fuming inside. Immediately she heard Francine's words, "You think you're the only one?" Of course she had known all along that Paolo must have other flings besides herself— she couldn't imagine where he found the time— but still, she felt angry and foolish and and annoyed with herself for letting the daydream carry on for so long.

"I heard they had a threesome with one of her friends. Paolo's wife told me one night when she was really drunk. Do not repeat this," Taddeo said, very calmly.

MILANO, LOMBARDIA

2017

SHE WAS LATE. She skidded from kitchen to bedroom, bathroom to living room, looking for everything that had been in the wrong place: make-up, heels, flats, laptop, wallet, keys, all scattered. She grabbed a handful of walnuts she had bought at the market on the way back from her run in the park that morning and rushed out the door, down the tiny neon-lit elevator to her palazzo's stone-laid internal courtyard, past the grumpy portaio *doorman* who was possibly the only grumpy person she had encountered in Milan, and out the front gate. She turned left on Corso di Porto Nuova. She would take the metro from Montenapoleone. Why in hell did the Lolato jewelry headquarters have to be at the very edge of the city, as far as possible from civilization?

When she arrived in the not-so-beautiful neighborhood, she stood on the sidewalk and leaned against the cement façade of Lolato's offices. She had never been here before, on this dead, wide street where there seemed to be almost no one and nothing. Elisio was running quite late, later than she had been. The nine a.m. sun hit her cheek and the tops of her thighs, and she closed her eyes for a moment. October had just begun and the transition had been gentle…summer to not-quite-summer to slight breeze.

Elisio: Five minutes. Did you bring the plans?

Cavolo *Crap.* She had not brought the physical floor plans, no, but she had a copy on her laptop.

Margherita: On my laptop

Elisio: I have them. Hard copy. Always.

Margherita rolled her eyes at her phone. *Well if you have them, why do I need them too?*

Elisio: Meglio un giorno da leone che cento da pecora…

She rolled her eyes again.

There was a message from her father that she had not opened. She had seen the notification pop up on her screen the previous evening when she was leaving Camilla's apartment.

Tommaso: Marghe call your mother. She says she hasn't heard from you in a week…

He was always doing that, playing messenger. Margherita was avoiding calling her mother, who seemed to have a one-track mind lately: her trades. If she managed to get Francine to talk about something else, the conversation inevitably returned to the subject of Margherita's meager

Italian paycheck, of her inappropriate escapades with the wrong men, and how she was stalling and damaging her potential career. Then a fight would erupt and Margherita would grow impatient and angry and hang up, only to face tired disappointment from Tommaso, who bore the brunt of the exchange between mother and daughter.

"I keep telling you, you should be grateful that she is so focused on her work lately. It could be a lot worse," Tommaso had said the last time they spoke.

Elisio finally arrived, exiting the Uber briskly with his typical nervous energy and a smile that came quickly to an otherwise stern face. She had grown accustomed to his abrupt mood shifts. They checked in with their IDs and were let through the gated entrance.

Through the internal gate sat a Japanese-style courtyard garden. There was a sudden, unexpected silence and arrangement of eastern plantings, a stream and a waterfall and a few Rosella-designed wooden seats. She could not imagine who would dare to sit there, surrounded by and exposed to the windowed walls of the headquarters looking down on it. *Who decided on this juxtaposition to Italian effervescence,* she wondered, *within this Italian company.* How daring.

Upstairs, Margherita and Elisio were ushered into a cold, stark meeting room made of glass and steel. The light fixture overhead was ultra-contemporary and she noticed as well the beautiful, delicate drinking glasses set for them, their unusual imperfect shapes. She made a mental note to hold her water carefully. There were far more respectable ways to get all eyes on her than to shatter a hand-blown, Zalto drinking glass.

Elisio laid the plans out on the glass table, which was big enough for twenty people. He pulled at his tie and sat upright, his lips pursed together, waiting for the others. Margherita turned her head toward the floor-to-ceiling window, which revealed the waterfall running silently below them. She knew she would not play an active role in the meeting, though she had been working on the project for over a year. It was an entirely legal discussion having to do with the licenses and insurance necessary to have a jewelry boutique of such worth within the Via Santo Spirito space. The hotel's legal counsel had cancelled at the last minute, and Elisio had decided to keep the meeting and come himself instead of rescheduling. Hence his nerves, she assumed. He wasn't a lawyer.

"Buongiorno, direttore," a young woman appeared through the glass doors.

"Monseiur Le Foll is just finishing a call with Seoul and Tokyo. Can I get you an espresso? Signorina?" Three other gentlemen and one woman walked into the room and everyone introduced themselves. They were part of the international legal team.

"No, grazie," Elisio said, growing impatient. Margherita politely shook her head. Elisio cleared his throat loudly.

"Non per me, grazie," she said quietly. When Elisio was agitated, she tried to be as undetectable as possible.

God, please let this man arrive soon, she thought. Elisio hated to be kept waiting. He was one of the most perpetually and shamelessly late people she had ever met—at least one hour if not two, was the norm—but he absolutely despised being on the receiving end of even a measly fifteen minutes.

"Excuse me for the wait, my plane from New York landed about an hour ago." A French accent. Elisio stood and she followed suit. A very tall, slender, early-forties man with thick, black Tom Ford eyewear and straight chestnut hair leaned over the glass table. He wore a button-down and a sports jacket and a beautiful Patek Philippe watch on one of his long arms. He had a long narrow nose and very blue eyes. "Alexandre. Enchante."

"Shall we?" he said after shaking both of their hands, and he sat down across from them with a small leather notebook and pen before him. Long slender fingers, very large hands. No ring. He must have been six feet three inches, Paolo's height, but such a different build, a long figure. He had probably been a gangly young boy, growing up in France somewhere in the countryside. Had gone to study law somewhere and assumed a confident, knowing demeanor, a sternness that commanded attention, but a nerdy coolness that made one wonder what kind of music was on his Spotify.

"Well, as you know..." Elisio began the meeting. Margherita looked on and inserted supporting commentary where she felt she could. At one point, when Alexandre and his team had gone off on a tangent discussing the cost of the build-out with their own architect instead of Elisio's, she had made a reference to the material used on the ceiling in the New York store, and he looked at her curiously, interrupting Elisio.

"Are you from New York?" he asked, his accent slightly muddled with something else, she couldn't quite make it out.

"Yes," she said.

"How long have you been in Italy?" He pronounced it with a staccato. It-a-l-ie.

"Two years."

"And you speak perfect Italian?" he asked, but it was more a statement.

"Well…"

"She speaks very well," Elisio inserted. "She loves it here. Never going back. We are never letting her." He smiled, proud of his protégé.

Margherita smiled. Alexandre watched her, intrigued.

"And how do you know about the ceiling of the New York boutique?"

"My father bid for that project. He didn't get it, but the team liked his idea for the ceiling, and they passed it onto the firm who got the job."

"Your papa is an architect?"

"Yes."

"Did you study it?"

She could feel Elisio slightly irritated at having lost the starlight.

"Yes, I went to the Yale School of Architecture," she said plainly.

"Aha." He said, as if she had suddenly passed a test she had not known she was participating in.

"Where did you grow up?" he asked her, unfinished.

"Manhattan."

"Ah, really? I lived in Manhattan for a few years when I was young."

"Ah small world."

"Seventy-first and Park," he said.

"I grew up on Ninety-second and Fifth," she said.

"Oui, the world is small. But not very. Coincidences are rarely coincidences."

She was unsure what to say. They had lived twenty blocks apart in different decades; where was the coincidence?

"Allors, what's next?" He turned his attention back to Elisio. She felt slightly dismissed.

After the meeting was over, Elisio rolled up the plans and Alexandre slowly edged to the end of the glass table, looking down at his phone. She was coming around from the other side. At the end of the table, he looked up, as if surprised to see her there.

"Ah, oui, so you will be at the site meeting tomorrow?" he asked. "I am interested to hear your opinions on a new layout I am considering for our Ginzeng store."

After the meeting, Elisio zipped down to Florence to be interviewed for a magazine article. He was nice enough to drive her as far as he was going; he was never one to go out of his way, and after all, he was the topic of the article, not her. She made her way back to the city center, wandering from Piazza della Scala toward Sant Ambroeus beneath the porticoes on Corso Matteotti, one of her favorite stretches of the city. She loved the way the wide marble sidewalk curved along, the ubiquitous lines of motorcycles and motos, the sharply dressed men walking briskly in groups of twos or threes, their navy suits perfectly tailored, their hair neat, their features irrefutably Milanese. She passed one of her favorite piazzas with its turquoise shutters and the out-of-place brick building that faced a large, quiet courtyard. Just beyond the porticoed sidewalk was the four-lane Corso Matteotti and the car and motos whizzing past the stern facade of the Banca Popolare di Milano. At Sant Ambroeus, she swung open the door with its thick gold handle and gave a smile and a wave to the young handsome man behind the counter who expected her on Sunday afternoons. A sporadic weekday visit was a rarity and he looked at her with raised eyebrows.

She approached the glass case where they displayed delicate cookies and house-made chocolates. The middle-aged woman behind the glass counter, a counter so tall Margherita had to stand on her tippy-toes to be seen, greeted her warmly.

"Buongiorno Signorina," she said with a gentle smile. The first few times Margherita had frequented that counter, the same woman had been brusque and unfriendly. After many visits, Margherita had won her over with loyalty and a constant smile.

"Il cioccolato?" the woman asked, knowingly.

"Si, per favore."

"Due?" The woman held the long silver forceps in the air above the dark chocolate made with espresso cream in the middle.

"Ahh…Si. Grazie," Margherita decided.

The woman placed them on a small round plate on top of a doily. Margherita took the plate to the counter where the young man was waiting, drying a tall drinking glass with a light pink napkin.

"Come stai?' he asked with slight disinterest, as was his style.

"Bene, tu? Come va lavoro?" *Good, you? How's work?*

"Eh, lo stesso." *The same.* He tilted his head, shook his hair from his face. "Caffè?"

"Si, grazie," Margherita assented.

He placed her espresso cup on its plate and a wrapped chocolate on its side, the norm at Sant Ambroeus. Bliss came in small packages evenly distributed between bitter and sweet. She loved the people-watching at the very smart caffè: businessmen and women, chicly dressed Milanese stopping in for a cake they had ordered, saying hello to all, the same way they had been doing for decades. It was a forever spot, an every-type-of-meeting spot. She took her last sip and crossed the floor to the cash register, where the chipper young girl sat with her long, thick, blonde locks. She gave Margherita a big smile as always.

"Come stai? Non lavori oggi?" *How are you? You're not working today?*

"I had a meeting. I'm just taking a little stroll before I head back," Margherita said.

"Hai fatto bene!" *Good idea!* The young girl said as she took Margherita's three euros and dropped them into the ancient register drawer.

"Buona giornata!" she said. And Margherita returned it with one of her own, and one for the young man who made her espresso, and one for the older woman who gave her the chocolates.

On her way out, she admired the window display with its exquisite cakes—not even the pasticceria was one to disappoint when it came to window displays in Milan—and she returned to the beautiful October day outside.

She strolled down Via Montenapoleone with a close-lipped smile on her face, taking in the beauty of her adopted city, of its fashionable and friendly people, of its elegant architecture. The Dolce & Gabbana building was being made up for an event, sheathed in a giant ribbon and glitter lights, and it looked like it was preparing for its own runway moment. She stopped on the narrow sidewalk across the street to take a photo on her phone. As she adjusted the frame, she felt the undeniable presence of a body next to her, looking at the same building. She turned to her left, phone still in the air.

"Ah, scusa mi, non sono una turista, promesso, ma è

troppo bello, no?" *Oh, excuse me. I'm not a tourist, I promise, but it's too beautiful, isn't it?* Margherita said to the very handsome, dark-haired man next to her, in his typically Milanese blue suit, crisp white shirt and silk tie.

"Ah, yes. It is," he affirmed with an English accent.

"Ah, sorry, I thought you were Italian," she said, now realizing how devastatingly handsome the man was.

"I am." He did not move from the sidewalk. "But I went to school in the UK. And New York. You're from the states?"

"Oh, I'm from New York. And tell me my accent isn't that bad?"

"Ehh...no, not really."

She was unsure what to do next, on that narrow sidewalk just wide enough for two. He had brilliant blue eyes that matched his tie, but surely he knew that. Dark hair, just long enough. A little shadow of a beard. Early to mid-forties, she guessed. Chic shoes, but of course, she was in Milan, and she didn't expect anything less. "What were you doing in New York, if you don't mind my asking?"

He opened his mouth to speak and then closed it, not taking his eyes off her, sizing her up, perhaps wondering how this conversation had begun on a Wednesday after-noon on the sidewalk of Via Montenapoleone.

"I was there for my MBA, and I worked for my family's company for a few years," he said, only slightly humble.

She nodded in understanding.

"And what do you do now? Here in Milan visiting? Or no, you said you're not a tourist." He said, glancing down the sidewalk to his right. She got the feeling he was looking for an out, to continue on with his day.

"I work for the Leonetti family hotels. We are developing

a new property, just around the corner actually," she said, gesturing toward Via Santo Spirito.

His face barely moved but he had a glimmer of something in his eyes, and she couldn't quite figure him out.

"So you work with Elisio?"

"Yes! How do you know Elisio?"

He held his hand out. "Beck. Nice to meet you."

She shook it. Tan hand but not too tan, firm handshake. "Margherita."

"I have to run to a meeting, but it was nice chatting. Hope you get your shot," he said, looking back up at the Dolce & Gabbana building behind her.

"Grazie," she said, not knowing how else to keep him fixed in his position, totally star-struck at his undeniably gorgeous looks and his discreet charm. She watched his blue suit as he strode quickly down the narrow sidewalk toward Corso Matteotti.

Margherita: Do you know a man named Beck-forties, dark hair, very good looking man, used to live in NY?

She would have to investigate.

Camilla: Beck Leonetti? Ugh so dreamy. Doesn't he look exactly like James Marsden?

She so much as slapped herself on the forehead. She began Googling immediately. There he was, the heir to the Leonetti fashion group. She found countless photos of him at events all over the world, with supermodels and Kate Winslet and the like.

She walked down Via Montenapoleone toward the satellite office in Via Santo Spirito, daydreaming about the beautiful man and writing to Francine about him. That would make her happy; Francine always relished a story with a devilishly handsome man with a big name. Oddly, Margherita found it made Francine more proud of her daughter to be in fashionable circles than to be doing the work that brought her great challenge and satisfaction.

Once inside the internal courtyard, she climbed the wide steps all the way to the roof, bypassing Lucas in the third floor office. The first thing she wanted to do was send Alexandre a thank you note for his time, as she always did after a meeting.

Bonjour Alexandre,

It was a pleasure to meet you this morning, and thank you again for your time. We appreciate your enthusiasm for this unique project, and we look forward to showing you the property on Friday. Every time I step inside this singular space, my breath halts for just a moment, and I have a feeling your reaction will be similar. To set a second flagship boutique within these ancient walls will set the brand apart in an intangible way; gluing it to a local's centerpiece in the center of the shopping district, and intrinsically tying it to a must-visit destination for visitors. It will be a win-win. Now if only I could brush up on my French and we could open a Leon Hotel Paris.

I look forward to working together.

My best,
Margherita

She had been a bit overconfident but such was her way with Alexandre's type, and she had learned to stop playing the timid young girl in these situations. Alexandre, being French, had to be slightly romanticized, didn't he? Or at the very least, he was more receptive to it than an American.

She was in the middle of a phone call to the site manager to confirm the Friday meeting when she received a reply from Alexandre.

That was fast, she thought.

Margherita,

Likewise, it was a pleasure to meet you as well. I am confident you are right, and your genuine passion for the space has left a mark. Looking forward to seeing you again.

Paris hotel project will be next, if you and Elisio have anything to do with it. I have no doubt that you are as lioness in your ambitions as you seem.

A bientot.
-Alexandre

Interesting. She sucked in a breath of October air, eyes darting around the rooftop terrace as if someone else saw that email too, though she was alone at the metal table set for six. Was this par for the course? Or was he flirting? Humph, she danced her shoulders a little, sat up straighter in her metal chair. She hovered her fingers over her keyboard with a pursed lipped smile.

So when you sign off on Milan, shall we include an exclusive for any future Paris hotel as well? :)

-M

She had deleted and retyped the smiley face at least five times, unsure how far to push into flirtation territory, but she was feeling confident and provocative and sent it along anyway.

Only if you improve your French.

-A

This was fun, she thought.

Not enough hours in the day. Also v hard to locate French teacher in Milan. Shockingly low French population here. I assume there to be a Paris/Milan bias.

-M

She smiled at her screen, awaiting his response. Five minutes went by and there was nothing, and she worried she had gone too far.

All you need is one. My number is +39 333 5500505, perhaps a little easier that way, if you would like to brush up. I can quiz you on your architecture knowledge...this will come in handy for me as I work on Ginzeng and Melbourne stores. See you Friday.

-A

Oh boy. Now what. It was in her hands. So if she wrote to him, she would be the one delving deeper into the flirtation. He had given his cell phone number, that was unusual, no? Who could she ask...who would know.... she could not share with just anyone, after all, he was deeply entwined in her work. Lolato was a very important deal for the project and Elisio's first choice jewelry partner. If she messed it up, it would be lethal for her career in Milan. It was a very, very, very small city in many ways.

Suddenly she felt a satisfactory *Paolo who?* Finally, *finally.* After a year and a half of being stuck in his orbit, she had finally found the clasp to the hinge. Or so she hoped.

NEW YORK, NEW YORK

2018

NICK HUNG UP the phone with his father, and a sliver of guilt hung in the air. He swiveled his chair around to face his desk. He had been bouncing a tennis ball off the wall, facing away from the hub of the open space where long communal tables were scattered with laptops and employees.

"Oh, you know your mother. Always has to moan about something," his dad had said while updating him about his oldest sister Emma. She had just found out she was pregnant again, and his mother was hoping that Emma and her husband and her two year old son would move back to Dorset. They were staying put in London, much to his mother's grim dismay, and instead of his mom being overjoyed at the news of another grandchild, she was bitter and lamenting about something inconsequential. She couldn't let everyone enjoy moments of happiness and celebration, could she. It irked Nick, and he simultaneously felt relieved to be living an ocean apart and yet guilt-ridden that he was not there for the rest of his family.

Callie: Hello lover. Are we still on for pizza tonight?
I am dreaming of anchovies and olives.

He looked down at his phone and smiled at her message.

Nick: And bears. Oh my.

Callie: See you at 8 lovebug.

Nick: See you at 8 my sweet.

Okay, three more hours of work. He needed to focus.

They had had sex three times in the past twenty-four hours. He was envisioning her long, athletic legs, her long torso, her pink nipples. He didn't really care about the anchovies and olives. He just wanted a slice of Callie in his bed, right then. There were moments when he felt genuinely happy where he was: his growing company, Callie, his life in New York, his three sisters happily married and child-bearing back in London, his future outstretched before him…granted, the latter gave him a fair amount of anxiety, but on a good day he viewed it with grateful excitement. He had not asked his dad about bringing Callie home for a few days over Christmas. He was reluctant to introduce anyone to his mother, and it would mean having to actually ask Callie, which admittedly he was not quite ready to do. For now, he only wanted to be thankful for anchovies and pink nipples. A fair combination for an evening, he thought.

NEW YORK, NEW YORK

2018

MARGHERITA TAPPED THE plastic floor of the taxi with her boot and sat towards the middle of the backseat, egging the traffic on as if she could move it with her mind.

"Let's go, let's go, let's go!" she repeated. She couldn't care less what the driver thought. She checked the time every minute. Seventh Avenue crept along and she felt she might scream.

"Fifth won't be any different, ma'am," the driver said in a thick Indian accent.

"Come onnnnn!" Her teeth ground together and she tapped her thigh spasmodically. All of the patience she had learned in Italy had gone to the crapper since moving back to New York. She felt her whole body had regrown the tension it had shed.

Her flight had circled LaGuardia half a dozen times before landing, and she had spent the last hour sitting in her economy-plus seat doing the same thigh tap, the same words constantly at the tip of her tongue as she stared at the window. "Come on, come on, come onnnn!" She was supposed to go to a dinner hosted by a professional league of women in the world of architecture and design. She had paid for her ticket, hoping to have the chance to meet like-minded peers, maybe to make a new friend. She had fewer friends in New York than she had fingers on one hand. All of her friends were in Italy, and she knew that she would have to make a serious effort in order to change that. It was easier to find a date in New York than to meet a potential girlfriend whom she could count on for coffee and lunch once every few weeks. She had been looking forward to the evening, really counting on it to meet new people. Successful, interesting women who weren't heading straight for a life of Lululemon, Soul Cycle, suburban gossip, and New Years in Lyford Cay.

At Nineteenth street, she paid the exorbitant taxi, shoving the receipt into her coat pocket (to be expensed the next day) and ran down the subway steps. The 1 train would take her a bit closer at least, and then she would run the last five blocks. The invitation had been very strict about timeliness. The dinner was beginning with prominent speakers from the industry, and they would close the doors fifteen minutes after the start. *Wankers,* she thought. She had paid two hundred and fifty dollars for the ticket. The cost of meeting new friends.

At Christopher Street she exited the subway and skipped/ran (she was in heeled boots and was carrying her tote, heavy with plans from her meeting in Dallas) towards Washington Square. Amazing how long it could take one to go less than forty blocks on the ridiculously aggravating island of Manhattan. The evening began at precisely seven p.m. It was now eighteen minutes past seven. She had a feeling she would not make it, but she fought the crisp air as it choked her throat and hustled on.

Two more blocks, one more block, move, you stupid tourists.

At 7:25, she arrived at Washington Square. She felt her body starting to slow down, no matter how many miles she ran every day, as she crossed the park to the NYU library on the south side.

At last. She hurried up to the second floor.

"Hi," she said to the young woman sitting at a white table clothed desk outside of a closed door. "I'm Margherita. I'm sorry—my flight was delayed. I tried to find a number to call..." she was breathless. The young girl stared up at her with a blank, pert expression.

"Is it this door?" Margherita began to move towards it. The young girl shot up.

"I'm sorry; it's after 7:30. The doors are closed."

"Please. I was on a plane that wouldn't land. And then there was so much traffic," she said, eyes begging.

The young girl shrugged. "I'm just the messenger. Sorry. We can't let anyone in after 7:15."

"But that was only fifteen minutes ago," Margherita pleaded.

"I'm sorry. The doors are closed."

Margherita inhaled and exhaled heavily. *Fucking A.* "Can I at least use the bathroom?"

She slowly washed her hands and looked at her reflection. She was annoyed. She would not go home to sit in her apartment by herself. There was a well of energy inside of her, and she desperately needed a drink. *This fucking city. Fucking ridiculous*, she thought.

She looked down at her phone, opened her WhatsApp. She had so few actual friends in the metropolis, she did not have one person she could call to hang out with on a casual, last minute basis. She opened up the chat with Nick, the chat that had been going nowhere for a few weeks, sporadic bursts of exchanged wit about mundane subjects.

Margherita: I need a drink. Or two. What are you doing tonight?

She took a chance. So he hadn't asked her out. She liked him. She had thought him to be funny. He would make for a funny friend. Why couldn't she casually ask a potential friend for a drink. She exited the library building as she awaited his response.

Outside she looked left and right. Where could she go to sit at a busy bar and have a drink by herself, where she might meet someone new like she had always done in Milan. New York restaurants had become so snobby with their bars. One had to have a reservation to sit at the bar, and it was used for dining as opposed to drinks. God forbid she wanted to sit at the bar to have a drink. What venom the bartender would greet her with. What begrudgement they would serve her drink with. What hurriedness she would receive her bill with.

She decided on Lafayette. It had a dark and ambient bar toward the back of the restaurant that was often an afterthought to its boisterous tables. She liked the after-work crowd there, the men dining in groups of six or eight in crisp suits, the women dressed well and speaking loudly. It had buzz. She managed to find an empty seat, perhaps the last one, and ordered a gin and soda.

Good karma was making a fleeting appearance in the form of the man next to her. She took note of the watch on his left hand, a beautiful Jaeger Lecoultre. Then she noticed his fine Italian shoes, his smooth skin, and his perfectly fitted suit. He was Italian. No doubt.

He had not glanced in her direction. He was waiting patiently for someone, she supposed, taking sips from his

Old Fashioned and looking toward the entrance once in a while.

"I think you are the only person who doesn't stare at their phone while sitting alone at a bar," Margherita said, not giving a hoot if he was interested in chatting or not. She had had such a long day by that point, she felt she had nothing to lose.

The smooth man smiled politely. "No, it is my time to give my phone a break," he said with an accent.

"Sei Italiano?" *Are you Italian?* Margherita asked.

"Si. Tu non sei Italiana…parli Italiano?" *Yes. You are not Italian…but you speak it?* He was intrigued.

"Ho vissuto a Milano qualche anno. Non la parlo mai adesso," *I lived in Milano for a few years. I never speak it anymore,* she said, suddenly happy, suddenly lighter, in the company of an Italian.

At that moment, another well dressed man appeared on her seat-mates right side. He turned away from Margherita to greet him. Margherita looked at the second man, cocked her head, and gave an incredulous smile.

"Ciao," she said to the second man. His dark brown hair exactly the same, his blue eyes enlightened by his silk tie, his shiny brown leather shoes, his James Marsden smile.

"Do you remember me?" she asked, just in case. Just in case after having a drink or two with Cristiano and Beck one very late evening—the two of them both discreetly vying for her attention—he had blotted her out.

"Margherita," Beck said with a smile.

"You two know each other?" her seat-mate asked.

"Yes, Margherita worked with Elisio with the hotels. We met in Milan. You're back? Living in New York?"

"Yes," she shrugged. "I'm back."

"What happened?" Beck asked.

"Oh, long story. I had an interesting offer with Lolato. Store design." she said, not a lie, not the whole truth, but enough to convince anyone.

"Brava. Yulia and I went to business school together. She is lucky to have you, although I am sure you are missed," Beck said. "Happy to be back?"

She raised her eyebrows, see-sawed her head.

He smiled knowingly. "Well, we are expanding our New York team, so I'm going to be spending more time here. Let's grab lunch next time."

"Certo." *Sure.*

"Is Eve here yet?" Beck asked his friend, looking around.

"She's running late, but our table is ready."

The gentlemen said their goodbyes, leaving Margherita alone. She checked her phone. Nick had read the message but ignored it. She felt like she could scream. She ordered another gin and left the bar ever so slightly wobbly but endowed with the numbness she needed to close the day.

NEW YORK, NEW YORK

2018

THE RESTAURANT WAS packed and loud. It was a popular spot for its overpriced Neapolitan style pizzas, and it was his and Callie's favorite. He sat across from her while she told him about her upcoming trip to Palm Beach for a pre-holiday event at one of the upscale department stores. She and Grace were hosting a lunch with Instagram influencers to launch the arrival of their brand in the store. He was genuinely happy for her. She might be a spoiled young woman but she *was* putting in a decent amount of time at growing her company. She was committed. That was a lot more than most girls in her circumstances could say.

"You sure you don't want to come with me?" she asked, taking her third slice of anchovy, the cheese dragging from the dish to her plate.

He shook his head gently. "I can't. Not right now. I'm going away for ten days for Christmas. I can't do anything more," he said, looking down at his slice and taking a big bite. He had brought up Christmas. It hovered over their pie like a fairy about to sprinkle hot pepper flakes.

She nodded. "Okay. That makes sense."

She didn't say a word about the holiday break. He wondered if she was waiting for him to bring it up.

"Are you going to Australia? You haven't mentioned it," he said. He felt it was the right thing to do. It would be strange to not bring it up at all.

"Yes. Daddy booked our tickets months ago. He would be devastated if we didn't go," she said.

Oh thank god, he thought. Relief, utter relief. Guilt rose out of him like a ghost.

"Aw, I would have loved to have you cozy up with me in Dorset. Next trip. I'll take you down to Durdle Door." He took her wrist across the table and rubbed her palm with his thumb. She kissed the air in front of her.

"Yes, next time. Cuddles in the countryside and doodle doors. I would love that."

He let the cultural blunder slip and held onto her hand as he looked into her oval eyes. Her blonde hair was pulled into a loose bun. She wasn't wearing any makeup except for a little mascara, he assumed, and she looked so pretty. His girlfriend. He suddenly felt guilty that he had been so hesitant to bring up their holiday plans. He should genuinely want to spend them with her.

"I'm going to run to the little girls room. Too much wine," she said, and she bent down to give him a kiss as she walked off to the bathroom.

He took out his phone while he sat by himself and checked his emails. There was a WhatsApp message waiting. He had turned the alerts off since meeting Margherita, whose name he had entered into his phone as Margo, just in case. He was worried he might get caught in a mess even though nothing had happened. He opened her chat.

Margherita: I need a drink. Or two. What are you doing tonight?

He closed it immediately, and put his phone away.

Hours later, with Callie asleep next to him in his bed, he wrote her back. He felt bad ignoring her, but he also didn't want to let the communication die.

Nick: Hello!
Nick: Sorry- I'm just leaving work and only just saw this.
Nick: How are you?

What am I doing, he thought, as he deleted the conversation from his WhatsApp, put his phone away, and tried to go to sleep.

MILANO, LOMBARDIA

2018

Alexandre: I am here. End of bar. Awaiting your presence.

Alexandre: You are right. It is a good bar. Tres bien.

MARGHERITA WAS SHAKING. Her fingers were shaking, her hands were shaking, her chest was vibrating uncontrollably. Nerves, all nerves, in the best possible way. What might happen that evening with Alexandre, a man with whom she should not be having a glass of wine or, more likely, two or more? Certainly in the States it would be inappropriate to socialize like this with an important client. In Italy, however, or in Europe, surely in France, the Inappropriate Line was nonexistent. It was fuzzy and often buried to suit one's desires. It was an Americanism.

No one was doing anything wrong. She could have a glass of wine with an intelligent man who was also a work contact. She was an adult. She had to think of herself too, right? What if one day he hired her to work at the jewelry company? It was simply networking. Yes. Networking.

Networking could sometimes entail five days of texting from morning to evening, sharing details of one's day, giving insight into one's interests, one's desires, allowing a man to make assumptions about her romantic habits and character traits.

Yes, she was simply networking. Networking without boundaries. Very European of her, actually.

When she arrived, he was sitting at the far end of the bar as promised. He had taken off his navy blue suit jacket, had draped it on the back of the bar chair and sat in a crisp white button down, navy pants, and beautiful Berluti shoes. He was wearing the same dark, thick Tom Ford glasses. There was a glass of red wine in front of him, and he was looking down at his phone.

She approached him and he looked up, gave her a smile, put his large hand and its long fingers on the middle of her back, and leaned in to give her a kiss on each cheek. She sat down next to him and she felt the intensity increase even more.

"Allors."

"Allora," she replied.

"Buona sera Margherita," Pasquale greeted her from behind the bar.

"Ciao Pasquale. Come stai?"

"Bene, bene, bene," he said, nodding and smiling bashfully, as was his way with Margherita. "Un pinot noir?" he asked.

"Si!" she said with a smile and held her palms together in gratitude.

"You are a bit of a regular here, yes?" Alexandre noted.

"Oui, monsieur."

They began where they had left off in their non-stop texting. She had just returned from Rome with Elisio and was telling him about her favorite property there. She showed him a few photos on her phone of a new hotel they had toured that day, always monitoring the developments in the major cities. She would go to Istanbul in a few weeks; Elisio would go to Amsterdam.

After this little shop talk, Margherita built up her courage to dig deeper. She had done her Googling, of course. Alexandre did not wear a ring, and she could not believe that a man of forty-four years of age, with such fine looks and sophistication, such education and intellect, such charm and worldliness, was not married, or at least divorced. Unfortunately, the Google search had left many questions unanswered.

She learned that he had studied in England, had done his MBA at INSEAD, and his JD at Harvard. He had lived in London for several years as a lawyer at a top firm. He had then lived in Paris to act as Chief Counsel of a fashion conglomerate, an umbrella company that held majority stakes in many of the world's top brands. From there he had gone to Tokyo (this explained the zen garden at the jewelry headquarters) to lead the acquisition of his company's main competitor in Asia. Then he had returned to Europe, and landed in Milan as CEO of arguably the world's finest jewelry company.

His Instagram was also frustratingly vague. Less than fifteen posts, most of them screenshots of lesser known musical artists playing on his Spotify, and one or two artsy photos from scenes in Japan. There was a child in one photo, standing on a beach in what looked like western France. This spurred her to return to her google search. Did he have a 10-year-old-boy? She dug and dug and dug until she uncovered a letter he had written to some kind of City

Hall in South Kensington, complaining about a neighbor's lack of building permits and the noise pollution they were causing the block to endure as they built a monstrosity that surely surpassed the allotted square footage for the lot. In the letter, dated nearly fifteen years prior, he had written the words "My wife and I."

She froze. She had sent him a message in the middle of an intimate exchange, a moment in which they were sharing their love for nature—he with photos of the forest he owned in France, she with photos of where she stood in the Doria Pamphili Park in Rome beneath the umbrella pines.

Margherita: Did you move to Milan alone?

She had thought and thought about how to phrase the question without sounding accusatory, or too nosey, or out of line. It had been only a few days but suddenly she felt extraordinarily close to him in a visceral way. She had become attached to his intellect, to how he spoke to her as if he knew her inside and out, as if he had known her for years, and yet they were doing the dance—not saying too much about certain aspects of their lives, leaving a few blanks in the mix.

Alexandre: Yes

He had replied yes. He had moved to Milan alone.

And then she thought more about that response—how vague, how selfishly vague it appeared to her. He knew she was looking for answers. He knew exactly what she was after, and yet he offered her no comfort, no assurance. He was suddenly in control. He knew, by her subtle inquiries, she had already given too much away, had become entranced, entangled, had unleashed a certain amount of emotion and hope, and now, he could share or not share whatever information he wanted, and it wouldn't make a difference. Maybe he had gathered that about her character; that she was aloof until she wasn't. She could be tilted, tipped. Maybe he had seen, or sensed, her weakness somehow. How, or why, she did not know, but for some reason it made her feel closer to him. He somehow knew her; she did not need to explain herself.

She was about to inquire as elegantly as possible about his family, as indirectly direct as she could be, when he began to speak.

"You and I have something. You feel it, oui?" he said, matter of factly. His eyes concentrated on hers from behind his black-rimmed glasses. She suddenly felt on the spot.

"We do?" she asked, a little snidely.

He took a sip from his wine, his gaze not leaving her. "I felt it in my conference room. You have an air about you."

His conference room, she thought. His. As if he owned it.

"*You* have an air," she said, laughing a little, taking a sip from her wine. Maybe two.

"Defensive. Okay. And quite intense. But I bet you can be like this wine—liquid. Whoosh." He tipped his glass precariously.

"Oh? That's quite a conclusion to draw after one conference room and a few days of texting!" She laughed.

He folded his forearms over each other, his long slender fingers a centimeter from hers. He raised his eyebrows.

"You think you know me very well, I see. Has anyone ever described you as presumptuous?" she asked with a hint of irony.

"Somewhere, somewhere," his eyes went to the ceiling, his long fingers wrapped around the stem of his wine glass. He refocused his eyes on her, refolded his arms, hand over forearm. "Somewhere, you can be soft. I know this because I saw photos of your father on your Instagram. You are obviously close. You love him very much. There is sweetness in your eyes when you are with him. There is a young girl, somewhere in there," he pointed towards Margherita's heart, his long forefinger coming into contact with her chest.

"No photos of your maman. I am not sure, yet, what this means?" he said, his French accent ending in a question mark.

She felt a bit taken aback, unsure what to say. Did she simply not have enough experience with Frenchmen or was he bizarrely frank, eccentric and pompous? It felt intense and manic and surreal; didn't that add up to something? Certainly it was a stark contrast from her emotionally minimal interactions with Paolo, and with others before and after him. But why did it *affect* her, make her heart race so? What did that *mean*?

His fingers enveloped her hand. His other hand pushed a strand of hair behind her ear. His sudden tenderness, that had to be a French thing.

She looked around at the bar to see if she knew anyone. They were speaking so intensely, so intimately, more so than the average work aperitivo.

Two days earlier:

> **Margherita:** I am just going to ask. Forgive my bluntness. And I hope you do not find this inappropriate. Are you married?

She had stood there in front of her terrace the evening she returned home from Rome, having thought all day about how to phrase the question, having typed it a dozen times in slightly different ways on her phone on the train ride home. Their conversations had been fluid, yes, but they had not been outrightly romantic. She was worried she might have misinterpreted him. Or worse, that he would suddenly show violent ego if he were put on the spot. He was an important work contact. She did not want to muddy the situation.

> **Alexandre:** I would rather speak to you about this in person. There is a short answer, of course. But the long answer is the one that means something. We have something here, Margherita, and I would rather you hear the long answer from me.

So, he was married. Still. Of course. Her heart sank a fair amount, like a block of cement being laid in the street. Plop. Boom.

The truth was that it was too late, either way. Short answer, long answer. In the moment, it didn't matter.

Sitting there, side by side, at the bar, listening to him, watching him drink his French wine, she felt that rush again. It wasn't hope for something romantic and everlasting. She was not sure she believed in that. She certainly did not dream of him leaving his wife. No, it was more…excitement, a rush, something for the right here and right now.

"You don't wear a ring," she said, eyeing his long finger.

His face scrunched up. "No, that is so silly. Like a dog tag. I do not need to show the world the decisions I have made. I do not belong to anyone."

Was he strange? Or very French? Or very modern? She was not sure. But for the moment, she was swept away, and that was all that mattered.

"L'occasione fa l'uomo ladro," she said with a hint of mischief in her voice.

She ached to tell Francine; she was terrible at keeping anything from her parents. She had always been a completely open book, always wanting to share the most mundane details and the most riveting. It felt like a terrible scratch she wasn't itching, to not share with her mom, but she knew it would bring more contempt for Italy. Sharing about Paolo had left a very negative mark. Alexandre was not a household name like Beck; he was simply a successful businessman with the faculty to have an affair with a young foreigner. Francine looked down on any relationship that might keep Margherita out of worlds she deemed acceptable, ie London or New York—whether it be romantic or professional, acceptable or frowned upon—anything that satiated her daughter in Italy was viewed as an adversary.

2018

Alexandre: Still on for this eve?

IN THE THIRD-FLOOR office, Margherita put the final touches on a PowerPoint presentation that reviewed the potential spa and fitness partners. They would host CEO's of prominent Swiss and French cosmetic brands in Milan that week to discuss the design of the future spa.

> **Margherita:** Oui, monsieur. 8? They don't take reservations.
>
> **Alexandre:** I am looking forward to it. A bit too much I think.
>
> **Margherita:** Moi aussi :)

She stared at her phone with her thumb nail between her front teeth. She had been feeling antsy all day. Daring, too.

> **Margherita:** Do you ever find yourself hopelessly lost in an exotic daydream at work? It is an awful

pickle to be in

Alexandre: Do you find yourself in this pickle today?

Margherita: Oh, I can't tell you that. I'm a lady.

Alexandre: Well, either way, yes, I do.
Alexandre: Especially lately.

Margherita: Rather distracting.

Alexandre: You are, yes.
Alexandre: Now I cannot stop picturing you.

Margherita: Picturing me?

Alexandre: Oui.

Margherita: May I tell you something

Alexandre: Always

Margherita: My panties have been very wet for about an hour. I will most definitely have to go home before dinner to change them.

Alexandre: You are perfect.

MILANO, LOMBARDIA

2018

SHE ARRIVED FIRST, knowing they would have to wait. The trattoria had been in existence for decades. The owners, an aging husband and wife, each had their parts in the establishment. He, full bellied, quiet, and discreetly jolly, cooked in the kitchen, once in a while making an appearance towards the end of the evening. She, gruff to those she did not know, smiling to those she did, bossy and lacking patience, took orders at the handful of tables. The menu changed every day, and a handwritten copy was duplicated on a copy machine and passed out to diners with a small basket of inedible Italian bread. If Agata knew and liked you, she would sit down at your table to chat, never mind the other patrons who might require her attention. The food was always simple and divine, layered with just the right herb and just the right amount of excellent olive oil, the height of the season for each ingredient. It was one of Margherita's favorite spots in her neighborhood. Alexandre had never been of course. He was not adventurous on foreign soil.

She waited for him inside, leaning against a small table next to the front door, hovering an inch or two from other tables; such was the Italian way. She felt something in the realm of elation, knowing she was waiting for a man for whom she had strong feelings, knowing as well that those feelings were reciprocated, and also knowing that he was a catch of a man—tall, intelligent, handsome, chic, and worldly. She played in her mind that she was waiting for a boyfriend. She was waiting for her tall, handsome, intelligent boyfriend. He had a busy job; he was always running late. She was understanding of course. In her story, he was separated from his wife. He had no kids. In her story, they took romantic trips to the Alps, where they made love for hours in an oversized bed overlooking the peaks, with a fire crackling. In her story, they spent a cozy weekend in the Rhône Valley and spontaneous getaways in Paris and Sevilla.

He arrived, finally, and dipped his head in to let her know, but he was still on a call. He held the phone to his ear and went back outside to finish his conversation on the sidewalk. The other dining patrons had seen the man for whom she had been waiting. They could now affirm that she and her partner were a fine looking couple, that he was older than her, sophisticated, handsome. Agata referred to him as her fidanzato. *Boyfriend.* She became friendlier towards Margherita after seeing him.

She hoped his being new in town would help them remain incognito, as there was always the chance of running into someone in a city as small as Milan. She suddenly felt worried and silly in equal measure. She was the other woman; she would *not* be the woman with whom he would actually go to Sevilla.

Finally, they were seated. The time was already nine p.m. and she knew what she wanted to order. He was tired, slightly agitated after a long day, and not comforted in the least by Agata's inability to speak English. He had not learned Italian yet. Margherita supposed it was his pride that stopped him. He did not seem the type to admit to an inability in a certain area. He was annoyed at the Italian menu; he could not fully understand it, and Margherita had to help him.

"I have been researching spas in Tokyo. At the big hotels. They do spatial design so well. Do you miss Tokyo?" She steered the conversation to a subject that he knew much about, a subject about which she knew very little. It seemed to pacify him, and he slipped his hand between her crossed thighs, resting it between them like a layer of thinly sliced mortadella in a panino.

As they were talking, or rather as he was talking, teaching her, or so he thought, she found herself growing increasingly languid, bored, tired. He was so serious all of the time, so overly pensive. So French. She wanted to laugh. She wanted a bit of silliness. She wanted a bit of Tommaso, her father, who always made her laugh, who never took much of anything too seriously, just enough to be respectable and successful, but not so much as to come off as wooden or wearisome.

She had stopped listening to Alexandre somewhere between his recommendations of onsens to visit, and the reasons why Japanese men were suicidal. He took every word so literally. He could not be playful. She knew in her gut that she had grown bored, and was disappointed. The evening had begun on such a different note. Suddenly she was alone again.

NEW YORK, NEW YORK

2018

"MARGHERITA…" YULIA'S VOICE drifted from her glass office, barely audible.

Margherita was convinced she did that on purpose—making it difficult for Margherita to hear her—so that the next time Yulia called her name, she had an excuse to yell.

"Yes?" Margherita appeared at her doorway.

Yulia's office belied nothing personal. There was not one picture frame, not one medal of any sort, not one token of anything sentimental. Her Georg Jensen espresso cup sat to her right, next to her Piaget watch which she sometimes took off when she typed, afraid it might scratch on her Dan Johnsson "Gazelle" glass desk.

"You are going to DC for the walk-through."

"Okay. When is that?" Margherita asked.

Yulia pretended not to hear her, leaving Margherita standing in the doorway awkwardly waiting. After a moment, Yulia looked up at her.

"Yes?"

"When is the DC walk-through?" Margherita asked again.

"You *are* capable of coordinating with the PM are you not? Did you confirm my reservation tonight with Alexandre?"

"Yes," Margherita said, *even though that's not my job,* she thought.

"It's just going to be him and I tonight, you know that right? Next time he's here maybe he'll take you for a little coffee," she said, passive aggressively wicked.

Margherita pursed her lips. *Wackjob bitch,* she thought, as she turned around and went back to her drafting desk. The last thing she wanted to do was spend additional time with Yulia outside of the working day. Besides, she had tickets to the ballet that evening.

Before the performance, she stood on the triangular green space between Broadway and Columbus and stared at the frenetic scene before her. Lincoln Center was a mash of taxi drop-offs and excited patrons standing in groups in the plaza. She could almost *feel* crossing the crosswalk on Columbus Avenue, watching Francine's silk or lightweight wool scarf fly backwards in the night air. She suddenly felt it difficult to inhale.

It had been something mother and daughter shared since she was a little girl. Francine had taken her to Broadway shows, ballets, concerts and orchestras, and Francine had shared her large scarves with her when they sat freezing in their seats due to the unnecessary air conditioning in the concert hall. When the show was over, they would leave brimming with exhilaration, discussing which performances and shows they would buy tickets for next.

She entered the hall by herself for that evening's American Ballet Theater performance, with everyone around her in pairs or small groups. She sat in her seat in the front center (she had splurged) while people around her gushed and gossiped. All she could think about was her mom; it was like a buzzing in her ears.

At the intermission, she quietly rose from her seat and walked toward the exit, along with the wave of other patrons who were eager to be the first to the ladies' room or stock up on chocolate covered raisins and cheap wine. Instead of joining them, she walked out the front door into the courtyard, with its spewing fountain and teenagers' voices in the night, and she didn't exhale until she got to Central Park, where she let the tears spout. She didn't think she could ever go to the ballet again.

NEW YORK, NEW YORK

2018

MARGHERITA AND YULIA climbed out of the Uber on the corner of Grand and Lafayette streets, Margherita's right arm wrapped snugly around four rolls of plans and Yulia with her hand wrapped snugly around a coffee from Sant'Ambreous, where they had just been meeting with a real estate developer visiting from Singapore. They crossed the sidewalk towards the front door of their building and as Margherita reached for the door, it opened from the inside.

"Hi!" Nick said, a glint of surprise in his eye.

"Hi…" Margherita said wearily, aware of Yulia.

"Hello…" Yulia said, a small grin on her face.

"Yulia, this is Nick; Nick, this is my boss Yulia. Nick launched a new co-working space a little while ago…the next big thing. Your office is around here right?"

"Yes but we've been scouring for new space as we are bursting at the seams. There is a gorgeous space for rent on the sixth floor. Bit pricey. You're in this building?"

"Yes, we are," Yulia said, eyeing Margherita and Nick, one and then the other.

"And you like it?" Nick asked Yulia. "Seems like good management?"

"Oh, yes, I think so. In fact, we are having a bit of a soirée Thursday eve, to celebrate my tenth anniversary with the company, if you'd like to see our wraparound terrace. The views are spectacular. And Margherita will be there, of course," Yulia said.

Margherita pursed her lips and held in an eye roll. Yulia stood there very pleased with herself and Nick must have noticed the awkwardness.

"Oh, wow that's very kind. I have a dinner Thursday, but I'll try to make it. Congratulations on ten years," he said, as charming and nonchalant as one could be.

"Ah well," Yulia raised her arms and shrugged, still with that proud smirk on her face. "I tried Margherita!" She embarrassed her completely. "Anyway, we are running late, aren't we M. Must dash. Ciao darling," Yulia said, and passed through the open door that Nick was still holding.

Margherita walked by him and quietly shook her head at her boss. He smiled and mouthed the word "Hello," as she moved the plans from her right arm to her left.

In the elevator, Yulia didn't say a word, making Margherita feel even more awkward. She assumed Nick was lying about Thursday. He clearly had never been interested in her.

NEW YORK, NEW YORK

2019

"So how was this week?" Jane carefully set her tea on the little table next to her easy chair. It was one of those university mugs, oversized and mass produced.

"Fine. Nothing too interesting."

"Any new dates?"

"Um, yes. One. I already forgot about it. Guess it wasn't so great." Margherita crossed and uncrossed her legs.

"Anyone coming up?"

"Um, yes…someone new this weekend. I think he said he's from Geneva?"

"Where do you find these international guys?" Jane joked.

"We floaters tend to find each other," Margherita said with a shrug.

"Do you still feel like you're floating? When you're here? Even though you grew up here?"

"Yeah, I would say so," Margherita said, slowly. "I'm not really attached to very much here. And I don't have very much attached to me. Now—even less."

Jane was silent.

"Anyway, she was always in and out, even when I was

here. Whether she was in and out in her mind or physically—with her work schedule. She wasn't a total fixture, so to speak."

"But she was something you felt tethered to," Jane said.

Margherita inhaled and exhaled. "Ugh. Whatever. Tethered. Untethered. We're all a little untethered, aren't we? Especially my mom. She always was."

NEW YORK, NEW YORK

2019

Nick: hello!

MARGHERITA'S PHONE PINGED on the arm of her chair. She had been lying in bed with her iPad, absentmindedly job searching out of curiosity, something she had begun to do more frequently.

Margherita: Bom dia :)

Nick: Funny running into you.

Nick: Thank you for the invitation

Margherita: You can thank my boss :) She invited you.

What does he want? she wondered.

Nick: Ah, true. I suppose you are relieved I am not going then?

Margherita: Al contrario…. I am so disappointed I don't think I'll go either!

Nick: Ha right. But you'll miss the terrace view.

Nick: Also

Nick: I feel like saying

Nick: And I meant to a while ago

Nick: I really wanted to go for a drink with you

Nick: You stuck in my mind

Nick: Ages ago

Margherita: Oh

Nick: Oh that

Margherita: Thank you for never asking me then

Nick: My having a girlfriend sort of got in the way

Nick: But I didn't want to presume

Margherita: Oh. Well you could have said so!

Nick: I suppose

Margherita: I wouldn't have been overly upset if you had

Nick: I think you're boyfriended up now?

Margherita: Boyfriended up

Margherita: You make it sound like bondage

Margherita: No…

Nick: You're not

Margherita: No I am not boyfriended up

Nick: It does sound like bondage

Margherita: So are you telling me this because you are finally revealing that you have a girlfriend

Margherita: Like an fyi

Nick: This is why I didn't!

Nick: It's presumptuous

Margherita: I'm just asking

Nick: I do yes

Margherita: Ok (thumbs up emoji)

Nick: ha

Nick: I guess it still hasn't watered down

Margherita: What does that mean

Nick: no idea

Nick: just I thought about you quite a lot after we met

Margherita: Ah, well.

Margherita: A man of little action then.

Margherita: Won't even come to an office 'soiree'

Nick: I know

Nick: No action whatsoever

Nick: Did you

Margherita: Did I what

Nick: Think

Nick: About our meeting

Margherita: Today? When you asked about management? And held the door open? Actually that was quite an action-man thing to do. Move over Tobey Maguire.

Nick: lol

Nick: No, not today. Did you, ever think about when we met. At the caffè

Margherita: I prefer to pivot

Margherita: Are you not allowed to have female friends?

Nick: Are you pivoting me away from what you deem to be flirtation
Nick: I certainly am!

Margherita: Because honestly when we met I thought oh he's funny I would hang out with him
Margherita: And you were not accepting of a new friend

Nick: haha
Nick: Problem is
Nick: I found you attractive

Margherita: so what
Margherita: I find a lot of people attractive and I am still able to interact with them

Nick: hahaha

Margherita: That's a shame. You must have a lot of unattractive friends

Nick: They're disgusting.

Margherita: C'est bon. Since you don't want to be friends and you have a girlfriend, I wish you all the best with the co-working company :)

Nick: I DO
Nick: Whoa
Nick: There
Nick: Be friends with me

Margherita: I will get back to you on that in like 4 months

Nick: oh shut up
Nick: Just cos I tell you I think you're attractive
Nick: and you tell me off

Nick: And give me atttitude

Nick: Doesn't mean we can't be friends

Margherita: Well okay. So what were you thinking.

Nick: When

Margherita: You said you thought about me a lot after we met. What were you thinking

Nick: hmm

Nick: Do you really want to know

Margherita: Don't be coy

Margherita: Spit it out

Nick: You're going to relegate me

Nick: Even further

Nick: Into typical boy category

Margherita: brits think too much

Margherita: Say it

Nick: hmmm

Nick: You're asking me

Nick: To just

Nick: Lay my cards down on the table

Margherita: I'm not cornering you I promise

Nick: what if I want to be cornered

Margherita: can you stop hiding

Nick: hi

Nick: I'm here

Margherita: what are these cards

Nick: I had incredibly

Margherita: incredibly?

Margherita: ok you are officially annoying

Nick: ha

Margherita: so glad we can't be friends

Nick: incredibly unacceptable thoughts
Nick: About you
Nick: While we were sitting there actually
Nick: If you must know

Margherita: I think that's allowed in life
Margherita: I think you will be forgiven

Nick: For which part

Margherita: Definitely NOT for shunning my friendship

Nick: Tell me
Nick: Why did you want to know my cards

Margherita: Because you said something and then let it dangle in suspense. I hate that.

Nick: I see
Nick: No more danglers

Margherita: Can I ask you something

Nick: Yes please
Nick: This is more fun

Margherita: not being an angler here I promise

Nick: Okay
Nick: I believe you

Margherita: is this a knock you off your feet kind of love
Margherita: Like a left you breathless kind of love when you met this girlfriend of yours

Nick: Meeting you?

Margherita: hahaha funny

Margherita: Your girlfriend

Nick: It was when we met

Nick: Doesn't feel like that anymore

Margherita: Maybe it can't feel like that forever

Nick: why do you ask

Margherita: Curiosity

Margherita: Ok person who is not my friend

Margherita: grazie for the info

Margherita: I'm not entirely sure where we landed here but am happy to be friends if you're up for it. Which means actually getting a drink or a coffee once in a while. And if that's not ok with you then that's totally fine and I understand. C'est bon?

Nick: Why don't you reveal your cards

Margherita: What cards do I need to reveal

Nick: What you thought

Margherita: I'm not the one in a relationship right

Margherita: What I thought when we met?

Nick: Yes

Nick: Or now

Margherita: Are you a generally greedy person

Nick: Interesting

Margherita: You have a girlfriend right

Nick: Maybe I'm finding myself in a greedy moment right now

Margherita: So it seems..

Nick: Are you greedy

Margherita: Depends how much I want something

Nick: what is your view on greed

Margherita: No I'm not having a long drawn out texting conversation

Nick: Just tell me your thinking then
Nick: You came back with a question

Margherita: When we met I thought oh he's quite funny and quite smart and enjoyable and I'd like to hang out with him
Margherita: That's what I thought

Nick: That's nice

Margherita: (angel emoji)

Nick: That's part of what you thought
Nick: I think
Nick: I hope

Margherita: What are you fishing for

Nick: Something

Margherita: What do you want right now
Margherita: In this moment
Margherita: Don't think just answer
Margherita: Stop thinking

Nick: I am thinking
Nick: I want to do something

Margherita: Such as…

Nick: Now you're fishing

Margherita: No. You're just vague

Nick: I don't think you actually mean this

Margherita: No I really do

Nick: You want me to be honest

Margherita: Always

Nick: I want to do something that I'll feel guilty about later
Nick: In secret
Nick: There's your answer

Margherita: That's the trick to what you're thinking though. You can only do it if you don't feel guilt
Margherita: If you do it's ruinous

Nick: I don't think I will feel guilt
Nick: Hence the greed

Margherita: You just said you would feel guilty later

Nick: I think I said that

Margherita: You are barking up the wrong tree

Nick: Why did you ask me

Margherita: Because this is my Tree historically
Margherita: So I'm going to repeat my little friendship message. Because truly. I would love that.

Nick: (Also I didn't assume you were a tree to bark up)

Margherita: Ok I hope you find what you're looking for tonight then :)
Margherita: Buona serata

Nick: haha
Nick: Shush
Nick: I'm not looking for it
Nick: You asked me
Nick: To stop thinking
Nick: And speak

Nick: So I did

Nick: I think you might have asked because you got a sense for the answer

Nick: Am I right

Margherita: I just wanted to see if you actually know, decisively, what it is that you're dancing around

Margherita: And I'm still not sure

Nick: And because it was of no interest to you

Nick: What are you not sure about

Margherita: I think you're just entertaining yourself right now

Margherita: I think you are unsure that you know what you are even saying or what you're getting at

Margherita: I don't know what you are doing having this "I'm not going to actually say what I mean" conversation

Nick: I have said what I mean haven't I

Nick: But I think I'm now slightly protecting myself

Nick: I was encouraged by your 'dont think speak'

Nick: Do you want me to say more

Margherita: which makes it impossible for me to respond. If you suddenly start backing up

Nick: I'm not backing up

Margherita: If you're looking for a girl to have some sort of flirtatious text conversation with and nothing ever comes of it then please find someone else because that's no fun/not fair to me

Margherita: And I genuinely would like to be friends but not the kind that you text once in a while when you get in a fight with your girlfriend and are seeking attention and excitement

Nick: Hey

Nick: I never responded to your message

Nick: Because I knew myself

Nick: And then today I saw you again

Nick: We got chatting

Nick: And I ended up telling you what was going on in the pit of my stomach

Nick: And the image that was playing out in my head...

Margherita held her thumbnail between her front teeth. She didn't know what he was getting at, being so vague. She hoped it was something in the realm of what she wanted to hear, but she knew the chances of that were slim; she assumed he was bored.

Margherita: Okay

Nick: I don't mean to be chasing you and being unfair

Nick: Enjoying telling you what's going on in my head

Nick: And chest

Nick: (You know that feeling?)

Margherita: What feeling

Nick: Of wanting

Margherita: You want because you are in a position where you can't have

Nick: Could be

Nick: Who knows

Margherita: Goodnight :) Sleep well. Take a Xanax

Nick: Incredibly punchy

Margherita: Just last thing. There were plenty of opportunities in our conversation where you could have seamlessly mentioned a girlfriend. It wouldn't have been presumptuous in the slightest

Nick: You asked me to level with you
Nick: And I did
Nick: Feel like you didn't want me to
Nick: But also did

Margherita: And I'm saying, light as a feather, you had plenty of opportunity to say something. You made it sound like it would have been an out of the blue thing
Margherita: Just saying:)

Nick: What if
Nick: What are you thinking
Nick: And what do you want
Nick: Right now
Nick: Regardless of anything

Margherita: it doesn't matter what I want. Moot

Nick: I'd like to know what you want
Nick: I've told you

Margherita: Not really

Nick: Explain
Nick: Not moot

Margherita: You didn't' say what you want. All you said was that you would feel guilty. So I'm led to believe you want something like a one night affair sort of thing

Nick: That was my way of labeling what I was thinking

Nick: Without saying

Nick: Cos I"m english

Nick: I'm not interested in one night

Margherita: I speak British- I get it. I just like to make you say what you mean because it's so very painful for your Nationality to do so

Nick: Ha

Nick: So you're sitting there

Nick: Without emotion or reaction

Nick: Teaching me to speak

Margherita: Have you ever cheated

Margherita: Tell the truth

Margherita: Not judging

Nick: Yes

Nick: I have

Margherita: On this same girlfriend?

Nick: Drunkenly and randomly

Nick: In this relationship

Nick: But before yes

Margherita: Multiple times? In this relationship

Nick: A couple

Margherita: Does she know

Nick: I feel cross examined

Nick: No

Margherita: Just getting to know my new friend

Margherita: Why do you think you do it if it's totally random

Margherita: What is the satisfaction

Nick: I don't know

Nick: Expression of some pent up energy

Nick: Naughtiness

Margherita: So you think you'll always have these little random one night stands

Margherita: No matter who you're with

Nick: No

Margherita: Maybe it's just your character

Margherita: Il lupo perde il pelo a non il vizio.

Nick: I don't know what that means.

Nick: but I don't know

Margherita: It's possible

Nick: Anything is

Margherita: You wouldn't be the first of this kind. But that's a shame

Nick: "Not judging" are we

Margherita: Not at all

Margherita: I understand it actually

Nick: mmm

Nick: What do you mean

Nick: You're making me feel

Nick: Judged

Nick: And like you're entertaining yourself

Margherita: Maybe you want to be judged

Margherita: I'm not at all

Nick: I want to be honest with you

But not with your girlfriend...she thought.

Margherita: I just don't want to be in a situation I've been in before
Margherita: And I have very minimal discipline so I am protecting myself now :)
Nick: Ah yes
Nick: I should have seen that
Nick: We're both protecting ourselves a little

Except you're protecting yourself from a potentially hurt ego, and I am protecting myself from actual, exposed feelings. There is a difference, she thought.

Margherita: Ok goodnight for real
Nick: Why
Nick: Because you have low discipline
Nick: This is the first real thing you've said in a while
Nick: And it's nice
Margherita: You like it because you think you found a possible weak spot
Nick: No
Nick: I'm at home now
Nick: Not trying to find your weak spot
Nick: Enjoying you being a bit vulnerable back
Nick: Rather than just me
Margherita: I am saying goodnight because this conversation isn't going to go anywhere really positive

Nick: I didn't think of you as a tree I would bark up

Nick: Hence why I left it

Nick: But seeing you today made me

Nick: Why not positive

Margherita: Are you going to be my friend now

Margherita: Legitimately

Nick: You are ducking

Nick: Out of my questions

Margherita: Like a 20 minute lunch to talk about location scouting and recruiting

Margherita: Was that girl you were having lunch with one of your random pent up energy outlets

Margherita: Or how come you could be friends with her and not me

Nick: hahah

Nick: No

Margherita: Not cool

Nick: An interview

Margherita: Really because I got the sense she was a little nervous and wide eyed

Margherita: Lots of eyelashes fluttering

Margherita: Did you catch that

Nick: I did not

Margherita: Sure.

Margherita: So are you going to be my friend now

Nick: Do you want to be my friend

Margherita: I always did

Margherita: You are the one who didn't, remember

Nick: Ah yes

Isabetta Andolini

Nick: The attraction was one way
Nick: I forgot that

Margherita: (eye roll emoji)

Nick: Silly me

Margherita: Don't fish

Nick: "He was quite funny and quite smart"...

Margherita: You can't fish if you have a girlfriend
Margherita: Greedy
Margherita: You haven't answered

Nick: What question

Margherita: omg
Margherita: Soon I give up
Margherita: Are you going to be my freaken friend
Margherita: Your British silence tells me no

Nick: You aren't being fully honest
Nick: With me
Nick: I want you to say what you want

What kind of idiot do you think I am, she thought.

Margherita: Why
Margherita: What for

Nick: Purely for academic purposes
Nick: Because I told you
Nick: And because why not

Margherita: So you can either be flattered for the sake of being flattered, selfishly, or so you can be unsatisfied with an answer you weren't expecting and then write me off

Nick: haha

Nick: Don't worry

Nick: I won't force you to do anything

Margherita: I don't think that's possible

Nick: You're so fun

Margherita: I want to get a drink like I did 5 months ago or whenever that was
Margherita: Basically

Nick: Okay

Margherita: Sorry to disappoint.

Nick: Not disappointing.
Nick: Wonderful chat

Margherita: Is this you writing me off like I predicted

Nick: No
Nick: Just retreating out of a slightly one sided exchange?

Margherita: I am not going to say things for the sake of saying them

Nick: Okay
Nick: You have no duty to

Margherita: You already know I was interested, I think that was quite clear...and I'm not going to put myself out there stupidly and unnecessarily to a person who can't or won't or doesn't want to do anything about it.
Margherita: So.
Margherita: It's not one sided.

Nick: I think I do want to do something about it.

Margherita: Maybe you think that tonight because you have pent up energy. And tomorrow you'll be singing a different tune. And that's where the whole greedy/unfair bit comes in.

Nick: No

Nick: I've thought about you since we met

Margherita: You don't know me at all

Nick: 100% true

Nick: You're a stranger

Nick: I feel like I'm disappointing you

Nick: 90%

Nick: And intriguing you

Nick: 10%

Margherita: I am practicing your British avoidance

Margherita: You have a girlfriend

Nick: I'm not avoiding

Nick: I know

Nick: We've established this

Margherita: So I don't know what to say

Nick: Well just talk with me

Nick: Explore this weird topic

Margherita: I tried a few times to talk to you

Margherita: And figure you out

Nick: I'm talking aren't I

Margherita: And you just brushed it off

Nick: What is unfigured out

Nick: You haven't said what you want

Margherita: When we met

Nick: Yes

Margherita: After we met. I tried a few times to talk to you and figure you out

Nick: I know

Nick: And I brushed you off

Margherita: Because I really wanted to get to know you. Whether just by being friends or not

Margherita: And you just totally brushed me off

Nick: I did

Margherita: So this is slightly unexpected

Nick: Okay

Nick: I didn't know what to do

Nick: But I decided

Nick: To be honest with you today

Margherita: And considering that I don't know you and what I do know about you is that you cheat on your girlfriend, my inclination is to say to myself, he's bored right now and this will fade by tomorrow.

Nick: *Quote:* **Margherita:** *Because I really wanted to get to know you. Whether just by being friends or not*

This is really lovely

Nick: *Quote:* **Margherita:** *And considering that I don't know you and what I do know about you is that you cheat on your girlfriend, my inclination is to say to myself, he's bored right now and this will fade by tomorrow.*

No judgement

Margherita: I'm not judging but it's a fact

Nick: Have you ever cheated

Margherita: No
Margherita: But I have been in situations like the one you are presenting.

Nick: hmm

Margherita: For long periods
Margherita: And I'm not putting myself in that position anymore

Nick: Okay
Nick: You don't have to

Margherita: Just sharing :)
Margherita: Over-sharing most likely

Nick: It's nice that you're sharing. Thank you
Nick: Not over-sharing at all.
Nick: It's weird
Nick: I've admitted stuff to you
Nick: And I feel shame
Nick: Rather than secrecy
Nick: Feel it's bounced off you
Nick: Which is ok

Am I his midnight therapist now? she thought.

Margherita: What's bounced off me
Margherita: What do you mean
Margherita: I'm going to sleep

Nick: My response to you asking what do you want
Nick: Dont think

Margherita: I still don't know what you want
Margherita: I doubt you know either

Nick: I don't think you want to know

Margherita: Why not

Nick: Because you react quite defensively when I'm honest
Nick: Or quite dismissively

Margherita: No not at all
Margherita: Tell me

Nick: I feel that
Nick: It might be wrong.

Margherita: I won't be dismissive

Nick: What shall I tell you

Margherita: What you want
Margherita: Try me

Please say something nice. Non-sexual. Please let someone that I like be interested in me for more than sex.

Nick: You want me to tell you again…

Margherita: You never did

Nick: You want to know?

Margherita: Stop it
Margherita: Annoying boy just tell me

Nick: I want to come over
Nick: To wherever you are
Nick: And take your clothes off you
Nick: And really slowly
Nick: Fuck you
Nick: But I think you already knew that

She felt defeated. They had been texting for hours, and she had convinced herself that no one would spend so much time in the conversation if all they wanted was sex. With his message, she realized she had been wrong. He was not interested in the way she hoped he was.

Margherita: That's what I thought

Nick: I took your word for it

Margherita: Little piece of me was hoping it wasn't what you would say. But I should've known better I guess.

Nick: Okay
Nick: Well sorry for disappointing you so much

Margherita: Not at all

Nick: A bit
Nick: It's okay
Nick: Your reaction cured me.
Nick: I won't try

Cured you? she thought. *Wow.*

Margherita: If I somewhere gave you the impression that I am the kind of girl who is up for a one night stand with a young guy who has a girlfriend and is looking for pure sex no strings attached, just to burn some energy, I apologize. I didn't mean to represent myself in that way at all.

Nick: You never did
Nick: Just me being a stupid boy
Nick: And me being really attracted to you

Nick: Not your fault
Nick: As in- no need to apologize

She had felt so much adrenaline throughout the nearly three hour chat, and then, poof, he pierced it.

NEW YORK, NEW YORK

2019

MARGHERITA FORCED HERSELF to lay in bed an extra hour. She had awoken periodically during the night to check her phone, but he must've gone to sleep, and the silence left her feeling blue and lonely. How was it that she was constantly in the same situation—wanting an unavailable man, someone who only wanted sex and secrecy? In the case of Nick, she hadn't gone looking, she hadn't known all along, she had even let it drop to the wayside when it clearly wasn't going anywhere. She had met someone by chance, had felt something click, a staggeringly rare feeling. Perhaps rarer was the fact that he was in her age group, a peer, someone with whom she might have a chance at something real. He was not married, with children. He was not fifteen to twenty years her senior. He was just another young, early-thirties guy, living downtown.

And all he saw in her was some kind of play thing. The same thing that she felt they all saw in her: a promiscuous toy. A smart one, but a promiscuous toy all the same.

An hour later she woke again and reached for her phone. Messages. Thank god. If he hadn't written anything at all, she would have felt seriously low. A stronger girl wouldn't care in the slightest, would have already deleted him from memory and categorized him as immature and idiotic. Margherita did not have the capacity to do that. She would dismiss when the other person did nothing to deserve dismissal. She could *not* dismiss those who unquestionably deserved it.

Nick: Hey
Nick: I'm sorry
Nick: Was in a very strange mood
Nick: I've never had the impression of you as anything but a lovely, respectful lady and please dont pay any attention to my meandering messages

She let it sit. It wasn't at all the apology she had hoped for; the words she had hoped would rescue her dispiritedness.

Margherita: They were quite productive messages actually…'cured' me of you as well.

Nick: lol

Margherita: That wasn't meant to be funny actually.

Nick: Can I buy you a coffee and apologize
Nick: A lightly caffeinated one
Nick: Would a video of my nephew singing me a good morning song while visiting me from London help?

(Sends video)

She watched the video of what looked like a three-year-old Nick, blonde and darling, in a sweet pajama set, singing in a British accent with his uncle Nick. It was achingly adorable. But no. She wanted to be strong. For once.

Margherita: No thank you
Margherita: Why does a guy with a limited conscience feel inclined to apologize at all? All you want is sex. You're not going to get what you want here. So what use is buying me a coffee

Nick: You think you know me
Nick: I'm not after anything
Nick: I'm just saying sorry for being a Pratt last night

Margherita: k

Nick: Sorry for offending you

Margherita: All good

Nick: It's not all I want, it was me operating on a silly rush of hormones
Nick: Nothing to do with you
Nick: Me being a nob

Margherita: oh

Nick: ergh you know what I mean

Margherita: Thanks
Margherita: Please stop talking
Margherita: I don't usually let something like this get under my skin. but seriously?
Margherita: Are you that daft? Or do you think I am that daft?

Nick: hmm

Margherita: Don't answer that.

Margherita: It doesn't matter

You need to not care, Marghe, she thought.

Nick: hey
Nick: You're trying to prove to me
Nick: That I'm a total asshole
Nick: And you've got that idea in your head, and anything I say you take to mean the worst possible thing
Nick: I'm genuinely sorry to have caused you offense
Nick: I don't think anything about you which you'd take offense from
Nick: I think you're interesting, quite funny, and curiously beautiful

Margherita: 1. I wasted hours of my evening talking to you last night trying to figure out what was going on in your head like a kid on the playground and in the end all you want is to fuck me. And then you tell me you are miraculously cured of me. Which has got to be one of the most offensive things I've heard in a while

Nick: I'm sorry you feel you wasted your time

Margherita: Lets not forget you have a girlfriend
Margherita: 2. You dismiss it entirely with a 'i was in a weird mood whoops'

Nick: I feel like you entrapped me a little
Nick: You asked me to tell you what was going on for me
Nick: And I told you

Margherita: 3. Now it has nothing to do with me at all, just your own hormones. So you could've been talking to just about anyone

Nick: No

Nick: That's an example of you taking my comment the wrong way

Margherita: I genuinely wasn't expecting you to say all you wanted was to fuck me

Nick: I didn't mean it that way

Margherita: So I'm sorry if you felt I trapped you

Nick: I didn't say all

Nick: I was being honest in that very moment. About that very moment

Nick: In a way that you made me feel it was ok to do

Margherita: I didn't think it would take so long for that to be the culmination of that entire discourse

Nick: course it wasn't

Nick: I'm apologizing

Nick: And telling you what I think of you

Nick: And saying that I was acting stupidly

Margherita: yet it has nothing to do with me?

Nick: but got the impression that we were exploring a conversation of total honesty.

Nick: Which really appealed to me

Nick: Of course it does!

Nick: What I meant was

Nick: My desires didn't reflect an assumption of you being a 'type' of person (i.e. a tree to bark up)

Nick: All it reflected was my boyish desire which I was enjoying being honest about

Nick: Of course it's 100% about you

Nick: I'm not saying this to anyone else

Nick: And I'm apologising

Nick: The good stuff is 100% about you

Nick: The silly stuff is me

Nick: I'll shut up now :/

Margherita: You know what

Should I be honest? she thought.

Margherita: Whatever

Nick: :(

Margherita: pointless conversation

Nick: Don't say stuff like 'no judgement'

Nick: If you then judge

Nick: You're judging so hard

Margherita: I'm not judging you for your own business

Margherita: I'm genuinely pissed off by the things you've said to me

Nick: I said them

Nick: In reaction to feeling like you said 'this is a safe space'

Nick: So I felt a bit shit

Nick: For that

Nick: And for the 5th time I am sorry for those things I said in reaction

Nick: I would like to go for a tea at the caffè

Nick: If you ever would

Nick: and maintain that I'm sorry for pissing you off

Margherita: I'm going to make this super clear for you

She took a deep breath. *Why the hell not*, she thought. *I'll never see him again.*

Margherita: I don't ever meet anyone randomly who I seem to click with and who I think oh I liked that person I want to see them again. and I went out of my way to get in touch with you because you stuck with me. And you chatted me right along knowing full well what was going on and then you disappeared. Okay, fine. Then months later, you say these vague things to me and lead me on a fair amount for one conversation. And after hours of that, it really isn't anything more than, oh I wanted to fuck this girl and Now I'm going to tell her so. And then, oh wait never mind, woke up with a clear head and Now I take it back. And the whole while you knew perfectly well that yes I was attracted to you, but as a freaken human being with feelings, I actually had this, I don't know, little schoolgirl crush on you. And wanted to get to know you more. So I just feel a bit like, fuck you, right now. In this moment. That's sort of my general feeling towards you is an unladylike fuck you.

Margherita: I don't want to have a tea with you. I'm going to focus on my work now and forget this whole thing.

By that point, it was nearly time for her eleven a.m. meeting with Yulia. She could not seem to end the chat. It was the never-ending chat.

I will never be able to concentrate now. Why is he still talking? What does he want, other than to mess with me, she thought.

Nick: Owh
Nick: I'm really sorry Margherita
Nick: It's not nothing more, you've misunderstood me
Nick: I was acting stupidly last night
Nick: And with a clear head, what remains is a funny, interesting, kind-hearted girl that I'd like to take for tea
Nick: That's what remains
Nick: But I understand the 'fuck you'
Nick: And that's my fault
Nick: I have a school boy crush on you
Nick: But I'm not allowed to

Margherita: That's why this is a pointless conversation

Nick: But it's not at all
Nick: I'd like to be friends
Nick: And I think it's possible

Right. Not interested enough, she thought.

Margherita: Because you're cured of me?
Nick: no
Nick: I said that in anger at feeling coaxed into saying something that I was then judged for

Nick: I think it because I think you are interesting and funny

Nick: And I enjoyed our exchange at the caffè

Margherita: I really want you to understand I wasn't judging you

Nick: I do now

Nick: I felt trapped last night

Nick: So I said that

Nick: In order to piss you off

Margherita: Mature

Nick: And I'm sorry about it

Nick: Not very

Margherita: And hurtful

Margherita: Way to go

Nick: I know

Margherita: It wasn't judgment it was disappointment

Nick: which is a type of judgement I think

Margherita: no

Nick: It's like

Nick: Safe space here say whatever you want

Nick: Oh dear, wrong answer

Margherita: You dont get it

Nick: I do get it

Nick: I know that there was vested interest in the answer

Margherita: okay. Maybe. I wanted a different answer. fine.

Nick: But you're being v black and white about what I said
Nick: trying hard to cling to the most hurtful read of it
Nick: And denying me saying sorry
Nick: And explaining

Explain what, though? Is there something more? she wondered.

Margherita: Because you hadn't actually said anything else definitively. Just that.

Nick: fine

Margherita: whatever I don't want to talk about it anymore

Nick: Okay
Nick: I stand by what I said
Nick: I'm sorry for hurting your feelings
Nick: I'd like to go for tea
Nick: If you ever think that's okay
Nick: I'm in

Margherita: No i think I'd rather not

Nick: i see

Margherita: thank you for your apology
Margherita: Have a nice day. Do good work. Make good decisions

Nick: You too

Try harder. Make a point of it. she thought.

NEW YORK, NEW YORK

2019

HE DIDN'T WANT to push. She had said no; what was he supposed to do—beg? If she was interested, great. If not, okay. She had presented herself so flirtatiously, so suggestively. He was befuddled by the amount of emotion—the gamut—that they had uncovered between the two of them in the last twelve hours. He was at a loss as to how to redeem himself, how to return to a place of lightness, excitability, humour, and seduction. Maybe he should save his pride and let it go. He would probably never see her again anyways.

NEW YORK, NEW YORK

2019

A FEW HOURS later, Margherita was staring at the text conversation. She was not ready to let it go. She was convinced this sort of intensity didn't happen very often. He must feel the same. He must agree that it was unusual, and the fact that he made more effort than most guys to apologize...what could that mean? She hated herself for it, but she couldn't drop it. On the way back to the office from a materials meeting in Brooklyn, Margherita looked up and saw that the subway car was filled with advertisements for Nick's company. What were the chances? She huffed at them in disbelief and snapped a photo impulsively.

> **Margherita:** (sends photo)
> **Margherita:** You did this to the J today on purpose didn't you

He wrote back right away.

> **Nick:** I did, yes.
> **Nick:** Hello.

Nick: I put them up myself. I think one even has your name on it.

She laughed to herself.

Nick: In case you can't find it, it says 'Dear Margherita, I'm sorry. Have a tea with me.'

Margherita: I'd rather a drink. If we are going to imbibe anything.

Nick: Okay. Ladies choice.

Margherita: Only because
Margherita: (sends photo of Camilla in the hospital with baby Vittoria)
Margherita: My friend in Milano just had a baby today and I feel like a puddle of love

Nick: Oh my god how beautiful. Congratulations! You're an auntie

Margherita: I know! I am overwhelmed. Such a surreal feeling

Nick: (sends photo of his nephew as a baby)
Nick: They make you positively melt.

Margherita: Melting

Nick: So, drinks. When?

Margherita: Tonight?

She had her thumb nail in her teeth. She was nervous. And excited.

Nick: Okay. That could work. I have to go to dinner

with my sister and her husband. It's their last night.
But it will be done early.

Margherita: Va bene

She arrived twenty minutes late, hoping she hadn't ruined the mood. He was there, at the end of the bar, where a tall, overflowing arrangement of branches drooped a few inches above his head. He stood up as she descended the staircase to the hotel's lower-level bar. He was in denim, as promised, and the kind of white sneakers she imagined a successful Shoreditch techie might wear. He wore something soft and grey on top, something that immediately made her want to fold herself into him the way she folded her delicates into her sweaters when packing, to keep them from getting damaged and to keep the sweater from getting creased.

She was late because she hadn't actually believed the drink would happen. She had delayed her shower as long as possible, had told herself she was simply taking a shower and blow drying her hair because she needed to, for herself, to be ready for the next day, not because she was having a drink with him. Not until he texted to say he was done with dinner did she even put on make-up. How many times had she prepared herself for an evening with Paolo and been disappointed?

"What a whirlwind twenty-four hours you and I have had." He gave her a kiss on the cheek and a big, warm hug. She rolled her eyes and sat on the bar stool next to his, her bare legs crossed, her hair loose over her shoulders.

NEW YORK, NEW YORK

2019

HE WAITED BY himself at the bar, save for a grisly gent at the other end playing host to a decidedly unattractive girl. He glanced down at his phone. 9:25. He had said they'd meet between nine-thirty and ten, and he had finished dinner with his family early. His nephew, only four, was tired and drooping at the booth. As much as he wanted to spend his last evening putting him to bed, he had been counting down the hours until the drink with Margherita.

Nick had been hoping for an evening with Margherita since that day at the café when she had placed her colourful hat down on the high-top table and announced, with great aplomb, that the seat was hers. Her eyes had locked with his, those green eyes that reminded him with a shock of the glistening emerald pool he had swam in at his grandmama's house in Australia.

"Why is it green?" he had always asked. "Aren't all pools blue?"

"Isn't a green pool more enticing?" She had said. "Don't you just want to dive right in!" His grandmother had been a very animated woman, always using her arms and hands to demonstrate her words, such a far cry from his mother.

"From my window it looks like a giant green jewel, an emerald maybe. Isn't it marvelous?" And she had wrapped him up in her arms and kissed the top of his blonde head.

He looked at his phone again. 9:29. For a second he wondered what Callie was doing in LA. He hadn't heard from her in hours and had avoided her all day, feeling as if conversing would distract him, would alter the mood, would yank him from his fantasy. He didn't want to hear from Callie. Not then.

Margherita arrived at 9:40. As she descended the stairs and came toward him, he felt his chest inflate. She wore a long, navy, wool coat and gave it to the coat check with a natural grace, like she was there all the time, even though she said she hadn't been in years. Her dress showed off her bare legs, it fluttered at the wrists, like a dance. She swept a hand through her hair and the dancing fabric on the sleeve followed her, like an entourage.

"What a whirlwind twenty-four hours you and I have had," he said, as he stood to greet her and give her a kiss on the cheek.

As she sat down, her lips so close to his, her legs grazing him, her green eyes tantalizing and addictive, he had to talk himself down from the urges that spread within him.

"Sorry to be late. Traffic. What are you drinking?" She looked down at his iced tea. "Is that a Shirley temple? Oh gosh, are you underage and I didn't realize?" She tilted her head, teasing him.

"Was waiting for you."

She motioned the bartender over, never one to be categorized as shy, and ordered an Americano cocktail.

"What's that?" Nick asked.

"Campari, sweet vermouth, and soda water."

"I'll have one too." He trusted her taste. She gave the impression that she knew what she was doing.

"So! Your family is in town. Until when?" She clasped her hands over her knee, which was folded over the other. She seemed completely in control. Happy, up, flirtatious, fun. He had been wondering if the attraction had held; would she be the vivacious, whip smart, witty Margherita that he had fixed in his head? Or would she be the protective, unpredictable person he had conversed with the previous evening and that morning? Had he ruined it with his idiotic, immature comments? He could not remember the last time he was nervous to meet a girl for a drink.

"Yes! My sister, her husband, and my nephew. He's heaven. Look." He showed her a few more photos of his darling nephew. "I feel my heart literally expanding when he visits."

"Oh what a sweetie!" She clasped her hands at her heart. "He looks just like you." She showed him the photo Camilla had sent her from the hospital with baby Violetta. "It's wild, isn't it? I never imagined the happiness I would feel at someone so close to me having a baby. Look at this little nugget."

"Beautiful. Little nugget. That's what I call my nephew." His eyes rested on her face for an extra beat.

"You cut your hair," she noticed. She tugged at her ear lobe.

Nick stared at her eyes, alight and taunting, and at her full lips. She seemed to have lust written all over her. Margherita placed her hand on his jittery leg. He hadn't noticed he was shaking it.

"Yes. I had to. Family."

"Explain."

"Well, they will go back to England and tell my parents how they found me. The state of Nicholas's life. They are like spies." He made an imaginary telescope in his hands and zoomed it in on her eye. She laughed. "So I cut it to seem more responsible. So they can go home and report back—*Nicholas is fine. He looks more responsible.*"

"So it's all a cover."

"Mmhmm. Totally."

"What would be the responsibility level on this encounter right here? On a scale of one to ten."

"Oh, well we are still on the first round, so quite responsible indeed, especially since I started with a Shirley Temple..."

She twisted her lips to the side of her mouth, a feigned look of disbelief. He smiled. She was charming.

"Wasn't heading in that direction last night..." she said.

He gave her a look—a slightly embarrassed, slightly humble, slightly playful look.

"You were encouraging me," he said, carefully.

"I was encouraging you to tell me what was on your mind, yes."

"And you made it feel like a safe space."

She didn't say anything, just regarded him with her strong eyes.

"And when I said what was on my mind- not to be taken the wrong way, as it was just what was on my mind *in that mom*ent, not the *only* thing on my mind when I think about you- it was suddenly: "oh no!" He pulled away from her abruptly. "Wrong answer!"

She stretched her arm out and grabbed his wrist, which he had pushed out behind him to demonstrate his point. She pulled it back in to their tight little space.

"I'm sorry. I didn't mean it that way."

They sat for a moment in silence, neither wanting to be the first to break it, staring into each other's eyes like a challenge.

"Why do you not have a boyfriend?"

She threw her chin back in a petite guffaw and took a sip from her drink.

"When was your last relationship?"

"Does this mean you are going to be my friend?" she asked facetiously.

"Seriously. Tell me."

"Why so curious?"

"Because, why not?"

She asked him how long he had been in New York, about his company, about why he didn't live in London. She asked him about his family, about where he grew up, about his parents.

"Do you think you'll go back to London?"

"Not right now. I feel like, it's New York right now."

"Really? I always loved London."

"Do you know it well? I was wondering where your slightly British vocabulary came from."

"My mom grew up in London. And she went back and forth a lot for work. And for my brother. He lived in Greece. It was a halfway point."

"You have a brother?"

"Oui."

"Where is he now?"

"London."

"And you don't want to live there too?"

"I happen to like the sun."

They had been speaking for an hour, at least, and she had inquired more about him than Callie had in their first month of dating. Nick felt he knew little to nothing about Margherita.

"Are your parents still married?" he asked her.

"You have very white teeth," she said.

He sat back, his eyes enlarged.

"Well. Thank you. So do you. Your teeth are perfect." He leaned in closely to inspect them as she gave him a silly, exaggerated smile.

"So, no boyfriend," he started again.

Margherita took a sip from her drink.

"Why not?"

She shrugged.

"Why do you think not?"

"Maybe I haven't met anyone yet."

"When was your last relationship?"

"Why do you need to know this information?"

"I don't *need* to. I want to." He felt embarrassed, he had asked too many times, but she was such a mystery.

"But why? You don't want to be my friend. So, you don't get to know this stuff," she quipped. She spun her head around and eyed the bartender at the other end of the bar, willing him over with her impatience.

"Come on. When was your last relationship?"

She was simultaneously dismissive and flirtatious, and it confused him. Maybe he didn't have a right to ask, but he felt they had already crossed over whatever line might have once existed. The undercurrent had zapped it like a cut wire. He had felt that undercurrent in the café in November, and they had confirmed it in their five-hour texting the previous evening, in their ability to switch with such ease from witty banter to serious and personal admissions, to high emotions, anger and grief and shame and apologies—to vulnerability, and back to sharing tidbits about the day, teasing each other, and making each other laugh. He had felt it all, and all of it layered in suggestiveness in its most obvious and opaque forms.

"Where is your girlfriend right now?" she asked.

"You are very good at asking questions and evading anything and everything personal about yourself." He knocked her on the knee with his two fingers.

She had been casually leaning toward him, with her chin resting on her hand as she listened to him talk about himself. At that comment, she straightened up again, her spine aligned with her neck. She feigned seriousness. "Oh, I know. It's a talent. I've been working on it for years."

He wanted more. He wanted to know things. Why? He could not say. It was odd; she was basically a stranger, yet in the past few months he had not been able to jettison her. He felt he had very little leverage. After all, he was the one who had, less than twenty-four hours earlier, admitted to wanting her, to having thought about her for months, to not being able to get her out of his head.

She had offered far less than he had, until he had offended her with his admission, until he had said something immature to band-aid his pride. It had left him embarrassed. Not for sharing his desires, but embarrassed that he had been so infantile to a woman who seemed so much more cosmopolitan and impenetrable than the typical twenty-nine-year-old woman he met in New York. The only thing she had revealed was that she had had affairs, and this had intrigued him. He felt something with her, some sort of openness. Yet it was becoming clear that she did not open as easily as he hoped. She was the enigma.

"So where is your girlfriend tonight?" She asked again. "Come on. We know she exists. We don't have to pretend."

"She's in LA." He felt a bit jolted once Callie became an actual person again.

"Do you live with her?"

"No. She lives with her sister."

"Do you think you're going to marry her?"

He could not remember meeting anyone so direct.

"Umm, no. I don't think so."

"Then why are you with her?"

"It was very intense in the beginning. She had a boyfriend. It was exciting."

"And now?"

"Not so much anymore," he said, suddenly feeling a pang of guilt about his old friend, Callie's ex-boyfriend.

"Interesting."

He sensed she was taking mental notes. She was writing things down somewhere inside her brain. She was going to remember every word; she was going to cast a judgment on every remark. Why, though? Was she going to use it against him somehow?

"But really…why don't you want a relationship?" He asked, trying a passive aggressive smile, a raised eyebrow, going for playful.

"Ah, someone likes to make presumptions. Well, let's put it this way. Person in a relationship, how often have you cheated on her?"

It was back to him. The judgment. Her impenetrability. Why did he care so much what she thought?

It bothered Nick; her knowing these things about him, about his indiscretions and his foolish acts. It was uneven. He felt she was looking down on his frivolities, his immaturity, or was she placing him into her bucket of cliché and untrustworthy males? She sat there, upright, with those green eyes, that wave of dark hair, those perfect lips that curved up slightly, challenging him to be truthful. Had he ever shared so much with anyone after meeting them once or twice completely out of the blue?

"Twice. Both random."

"What do you mean, random?"

"Just random girls I met out. Two random encounters- never spoke to them again. I was just being very drunk and stupid." He would have kept defending himself, but she had focused her attention on the absent bartender. There. He felt frivolous and immature right then. How she flitted her attention away from him, as if she was collecting information about him to fill her evening, to have something to do. He remembered how she had referred to him multiple times as a young guy, a 'boy.' He supposed she was accustomed to older men.

"Can I get another?" she asked, listing the ingredients again in case the barman forgot. She turned her head back towards Nick. He sat there looking at her, into her eyes, feeling like they were at a stalemate. What did she want? He wondered.

"Tanto va la gatta al lardo che ci lascia lo zampino," she said with raised eyebrows.

"You know I don't speak Italian, right?"

She turned up the corners of her mouth and gave a slight, mysterious shrug.

"So what made you want to come back to New York?" he asked, ignoring her Italian statement, which she did not offer to translate.

Margherita taunted him with her silence, her composure. Her hands were clasped over her knees, and she was enjoying herself, as if their little dance was pure entertainment. He suspected that she wasn't actually interested. If she was, she covered it expertly. Intuition told him she was filling the time, a few hours at the bar, only to get to the other side of what was to come. She had had affairs. He was positive she knew the game better than he did.

Nick sat there, looking at her. Margherita looked at him back. He didn't know what to do with her—what to say to her, or how to read her. He remembered a scene from the film *On the Beach*:

"A nice man asked me to wait here. I don't think he knew what to do with me." They had studied it in film school before he moved to New York, when he had spent a year in LA.

"I wanted to be better behaved," she said, vaguely.

"Oh? And are you?"

"Hmm…the jury is out."

Was he intrigued, he thought, *because* of her affairs? No, their connection intrigued him. That she had been the other woman, a few times, as she said, that came later. He hadn't known that when they met. It couldn't have had anything to do with his interest, could it?

There was a reason for it. She didn't appear reckless. She appeared quite the opposite: protective, thoughtful, purposeful. A little wild maybe, but not reckless.

"How about relationships that were *not* affairs?" he asked.

Margherita swirled her head towards her drink. She watched the large ice cubes in the glass; they were too big, too unwieldy, to move around each other. She took a sip. She looked back at him with a straight face. Silence.

"You seem a little fixated. Did you take a Xanax last night? Hey—why not come to bootcamp with me? You don't even have to talk to me, you can just work out your pent-up energy and eye me from the other side of the room," she diverted.

"Bootcamp. Is that how you work out your pent-up energy?"

"I love it. Work it all out. I actually love to run, but in the winter my legs go numb, so that can be rather challenging. What do you do?"

"Not much lately."

"How do you stay fit?" she asked.

"I used to run a lot more. I haven't in a while. I run at home. In Dorset."

She flexed her bicep playfully, grabbed his hand and placed it on her arm. He felt the definition under the sleeve of her dress. "I could kick your tush in bootcamp," she said.

"I bet you could!" He didn't doubt it.

She grabbed his hand with hers, palm-to-palm, and knit their fingers together, closing his grasp over hers with her other hand.

"Are we arm wrestling?" he asked incredulously, a smile growing on his face to match the smile on hers. She oscillated between sexy and adorable, and he felt his heart beat in his palm. He hoped she couldn't feel it.

She pushed into him with her weight, so much so that her bar stool tipped forward and she had to reach her other hand out to his chest to keep herself from toppling over. She laughed and righted herself before trying the match again. They had been sitting there at the nearly empty bar for almost three hours by then, and they were both a little tipsy. His eyes locked on hers. She stared back, challenging him, burning into him like desert noon sun. He watched her smile spread across her face and crease the corners of her eyes, her eyebrows raised and her gaze locked with his, as if to say, *stop overthinking it, just go with it.*

Margherita's stool tipped forward again, and she caught herself by placing her hand on his leg. He helped her find her balance. She righted herself and gave him a mischievous grin with her perfect white teeth, her hand still enclosed tightly within his. Her lips were full and curved, as if someone had drawn them on her face. They had spoken no words in what felt like thick, heavy hours, but, in reality, was probably only a moment or two. He wanted her.

He pulled her forward on purpose, the bottom prongs of her stool coming off the ground, and her lips impatiently found his. He kissed her gently. The moment had been coming. It had been coming since November at the café. She responded with pressure and leaned into him. She raised herself and stood in front of the stool, placing her hands on his shoulders, then around the back of his head. The undercurrent. He could feel her fingers trembling behind his neck. He was sure of it.

"Oh, this is bad," she inhaled, exhaled, pulled away. He wasn't sure what she was afraid of. He was the one who should be apprehensive, conflicted. She was quicksand, and he could not get stuck in it.

Nick had one hand on the small of her back, the tips of his fingers on the sway where her bottom began. With his other hand, he grazed his thumb over her bottom lip, tugging it down gently. He leaned in to kiss her again. She kissed back. They stayed like that for what felt like a lifetime and yet no time at all. Kissing. Tingling sensations running rampant. He was getting hard; she could feel it, surely. She stood, and she wrapped one leg around his waist as he sat there on his stool, He ran his hand over it and moaned.

"Your skin is like butter," he said.

She pulled away, breathless, shaking. He could feel it, her quiver.

"Why is it bad?" he asked.

He tried to find her eyes again. She appeared shaken. Maybe the alcohol had just hit her.

She sat back on her stool, running her hands through her hair, taking a sip from her drink, composing herself.

His eyes stayed on her. He could not figure her out. What was she afraid of, wary of? He wanted her. Badly. Uncontrollably.

"Because you have a girlfriend."

He said nothing, just watched her.

"So, this," she wagged her pointer finger between herself and himself. "This. Is bad. A bit of a rattle, no?"

He didn't say a word.

"You're not scared? That you could be seen?" she asked, looking for a droplet of liquid in her glass.

The bartender pushed the bill in front of them. He had been hovering nearby. They were the last ones in the restaurant.

"Does it rattle you?" he asked.

She looked down at her empty glass, swished the ice cubes around.

"It won't end well," she said with a hint of flirtation.

The bartender hovered.

"Oh. You want us to leave, don't you?"

"We closed five minutes ago," the bartender said.

"Who says? It won't end well?" Nick asked.

She raised her eyebrows and gave him her look of

silence; her closed door expression. He had come to know it well, already.

Nick paid the bill as Margherita played with the straw in her glass and ran her hand along his thigh, torturing him. She appeared in the mood to taunt again. He felt he had just taken a hit of something strong; he needed to get her out of that restaurant; he needed to fuck her.

"So? Why won't it end well? You haven't said," he asked again.

"When does it ever?" She leaned her hands on the top of his thighs and dismounted her barstool.

She felt relief that she had not allowed him to come home with her. He had asked, and she had said no. The truth was, she had her period; at least that had allowed her to exert some control over her low discipline. At home in the silence, without an object for her flirtation, no means with which to entertain herself, and wide awake at two a.m., she felt, suddenly, very alone. She felt upside-down, ensnared, and terrified all at once, and as she looked at her reflection in her bathroom mirror, her eyes reddened and filled with salty tears. It was some kind of knee-jerk reaction to the intensity of the evening. It was that old, familiar manic feeling. She knew he would never choose her over his girlfriend; he would never view her as anything more than a diversion from his life. It was a life that she would never fit into. Yet she had fallen for him, against her pretend strength of will.

She didn't want to fall for anyone. The mania would haunt her, it would prey on her lack of discipline, it would purloin her freedom, her insouciance, the carefree magnetism she was able to keep up thanks to few attachments.

Isabetta Andolini

Too many feelings ruined things. They ruined the fun. They muddied her thoughts and made her foggy.

She stared at her phone, wanting to say something but not knowing what. A message appeared.

Nick: Thank you for the drink. I had a lot of fun
Nick: I hope you got home okay.
Nick: Xxx
Nick: Goodnight Margherita

She couldn't handle it. Didn't know what to do with it. Didn't know how to act. She knew only mischief without cumbersome emotions, and she could feel already that whatever was happening with Nick did not fall under that category.

She typed quickly, without hesitation. She needed to tame her recalcitrance.

Margherita: I don't want to do that again.

I don't want to be a girl you keep a secret. I don't want to feel that rotten, empty sting again. I want to be the girl you want, not the one you hide shamefully, she thought.

Margherita: That's not what I want.

NEW YORK, NEW YORK

2019

Nick woke with a start, feeling excited, energized, nervous. He had had a hard time falling asleep, all worked up, thinking about Margherita. He reached for his phone, wanting to write to her. There were two messages.

> **Margherita:** I don't want to do that again.
> **Margherita:** That's not what I want.

His energy swiftly depleted.

He would not chase a girl who was not his girlfriend. That would be ridiculous. Maybe she was saving him a lot of strife, doing him a favor.

Okay. Easy out. Keep it light. Walk away now. Keep your pride, your sanity, he thought.

NEW YORK, NEW YORK

2019

SHE WAS AT work when her phone beeped; the beep she had been waiting for all morning. Her head jolted upwards from the plan she was reviewing, praying it was Nick, praying he had said something to prove genuine interest, to make her feel it was more than sex and secrecy.

Nick: Okay.
Nick: I don't want that either.

She felt immediately flattened. The high of the previous twenty-four hours had left her very low. She could not concentrate on her work. She kept her phone nearby for a few minutes and then shoved it in a drawer in an attempt to be as independent from her own feelings as possible.

Yulia called her into her office. Margherita rose, flattened her skirt, and stood at the doorway.

"The Dallas plans," Yulia said without emotion, not looking up at Margherita.

Is that going to be me in ten years, so hard you could tap on me and I would make a glass sound, she thought.

Margherita returned to her desk to find the rolled plans

for the Dallas boutique, suddenly feeling very disjointed from her work. In Milan with Elisio she had always felt so engaged, so excited, so involved and necessary.

She felt a hollow in her throat. She missed her mom, all of a sudden, and felt like a door had slammed on her head. Her eyes burned. She took a sip of water and walked toward the hard Roche Bobois chair in Yulia's office.

NEW YORK, NEW YORK

2019

Nick: I don't want what you don't want.

Margherita: These vague conversations get more and more riveting.

Nick: I know

Margherita: How do you know what I was referring to

Nick: I don't. Why don't you tell me

WHY DIDN'T HE *ask?* she thought.

Margherita: It doesn't matter. Why don't you tell me what it is you don't want?

Nick: It does matter. And I don't want a situation where I'm trying to persuade you on something you don't want.

Margherita: Vague

Nick: What do you want?

Margherita: Nick it really doesn't matter. Given the circumstances.

Nick: Yes it does.
Nick: What do you want?
Nick: Selfishly

If he wanted something, he could say it. He doesn't need me to go first, she thought.

Margherita: I definitely don't want to fall for someone who has a girlfriend. How's that?

Fuck. I shouldn't have said that. Now it's totally in his control, she thought.

Nick: Okay
Nick: Maybe let's leave it then.

NEW YORK, NEW YORK

2019

Nick: I mean that for our own health and stress.
Nick: Not because I don't want to.
Nick: I think you've taken offense.
Nick: I'd so much rather you say what you want.

WHY ON EARTH does he keep asking me that, she thought. How much more obvious can I be?

Margherita: No offense taken at all.

Don't show that you are upset. Be indifferent. You don't know him. This won't matter in a little while, she thought, knowing she would never roll on so easily.

Nick: Okay.
Nick: Will you tell me what you want?
Nick: Or shall I stop asking?

Margherita: Why do you want to know so badly?

Nick: Because I want to figure this out

Is he bored? she wondered.

Margherita: Figure what out

Nick: This

Margherita: What is "this"

Nick: I don't know yet.
Nick: Maybe nothing.
Nick: Maybe something.

Margherita: You said let's leave it. I think that covers it.

Nick: You have more interest in being aloof
Nick: Than in leveling with me.
Nick: You won't level with me

Margherita: You're saying let's leave it. no leveling necessary.
Margherita: I'm not being aloof. I'm not going to be foolish just to flatter you and have you turn around and say oh that's nice, I have a girlfriend though.

NEW YORK, NEW YORK

2019

A FEW DAYS later she was wavering again. It had felt too momentous to amount to nothing. At the very least, she would enjoy the immense sexual attraction. Why shouldn't she? She wasn't the one in a relationship; she wasn't going to be unfaithful or irresponsible, or whatever the right word was.

To hell with her feelings, with his relationship, with the fact that he was willing to risk hurting someone else. Maybe her mind was playing tricks on her; maybe she didn't have any strong feelings for him—maybe it was just chemical.

Or maybe he wanted more but didn't know how to say it. She knew the only way to keep him interested was to play the card he wanted to play. But she needed to lighten the situation again. They had become too heavy, and she was worried he would grow weary.

Margherita: I feel a little fluttery. Is that the right word

Nick: In what way?

Margherita: Good, but frustrated.

Nick: Explain

Margherita: No way.

Nick: Okay.

Margherita: Just need to vent for a sec.

Nick: Don't explain

Margherita: It's very distracting.
Margherita: It's somewhat your fault.
Margherita: How am I supposed to resolve this flutter

Nick: What type of flutter?
Nick: A pang?

Margherita: More like constant.

Nick: Ache

Margherita: The best kind of ache

Nick: What do you picture
Nick: That makes you ache

Margherita: Something I can't have

Nick: I pictured something yesterday.

Margherita: I have to change my panties. That's how intense my flutter has become.

Nick: I had started to make a mess of my boxers by the time I got home the other night.

Margherita: I feel like I'm being slowly tortured.

Nick: Show me.

Margherita looked up at Yulia in her glass box of an office.

Margherita: I can't. I'm not alone.

Margherita: Can I ask you a real question.

Margherita: No judgement

Nick: As if. But yes.

Margherita: I Promise I've never judged.

Margherita: How often do you find yourself having these little flirtations. For lack of a better word.

Nick: Not often. Not really at all. Not in the last year and a half. I've been too focused.

That wasn't the right answer, she thought.

Nick: Are you going to tell me what you are picturing?

Margherita: Oh, sigh. Just a few overactive daydreams. Of the distracting nature.

Nick: Share one.

Margherita: What's the point in sharing with someone who I can't ever bring them to life with?

Nick: Why do you make that assumption?

Nick: I don't think that assumption is correct.

Margherita: Of course you don't.

Nick: I don't think you do either.

Margherita: If I was smart I would stop talking to you right now.

Margherita: Or 48 hours ago.

Nick: But we both know

Nick: What we want.

Margherita: You do.

You want sex, she thought. *I want more.*

Later that evening, with the momentary excitement of their fleeting exchange having ended unsatisfactorily, her feelings of loneliness returned. She had been hoping that he would say something to prove reciprocation. She struggled to maintain the distance she had talked herself into; in her truest moments, she knew she would never be able to approach him in a hard-boiled way.

Margherita: I should never have told you what I told you.

Nick: About being the other woman?

Margherita: I think this is not a good thing. Maybe we should just leave it like you said the other day.

Nick: Okay.
Nick: I assume this isn't a test.

Margherita: No.

Nick: Good idea then. Let's leave it.

Margherita: I don't want to be a random. Does that make sense?

Margherita: For some reason I want to explain this to you and then I stop myself because I don't think it's at all necessary.

Margherita: Which is in itself problematic already.

Nick: You aren't a random.
Nick: Already.
Nick: It does make sense.
Nick: what do you want to feel?

Margherita: What do you mean

Nick: What do you want to feel

Nick: Do you want to be in my life

I'm not going to answer that until he says something real, she thought.

Margherita: I think it's interesting how you write it off so quickly and easily

Nick: You were testing me.

Margherita: Not at all

Nick: Yes. You were taking data from it.

Nick: Do you want to be in my life Margherita?

What kind of question is that? And why is it all on me? she wondered.

Margherita: But that's telling. it's sort of like ok I made the right decision if this is an eh ok whatever, next situation to you.

Nick: It is not.

Nick: Stop trying to figure me out.

Nick: Using these traps

Nick: It's not that way.

Margherita: I'm going off of what you say.

Nick: I'm not going to force something if you don't want it.

Nick: And I'm going off of what *you* say.

Margherita: But you just copy whatever I say.

Nick: Marghe do you want to be in my life

Nick: Just be straight with me

Margherita: What kind of question is that

Nick: you aren't a random.

Nick: And it's up to you if you want to be involved with me in some way.

Margherita: You have a girlfriend. Have you forgotten?

Nick: I haven't.

Margherita: You can't go around collecting people.
Margherita: That's insulting. You're an asshole.

Nick: I don't think I can.
Nick: Which is why it's up to you.
Nick: So if you say no thanks, then ok, I'll respect your decision.

Margherita: I don't understand this game.

Nick: Im not trying to play a game.
Nick: I don't know you.
Nick: I don't know what you want.
Nick: I'm trying to be fair and honest.
Nick: Which might be helpful

Margherita: You are trying to have your cake and eat it too. You are such a cliche it's pathetic.

She tried to corner him into disagreeing with her, into saying what she wanted him to say.

Nick: That's unfair.
Nick: I don't think we should continue this conversation. It will just go on with weird tests and things to fail when I trust you are being open.

She sunk into her chair in her tiny apartment.

I'll always be the other girl, she thought. She wondered how it would have unfolded if she hadn't been so forthcoming about her past. She had felt a natural comfort with him, an openness, and it was so rare she had jumped right into it.

She bit her thumb nail between her upper and bottom teeth and typed out a message that caused her to inhale and exhale many times.

> **Margherita:** I like you. I liked you when we met. A totally random chance encounter that I personally think, and maybe it's different for you, is kind of rare. The kind that gets under your skin and makes others feel a bit inconsequential. Precisely the kind that I have always tried to avoid. What I confided in you is basically my way of keeping messiness at bay and protecting myself. But those were very different situations. And if you think that that's the only kind of situation that I want, then I'm sorry to burst that bubble, but it's not.

He read the message but didn't respond.

NEW YORK, NEW YORK

2019

Margherita: Okay. I thought about it. I'm up for it if you are.
Margherita: And I am sorry for swearing at you. Wasn't right.

S<small>ILENCE</small>

Isabetta Andolini

NEW YORK, NEW YORK

2018

ALEXANDRE CALLED HER three times that Sunday morning. He sent her a few thoughtful messages and made a sincere effort to reach her, but she did not want to speak to him. She did not want to get stuck under his giant hand, under his stare, under his overly deep and heavy demeanor. She assumed Elisio had told him the reason for her absence the past two weeks. She wondered who else Elisio had told—who else would she have to accept pity from upon her return to Milan.

That evening, laying on her side in bed, her face pushed into the pillow, her eyes raw from crying, she wrote Alexandre back.

Margherita: Grazie. I really appreciate it.

It was all she could muster. She wanted to be grateful but distant.

Alexandre: You are not alone Marghe.

It frazzled her how he had a secret doorway into her heart's mind, her mind's heart, whichever was the twisted place inside of her where those feelings lived, the ones she could not decipher. He seemed to know what she was struggling with before she put it into her own words. She began to cry again.

> **Alexandre:** I am in NY this week, as it happens.
> Have lunch with me? We don't have to talk about
> it. Just wine and oysters at a fabulous restaurant of
> your choosing.

She agreed, in her moment of vulnerability, even though it made her feel guilty to leave her father alone for a few hours. She hadn't seen any friends in the two weeks since she had returned to New York. She didn't have any there.

At a two-person table at Le CouCou, with wine and oysters set between them, as promised, and a tartare on its way, Alexandre slid a piece of paper across the white tablecloth.

She picked it up to read the other side. It was three times her salary in Milan. The irony; Francine would have been so thrilled. She thought of her father, laying on the sofa every night to watch television, with the sofa opposite him empty.

Margherita looked up at Alexandre with sealed lips and sad eyes. She felt her former life slipping away from her as if it had never happened at all, down like a Maine oyster.

"So you have an option," Alexandre said.

He thinks he is my savior, Margherita thought.

She wished she could ask her mom what to do.

NEW YORK, NEW YORK,

2019

Nick: Hey- I don't mean to be an ass by not responding, but I've had a reality check that I can't behave like this and respect my girlfriend too much to do that to her. It's just not how I want to treat her and go about things. You're lovely and deserving, it's just me and where I'm at. I'm sure (hopefully) you understand.

I'M NOT WORTH it. The play thing isn't worth it, she thought.

Margherita: Of course I understand.
Margherita: I meant what I said though. I genuinely enjoy you and would love to be friends. Up to you :)

She stared at her phone, disappointed, dejected, rejected.

She reflected on the intense conversations she had had with Nick in the past week. Why would anyone give her that much attention, devote that much energy to it, if all they were after was sex? She had felt in her bones that he had felt something.

Margherita: Can I ask you one question though? As someone who is working on practicing discipline as well.

Margherita: Why was this so easy/okay for you the other times you told me about. And so not this time

Nick: Yes, we can be friends. I'd like that too.

Margherita: You're not going to answer my question are you

Nick: I am!
Nick: The other times felt like 'in the heat of the moment' hormone-driven mistakes
Nick: This felt like a calculated plan.

An unsuccessful femme fatale, a less villainous Phyllis Dietrichson. she thought. *Wow I feel like a shit person.*

Nick: With more meaning
Nick: More intentionality
Nick: More significance

Keep going, she thought. *Make me feel better about this.*

Nick: So it just didn't pass my moral compass

Suddenly you have a moral compass? she wondered.

Nick: It felt more like- I should only be doing this - if I'm truly unhappy in the relationship
Nick: And If I'm unhappy, I shouldn't be in it

So why are you? she wondered.

Nick: ya know?

She sat there, in her chair, staring at the chat, regretting that she'd let it get as far as it had. She regretted allowing him to reach a place where he could affect her. She wanted nothing more than to show him that she didn't care.

Margherita: Yeah
Nick: what do you think

Does it matter? she thought.

Margherita: About what
Nick: the above
Margherita: well
Margherita: I feel a bit like a terrible person. But it makes sense. And I'm glad you're going to be my friend, despite my own misguided moral compass :)
Nick: No
Nick: You're not
Nick: why do you feel like a terrible person

Why do you care? She desperately wanted to know why he was still bothering.

Margherita: oh I don't know. Can we go to the next subject please
Nick: tell me
Margherita: Because I don't seem to have the 'that's wrong' flag

Margherita: Maybe one day
Margherita: I'll find it

Nick: No
Nick: don't need to find it
Nick: Necessarily

NEW YORK, NEW YORK

2019

NICK DIDN'T KNOW what to say. He only knew that he had
not intended it to be a destructive situation. He wasn't sure
why she thought of him that way, and it made him all the
more certain that all she had wanted was an affair, yet part
of her seemed to be struggling with how she felt about it.
He found it rather confusing.

> **Nick:** Anyway. Gorgeous day out. I'm about to go
> for a run.
>
> **Margherita:** so good to sweat. The best release. I
> am always a new person afterwards.
>
> **Nick:** Me too.
> **Nick:** So good for endorphins and synapses
> **Nick:** And cortisol levels
> **Nick:** And general appearance
>
> **Margherita:** Synapses.
> **Margherita:** You nerd

He smiled at his phone. He didn't know what she wanted,
but he wasn't ready to give her up.

NEW YORK, NEW YORK

2019

THE NEXT DAY Margherita was once again feeling light and flirtatious. She had dismissed the vulnerable slippage and decided to test the dalliance once again. The addiction was real.

She sent Nick a photo of herself in her sports bra at bootcamp.

> **Margherita:** Did we decide when you're coming to bootcamp?

He responded straight away.

> **Nick:** Is this what friends
> **Nick:** Who secretly (or not so secretly)
> **Nick:** Fancy each other do?

She ignored the message, not wanting to admit to anything.

NEW YORK, NEW YORK

2019

Margherita: Have you ever passed a sketchy looking massage place on 1st ave near 6th? I got one there years ago and am walking in circles trying to find it.

Nick: Sounds like you need the Xanax

Margherita: I have something for you.

Nick: I'm beginning to think you are some sort of fancy Connecticut drug dealer.

Margherita: no you oaf. Check your email

SHE SENT HIM the email she had drafted. He had mentioned that he was working on the new Chicago space for his company, and she had volunteered to look at the plans. She had made quite a few notes on them.

Margherita: Told you I'm a good friend

Nick: Wow. You are amazing. I am going to look at this tonight.

Nick: What a wild ride you and I have had.

Margherita: Is it over yet?

Nick: Never will be.

2019

Margherita: Am letting alcohol speak for me for a sec. Tell me something and be honest- jerk level honest if need be. Are the things you've said to me genuine, as in was there anything actually *actual* there, or do you have a habit of dangling forbidden fruit and snatching away when bored. Am I that gullible, basically. And don't pitter patter around my feelings.

Nick: Hello
Nick: Yes I am being genuine.
Nick: No I do not make a habit of that
Nick: I don't have the time or headspace for it
Nick: how are you?

NEW YORK, NEW YORK

2019

SHE SAT ON the bench opposite the Jefferson Market Garden, facing Ninth Street, where she had once lived in her early twenties. The apartment was a sliver of a thing in an old decrepit building opposite the PATH train station, and her bedroom barely fit herself and a full size bed, but her very tall roommate had decorated it in a cute way and she loved the location. After a few months of living there she had somehow contracted mono, which caused her to miss weeks of work and enter into a sort of dazed, sleepy depression. She slept most of the day and left only for a very slow lap around the neighborhood, and a trip to Three Lives Books on Tenth Street. She was at the lowest weight she had ever been, hardly ever eating, and her roommate passive-aggressively parlayed her annoyance that Margherita rarely left the apartment.

"So you're just going to stay here tonight?"

"Yes…"

"Okay, well, I am going to go out. With friends. You know. It's nice to go out. With friends." Alexa said.

Margherita always remembered that feeling—how alone she had felt, how strange and abnormal Alexa had made her out to be. She wanted friends, but everyone around her seemed to already have theirs, and she was hardly ever included, no matter how hard she tried. It appeared to her that most girls in her age group just wanted to get drunk and be silly, as if they were still in college. She felt out of place amongst her peers, and the last thing she needed was a Mean Girl roommate, straight out of her high school nightmares.

She remembered sitting on the sofa after a day with Francine, who hardly ever came downtown. She had felt happy all day, until Francine was getting ready to leave.

"What are you doing tonight?" Francine asked.

"Nothing."

"Does Alexa invite you out?"

"No."

Her mother delayed her departure.

"Marghe doll, I can't be the filler in your social life. Your mommy can't always be with you."

"I know. But I'm always alone," Margherita said softly, like a little girl, looking down at her knees.

Her mother had put her hand on Margherita's head. "I was a bit of a loner too. Don't worry. You just need one or two good girlfriends. You will find your people."

On Greenwich Avenue, nibbling at a mediocre takeaway sushi roll from Citarella, she thought about how immediate, and close, her friendships had been in Italy, how convinced she had been that she had finally found her people. One of her greatest fears about living and dating in New York was that a guy would judge her for her lack of close friends in the city. She knew she would never have a big wedding, if ever that day came; who would she invite?

A window washer a few feet away from her moved closer. He was cleaning the store front behind her, and she wondered if she would have to get up and change benches.

"Oh no, you're fine where you are. I can go around you." He read her mind, and he moved to her right.

"Thank you. Just let me know," she said, putting the empty sushi tray back in the bag.

"You know, you are beautiful. Do you ever take your photo? You gotta remember your youth," he said kindly.

Margherita smiled bashfully. "Oh, well...thank you. That's very sweet." She felt like she looked a mess. Her hair was dirty and she had just finished taking very large bites of sushi roll.

One day I won't be young anymore, but I'll probably still be eating takeaway on a bench by myself, she thought.

It had been a week since she heard from Nicky. In other circumstances, Margherita would have asked *How are you,* or *How's your day,* or similar niceties, not just to be polite but because she really did care. It was delicate, however, because she didn't want to appear too interested, too attached on a personal level. She was not sure how much sweetness, in their particular situation, would scare him away. Besides, she thought she should wait for him to initiate once in a while. He was the one in a relationship. Maybe he was away. He might be in another country. He might be visiting his family in Dorset, or he might be on vacation with his girlfriend. She couldn't ask these questions. It wasn't any of her business.

They weren't friends. They weren't anything.

MILANO, LOMBARDIA

2018

MARGHERITA CHECKED HER reflection in the beautiful dark wood elevator. She was wearing a little white cotton dress and her shoulders had a few new freckles after the past Saturday at the beach club in Paraggi. Her stomach grumbled. She had eaten nothing but a few grapes and a cucumber for dinner, feeling hungrier for socialization than for food.

At the penthouse floor—the seventh, a very high number in Milan—she stepped into Cristiano's entryway.

"Eccoti," *There you are,* she heard his deep voice vibrate from the living room.

"Eccomi!" She said as she took a seat on one of the velvet sofas next to him. He gave her a kiss on each cheek and poured her a glass of wine from the bottle on the tray before them.

It had become a frequent occurrence, to join Cristiano on a weeknight, usually after nine p.m. In his living room, or on his terrace, overlooking the verdant neighborhood of Brera. She knew he had a reputation of being a little strange, a little lonely, but in truth she really enjoyed his company. He had been a good friend to her, though she was a secret friend to him. He did not acknowledge their friendship in public, but between the two of them, he helped her with things like renewing her apartment contract and asking for a raise (in vain). He often listened to her vent about men, and, on occasion, about her mom, something she rarely felt comfortable doing with anyone.

So an hour or so later, as Margherita leaned forward toward the coffee table to reach for her glass of wine, and Cristiano leaned forward and gently wrapped his large, tan hand around her slight wrist, pulling her towards him, she felt disillusioned.

At first, she let him put his other hand on the back of her head and bring her toward him. His lips were full and he tasted of red wine. She let him kiss her for a moment or two before pulling away, trying to laugh it off.

"Wait a minute..." she said, and he pulled her toward him again.

"I thought we were friends," she said as lightly as she could. "I don't want to mess with that."

"Come on, you're a smart girl. Don't be stupid."

Had she been cozened into believing that their interactions were based on friendship? Was she that foolish?

MILANO, LOMBARDIA

2018

"Maybe we need boundaries," Margherita said.

They were seated at the bar at Langosteria Caffe near the Duomo. It was late, a Thursday, and Margherita was tired from a long day with Elisio. In truth, she hadn't been looking forward to the evening at all. Her interest in Alexandre had seriously diminished, but she was hesitant to end it for fear of what his bruised ego might do. He was too tiresome, too cerebral.

"I don't think so," Alexandre said, dismissively, matter of factly. "Whatever we do, I do not think they are of any use. The mere fact that we say we need them defies their purpose."

She crossed her arms, ran her palm along the side of her neck, up towards where baby hairs grow at the base of her scalp, her eyes grazing the other patrons of the chic restaurant, the same one Paolo had brought her to on that hot summer night.

Alexandre eyed her.

"One could spend hours clawing at the Margherita that you present, peeling back these layers. But you are iron-clad. We are similar in this way," he said, knowingly, a smart little grin on his face.

She was too tired to interpret his cryptic oppressiveness.

"Would you like another glass of pinot noir, signorina?" the waiter thankfully inquired.

"Non—try the Muscadet—much better with these oysters," Alexandre answered before she could. Margherita eyed him viciously.

He looked away from the waiter who had brought over a beautiful tower of oysters. "Do you honestly think you will ever let yourself *be* with someone?" He reached for the lemon. "So you see, what is the point of a boundary?"

She hated the way he spoke about her, as if she were a curious zoo animal, how he assumed to know how she worked, how her heart and mind strummed together. His preposterous observations were an affront. He was pompous, a cliched forty-six-year-old successful lawyer with some sort of complex, and she suddenly felt repelled. She no longer felt the attraction toward his tall slender form, and she no longer appreciated how he always hunched over when they dined together, in order to be closer to her and to put his long fingers on the small of her back or on her upper thigh. She now found this intrusive and irritating. He assumed her to be in love with him—in his mind, a sage, dreamy, savior, in possession of more worldly wisdom than she would ever acquire. His gall was no longer striking; it was antagonizing.

"Desire is messy," he said with a smirk, sucking back an oyster.

"Where are you going with this?"

"So defensive!" he mocked, half ironically, and she knew his pride had somehow been pierced. Her face belied her disinterest. "I am only saying, you are someone who enjoys desire but does not know sacrifice. You do not know serious relationships, commitment, the ugly side of love. So for you to attempt to create boundaries for yourself, at this point, mon amour... what are you protecting yourself from?" He picked up another oyster. He sucked it down. French oysters. From Bretagne.

She felt a scream building in her throat.

She watched his Adam's apple rise and fall in his long thin neck.

NEW YORK, NEW YORK

2019

THERE WERE MOMENTS when she would be sitting somewhere, anywhere—on a train, at a manicure table, reading a book at La Colombe, at her desk at work—when she would think of him. A pulsating feeling would begin between her legs. Something would swish in her chest. She would envision him standing over her, the first kiss of the evening, or she would see him sitting next to her at the bar, saying something that made her laugh. She would see his blue eyes, the upturned corners of his mouth, and she would hear his voice, his words, and she would feel his touch, his shoulders, his soft hair. Then a daydream would begin, in full swing, and a beating between her legs would send her off to another world, one of wanting... and getting.

It was after these physical feelings of internalized ecstasy and torture that she talked herself into being okay with the situation. She told herself a number of things:

- *There was undeniable sexual chemistry. That was not easy to find.*

- *She was very attracted to him. He was objectively very good-looking.*
- *What was so bad about having sex with someone when you are young and single?*
- *Why should she deny herself great sex with someone with whom she felt comfortable?*
- *Shouldn't this time in her life be lightweight and fun?*
- *She didn't want him, anyway. He cheated. He was a cheater. He always would be. He was also capable of being immature and selfish and self-centered. So she did not want him.*

Margherita: I have the most amazing imagination

Nick: Go on…

Margherita: Beach fantasy

They spent the next hour in full fledged sexting, completely free on both sides, a liberating afternoon. It only increased the temptation.

Margherita: You think this will ever happen?

Nick: 100%

Margherita: Why 100%
Margherita: Those are pretty strong odds

Nick: I just know
Nick: It kinda has to
Nick: So it will

Margherita: Oh does it?

Nick: Soon probably

Margherita: Oh I kind of like letting it build.

Margherita: It's a bit torturous

Margherita: Although you told me you didn't want to...

Nick: I do

Nick: Trust me

Margherita: I don't want to make you do something you don't want....

Nick: You wouldn't be

Nick: Do you think I'd be able to write what I did if it didn't really appeal...

Nick: Or wasn't on my mind

Margherita: Okay. Well thank you. For contributing to my fantasy.

Margherita: Last thing.

Margherita: Does this mean someone has misplaced their moral compass, somewhere along the way?

Nick: Don't worry about me.

Nick: Just take me at face value.

Margherita: Meaning?

Nick: To not trouble yourself with this.

Margherita: I'm not troubled. I just never know which side you're playing on.

Nick: I'm on the adventurous side.

Margherita: Okay. No backsies on that one

Nick: There won't be.

Later that night, after dinner with Tommaso, Margherita decided to sleep uptown. She lay stretched out on the sofa after Tommaso had retired to bed, and a dip of loneliness mixed with sweetness set in; she ached for company. The feeling became stronger after watching a romantic movie set in England. She wished she could chat with Nick about it, just as friends.

> **Margherita:** Does no backsies mean you're also going to be my friend
> **Margherita:** Beyond the mid-afternoon sexual fantasies

Silence.

> **Margherita:** I did very much like the sweet apologetic Nicky
> **Margherita:** He felt very human to me

Silence.

From the doorway of his bedroom, Nick watched Callie take a pot out of the cupboard to boil water for pasta. She had her hair in a bun on top of her head and she was quietly singing along to the Bob Dylan music playing on her iPad on the counter.

> **Margherita:** Can you relay a message to that person
> **Nick:** Sure

Margherita: Somehow I missed this most adorable sweet funny thoughtful movie. With Bill Nighy, so you know it's gotta be good. British of course. 'About time.' So if a potentially thoughtful, witty version of you hasn't seen it, I recommend.

Nick: I've seen it
Nick: I mean, He's seen it
Nick: Gorgeous isn't it

Margherita: How have I not seen this
Margherita: Why didn't he tell me??

Nick: No idea.

Margherita: Why can't you let him come out to play once in a while
Margherita: Omg the slutty friend is Vanessa Kirby- I knew I recognized that voice.
Margherita: You could've told me that too, jeez you're a bad bad friend

Nick: So bad. So very bad.

Margherita: But why

Nick watched Callie peel a clove of garlic with her fingernails. No matter how many times he showed her how to smash it with the side of the knife, she insisted on doing it her way.

Margherita: In that case maybe I give up on this little situation

"Pesto or tomatoes?" Callie called out.

"Pesto," Nick said, as he joined her in the kitchen and put his phone in his pocket.

NEW YORK, NEW YORK

2019

SHE WAS RUNNING late but was not stressed about it. Julius had been waiting for her at the bar at Frenchette for a good twenty minutes. It was the most packed she had ever seen it, and she magically got a bar seat within a few minutes while Julius remained standing next to her. He was drinking an Old Fashioned, and Paul immediately handed her an Americano.

She looked up at his blonde locks, neatly combed back. He was very good looking, she had to admit, at over six feet tall and with gentle but strong features. He looked very Dutch actually, when in truth he was born and raised in Melbourne. She had gone for a casual Sunday afternoon tea with him for their first date and hadn't bothered to put on anything special, as he was only a few years older than her and struck her as a bit of an Aussie party boy—not her type. He had, however, been organized and unusually polite about the date, so she figured why not? He was actually very smart, ambitious, quite courageous for making the big move, and had the manners of a gentleman.

At Frenchette she was in her element; they flirted and chatted about work and New York things—gyms and restaurants—before heading next door to Stannie's Lounge, where they were the first patrons of the evening in the cozy underground dance club. They sat down at the four-seat bar for another round of Negronis served by the white-jacketed barman.

They ended up having fantastic conversation and laughing quite a bit. The subject of infidelity came up, as it had a habit of doing.

"I can't tell you how many men in the banking world are cheating on their wives on work trips. I have seen so much, you don't want to know," Julius said.

Margherita shrugged. "It seems inevitable. I sometimes wonder what's the ideal situation—knowing about it and letting it bother you, or remaining ignorant and knowing they still love you but have a little indulgence now and then."

"Wow, I've never heard a female with that perspective before."

"Well, I've seen a lot too. I think it's a realistic perspective. Do I love the concept, no…but? And surely women are sneaking around too…"

"Right! I hope they are!" Julius said. "Why shouldn't they?"

It was an odd but refreshing conversation, and as the tiny club began to fill up and the third Negroni went to her head, they got up to dance. She stopped him at every other song or so to make out, and they took only one break from sweaty dancing so that she could pee. The bathroom spun around her and she typed out a message to Nick, but ended up deleting it. *Fuck him. I'm having fun*, she thought.

LAGO DI COMO, LOMBARDIA

2017

MARGHERITA LAY AWAKE in bed scrolling through Paolo's nine Instagram photos, as she often did. Her mom was asleep in the bed next to her. She opened the chat with Paolo and clicked on his profile photo—the endlessly sexy one that she showed to Chiara whenever her friend tried to tsk-tsk her for continuing the affair.

> **Margherita:** I can't sleep.
> **Margherita:** I feel like dancing.
> **Paolo:** Balla. *Dance*

Margherita smiled at her screen. She saw him go off WhatsApp and her smile turned into a small pout. She pushed her phone under her pillow and turned towards her mom.

When Margherita was little and couldn't sleep, she'd wander into her parents' bedroom and stand at the bed, tapping one of them ever so gently until one of them woke up. If her father walked her back to bed, he would tuck her in and then go back to his own room. If Francine walked her back to bed, she would climb in and sleep the rest of the night cuddled around Margherita's small body. Her protector.

NEW YORK, NEW YORK

2019

MARGHERITA EYED HERSELF in the office bathroom mirror. She pulled a few strands of hair at her scalp left and right, inspecting for a gray hair. She found a few once in a while and it terrified her. She tousled her hair back into place and picked up her phone, which was sitting on the marble counter.

Margherita: When's the last time you went dancing?

Nick: At a wedding in Baltimore last weekend.

Reminder that I know nothing about you. That I am not invited into your life in the slightest. Did you go with your girlfriend? she wondered.

Margherita returned to her drafting desk and found Yulia hovering over her work.

"I was just about to ask you to bring these in to review, but you were no where to be found. You seem to take a lot of bathroom breaks. Is everything…ok?" Yulia's eyes traveled down Margherita.

You are vile, Margherita thought.

"Sorry. I have a small bladder."

It was a good thing Yulia wasn't running a team in Milan. With all of those cigarette breaks, how would her boss possibly control her pupils?

NEW YORK, NEW YORK

2019

THAT EVENING, AT the launch party for the Xiolitti collection, Yulia gave Margherita a startle when she silently appeared at her side, looking gorgeously sleek in a floor-length Valentino dress.

"This dress is adorable," Yulia said, giving a playful tug to the bottom edge of it, passive aggressively suggesting it was too short. "You won't even have to lift it for all your bathroom breaks."

"Yes. It's rather convenient." Margherita side-stepped one inch farther away from her boss.

Yulia surveyed the room at the top of the Grand Street Hotel. She looked pleased with herself.

"I didn't realize Beck Leonetti was coming," Margherita said, carefully eyeing him as he stood next to the CEO of the private equity firm that owned Barneys. He laughed along with a joke in his gorgeous blue suit and striking blue eyes.

"Is there a problem?" Yulia asked with knife-sharp attitude.

"No," Margherita said immediately. She bit the inside of her lip.

"Beck! Ciao!" Yulia called to him as he looked up and noticed the two ladies facing him. He politely exited his conversation and gave Yulia a kiss on the cheek, then Margherita.

"We were just talking about you. I didn't realize you and Margherita knew each other?" Yulia said, demonstrating Margherita's presence with her prosecco glass.

"Yes, of course. She was hard not to know in Milan—was quite a success with the new property," He gave Margherita a gracious nod.

Margherita pursed her lips. It was precisely the kind of comment that would irritate Yulia.

"She certainly makes waves, our girl, doesn't she?" Yulia let out a conniving laugh, as if Margherita weren't standing right there. Beck looked uncomfortable but in his aristocratic way knew how to hide it. Yulia hooked his elbow and led him away toward the bejeweled and bedazzled long tables that were expertly lit and set.

Margherita had made attempts to ingratiate herself with her colleagues at Lolato, but none of them seemed interested in extending their office friendliness outside of the glass walls. She made small talk with one of the material scouters but truth be told she had very little in common with the Arabian princess (literally, she was a princess). She couldn't tell if she were relieved Alexandre was not in attendance, or disappointed not to be able to chat with him.

At the exquisitely designed table, Margherita sat next to one of the head jewelry buyers from Barneys who recounted his Hawaiian elopement.

"And you, mon amour, are you married?" He picked up Margherita's naked hand. "Ah! Not even a Lolato ring!"

Across the table, a few seats down, Yulia seemed to have one ear permanently open to Margherita's conversation.

"Margherita isn't interested in marriage: isn't that right darling?" Yulia said, sliding her chin into the palm of her hand and resting her elbow on the table, turning her attention towards her employee and encouraging everyone between them to do the same.

Margherita shook her head and pushed her eyebrows together. "Not sure why you would say that?"

"Oh come, dear. I've heard all about your escapades! No, Margherita is a girl about town, if you know what I mean," Yulia said to everyone listening. "Oh don't be ashamed darling. You have your fun. Who was that adorable young man we met at the office? What happened with that?"

Margherita inhaled deeply. She watched Yulia take a long swig from her glass of gin. Surely it was purely gin.

"I am not a girl about town," Margherita said, as politely as she could.

"Of course. Of course. Beck, you knew Margherita in Milan. How many men were there exactly?" Yulia turned her focus on Beck, who was clearly, once again, uncomfortable.

"Does anyone know?" Yulia addressed all who were listening.

"Holy shit, she's wasted," the jewelry buyer said.

"Alexandre inserted you into this company in a wild hurry. I've always wondered why. Would you tell us the story, lovey?"

"Excuse me," Margherita gently pushed her chair back from the table.

Yulia shouted at Margherita as she walked away from the table. Margherita felt something sharp hit her back. Yulia had thrown one of the decorative crowns at her.

At the coat check, Margherita was hot to the touch and red in the face.

She felt vexed all over, not ready to go home and sit in her apartment. She wandered around the corner to Frenchette. She knew what she wanted at that moment, what she thought she *needed*. She was aware of how her emotional state had depleted her pride and inhibitions time and time again, but in the moment, she just couldn't be bothered with the aftermath.

Margherita: Hi
Margherita: Drink? Need it

She sat down at the bar with the last of the late diners and imbibers. Paul was just leaving for the night and left her in good hands with his colleague. She ordered a gin and soda and glanced from left to right, her leg practically shaking under the bar, willing her phone to murmur.

"There she is."

NEW YORK, NEW YORK

2019

BECK APPEARED AT her side, slightly out of breath. She was momentarily caught off guard, disoriented. Was he really standing there in the mostly empty bar?

He slid onto the stool to her left.

"Old Fashioned, please," he asked the bartender, unbuttoning his top collar buttons, folding his hands over one another, and turning towards her.

"Don't take her personally. She's always been like that. You know her husband divorced her very publicly last year—married their at-home yoga instructor. I think she just hates any woman under the age of forty."

Margherita shook her head and rolled her eyes. "I don't take her personally. Women don't have a tendency to like me."

"I can see that."

She raised her eyebrows in mock defense. "Oh, yeah?"

"I mean, I can understand how that happens. They are threatened. And you don't falter under them, so they immediately view you as competition."

"Such bullshit. Damned if you have no confidence, damned if you do. Damned if you don't know what you're doing, damned if you do."

"Well, better to be damned in the latter," he said and clinked her glass.

"How did you find me?"

"I snuck out when you did, wanted to be sure you were okay. Saw you in the window." He motioned toward the large windows on one side of the bar.

"Come on. Fuck Yulia. Tell me about life in New York."

"Life in New York. Okay. Well, I pass a fair amount of time at this bar. I spend an inordinate amount on espressos. Sarcasm flows easier here. But I have to say—it's very disappointing the lack of men's dress. I mean, there are very few Beck Leonetti's dashing about."

"Dashing?"

"Dashing."

"Who *is* dashing about, then?"

"Ill-fitting pants, too-short pants, too-long pants, horribly embarrassing shoe choices, horrific socks, god-awful sunglasses—the kind with the string—the works."

"Americans aren't known for their style, are they."

"What are Americans known for? Anything positive, I mean?"

"Yes."

They sat in silence, pondering.

"Well, can we narrow that down…New Yorkers," he said.

He made her laugh, and he was a mediocre distraction after an awful evening, but underneath it she continued to grow frustrated by Nick's silence.

The bar was closing and Beck suggested one last drink at the Mercer Hotel. She didn't want that. She wanted to climb into bed with Nick. She didn't even really want to have sex, she just wanted to be with him. She wanted someone to look at her the way he did. The way she imagined he did.

"Quick visit to the ladies' room before they kick us out and then I'll decide," she said.

In the gold-piped bathroom downstairs, she finally heard her phone beep.

Nick: Hello
Nick: Can't
Nick: Right now
Nick: Speak tomorrow

She could barely see herself straight in the mirror, but she knew her face belied such incredible disappointment she might as well have been crying. She sucked in a deep breath, yelled a profanity at her phone, and returned to Beck, who sat alone and devastatingly handsome at the empty bar. Devastatingly handsome…and married. Her eyes lingered on his wedding ring as she seated herself again.

"Hey," he started, casually bumping her shoulder. "I have a question. Why *did* you leave Milan so abruptly? Last time I saw you there, you seemed so happy, and you were just about to close that partnership deal for the spa. It was like one day you were there, and the next you weren't." He looked into her eyes, at her forehead, at her lips, and back to her eyes.

She watched his eyes flit about her face. He opened his eyes widely, a fake staring contest.

"My mom died. Abruptly," she said, with little emotion.

"Oh, Marghe." There were suddenly creases in his forehead and concern in his eyes. He placed his hand over hers. Pity, she assumed.

She finished her drink. "Okay let's go," she said energetically, shattering the silence.

His face was still piteous. She hated that look.

So she kissed him.

She kissed him with strength and purpose, as if his lips were the exit door to the pathetic, frustrated feeling she couldn't shake. He kissed her back. He took her hand and guided her out of the restaurant, back to his hotel.

NEW YORK, NEW YORK

2019

MARGHERITA SNUCK OUT at sunrise, having quickly and quietly escaped without waking him. She walked across Prince Street to the subway, relishing the empty blocks and the morning silence in Soho.

At home, she immediately took her dress off and stepped into a scalding hot shower. She stood under the running water, letting it fall on her chest and her shoulders, never wanting to get out. She let out a cry, a heaving cry.

Wrapped in her towel, she looked at her reflection. *Am I being young and carefree or am I being destructive? What was my mom like at my age? I never asked her enough about it,* she thought.

Isabetta Andolini

NEW YORK, NEW YORK

2019

Nick: How was your night

MARGHERITA LOOKED UP from the travel itinerary she had been pretending to double check. Yulia had a personal conflict the same dates as an installation in the Paris boutique. Alexandre ruffled Yulia's feathers when he suggested Margherita go in her place, and Yulia had been treating her with ice cold contempt since. Margherita couldn't imagine what the conflict was. She assumed it was plastic surgery.

She slid her phone in front of her and stared at the screen, still feeling extraordinarily blue after a sleepless night in a hotel room that wasn't hers.

Margherita: Have you ever had your heart broken Nicholas
Margherita: I feel like that's probably never happened to you
Nick: Why do you ask?

Silence.

Margherita: Ciao

Margherita: Think I had a bit too much to drink last night

Nick: why did you ask though?

Margherita: No idea

Nick: Okay
Nick: No I don't think I have
Nick: Not truly

Margherita: You would know. If you have

Nick: No then

Margherita: How did I know

Nick: Because
Nick: You think I'm arrogant?
Nick: Like someone with no scars

Margherita: Your words not mine
Margherita: I just sensed it. no particular reason
Margherita: Maybe you're just very smart in your decisions
Margherita: Or too safe. Orrrr maybe it's comin for ya. Who knows

Nick: You are funny.

Margherita: I made a crap decision to see someone last night who I shouldn't have. Made me think about it. I think we all step on hearts like little eggshells at some point in our lives, not purposefully.

Nick: Who why?

Nick: Why shouldn't you have?

Always asking questions, never revealing why he is so curious. Never revealing anything about himself, she thought.

Margherita: Who why what when Where
Margherita: 5 W's of storytelling

Nick: Whence*

Margherita: Bravo

NEW YORK, NEW YORK

2019

Margherita: ((Sends song "Wear Sunscreen" tropical mix.))
All the wisdom you will EVER need in life in one Tropical Mix

Nick: how are you

Margherita: we are so random aren't we

Nick: We are, yes.

Margherita: Listen to the mix. It's very wise.

Nick: You saw someone the other night
Nick: So you wanted to speak with me
Nick: About what

Margherita: No I wanted to distract myself and have fun

Nick: Oh

NEW YORK, NEW YORK

2019

THAT EVENING MARGHERITA found herself on one of the best first dates she had ever been on. She had learned to not set expectations for first dates; she approached them with a positive mindset and nonchalance, always choosing someone handsome, intelligent, and international. She knew then at the very least she would have an interesting evening with someone smart and cute.

She sat at the bar at one of her favorite spots on East Houston and enjoyed an Americano cocktail before Harry arrived. He was running late but she didn't care; she was happy to be out. They had matched on a dating app, and he had come across as a little overeager and slightly nerdy; a thirty-something investment banker from London with dark brown hair and thick-rimmed glasses.

When he finally arrived, however, with his bank-logo duffel and in casual Friday dress, he was taller, more handsome, and far more charming and easygoing than Margherita had anticipated. They flirted, dove from subject to subject, interrupted each other with keenness and enthusiasm, and shared nearly half the menu, though their appetite was more for each other than the food.

At dessert, Margherita encouraged Harry to order the chocolate cake.

When it arrived, the decadent scent wafted her way. She let out a little moan. "But you can't have any, right? It has dairy and gluten, and—holy hell—maybe even almonds..." he said.

"You enjoy it," she said.

He delicately swiped his fork through the layers. "Oh my god. I feel bad saying this, but that is incredible. Are you sure? You can't have even a taste?"

They had become increasingly close to each other over the evening. His large hand had lain on her leg many a time by then, and she had many drinks and glasses of wine in her.

"You can kiss me. Then I'll be able to taste it," she suggested, wondering why he hadn't kissed her at least an hour earlier.

"I would like that very much."

After midnight, the bartender managed to interrupt them with a check, wanting to close out. They noticed they were the last two in the restaurant and were both hesitant to call it a night.

"I don't feel tired at all," she said.

"Me neither. I am wide awake. Do you want to go somewhere else? There are a few spots in Williamsburg I know..."

"What about your place? You said you just finished decorating. I'd love to see it." *So what*, she thought. Why shouldn't she enjoy the chemistry?

They could barely keep their hands off each other in the taxi as it made its way across East Houston and over the bridge, and at his one bedroom in a beautiful building on the river, they began to drunkenly ravage each other. Harry was tall and able and picked Margherita up with ease. She was over the moon at having found someone smart, successful, well-mannered, well-read, cultured, fun, and incredibly handsome. She could not remember the last time she had clicked with someone, the last time she had such a chemical charge.

Well, yes, actually: Nick.

On his sofa, Margherita was feeling generous and free with Harry. "Holy hell, you're amazing," he said as he tousled her hair. She brought him a tissue and excused herself to the bathroom. She was shaking with adrenaline as she checked her phone.

Nick: Hello
Nick: how are you?
Nick: what are you up tonight?

What were the chances? It was like he had radar. *Well F him*, she thought. She had finally found someone new to be excited about.

As she said goodnight to Harry, he picked her up once again to give her an enthusiastic kiss. "Let's go to dinner next week. And then come back here. And do more of this. There are so many good places in Williamsburg. We'll go to all of them. And do lots more of this," he repeated. She giggled and called an Uber to go home and sleep in her own bed.

———

The next morning she woke up with a massive, stupid smile on her face. She was positively dancing as she brushed her teeth.

"Dad, guess what!" She said into the phone. "I met my future husband."

Tommaso laughed. "Oh? Is that so? This is the guy from last night? And does he know?"

"No not yet. But it's decided. He is so cute. Tall. Already super successful. Smart. Has lived all over. Speaks like five languages. We have so much in common. He asked questions. He listened. We laughed. He has a decorated apartment. And he has a gorgeous accent," she gushed.

"Sounds like a catch. I hope he keeps this impression up. When will you see him again?"

"This week I hope."

"Okay. I'm happy for you."

She was about to say *Can I talk to mom?* but caught herself. Suddenly her mood shifted like a slammed door. She always used to tell Francine about those sorts of things.

"What are you doing today? Do you want to drive up to the house with me?" Tommaso asked.

Margherita didn't reply. She stared at her reflection in the bathroom mirror.

"Marghe? Did I lose you?"

"I miss Mom," she sobbed, and she cried into the phone.

NEW YORK, NEW YORK

2019

Nick: What are you up to

Margherita: Can I tell you something

Nick: Yes

Margherita: I met someone who I really like. And it makes me think maybe I need to force myself out of this habit I have. To stop doing this I mean

Nick: This
Nick: As in
Nick: Me

Margherita: As in sneaking around with someone who I shouldn't be sneaking around with. And I know in this specific situation nothing has really happened but I know it could and it's just a rabbit hole for me

Nick: I would like to sneak around with you.
Nick: I see

Margherita: That's not helpful Nicky

Nick: What isn't
Nick: Saying that I want to

Nick: And that I want to this week
Nick: I'm being honest

SHE SAT ON the arm of her chair, her thumb nail at the edge of her teeth.

Margherita: I hate feeling cheap

Nick: But I won't force you to do anything you don't want to
Nick: You aren't cheap
Nick: At all

Margherita: It's hard to explain

Nick: I'd like to hear
Nick: I'm sitting in my office
Nick: On my own

Margherita: I can never tell when you're being genuine

Nick: I am
Nick: Right now

Margherita: You want sex. Come on!
Margherita: I do too honestly. Of course

Better keep this light, she thought.

Margherita: But I feel like I need to teach myself to not constantly seek out this kind of situation

Nick: You didn't seek it out
Nick: Neither did I

Margherita: Ok but it became that

Nick: I don't want you to feel cheap
Nick: It's not how I view you
Nick: I was about to use a word you don't like

Margherita: Which word don't I like

Nick: Delicious
Nick: :/

Margherita: ha

Nick: I sort of
Nick: Just want to disappear
Nick: Into a pillow fort with you
Nick: And put my mouth all over you

Margherita: This is what I mean though

Nick: go on

Margherita: I put myself in situations where it's only this
Margherita: And I need to stop

Nick: :(
Nick: It's not only this
Nick: But okay

If it's not only this, then what is it? she thought.

Margherita: I have a question
Margherita: That's really none of my business and you can tell me so if you want

Nick: go for it

Margherita: Why do you stay with your girlfriend if you're so okay with cheating on her

Nick: Because

Nick: I have sides to me
Nick: That I want to explore
Nick: That are real
Nick: But separate

Margherita: What does that mean
Margherita: Sides to you

So it's not about me, specifically. That's just a British way of saying because I want to eat my cake and have it too, she thought.

Nick: different parts of me
Nick: A side that wants to disappear from my office
Nick: And meet up with you

Margherita: To have sex
Margherita: That's not sides

Nick: your questioning
Nick: Sometimes
Nick: Feels
Nick: Like
Nick: Judgement
Nick: And I hate it so much

Margherita: but that's just cheating
Margherita: I'm not judging you
Margherita: I guess I am a direct texter
Margherita: I think if you were sitting in front of me talking in person you wouldn't feel like that

Nick: Not really direct
Nick: You're skirting around things a bit
Nick: And you're very

Nick: Inconsistent.

Margherita: I think you've also been a little inconsistent

Margherita: It makes me unsure

Nick: Okay

Margherita: chicken or the egg

Nick: I'll play the egg

Margherita: But I still don't understand this

Nick: Why I want to cheat

Margherita: If you want to spend time with this girl and that girl and this girl and that girl then why not just be single

Please tell me it's not this girl and that girl, she thought.

Margherita: Do you think you are someone who needs a girlfriend

Nick: No
Nick: I do not feel the need to explain
Nick: Defend* myself

Margherita: I guess I am wondering if I were in a relationship would I be doing the same thing

Nick: I don't want to tell you all this if you are just using me as a test subject

Margherita: No I'm not. That's not fair.

Nick: Okay but it doesnt feel nice for you to say
Nick: Basically: I'm out
Nick: Oh and by the way, why on earth are you still up for it?

Nick: When two days ago it was different

Margherita: I didnt mean it that way at all
Margherita: I am struggling over here

Nick: I'm sorry that you are

Margherita: This is sort of a new one for me in its own weird way

Nick: How so

Margherita: I feel like every time I answer honestly, I am somehow reminded that you are here just for sex and then I feel really silly having just been so honest with you

Nick: I'm not going to play roulette with how you want me to talk to you
Nick: It's so unpredictable
Nick: I'm not here for the sex- nothing has happened
Nick: Maybe we'd cuddle and talk
Nick: Maybe we'll do loads of sex
Nick: I don't know

Margherita: That's why it's new to me
Margherita: It's grey
Margherita: That's different

Nick: Okay well
Nick: It's very easy

For you. It's not that easy for me, she thought.

Nick: If you would like to see me, I would too
Nick: If you don't, then I dont want to either
Nick: I'm not going to force it

Then he obviously isn't interested, she thought.

Margherita: You know I do

Nick: I don't
Nick: I do take you at your word
Nick: So maybe I do again

Margherita: I can't even take myself at my word
Margherita: I would absolutely not be speaking to you still if I didn't want to

Nick: Fair
Nick: You're playing with me a little
Nick: You know that

Margherita: Youve been playing with me for a very long time
Margherita: Maybe that's the attraction

Nick: Ah yes
Nick: Patience

Margherita: I'm not generally known for my patience
Margherita: Okay I'm going to sleep.

She turned off her lamp and rested her head on her pillow. She did not feel satisfied by the conversation; it left her just as confused as before. Trying to figure him out was like unsuccessfully yanking a weed, and she already revealed much more than he had. She told herself to drop it. Let it go.

A few minutes later, the blue light from her phone lit up her room. Was he calling by accident?

"Hello?" she answered.

She heard a whishing sound, pedals in the night.

"I'm biking home," he said, somewhat breathless.

"You're not supposed to chat and bike. That's dangerous."

"Oh? I do it all the time. There's hardly anyone on Lafayette right now."

She turned over on her side and rested the phone on the mattress. "You work so late," she said.

"Yeah. Well, I went to dinner with my mate and then we went back to the office."

"Uffa long day."

"How was your day?"

Why the sudden attention? she wondered.

"Ohh...it was fine. Went for a long run this morning. Got to leave the office before six, unheard of," she said, thinking about Yulia's imminent return from Milan the next day, reminded of how she was not allowed on the trip.

"Where did you run?"

"Over the bridge, to Battery Park and back."

"And you did a lot of thinking on this run, I suppose?" He seemed to be hinting at something.

"Oh, I think a lot," she said flirtatiously.

"Yes, I noticed. Your brain has been quite fiery tonight."

"Mmm."

"Why is that?" The background noise was quieting down. "I'm going inside my building now. Going to be winded with these five flights."

"Keeps ya young."

"Deflecting."

"I don't know. Sometimes I think."

"Yes. It comes on rather suddenly," he said, going up the stairs.

"Mmm."

"This is my least favorite version of you."

"Did you really just say that?"

"You mull things. And you draw conclusions. And then you mull your conclusions. And you push them onto others, unfairly."

"Others? Or you?"

"Well I assume others, because you do it with me," he said, facetiously.

You don't know me, she thought.

"You *can* step in you know, and help me draw those conclusions."

"I suppose."

She heard him punch an alarm code at his front door, and then the door opening and closing.

"I'm going to make a tea," he said.

She laughed to herself. It was sort of sweet how he wanted to stay on the phone with her for no reason in particular.

"What's your bedtime tea of choice?" She asked.

"Tonight it's a Sleepy tea," he said. She could hear a cupboard opening, a tea box sliding off a shelf. "But sometimes chamomile, sometimes mint. What's your nighttime tea of choice?"

"I like mint. Lemon and ginger. Maybe licorice and fennel."

"Oh very nice, my little thinker. I love my tea before bed. With my book. I feel like such an old man lately. You wouldn't believe how much I look forward to getting into bed with my tea and my book."

She smiled to herself. "What are you reading?"

And they stayed like that, each in their own beds, chatting about nothing, until they got too sleepy to keep it up.

As Nick was about to say goodnight, he asked an impulsive question.

"Would you like to meet for a drink tomorrow eve?"

"Sure," she said, surprised.

"I think it's due, don't you?"

"I do." She tried to remain even.

"Eight?"

"Perfetto."

And they said goodnight, both too excited to fall asleep.

NEW YORK, NEW YORK

2019

THE NEXT MORNING she woke with a start. She tried not to be excited, to get ahead of herself, to jinx the evening's plan. She made an espresso and put her sneakers on. She started the day with a run, a good sweat, something to get the blood flowing, something that wasn't Nicky.

Next, she opened the chat with Harry. They had spent the previous week texting intermittently, but he hadn't made any plans with her after he had canceled their second date due to an unscheduled work trip. He hadn't responded to the last message she had sent the day before, and she was genuinely confused as to what had suddenly shifted the dynamic.

A new message appeared on her screen.

Nick: I'm wearing flip flops

Margherita: well that is fascinating!

Nick: I just wanted you to know
Nick: because we are meeting tonight
Nick: and I just realized
Nick: that I'm wearing red flip flops

Margherita: oh they're red thank god

Margherita: that's totally fine then. should I bring a floatie?

Nick: lol shut up

Margherita: I'll be wearing heels, as one does

Nick: I should go home after work and change shouldn't I

Margherita: I'm sorry, I didn't realize I was having a frantic chat with one of my girlfriends…I think there was an article about which shoes to wear on which kind of date in the last Seventeen magazine. Shall I forward?

Nick: flip flops is what you're getting then

Nick: what kind of date is this

Margherita: Let's write to the advice column and see what they say

Nick: Surely they would advise you against seeing me

Margherita: are you reverse psychology-ing on me

Nick: no

Nick: Is it a date

Margherita: Is it

Nick: I don't know

Nick: but I'm looking forward to it

NEW YORK, NEW YORK

2019

SHE ARRIVED FIRST, wanting to snag two good seats at the small bar. She worked hard to save the seat next to her, fending off many determined people who hovered behind her. Paul allowed her to hog the empty seat, even though it was very much his job as bartender to fill them. Paul had been witness to many of Margherita's dates but had never seen her so rosy and aflutter.

When Nick finally arrived, she introduced him to Paul. "See? I told you there was a real person coming!"

"Yes, yes I am a real boy," Nick said.

"To be honest…for a while, we were doubtful. We had a bet going back here," Paul joked. He outstretched his hand. "Paul, nice to meet you."

"Nicholas. Thanks for keeping the seat," Nick said.

"You can thank our Marghe. She's feisty. What are you drinking?"

"Umm…what are you having?" He turned to Margherita's drink.

"Gin and soda," she said, noticing it was basically empty. "Perfect."

"So, red flip flops. Let's see 'em," Margherita looked

down to inspect.

They carried on for an hour or so before Paul returned for the fourth time with menus. No matter how infrequently she and Nick actually saw each other in person, it was always as if they had known each other forever…and yet it was also just as clear that that they hadn't, since each was such a mystery to the other.

"Okay, focus," Nick said, sliding the menu between the two of them. They huddled their heads together. Neither of them had dared touch the other, even though Margherita wanted to so badly, to lay a hand on his knee as part of a gesticulation, or touch his hand in some way while listening to a lively story.

"Do you know what you want?" Nick asked after a studied pause.

"In life? I am still not sure, what about you?" She responded dryly.

He looked at her and smiled. "Oh, psst."

"You know those menus where you want—or could eat—almost everything on it?" Nick asked.

"Yes."

"This is not one of them."

"I know. I only ever come here for drinks and for Paul. But the menu blegh. Too French. What about oysters. Oysters are safe."

"Done."

They gave the menu back to Paul and turned back to face each other.

"Do you think you know what you want?" Margherita asked.

"Yes, oysters."

She rolled her eyes. "In life. In work."

"Oh, whoa. Okay." He faced her, his eyes fully on her; she had his undivided attention. She loved that about him.

"IF someone were to ask you, *What is it that you want? What do you imagine you'd say?*" she quizzed, staring into the blue eyes that were staring into hers.

"I want to act," he said after a moment's thought. "I'd like to do theater. I'd like to be gloriously successful, make a ton of money—" He outstretched his arms very wide, accidentally brushing the woman seated next to him. "Oh sorry," he said to her and patted her shoulder to make it better, after which he turned back to Margherita with a *Whoops* expression.

"—Or at least a lot of money," he said, picking up the thread again, with his hands shrunken inward. He was always gesticulating. "I don't want to be a struggling actor. I just want to do it and enjoy it."

She nodded at him, regarding him very seriously, her eyebrows scrunched together and her head moving slowly up and down, in mock deep pensiveness.

She is adorable, he thought.

He looked at her eyes, and the right side of his mouth slightly curled upward, expectantly, happily.

"Would you want to be alone in this adventure? Do you see yourself...with someone?"

"Well, yes," he started without hesitation. "No one wants to be *alone*."

"Someone who's a *real* partner I mean. In life and in love. Not just any Sally or Elizabeth," she clarified.

"Well, you don't think I'm not choosy when it comes to spending time with someone, do you?"

She tilted her head, and rolled her eyes. "How would I know?"

He softened. "Do you see yourself with a partner?"

"You are evading," she said, stabbing him playfully with her pointer finger.

"I learned it from you, Master Evader."

"I prefer Madame Evader. And I asked you first."

"Yes. I see myself with someone. Someone specific. No one named Sally or Elizabeth, that's for sure," he said.

She smiled.

"Now you."

"Now me?" She took a sip from her third drink of the evening, a tangy Americano cocktail.

"Do you. See yourself. With someone. A partner. No random Emiliano or Jean Paul."

She sat back in her bar seat, breathing in a bit of air.

She shrugged.

"What would happen if you were to answer a question?" He leaned his chin on his fist, professorially.

"What if, what if, what if. We can't live in hypotheticals. What if Katharine had an iPhone inside the cave. She could have just called Almasy—*I'm dying, dear; please bring water.* What kind of love story would that have been!" She threw her hands in the air with a smile.

He watched her, studying her eyes, the curve of her lips. In that moment, he could see her zip up, and re-spool the thread.

It was that, that right there, that made him doubt her position entirely. She either had no idea what she wanted, or she knew and was leading him in the wrong direction.

"Do you see yourself in spawning years? Spawning?" he asked, motioning a pregnant belly.

"Do I see myself spawning…" she pondered very seriously, mocking him in her charming way.

"Yes, spawning. I picture you with a pitcher of lemonade and a broad brimmed hat. And Little Margherita's. Little Margheritos running around in pastel outfits."

"Oh, well, that's bound to get confusing. I should hope I can differentiate their names a bit more than that." She said, decidedly. She took a sip from her drink.

He watched her, his body turned toward her on his bar stool. She took a sip of her drink, looked up at the bartender, purposefully listened in on the conversation next to her, and inserted something witty and flirtatious. The bartender gave her a quip back and she laughed, showing her perfect teeth and dimples. She turned her head back to Nick, her chin rested on her hand, while her eyes waited for his next move.

"What?" she asked, as if she had no idea the little game she was playing, and always winning.

"Nothing, nothing. Just wondering about you," he said.

Her brows raised. "Don't think too much. It's bad for you."

"Another round?" Paul asked. They both acquiesced. She squeezed his thigh under the bar, a mischievous grin on her face. It was the first time either of them had laid a hand on the other that evening.

The conversation moved to their favorite actors, currently—who was aging and who was getting too much Botox (Leonardo DiCaprio and Nicole Kidman, but they both loved them regardless). Nick told her about his stint playing assistant to the star of a hit HBO show and the actor's foot fetish. They discovered they were both living in San Francisco at the same time, only a few blocks apart.

He had been working on a personal film project after grad school.

"I actually made quite a poignant little film," he said.

"Ohhhh! Tell me about it!" Her eyes widened.

He felt her excitement; it was contagious. He was happy that she was so curious. She seemed to really want to know things about him.

"Isn't it funny how we've both hopped around so much, trying this and that, always looking for a fit?" He gesticulated *this* and *that*. He made the comment with joy, not sadness or nostalgia. She, on the other hand, had always regarded her flitting around as rather lonely.

As the evening sped on, the other patrons began to leave. They decided they had both drank too much to order anything else, and asked for the check.

"I'm going to call an Uber," he said. She looked down at his phone, watching him.

"Am I invited in this Uber?" she asked, playfully.

"Yes of course. Okay, two minutes away."

They descended from their bar stools and said goodbye to Paul, who, raised his eyebrows. Nick took her hand as they wound their way towards the door. Outside, he walked one pace ahead of her, still holding her hand, guiding her towards the car waiting across the street. They got in, and in the backseat, he reached for her hand again. It was a strange sensation. She was not used to someone holding her hand in such a seemingly tender way, let alone in the back of an Uber. What was she supposed to do, let it sit limply in his? Give pressure? Rub him with her thumb? She swept one finger back and forth on his palm, tickling him.

They climbed the stairs to his loft on the fifth floor. She walked in front of him, up the stairs in her heels, he clipping and clapping along in his flip flops like Daffy Duck. He opened the door with a code. She went to the bathroom to wash her hands and check her reflection. When she came out, he was sitting atop the kitchen island, a large island, a large kitchen for New York, a huge space.

She approached him, holding tight to the laughter that they had enjoyed at the bar. He turned on a random playlist on his phone, which sat next to him. She scrolled through and found "Mama Said" by The Shirelles. She turned up the volume and started to sing along and dance, watching him.

"You're nuts," he said, laughing. He couldn't help but hop down from the counter and dance with her, each of them singing the words, often messing them up and laughing. They kept going right on through "Groove Me" by King Floyd and both had gotten their heart rate up by the time "Gimme Little Sign" by Brenton Wood came on. On a twirl, as she started to come towards him, he wrapped his arm around her waist and brought her body towards his.

"Just gimme some kind of sign girl," she said very seriously, her face barely a centimeter from his.

"To show me that your mine girl," he replied, and he kissed her gently. It was the first time they had kissed since their late night drink at the Mercer two months before. He kiss-walked her towards the counter and picked her up so that she was sitting on it, with her legs wrapped around him. There was a tingle everywhere.

They separated from each other's lips to take a breath. He caressed her thighs with each of his hands, running his hand along her calf while she tousled his walnut-colored locks. She reached for the hem of his t-shirt and pulled it over his head. His shoulders were tan and freckled from the sun and soft like butter. She ran her hands from the crests of his shoulders to his upper arm, feeling nervous.

She slid down from the counter, and her dress fluttered upwards. He lifted the edges of it gently and, while looking her in the eye, felt her lace underwear where it met the skin of her hip bones.

He picked her up and carried her to his bedroom.

NEW YORK, NEW YORK

2019

THEY LAY THERE next to each other, he on his stomach with his face turned toward her, one cheek buried in the pillow, she on her back, glancing between him and the ceiling.

"Tired?" she asked.

"Just enjoying the moment. Post ejaculation," he smiled.

She smiled back. She ran her fingers lightly across his arm. He closed his eyes.

That feels good, he thought.

What do I do now, she thought.

He opened his eyes and looked at her. Those blue eyes.

"You can sleep here," he said, quietly, tenderly.

"No, no, I'm going home."

"Okay. Do you want water?" he asked.

"Sure."

He went to the kitchen and came back with a tall glass of water. He passed it to her in bed and she took a sip and gave it back to him. They shared it.

"Do you like my room?" he asked, more awake.

She wished it had never started, that nothing had ever happened—but it did, and it would again.

NEW YORK, NEW YORK

2019

MARGHERITA SAT ON MetroNorth on her way to her parents' weekend home in Connecticut. She hadn't been to the house since after Francine's funeral, and she told herself she needed to rip the band-aid at some point. Her phone was on her lap, and she willed Harry to write to her. She had sent another message—*What are you up to this weekend?*—which he had read and ignored.

The train made a stop at 125th street. Her eyes fell to the street below the concourse, where a young boy ran behind an older boy; they both wore backpacks, and were probably on their way home from some sort of after-school activity. It was so much easier to be young, and she found herself jealous of them, of their unencumbered youth. She felt melancholy from her toes to the hair on her head. It soaked her.

Endings. She hated them. A beginning was all she ever wanted—lots of them. The endings had a habit of breaking her, and she pushed them off as much as she could, even if it meant butchering something until it was barely recognizable. Nick would carry on with his girlfriend. They would move towards something, together, and she would be alone, as always. She would not carry on with anyone. Whatever they had was something that felt like something, but in the end, it was nothing.

She told herself that she was better off closing the door on him altogether.

That night she went to sleep early, hopeful for a solid nights sleep in the country and looking forward to going for a run around Lyme the next morning. She hadn't heard a peep from Nick. It made her feel rotten, knowing he was spending the weekend with his friends, with his girlfriend, living his other life that she wasn't a part of.

When she woke up, she saw two messages, sent at four a.m., but they weren't from Nick.

Harry: Hi
Harry: Come over

She stared at her phone with her head still on the pillow. She felt she would always be that girl—the one that guys texted at four a.m. and asked to come over. She couldn't understand why. She was smart, and she could be sweet, and she had interests, and she had a fun personality…she believed these things about herself. So why was she the one they texted in the middle of the night?

She rose from her bed and sat on a wicker bench in front of three side-by-side windows overlooking the garden. Her father stood in the center, coffee mug in hand, surveying his flowers. Her sweet, loving, widowed father, who believed his daughter to be mostly innocent still.

She composed a new message.

Margherita: I don't think I can do this. Whatever this is. Mostly because I really like you as a person,

and I really enjoy you and I want to be your friend as much as I want other physical things and it just gets too messy. Honestly, I would have rather had you as a friend than whatever it is we're doing now.
Margherita: And I'm not sure I want to be the person who enables you to do what you're doing. Not because I'm "judging" you, but because I think you are really wonderful and it makes me sad to think that you can hurt this girl so easily.
Margherita: I can't help feeling conflicted. I want the fun but I don't want that crap feeling afterwards. I'm sorry for being inconsistent, but put yourself in my shoes Nicky. It kind of sucks. I don't want to be 'girl on the side'. I just can't stand that feeling anymore.

Nick: Marghe, I'm sorry.
Nick: I don't want to be the one who makes you feel something you don't want to feel.

Margherita: How am I the only one who feels conflicted.
Margherita: You're like plain sailing over there.

Nick: Assumption.
Nick: Assumption.

Margherita: Yes, assumption, I know. I don't have anything else to go on.

Silence.

NEW YORK, NEW YORK

2019

Nick: I'm knocking around an empty apartment.
Nick: And wish that you were in it.

Margherita: You can't do this with me.
Margherita: I meant what I said.

SILENCE.

Isabetta Andolini

NEW YORK, NEW YORK

2019

Nick: Let's just leave it I think. You're right. Bad timing in general.

Margherita: It's not about timing in the slightest. But doesn't matter at this point.

Nick: It does

Nick: Why do you keep talking to me?

Nick: I thought you wanted rid of me

She sat in the back of her yoga studio with her thumb nail in her mouth, staring at her phone. *Why is he still conversing*, she wondered. She had to put her phone away; the class was about to start.

She picked it up immediately once it was over.

Margherita: It's not timing. It's a choice. And I want something real with someone who chooses me. Otherwise it's not anything more than convenience. You can keep saying that all you want but I will never see it that way.

He didn't reply.

NEW YORK, NEW YORK

2019

MARGHERITA SAT ON the sofa in Jane's office, pushing her thumb nail cuticle back unknowingly.

"So, you're sure?" Jane asked. "You're not going to see him anymore?"

Margherita's lips pursed into a 'Yikes, I'm trying,' expression.

"Is that what you really want? To end it?"

"Well, I should, shouldn't I?" Margherita asked.

Jane was silent, in that typical, rather infuriating, therapist sort of way.

"He should prove it. Prove something. If he wants something. If he doesn't surface, then that says everything."

"Why is this one so hard to let go?" Jane asked with curiosity and a slight smile on her face. "He has really gotten under your skin."

"Have I shown you a photo?" Margherita thought of Jane as a girlfriend she had to submit an insurance claim for. Sometimes she genuinely looked forward to seeing her therapist, to have a female to chat with. She pulled out her phone and brought up Nick's photo.

"Oh. Wow. Okay. He's really, *really* cute," Jane said,

zooming in on the photo.

"Okay, so you see!?"

"But it's not all looks. He is really getting to you. I think you really like him."

"Well. That cannot be. Must end that."

"Why? Why is it bad to fall for someone?"

"Because. Because…because he's not going to choose me," Margherita said defiantly, "and I'll just end up really freaken' upset and I just can't go through that again. Enough with that."

"Too much loss for one year."

"He is a good distraction for me. If I'm not thinking and obsessing and daydreaming about someone, I'm just going to think about my mom. And Italy. So for now, he keeps my mind busy."

"What about a hobby?"

Margherita rolled her eyes. "Ugh. Hobbies. You sound like my mom. She kept telling me to go up to the Y on 92nd street and 'join something.'"

"Well…" Jane obviously agreed.

Weeks went by and neither of them surfaced. Margherita wondered if he went somewhere for an August vacation with his girlfriend and their group of friends. She would never know.

One evening, alone on her building's small rooftop overlooking the Manhattan skyline, feeling left out of the gorgeous summer holidays her friends were having back in Italy, she gave in.

Margherita: I can't get sleepy.

Margherita: I would like it if you were in front of me.
Margherita: I would like you to kiss me. And talk to me. And kiss me.

He read the texts but didn't respond. She felt that sinking feeling immediately. That disgraced, embarrassed, frustrated, angry feeling she felt whenever he ignored her. She deleted the chat thread and put the phone face down on the deck chair. *Fuck you,* she thought.

She heard her mother in her head.

"The problems you have in the beginning of a relationship will never go away. That red flag you saw in the first few dates—it will be there forever. You just have to choose what you are willing and able to deal with. What are you compromising?" Francine had said to her one evening over sushi at a sub-par restaurant on Second Avenue. Margherita had been home from Italy for Christmas and had managed to get her mother to herself for an evening, away from Benjamin and his ever-so-perfect Alice.

"How do you know what you're compromising now won't bite you later? You think it's the right combination of things now, but then later everything can change," Margherita had said. "It sounds awfully precarious to me."

"Just think, daisies are truer than wildflowers. All those qualities that blow away in the wind. That wash away unexpectedly. What are the qualities that you want forever. Look for those."

It sounded like an impossible puzzle to Margherita. A headache, that's what it was.

NEW YORK, NEW YORK

2019

"PAUL," SHE SAID in greeting, a sly grin and a nod.

"Margherita," Paul said, barely smiling, begrudging her a nod. Holding back was typical Paul.

She slid onto a bar seat and took a peek around. The September light outside was beautiful, and she smiled towards it.

"Drink?" Paul asked.

"Americano please," Margherita said. She took stock. There were two twos on her right: one comprised two young thirty-something women having an after-work drink; the other was a forty-something couple diving into what Margherita believed to be a way too early in the evening duck and frites. Duck and frites felt like an after nine p.m. affair— when the restaurant was full and booming, when it was dark outside, when a certain number of drinks had made laughter a little louder, and the duck a little more tender.

There was one man at the end of the bar where it hooked around, and he faced inwards toward the restaurant. He glanced towards the door periodically, and she assumed he was waiting for someone. He was cute in a suit and dark hair, although a bit too Park Avenue perhaps. As she nonchalantly tried to catch his eye, a plain Jane blonde approached him with that shiny hair that looks impossible to achieve. *Oh fuck them*, she thought.

"Your friend from last time was very pretty. Good hair," Paul said, detached.

"Yes, I know," she said. "He knows too."

"Why aren't you two a thing? Seemed pretty obvious."

"He's too pretty," she said with a wink. Her mother's words echoed in her head: "Never date a guy who is too good looking. They know it, and it's dangerous."

She texted Noah. Noah was always a reliable chat when she was alone at the bar.

Margherita: How is wedding planning going

Noah: Horrible. I have not eaten carbs in weeks. I am miserable.

Margherita: Why not? You look great. You don't need to eliminate.

Noah: I can't even have rice cakes. Or wine. Life is so dull.

Margherita: This sounds precarious.

Noah: People who don't drink are terribly drab. How are you

Margherita: Have taken myself for a September cocktail. September is here. It is lovely.

Noah: You never drink with me.

Margherita: What do you talk! I always have something. I just don't drink A LOT with you.

Noah: Dull.

Margherita: I don't like to steal your spotlight my dear friend. So how many people are going to the wedding- need to know how upset I should be that I'm not invited.

Noah: No one is invited who doesn't know us both.

Margherita: Humph. Shall hold it against you for decades. Will never drink with you again.

"Sorry," a man's voice came from behind her, followed by a hand reaching through to grab a glass from Paul.

She turned her right shoulder to see a handsome blonde man in a white button down, holding a tall glass of something clear with a lime. Hopefully a gin drinker, not vodka.

"Well done. Not a drop on me," she said.

"Oh maybe you haven't noticed it yet."

He was rather cute. She guessed he was six foot one, with blue eyes and straight blonde hair, as if he were straight out of Laguna Beach.

"Do you want to sit here? I can move over one," the fifty-something woman to her left interrupted their meet-cute moment.

"Oh, thank you, but I'm waiting for someone," cute Californian said. He sounded intelligent.

He looked at her and smiled shyly. "Unless you want to save it for someone?"

"Oh, no, that's okay," she said. He might be waiting for a date or a girlfriend, or a wife, most likely, given Margherita's luck.

"You're not waiting for anyone?" he asked, as if he were surprised.

"No?" she replied. "I like to take myself for a drink once in a while. Chat with Paul."

"I do the same. I travel a lot, and I can't hole up in a hotel room all the time. Although I have been mistaken for a male prostitute on more than one occasion," he added.

"Oh? What does that say about your bar presence? Do you think you are putting those vibes out there?"

Cute Californian Guy cocked his head and gave it a ponder. "I think I'm just a natural smiler. I smile at people who make eye contact. Maybe too often. Might give the wrong signal."

"So, this here," Margherita swung her finger between herself and the cute blonde. "Just to be sure—it's not about to be some sort of proposition, is it?"

"Oh—this—no. This was more like, *I hope I don't spill my drink on this very pretty woman sitting by herself at the bar, but if I do, it might be a good conversation starter*," he weighed these two possibilities in his hands.

"We've got a real analytical one here, haven't we?"

At that, a suited male figure appeared next to him. He clapped the blonde on the back of the shoulder, and shook his hand with his other hand.

"Sorry man, traffic." He was a little paunchy, roughly the same height as his friend, with brown hair, and very white teeth. He looked at Margherita and sized her up.

"Has he been disturbing you?" Margherita immediately did not like him.

"Not at all," she said. She looked at Cute California Guy and locked eyes with a knowing look. He extended his hand.

"I'm Derek, by the way."

"Margherita," she said, and shook it, her hand cold from her cocktail.

"This is Pen." Margherita shook Pen's hand. Of course his name was Pen. He probably was a Brunswick kid from Greenwich.

"Margherita. Is that Italian-o?" Pen asked, rather loudly. Cringe.

"Yes, yes it is," she said. Derek watched her, suddenly shy.

"Beautiful. I just went to Capri in July. Gorgeous place," Pen said. He pronounced Capri incorrectly, with the emphasis on the second syllable, as most Americans did. Her opinion of him continued to plummet.

"Yes, it is," she said with feigned interest.

"I'm gonna go see if our table is ready. Are the other guys here?" Pen asked Derek.

"No, I was the first," he said. Pen left them alone again.

"He's one of my most…boisterous friends," Derek said, turning to watch Pen speak loudly with the hostess.

"Ah, yes. Well enjoy your dinner," she gave him a smile.

"Thank you. I would rather finish this drink here with you, but something tells me you won't be sitting by yourself for very long."

Ah, so maybe he is single? she thought. *Although that doesn't necessarily mean anything.*

"Well, I can save you a seat for next time. Safety in numbers. Wouldn't want anyone to think you're a prostitute…"

"Here. Have to do this quick so Pen doesn't see me. I'll never hear the end of it," he fished for his wallet and retrieved a card.

She looked down at it.

"Derek Vanden Dahl. KKR. Fascinating," she said. A private equity guy. Of course. "That explains Pen."

"Hey—it can be! Fascinating. And unfortunately nothing explains Pen…"

"Okay. Mr. Vanden Dahl. Go enjoy your testosterone heavy dinner. Have the duck."

"Grazie," he said with a perfect accent. She tilted her head.

"Bravo!" She turned back around to the bar and Paul's raised eyebrows.

NEW YORK, NEW YORK

2019

IT WAS THE third morning she had woken up in Derek's apartment. She could not remember the last time she had slept at a guy's apartment so many times. She was restless and wanted to get up, but he clearly wanted to sleep in. She decided to take a shower.

"Do you have a hairdryer?" she asked quietly as she ran her finger down the length of his back.

"Yes, I think there's one here, under the sink," he said, still half-asleep, his mouth buried in his pillow.

In the bathroom, she found the cheap fold-up hairdryer under the sink. She also found a small cosmetic bag with stray plastic hair clips, a mini shampoo and conditioner from a good brand, and a travel-sized Sensodyne toothpaste. Hmm. Whoever the ex-girlfriend was, she had Margherita's same taste in toothpaste and hair products. Well, at least it was handy for her shower.

She climbed into bed with her hair a little wet; the hairdryer was shriekingly loud and she didn't want to be a nuisance. He was more awake and rubbed his hand up and down her soft arm.

"Mmm so fresh," he said sleepily.

"Are you awake yet?!" she asked. "I've lived nine lives already."

"Oh shove it. Come here," he pulled her entire body on top of his so they both faced the ceiling, and then wrapped his arms tightly around her. "It's a Margherita lock."

She laughed. "You dork. She rolled over to lay next to him. "Can I ask you something?"

"Just nothing serious before I'm completely lucid," he said, picking up his watch from the bedside table.

"Is there still another female using that cosmetic bag under the sink?

"I can toss it actually."

She looked at him, waiting.

He looked at her.

"Actually there are some goodies in there."

"Well. All yours, then."

"Can I ask when that ended?"

"You can ask. I'd rather not talk about it. She cheated on me. With one of my friends." He sat up and put his feet on the floor.

Margherita scooted toward the end of the bed to sit next to him. She put her little hand over his big one.

"I'm sorry amore. That's awful."

"Yes, well. They're together. Still. So it all worked out," he said, and he stood. She quickly stood on the bed to keep hold of him.

"She was a twat idiot," Margherita said, simultaneously serious and playful in an effort to extract a smile.

"Well, you said it darling. Twat Idiot. Okay, you want to go for a bike ride?"

"I just showered!"

He threw her over his shoulder and walked her out to the living room.

"So? We're gonna sweat."

Hanging upside down, beneath her laughter, she had a fleeting fear that Derek would never understand, or forgive, her if she ever told him her history.

"By the way, I have dinner plans tonight with my old college roommate. Do you want to come? He would love you." He placed her on a stool at the counter, and he retrieved the coffee beans from the cupboard.

"Oh, I'd have loved to, but I promised my dad I'd go uptown to see him," she lied.

NEW YORK, NEW YORK

2019

Nick: Hiya
Nick: How are you

IT's LIKE HE *knows. Marghe is finally maybe just maybe getting over you. Has maybe met someone new. Swoop in and mess with her,* she thought.

Margherita: Good :)

Nick: Tell me more

Margherita: Goodnight Nicky.
Margherita: Can you do something for me
Margherita: Can you not write me anymore

Nick: Okay

NEW YORK, NEW YORK

2019

Margherita: I still want what I want

Margherita: Right now. I kind of want it right now.

Nick: What do you want

Margherita: Something that belongs to you

Margherita: I want to make it stop

Nick: Do you want me to stop

Nick: You are confusing and inconsistent, you know that

NEW YORK, NEW YORK

2019

Margherita: I don't know how to end it. I don't know why he still keeps it going. I don't get it. I am kind of a pain in the ass sometimes

Noah: I bet you are
Noah: he's still getting something out of it

Margherita: I wish I knew, very concretely, what that was

Noah: Why do you need to understand it or know what's happening? Maybe that comes later

NEW YORK, NEW YORK

2019

NICK LAID ON his side, with his arm resting on the pillow above Margherita's head. He gently brushed his thumb over her jaw line towards her ear and came in for a kiss.

"You can sleep here if you want. I know you're probably going to say no. But you can."

She shook her head, rolled over onto her back and looked at the ceiling. It was such a big room. She couldn't imagine having such a large bedroom in the city. She felt him looking at her still, his hand left to fall to the mattress in the space she had created between them.

"Why not?"

Margherita inhaled and sat up. She glanced around for her clothes. She could feel his eyes still. His hand brushed the space right above her tail bone.

Because I'm not your girlfriend, she thought.

"Hey…" he said to her back.

"I should go." She started for the edge of the bed and he sat up, one hand on her back and one on her chest, blocking her. "Come here." He brought her back to horizontal. She let him.

His hand held the back of her head, his thumb was on

her jawline, and he kissed her collarbone. She felt her heart in her chest. She had been very quiet all evening, wanting to withhold but not wanting to appear too icy. She couldn't find the middle ground.

He looked at her with his big blue eyes. His nostrils flared.

"What?" she asked, a coquettish smile on her lips.

Don't say a word. He will not reciprocate, she thought.

"I should go. You need to sleep. I need to sleep." She tried to sit up again. He sat up next to her and put his hand over her hand. They played with each other's bodies because it was safer than playing with words.

"You're a runner," he said, a lightness to his voice.

"I'm not. I'm just going home. Sleepy time."

What do you want from me, she thought.

"What?" She could feel him thinking.

"How are the boys?" he asked playfully.

Her eyebrows furled. She looked slightly offended.

"What?"

"The boys?"

His nostrils flared as he caught her eye. He smiled with an innocent look.

"Kind of an odd question, no?"

"I'm just curious."

"Why? What's the point of being curious about this subject?"

"Just, to be honest, I guess. I'm honest with you."

He uses it like a badge of honor, his supposed honesty, she thought.

"You're strange." She wanted to lay back down with him and snuggle into his arms as much as she wanted to run far, far away from his bedroom and erase him from her memory. She wanted him to stand up, on his feet, and grab her shoulders, and look her in the eye and tell her that he wanted to be with her, as much as she wanted to walk away with her chin up and never speak to him again. She knew she needed to leave. She had barely an ounce of pride left but an ounce was something.

She put on her clothes, and he sat there, leaning into his knees. His tan shoulders taunted her. That pursed lip expression with the edges slightly curled up, that maddening, unknowable face tortured her.

"Goodnight," she said, as she slipped her shoes on.

"Goodnight."

On her walk home she reviewed one of their first text conversations from the days after their drink at the Mercer. It was the one where he'd admitted that he wouldn't leave his girlfriend, but wondered whether Margherita would be interested in seeing him anyway. At the end of the conversation, he said he'd leave her alone. *You deserve more than what I can offer*, he'd said.

If she had let that be the end, if she had *listened* to him then and trusted that he really was being honest, that he was not going to leave his relationship, she would have saved herself time and trouble, plus a great deal of disappointment, emptiness, and loneliness. She would have also missed that drug-like feeling when one falls in love and knows nothing can be done about it.

NEW YORK, NEW YORK

2019

"Have you ever thought about leaving New York?"

"What?" Derek yelled over the sound of the whirring Vitamix.

Margherita flipped through a beautiful coffee table book on mid-century architecture in Europe. He had bought it for her the previous day at McNally's; she had been glued to it for the better part of an hour, and it seemed the only way to pry her from the store.

"Have you ever thought about living somewhere else, not New York?

Derek placed a glass filled with green juice before her.

"Grazie amore." She took a sip.

He awaited feedback with raised eyebrows.

"Yummy scrummy!"

"Um, leave New York? Why?" He poured himself a glass.

"Just to try somewhere else? Live in a different culture? Different lifestyle?"

"Like LA? Maybe LA, for the weather."

"Like outside of these delightful fifty states."

"Oh. Like Italy you mean."

"Well yes but no, not necessarily."

"Where?"

"Anywhere! Has anywhere ever excited you, that wasn't New York? Anywhere ever intrigued you?"

"Hmm. Not to live. No. I don't think I would leave the States. My family is here. My career. I could see leaving the city eventually..."

Please don't say Darien...New Canaan...Westport, she thought.

"My buddy just bought a huge house in Westport. With a pool and a yard overlooking the water. It's insane. That's a nice life."

She looked at him with a poker face.

"What about you? You want to leave New York?"

"I didn't say that. I don't think I'd like to commit permanently to any one address. I like being a little open-ended."

"But what about when you have a family?"

"Well...what about it? Kids don't move?"

He pursed his lips as he analyzed this.

NEW YORK, NEW YORK

2019

"SHE IS A bit brusque sometimes. I don't know how to explain it. It's like she has five voices in her head. I'm not saying she's crazy. More that she just doesn't know how to represent herself. She'll say something that feels very open and honest, and then she will tighten up, ready to go on the defense, before I've even said anything." Nick sat on Sundeep's sofa. He was tired. It was his first session in three weeks; he just hadn't had the time.

"Do you want her to be open?" Sundeep asked.

"Yes," Nick said immediately.

"And how would that change the situation, for you?"

"I'm not sure." He thought about that possibility. If it actually happened, would he view her differently? He thought about Callie.

"Maybe it would make things even messier? Or harder? I don't know."

"How is Callie?" Sundeep asked, one leg crossed over the other, a small notepad resting on the arm of his chair.

"She's great. We went to Maine a few weeks ago with some friends. It was a lot of fun." Nick paused. A thought seemed to occur to him.

"See, that's the thing, isn't it? Margherita feels so…heavy, sometimes. It's all so dramatic and frustrating. And then she can be so fun and funny and spontaneous. And then she shuts down again—becomes cold and distant and almost angry. And then she reappears in a purely sexual way. It's starting to give me a headache," he said, growing more and more aggrieved.

"And Callie?" Sundeep asked, perfectly stoic.

Nick shrugged. "It's easier."

Sundeep was silent.

"And how do I know she's not sleeping around with other guys- married men and blokes with girlfriends and maybe even single guys too. She dates. I know she dates. She's told me she has terrible discipline. She's admitted to not being able to say no or walk away. So she could be playing this game with multiple guys, for all I know. I'm just one of them."

"Do you think," Sundeep said slowly, "Margherita's behavior could be a product of this situation?"

"No. I don't know. How should I know? I don't really know her outside of this situation. But based on the information that she has given me…it doesn't sound like it."

"Is it possible to separate her past and the information she has shared with you from your relationship with her? Is it possible that she wants something different with you? And maybe she is apprehensive, or unsure, about how to go about it?"

"I've no idea." Nick leaned his elbows into his knees.

"You have also admitted truths to her, haven't you? That you've cheated."

Nick nodded.

"Do you think that is getting in the way of her judgment of you? Of how she acts with you?"

"I don't know. She is constantly changing her approach, so I really don't know."

"Maybe you are both placing too much emphasis on the truths that you have shared, maybe it is souring things for both of you. Isn't it interesting, how two people felt so immediately comfortable to share with each other? And yet you are possibly both faulting each other for doing so. It's a bit of a Catch-22. Have you tried just *being* with her? Putting aside the clandestine sex for a moment, and just spending time with her?"

Nick's lips parted slightly. He breathed in and out until his tongue became dry and he closed his lips. "Not really. Once."

"And what was it like? That time?"

"A lot of fun."

Sundeep nodded with a straight face.

"If she had at any moment—sporadically or consistently or what have you—felt safe to reveal parts of herself to you, it certainly says something. And if she suddenly shuts down, as you say, then I wonder if there is a reason that, in that moment, she no longer feels safe," Sundeep said.

Nick suddenly envisioned Margherita sitting at the bar at Frenchette, laughing. He smiled to himself.

"What?" Sundeep asked.

"Nothing," Nick said, and he shook it off.

NEW YORK, NEW YORK

2019

Margherita: (Sends a song)

Nick: Hello

Nick: How are you?

Margherita: Good!

Nick: Tell me more.

Margherita: Just kicked some ass at boot camp. Feels so good.

Nick: Yes. Well done.

Margherita: Are you still at work?

Nick: Yes.

Margherita: I have always had an office fantasy. Shall I show up one day for an interview? Do you have a good stairwell?

HE GRIPPED HIMSELF hard under his desk. Feelings of eroticism invaded.

Nick: Multiple stairwells.

Margherita: By the way there is a Leon Bridges concert next month. Just learned. Jump on it.

Nick: Ohhh, fantastic. Will do. Thank you for the head's up.

Margherita: Okay heading home to shower and bask in my fantasies for an hour or two

Nick: That's a lot of time in a stairwell

Margherita: Well…it could evolve…

Nick: I am on my way to a meeting or I would gladly schedule a last minute interview

Margherita: That's okay. How's the second round of investment going? Any potential takers?

Nick: It's going…hopefully soon. I have a presentation this week actually.

Margherita: Oh that's great! Have you practiced?

Nick: Oh yes.

Margherita: Okay. Fingers crossed. You'll be smashing, I know it.

Nick: That's sweet. Thank you.

Margherita: (kiss emoji)

Nick: We have the most delightfully random conversations.

Margherita: I know :) I like it.

NEW YORK, NEW YORK

2019

SHE RUSHED OUT of the Lolato offices toward the elevator bank. She was late for her session with Jane. Yulia knew she had somewhere to be, but kept her prisoner at her desk, reviewing the Aspen renovation, centimeter by centimeter. Her boss had been on the phone with Alexandre when Margherita arrived at her door for their scheduled meeting. Yulia had put the call on speaker, then motioned for Margherita to sit down and close the door behind her.

"Alex—escusez moi, Marghe just stepped in," Yulia said with a false smile, her eyes alight. Margherita internally rolled her eyes. She knew Alexandre hated to be called Alex. She often detected that Yulia was trying to make her jealous, only she clearly didn't see that Margherita did not care. Besides which, Alexandre would always be a little in love with Margherita; she had him in her palm whenever she wanted.

"Ah, ciao Marghe. We were just finishing up. So I will see both of you in a few weeks at the Prince Street soirée," he said through the speakerphone.

"Oui. And we have agreed to do the private dinner the evening before, yes?" Yulia asked.

"Yes. Marghe, will you be joining us? It will be an intimate dinner. Only forty people," Alexandre said.

Margherita looked at Yulia. It was the first she'd heard of the dinner. She thought the event was only one evening, an aperitivo with about three hundred invites to celebrate the opening.

"Oh, Alex, I do not think there is room. The dinner is already set. I am sorry Marghe." Yulia looked at her with falsified pity and regret. Margherita pursed her lips.

Stronza, she thought.

"Ah, what a shame. Okay. Next time. Aspen. I'll let you ladies get to your meeting. A bientot," Alexandre said, and hung up.

"Sorry, Margherita. I just thought.... it would be better this way," Yulia said, the corners of her eyes creased in feigned apology . "The last dinner was a bit...awkward for some of our guests, with you being there. You understand, of course."

Yulia turned her attention towards her laptop screen. "Just finishing this email, and we can get started."

"I don't, actually. Understand," Margherita said.

Yulia looked up, surprised. "Well, I think your past precedes you, don't you agree? We can't jeopardize our relationships quite like you can."

"Excuse me?" Margherita challenged her as politely as possible.

Yulia sighed expressively. "Was it not you at the bar at Frenchette with Beck after the Xiolitti launch party? Or during it, rather. How *do* you do it?"

"Do what?" Margherita stiffened.

"Well, the evening was not over, and yet Beck dashed out to your rescue. You don't think that's a tad inappropriate? Why would Beck be sitting knee to knee with you at an empty bar?"

Margherita clenched her jaw and didn't say a word.

"Or might you have had drank too much- oh darling do you even remember?" Yulia laughed. "I'll let it slide this time, but that kind of behavior is not acceptable here. It might have flown in Italy, but this is New York. Let's start this meeting, shall we? I have an appointment with my dermatologist soon and I cannot be late."

Margherita's teeth clenched firmly. She wanted to get up and storm out. She bit the inside of her cheeks and regarded Yulia with narrow, slitted eyes for the rest of the meeting, ready to explode.

NEW YORK, NEW YORK

2019

"WHAT ARE THE reasons that you stayed in New York this time?"

Margherita contemplated the question. Really, she was not entirely sure what the answer was.

"Well, it was a good job offer," she said, nebulously.

Jane sat there, watching her, waiting in that way she did.

"I have health insurance now. I am closer to my dad," Margherita listed. "It would have made my mom happy, I think."

"If you had stayed in Italy, what would you have given up?" Jane asked.

"Um. Health insurance," Margherita said. She smiled, trying to lighten the mood.

"So what did you give up by moving here?"

Everything, she thought.

"My friends. My network. Constant beauty and inspiration. Constant culture and travel. Newness. Discovery. People who I felt connected to. My routine that I loved. My places. Great food. Happiness. Appreciation for the little things."

She paused a moment and then continued. "Patience.

Fulfillment. Relationships with meaning and longevity. Feeling like I belonged somewhere. Finally. Feeling happy."

She felt she could go on but she stopped. What was the point, really. She didn't live there anymore. She wasn't sure where Jane was leading.

"Can you find these things here? Can you find contentment and fulfillment and discovery and newness here? Or do you think you are blocking yourself?" Jane asked.

She was suddenly tired. *It's so much easier for everyone else. Why is it always so much easier for everyone else,* she thought.

"I don't know. I just feel alone here. I can be okay for a few hours. I can fill my time with exercise and a date, and I can flirt for a few hours and laugh and enjoy myself. I am really trying with Derek. He's really great. There's nothing wrong with him. But it all feels so shallow here, like I'm floating on top of it or something. In Italy, it was deeper. I know that sounds weird, but I was really, genuinely happy. It just worked." She picked at her cuticle unknowingly. It suddenly stung and she stopped, rubbed it and slid it between her thighs.

"And being closer to your dad doesn't make you feel more connected," Jane said.

"I feel like a horrible person saying this, but it makes me more anxious and stressed and heavy-feeling. I feel heavier." *And it's so hard to see him without her,* she thought.

"How is your dad?"

"He's fine, I think. Quiet. Lonely, probably." She felt a gaping hole in the back of her throat.

"So the biggest reason you came back was for him? To be near him? So he wouldn't be so alone?"

"Well, of course. He's my dad. He would do anything for

me. But he's still…alone, and it breaks my heart to see him that way. I don't know what was worse—seeing him pretend to not be worried or stressed about her, or seeing him sit down to the breakfast table by himself, turn on the news by himself, make coffee for one, not really sure what to do with his Saturday." Tears burned in the backs of her eyes.

Once outside, she felt a surging guilt for the things she had said about her dad; she would never want him to know how unhappy she felt about living in New York again, and that she yearned to return to Italy even if it meant leaving him. She could not decipher how much the weight of her sadness had to do with her mom and how much of it was due to leaving the life that she had made for herself.

She felt that she should call her dad, to alleviate the guilt of the moment, but the noise of passersby, trucks unloading and men laying pavement distracted her. She was rattled by the sirens and honking cars. It occurred to her that the person with whom she actually wanted to speak was her mom. Her mom would have complained about the background noise. She would have asked about work and inquired about Derek. She would have been so happy that Margherita was dating a New Yorker. Margherita might have asked her mom if she wanted to go to the ballet soon, they would have both decided to check the programming for the next month. They would have texted back and forth about it for a few days until they would finally cave and buy the exorbitantly priced tickets.

But she couldn't. She couldn't call her mom.

She walked down Fifth Avenue towards Washington Square Park, wary of the strain in her throat. She tried not to cry in the street in broad daylight. She ached to go for a run, to run hard and fast and swiftly, to unravel herself from everyone and everything for an hour. She checked the weather: chance of rain later in the evening, so she had a few clear hours.

At home, Margherita quickly changed her clothes. She ran over the Brooklyn Bridge and crossed Tribeca on Chambers Street, filled with construction trucks and dust. She felt men watch her as she jogged past, their eyes burning into her, their wicked smiles. It disgusted and angered her, and she felt ready to snap.

At the fourth mile she stopped to walk for a minute and looked down at her phone. Not a peep from Nicky in weeks. She wanted to scream—at him, but mostly at herself for letting it happen all over again.

At the fifth mile, the storm clouds rolled in earlier than expected. She was on her way back up Battery Park City Promenade. She ran faster to get back to the A train on Church and Warren before the skies opened.

The clouds unleashed their wrath, and it started to pour. She heard thunder coming from the West Village, and she felt her sneakers slip on the ground. Her ponytail whiplashed blots of rain water in her face. She swatted her eyes with windshield wiper motions.

She found an awning at one of the rental buildings in Battery Park North and stood there, breathless, dripping. Her sneakers were soaked, her feet in puddles inside her socks. It was such odd weather for that time of year. After fifteen minutes the rain began to slow, and chilled to the bone, she stepped out from under the awning and walked at a brisk pace toward the subway. She was scared to run in case she slipped.

At home, she disrobed, threw her soaked clothes in a plastic bag, and jumped into a steaming shower. The heat mixed with the cold temperature of her skin. But the run hadn't relieved her nerves.

She texted Nick on her way to dinner that evening with Derek, her willpower evidently washed away in the storm.

Margherita: I can't concentrate today.

Nick: Hello
Nick: What would you like to concentrate on

Margherita: mmm…the best kind of activity for a thunderstorm

Nick: mmm yes. me too

Margherita: Is Nicky going to come out to play ever again or should I keep my daydreams to myself?

Nick: Nicky was just now thinking of where
Nick: I wish there was a place

Margherita: Are you recently homeless

Doesn't he want sex? I am giving it to him on a platter, she thought.

Nick: No

Margherita: Or have you moved in with your girlfriend

I don't even want to know, she thought.

Nick: Neither

Nick: No change

Margherita: So

Nick: A different place

Margherita: What are you hiding

Nick: Nothing at all
Nick: A different place appeals tho

Margherita: mmm okay. Well. I'm meeting a friend in Nolita tonight. so if nicky is around after and feeling friendly...let me know :)

Nick: Did you know
Nick: today is national orgasm day
Nick: (yes it's a thing)

Margherita: do I even want to know how you know this

Nick: just googled it to confirm

Margherita: Who. Just who. googles National Orgasm Day
Margherita: You are strange
Margherita: So what you are saying is you're not free tonight
Margherita: But sharing this vital news
Margherita: Cool

Nick: A friend told me, so I fact checked
Nick: I mean...
Nick: I wish we had a space
Nick: to shelter from the storms

Margherita: You are making excuses
Margherita: I don't get why

This is so fucking frustrating, she thought.

Nick: No
Nick: I'm not
Nick: I would like

Margherita: You have an apartment
Margherita: So do I
Margherita: But okay

Nick: Your apartment then
Nick: I keep on writing
Nick: What I plan to do with you
Nick: But then deleting it

Margherita: How come
Margherita: Why suddenly so shy Nicholas

Nick: Where do you live

Margherita: Is that how you're going to make your decision?

Nick: I want you to be very direct with me
Nick: I'm in that mood

Margherita: I am…I'm always very direct ;)

Nick: Ne-ver

Margherita: Always
Margherita: I just change direction periodically

Nick: Sure
Nick: And in this direction

Margherita: I want you. Tonight.

Nick: Hmm yes.

Margherita: Okay yes you'll give me what I want?

Nick: What exactly do you want to do with me

Margherita: Nicky

Nick: Hiya

Margherita: You are being a pain

Nick: I want to picture it
Nick: Is that so bad

Margherita: I would like to know if I'm going to see you
Margherita: I'm not going to say another word unless you tell me

Nick: ooh ultimatum. on a day like today

Margherita: yes

Nick: gosh
Nick: so strict

Margherita: I am really at the edge

Nick: Okay

Margherita: So can you stop being a royal pain in the ass. Yes or no.

Nick: Likely
Nick: what time
Nick: I need to play by ear

Margherita: idk like 10. Why

Nick: Cos

Margherita: Why
Margherita: You're being really annoying

Nick: I'm not

Margherita: K whatever

Margherita: This game isn't fun ps

Nick: Genuinely not trying to play games

Nick: Just not able to commit this minute

She was standing outside the restaurant as she texted Nick, delaying going inside. She wasn't hungry for food; she needed a release. She needed to see him; she just needed it.

After dinner, she kissed Derek goodnight at the corner of Mott and Prince Streets.

"I think you're the first guy I've dated who still has a bedtime," she said sweetly.

He rolled his eyes. "It's not like it's official. It's a goal."

"I know! Don't worry. I'm all for eating early. Buonanotte handsome," she said, and she walked south as he walked north.

Margherita: What does your ear say?

He read the message but didn't respond.

Frustrated, disappointed, slightly angry. They were familiar emotions.

She felt outside of herself as her Uber headed down an empty Broadway. She watched the tall buildings of Lower Manhattan loom closer, and she thought, *How long am I going to let this last? When do I fall for someone who wants me back? When does that happen?*

She argued with herself that the sex was great, so she should at least take advantage of it, but could she? Could she separate it? Could she disengage? She felt numb.

He always said it was in her control. Bullshit. It was never in her control. Never once had it felt that way.

Such a sickness, wanting.

Margherita: is that a no

Nick: Hello

Nick: :(

Nick: I think it is

Nick: I can't

Nick: Im useless I know

Margherita: Yes. we agree on something

Margherita: This is such bs isn't it

Nick: !

Nick: Don't be angry at me

Margherita: No fun at all

Margherita: You know what

Nick: yes

Margherita looked down at her phone and wanted to scream at it and throw it out the window. She wanted to tell him everything, and then she wanted to tell him nothing. She wanted to tell him off, but she didn't want to be too emotional. What for.

How many times did she receive a message from Paolo in Milan—*Non riesco*—after hours in limbo. How many times was she disappointed by that last minute news, as if it didn't matter to him one way or the other.

Margherita: I've had such a shit week already and if you were in front of me, I think I would boil over with all the things I'd like to say

Margherita: So im not going to say anything

She got out of the Uber in front of her building and lingered. The street was quiet and she felt robotic. They were both typing and stopping, typing and stopping. She suspected he wanted to say something about her being mad, that it wasn't a big deal. She continued to type a long message.

Margherita: Except that I don't like your selfish head games and your cryptic personality and I am not the one playing with someone here and its just dumb and a waste of time and I'm over it. Not because you can't meet up tonight but because it's your schedule always and you disappear when it suits you and reappear when you're bored. And I don't know anything about you because I don't get to because that's not what I'm here for. It's so incredibly one sided and immature and cliche and I have been here before and I know how it goes. And I'm just so fucking over it. You make yourself so vague so that you can always somehow get your way. I keep thinking ok whatever I want what I want too, but it's STILL one sided
Margherita: I am too smart for this shit
Margherita: Goodnight

She unlocked the door to her apartment as he began to type something. She threw her phone down on her chair. She didn't care anymore. She washed her hands, put on her pjs, and picked up her phone again. Maybe that's what she needed to do—get angry enough at him to turn him off once and for all. She needed him to end it. She knew herself—if she ended it, she would never stick to her word.

Nick: What's your address

Was he serious? Suddenly he was willing and able? After she said all that? She didn't understand. She didn't understand at all.

Nick: you're projecting so much, not sure where to even start. You assume this is every past experience you've had. It's not.

Margherita: Hardly
Margherita: But it is an absolutely pointless thing to argue over

Nick: I have to be more careful than you do.

Margherita: Okay. You do that—Be careful. I don't care anymore. You can surely find whatever it is you're doing here with someone dumb enough to put up with it

Nick: You're being excessively dramatic tonight.
Nick: put up with it?
Nick: my gf is in town
Nick: and I'm not of the habit of disappearing
Nick: you assume its mind games.

Margherita: because you don't tell me anything. you just go vague or silent

Nick: whats your address
Nick: I don't mean to

Margherita: And I'm left guessing
Margherita: Im so sick of it

Nick: I'm sorry. That's not my intention.

Margherita: whatever

Nick: I literally worked out this evening
Nick: and am working

Margherita: I don't care Nicky its not about tonight its really not

Nick: Can you pick a side. You keep switching on me.
Nick: you've done this 7 times now?!
Nick: I ask for your address thinking I would put my clothes on and get in an uber and we would just enjoy ourselves
Nick: But you start slashing at me for shit I really don't understand
Nick: I'm not overthinking this or trying to play with you
Nick: but if you're not interested then okay

She hated it. At that moment, she hated it so much. She felt misunderstood. She knew she was coming across as slightly crazed and that was not what she wanted. She wanted him to see her as worthy of making a plan. She had told him from the beginning that she was game as long as he didn't call her only when his girlfriend was out of town. She didn't want to be treated with such a flippant attitude.

Margherita: I feel like you enjoy the drama
Nick: Hardly
Nick: I could say the same of you
Nick: I do not enjoy it

Nick: I do not turn on you

Nick: I'm consistent

Nick: You turn on me

Nick: And twist this into some sort of game

Margherita: you are consistent in making me feel cheap

Nick: You cannot go into this and say "I'm game"

Nick: and then have all these expectations

Nick: when did I set expectations?

Nick: I didn't

Margherita: You are as vague as can be

Nick: yes

Nick: because I can't commit sometimes

Nick: I don't want to be having this conversation

Nick: I either want to be diving in between your legs

Nick: or

Nick: not

Margherita: then why did you say no

Nick: because I couldn't commit right then

Nick: I'm operating on hour by hour context

She was exhausted by it all, but she decided that she wanted the release, and nothing could dissuade her from that.

Margherita: So what now

Margherita: Are you coming over or am i making a tea and going to sleep

Margherita: would love to know

Nick: May i?

Nick: We have 48 minutes left of national orgasm day

Margherita: ha

Margherita: fine lets make the most of it

Nick: putting clothes on

Margherita: k

Nick: 14 minutes away

By the time he reached her apartment, her nerves had muted her stormy frustration and annoyance and she felt instead shy and nervous. She was self conscious that perhaps she had become too emotional, that she had gone overboard in her angry texts. She masked it as best as she could and sat at the edge of her bed as he checked out the kitchen, only a few steps from the door. The apartment was so small that he had few other places to go except to stand in front of her. He cupped his hands around her face and kissed her softly and slowly, the way that made her heart beat twice as fast, made her aware of each millisecond. It was like being in slow motion in the best possible way. It made her think she could hear the whoosh of blood in her veins, made her want to give up control entirely, let go, and let him guide her at his speed.

Her hands ran over the crescent of his shoulders; she squeezed them, but he held his steady pace, forcing her to slow down. She felt a tingle in her tummy, in her thighs, in the space between. He leaned her backwards onto the bed, his hands on the underside of her legs, lifting her calves upward in the air. He shifted on top of her, gently kissing her still, his hand running down her leg, so lightly and so slowly.

He looked into her eyes. They were so blue, his eyes. His blonde hair was shorter. He had the upper hand, always. In that moment, with her heart beating so fast, and his motions so slow, it was so clear, as to who stood where.

Her hands gripped his back as he kissed her neck. "Aren't you boiling in this sweater? It's so hot," she said, breaking the moment ever so slightly—to keep it light, to keep it nonchalant, or to calm her nerves, she was not sure.

He kissed her on the mouth. He was so quiet, and he looked a little tired. She felt a large hole in the soft navy sweater, just under his left arm. She smiled.

"Ah, that's how you stay cool!" She pulled it off. His chest was tan and his skin was soft, his form was flawless. She ran her thumb down the slope of his shoulder to his chest, like running downhill.

It was all nerve endings, until she suddenly thought about the moment that he would leave. He would go home, back to his life, back to thinking about his girlfriend, to waking up and making plans with her. His girlfriend.

She was lost in the thought as he slid off her silk pajama shorts, as he gently pulled the strap of her pink silk top off her shoulder, as he kissed her nipple. She looked down at the top of his head, his soft blonde hair. Why was he torturing her, playing with her, making her second-guess his intentions?

She rose, naked, and poured two glasses of water in the kitchen. He leaned into a pillow and she laid next to him, on her stomach, always slightly unsure what she should do or how she should act; she didn't want him to think that she thought it was more than it was. She didn't want to ask too many personal questions, to make him think that she cared too much.

"How long have you lived here?" he asked.

"Too long."

"Do you like it?"

"It's fine. I don't spend that much time here."

He looked around, toward her framed photographs on the walls—a market scene in Brussels and a rocky beach on the Ligurian coast.

"How's your dad?" he asked.

"He's good."

She could see the circles under his eyes. "You tired?" She asked.

"Mm hmm. I swam tonight."

"You swim?"

"Yeah."

"Where?"

"The local." He brushed his thumb along her forehead. She loved when he did that, but she wished he wouldn't; it made her hopeful.

Margherita picked up her phone and scrolled through her Spotify. "This is a funny one." She turned up the volume on "Lime and the Coconut." Nick started to mimic the deep voice, always ready to play along, always ready to sing and perform. He tapped her butt, one cheek and then the other.

She played another she thought he might like, and he shared a few songs with her as well. They moved onto Elton John, and then to his performance at Princess Diana's funeral. Nick held the phone as they lay on their stomachs watching it. Margherita felt tears in her eyes. Her hands rested on his forearm as he continued to hold the screen for her. The emotions of the day hit her.

"Oh, I can't watch it, it's too sad," she rolled onto her back and faced the ceiling.

At Francine's funeral, Margherita had held her fingers limp in her lap. She wore an awful black wool dress; it had taken so dreadfully long to pull on her tights. She couldn't stop crying and the muscles in her arms seemed to have stopped working. She remembered all of this, but especially her fingers in her lap; the memory was so vivid at that moment as she lay in bed with Nick. She had been thinking, during the funeral, about her mom's hands, remembering them. Francine's hands were so delicate; her wrists so small. Tommaso used to hold them and admire them. Laying next to Nick, she suddenly couldn't visualize her moms wrists, and she felt sick to her stomach. She held her hands up in front of her face.

Margherita remembered, as she was getting ready for the funeral, picking up the serpent ring, wanting to wear it but not having the energy to put it on. She remembered how old and fragile Tommaso looked. Francine's wrists.

"But it's so beautiful, isn't it? Fucking beautiful as hell." Nick turned off the video.

She held her eyes shut to stop the tears from coming. They would arrive so suddenly, without much warning, triggered so easily. She sat up to get more water so that he wouldn't see.

When she returned to the bed they traded a few more songs. "Sparring Partner" by Paolo Conte, and "Cheer Up, My Brother" by HNNY, "Coming Home" by Leon Bridges, and "Bless the Telephone" by Labi Siffre. "Cucurucu" by Nick Mulvey.

"I should go home." But he didn't. They passed an hour listening to music and chatting about random things.

"Okay I have three questions for you. Can I just ask you these?"

He was wary, she could tell.

I have so many questions, actually, she thought.

"Where does your girlfriend live?"

"Here."

"So why do you say, She's in town? Of course she's in town; she lives here."

"Well, sometimes she goes out of town."

"Okay, but you make it sound like she doesn't live here."

"She does, sorry." He was suddenly quiet. "What are the other two questions?"

"Oh," Margherita said, looking at the ceiling. "I don't have any others. Just that."

He turned his head to face her, and she glanced at him, then looked away.

She put on "Boa Sorte," one of her favourite songs, and she was amazed to learn that he knew it. He sang along immediately, skipping ahead and singing the chorus before it came. How did he know it?

She put on her pajamas and went to brush her teeth, wandering out into the room to discover him in her kitchen peeking into her fridge.

"You can tell so much about someone by what they have in their fridge," he said with raised eyebrows.

"Are you judging my spaces?"

He went into the bathroom to pee, shutting the door.

"Hey—you can't shut someone out of the bathroom mid-tooth brush!"

He came back out, sat at the edge of the bed, and gave her an eye roll as she passed him to spit out the toothpaste. She returned to where he sat and stood in front of him. She felt silly, now that he had gotten what he came for.

"I cut my hair too short." He touched the smooth sides of his head.

"You cut your hair?"

"Yeah but it's so short."

"Oh, I like it," she said, touching the sides, soft as a baby's head. "And now you're ready for the Army."

He rolled his eyes and laughed, grabbing her wrists.

Francine's wrists. What did they look like? She couldn't see them anymore.

"Yes. I'm ready to be screamed at," he said.

"They don't always scream at you in the Army," she said, trying not to think about her mom.

"No, that's you. You do that."

"I don't scream at you."

"Scream in text, you do."

"Nooo..."

I'm not crazy. God, I wish I could explain this to you, she thought.

He stood up and put on his clothes. She lay down at the edge of the bed, her head on the pillow, and watched him get dressed.

"I have to wake up in four hours," she moaned. It didn't occur to her to ask if he wanted to stay, knowing that he probably wouldn't, anyway.

"I'm going to call an Uber and go to sleep too."

He buttoned the last button on his jeans and nestled in next to her, leaning back on the pillows and looking at her sleepy face. He leaned in to kiss her on the mouth, then on the forehead, then on the mouth again, gently.

"You smell good," he whispered.

"I do?"

"Three minutes away," he said as he looked at his phone, tracking the Uber. He appeared tired, a little melancholy, she thought, but she wasn't sure. She wondered what was going on in his life, what was going well and what was not, what was he stressed about and what made him anxious. She wished he would tell her, but he wouldn't.

He moved to the floor and put on his shoes. She sat at the edge of the bed, cross legged, watching him. She was not sure what it was about him that seemed to extract so many pieces of her at once, only to let them fall one by one to the ground…he never lifted a hand to attempt to rescue them.

He stood up, making sure the laces were tied tightly.

He gave her a kiss and left. She sent him two more songs, and he read the message but didn't respond.

NEW YORK, NEW YORK

2019

Margherita: I don't get it. If he just wants easy sex, surely he can find it elsewhere, with someone less complicated than me. Someone who gives him less strife.

Chiara: It's the endorphin hit from the intrigue and the flirtation. That's what keeps him going. Same as it is for you- only you expect more in the aftermath, and he doesn't.

BUT WHEN DOES he get bored? she wondered.

Margherita: Yeah. That makes sense.

Chiara: Get off the Nicky rollercoaster now. Before you go round and round again and miss other things.

Margherita: Surely it's better than the Paolo rollercoaster…at least there is a chance he will break up with his girlfriend. It's not like he's married with kids.

Chiara: Cara if he was going to break up with his girlfriend, he would have already

Chiara: The only 'at least' here is that you're not paying for hotel rooms again

Margherita: Well...I've thought about it...

Chiara: NO!

Chiara: What happened to Derek?!

Margherita inhaled and shrugged her shoulders to herself.

Chiara: I'm going to sleep...it's really late here. But NO. MORE. NICKY.

NEW YORK, NEW YORK

2019

DEREK EXITED THE bathroom and watched Margherita flirtatiously laugh with an older gentleman seated next to her at the bar. Her hair cascaded in waves and she let it dip in front of one of her eyes, ever so slightly without pushing it away. The man was clearly entranced. He had been eyeing her and evidently waiting for her age-appropriate boyfriend to exit the scene long enough to swoop in…him with his custom shirt, his fifty thousand dollar watch, and his Italian shoes. Margherita was clearly enjoying it.

"I love to flirt," she had once nonchalantly admitted, as if she was declaring a love of something as innocent as blueberries. She had shrugged her shoulders at him and changed the subject. It wasn't a confession; it was a part of who she was, and he would have to get used to it if he wanted to stick around.

He walked toward them in no big rush and placed his hand on the middle of her back.

"Derek, this is Hannes. He was telling me how gorgeous the Swedish lakes are in the summer. He swears to me he owns one—a lake!—but I think he's being a boring bragger." Margherita smiled warmly, wrapping her hand around Derek's forearm, inviting them both into her game.

Hannes, so obviously Swedish, with blue eyes, straight blonde hair and very long legs, faced Margherita in his seat. Her bare, crossed legs angled towards him.

"I've heard beautiful things about the Swedish lakes," Derek inserted dully.

"Yes, they are worth visiting for maybe a week—no more—during the month of July. Then you start shooting each other with boredom."

Derek nodded with a pursed-lip smile.

"Oh, sounds rather exciting actually," Margherita said.

"Well, I'll let you two get back to your evening. Margherita, it was a pleasure. I will certainly take a look at your father's website. I am thinking of building a new flat in Stockholm."

"Yes! Please do. He would love to do a project in Stockholm," Margherita said with glee.

Hannes signed his check and smoothly stood, his long Swedish legs barely straightening before they met solid ground. Margherita gave him a 'Ciao' and turned her attention back toward Derek.

"So, what do you think—another drink?"

Derek checked his watch. Nine-thirty. He had a 5:30a.m. wake-up the next day and was already fading. Margherita challenged him with a hard stare, her head resting on her hand, her face tipped.

"I can't. Not on a school night."

"I know. I just love to hear you say 'school night'." Margherita teased.

She sighed internally and surveyed the rest of the bar. How very dull her date was.

They walked towards Derek's apartment, just a few blocks away. He held her hand and she let him, although she was aware of it the whole time, like a bandaid that flapped in the wind.

"Do you want to sleepover?" he asked.

"I don't have anything with me."

"You don't need anything..." He pulled her towards him, his hands firmly on her hips, and kissed her on the mouth.

"You go to sleep. I'm going to go home and get back to my book," she said, her voice an octave higher than it had been at the bar.

He gave her a firm kiss, a bit *too* firm for Margherita's liking, and she pulled away gently.

"Buonanotte..." she said quietly as she walked away towards Bowery.

After a block, she took out her phone.

Margherita: Hi

Nick: Hello

Margherita typed and stopped.

Nick: Haven't heard from you in a while.

Again, Margherita typed. Stopped.

Nick: How are you?

Margherita: Good.

Nick: Where are you?

Margherita: Not far from you.

Nick: Oh. Alone, not far from me?

Margherita: Oui

Nick: Come over.

Nick: If you want.

Nick: I'm just reading. We can have a tea.

Margherita typed. Stopped.

Nick: I'd like to see you.

Margherita: Hmm

Nick: You don't have to of course.

Margherita: I know I don't have to.

Nick: Okay. Well

Nick: I'm here.

Margherita: Just for a tea.

Margherita reached the top level of the building. She climbed the final steps slowly. With each one, she felt herself slowing down. What was she doing? And why? What did she get out of it, really? Wouldn't he know by now if he wanted to be with her? Wouldn't they have passed the exploring phase and have made a decision? He wanted to "explore this thing with her." Vague. He was always so vague. Francine would have rolled her eyes. She would have said, *I told you so.* Her mother loved to point out Margherita's romantic blunders.

Nick stood in the doorway and held the door open. She stopped a foot in front of him and they stood there, facing each other. He gave her his irritatingly charming closed lip-smile.

"Ciao," Margherita said.

"Ciao," he replied. She took a step toward him, her lips inches from his. Nick put his hand behind her head and kissed her slowly and gently. He looked into her eyes, that closed lip smile again, and she looked down at the floor. He kissed her forehead, breathed in her rose shampoo, and she stepped passed him into the loft.

On his bed, she kneeled with her calves beneath her, facing the headboard. Laying next to her, he played with her hand as if it were a metronome.

"You know what?" she asked, suddenly gripping his palm. His eyes enlarged, playfully dramatic.

"What?" he said, returning the pressure.

"You know what I wish?"

He watched her, waiting.

"I wish you would say no to me," she declared, with a hint of playfulness.

"Why?" He questioned, searching for eye contact.

She loosened her hand from his grasp and looked down at his chest, running her finger in figure eights.

He took her hand in his. "Why?" he asked again.

"I just wish you would, sometimes. Just end it."

"Do you?" he asked. His eyes tried to penetrate her, but she wouldn't return his gaze. She looked at his face, or his mouth instead.

"I don't know."

"I'm not going to do that. You can do that," he said.

"I don't trust myself," she admitted.

"I know." He watched her. He watched her eyes wander over his chest, to her knees. She wouldn't look at him.

NEW YORK, NEW YORK

2019

"I CAN COME with you?" Derek suggested. "We can have a romantic weekend in Carnegie Hill…" he trailed off.

Margherita eyed him over her espresso cup.

"Come on. You can take me to your book shop. We can go for a run in the park. I'll cook?"

She placed the espresso cup in the sink and ran water over it.

"No…It's so very quiet up there. You'd be bored in seconds. And my dad has probably left the apartment a mess. He's not very tidy." *Anymore*, she thought.

The truth was she did not want Derek in her family's space, where Francine had lived. It felt like an intrusion.

"I don't care."

"You freak out if a piece of mail on your counter is facing downwards," Margherita said.

"Stop. I can handle it. We never go to your apartment, and I just thought—"

"—because my apartment is the size of your bathroom," she interrupted, as she reached for her bag.

"I just…I don't know. I want to hang out with you."

She wrapped her arms around his back and tipped her

face up toward him.

"Amore it's a few days. We'll have a romantic Il Buco dinner next week when my dad gets back. I'll send you photos of me and the pooch. I'm not leaving the planet."

He wrapped her face in his palms and looked into her eyes.

"You're a very different type of girlfriend."

What does that mean? she thought.

"Interesting. Okay. Have fun at b-ball today. I'll call you later," she said, and she left before he could say anything else.

On the subway uptown, she toyed with a daydream in which Nicky came to her parents' Carnegie Hill townhouse to stay with her for a few nights—just the two of them, with the dog, a few good movies, and morning laps in the park.

Then she caught herself thinking that it wasn't really her parents' townhouse anymore. It was her dad's. She swallowed back a hollow-throat tear.

NEW YORK, NEW YORK

2019

THEY SAT ON bar stools at his kitchen island with two cups of tea, swinging their legs towards each other like two kids on the swings. "Me and Magdalena" by the Monkees played on her iPhone.

"I meant what I said, you know," she said apprehensively.

"Which?" he asked.

"About ending it."

He stopped swinging his legs.

"If that's what you want," he said, somewhat straight-faced.

Margherita leaned her elbow on the counter and pulled at her earlobe.

He snagged her hand down to stop her from fidgeting.

She looked down at her finger and spun her grand-mother's serpent ring around. She didn't know the emeralds and diamonds were real until after her grandmother died.

"You always twist it around. Forget about what I want. What do you want?" she asked.

He placed his hand gently underneath her palm and held his thumb over the ring. She didn't look up.

"What's the story with this ring? You wear it everyday."

She didn't look up. *How would you know?* she thought.

He put his thumb on her bottom lip and his other hand at the nape of her neck. He pulled her toward him and kissed her gently, pulling his thumb ever so slowly down her bottom lip.

She wanted that, that right there, that feeling. But a thousand other feelings rose from her chest too. They swam to her warm cheeks, and she could feel them at her temples, and then a few at the tip of her nose. She wanted it so badly, more of it, but then she also wanted it to stop. She felt infuriatingly stuck in it.

She heard Alexandre somewhere over the noise in her temples. "You can't run on highs your whole life," he had said, his elbows on the marble bar, a glass of red wine in front of him, eyes tired from fourteen hour days.

Nick took her hand and led her into the bedroom. They had sex and afterwards lay next to each other chatting about random things. He asked about her dad, who she often mentioned. He asked about her boss, and what she was working on at the office. She picked a book up from his bedside table and read the back cover. She told him about what she was reading. He picked up her hand and fingered the ring.

"It was my grandmother's," she said quietly.

He looked up into her eyes. "On your dad's side?"

"No."

"Your mum's."

"Oui."

"You never talk about her," he said, watching her carefully.

Margherita sat silently, eyeing the ring.

She inhaled. "She died," she said, quietly, almost a whisper.

Nick inhaled and his entire face expressed pity. He searched for her eyes, but she wouldn't look up. "When?"

"Before I moved back."

"Oh Marghe, I'm really sorry. I had no idea." He held her hand in his.

Margherita shook her head in a small way, as if to dismiss it or wash it away. "She was ill."

"With what? If you don't mind my asking. Cancer?"

Margherita shook her head, just barely.

"No?" Nick rubbed the top of her hand with his thumb.

Margherita swallowed. The grief therapist at the hospital had taught her to swallow purposefully when she felt a powerful wave coming on. Breathe, yes, everyone always focused on breathing, but few people taught the importance of swallowing.

"She was bi-polar. Was having a really rough time of it the past few years. She overdosed. Died in her sleep."

Nick wrapped his arms around her and squeezed her into his warm body, kissing the top of her head and stroking her back and her hair.

"That's why you came back, isn't it?" He asked her, when she gently pulled away.

Margherita bit the inside of her cheek.

"Anyway, life is unfair. My mom was a tough cookie. She worked really hard. Fooled a lot of people. Do you have any chocolate?" She swallowed her tears and sat up, her eyes wide, trying, pitifully, not to cry.

Nick watched her, his face saying nothing, probably unsure what to say or do. He slowly sat up and kissed her forehead.

"I think I just might." He held out his hand. "Come," he said gently.

He took her hand and led her to the kitchen. His back was to her as he opened the fridge to retrieve Callie's bar of chocolate.

Margherita inhaled the hollow in her throat and shook a tear away. She clenched her eyes shut and opened them again, wishing she hadn't said a word. He would regard her differently now.

Nick sat on a stool next to her, the chocolate on the island, it's aluminum foil messily peeled back.

He reached for her hand. "You're a tough cookie, too," he said.

She pursed her lips. Truthfully she had no appetite for the chocolate, but she ate it anyway, wanting desperately to cry.

NEW YORK, NEW YORK

2019

SHE LOOKED AT her father at the kitchen table, still such a handsome man, widowed at the age of sixty-six. She wished her parents had had another child, so that he had more family around him—more support than just Margherita.

"Where is your new ragazzo tonight?" Tommaso asked her.

"He's on a work trip."

"Ah." Tommaso watched his daughter unpack the groceries she had brought from the farmers market. "You look so beautiful."

She looked up at him and rolled her eyes. She was in yoga pants with dirty hair and no make up.

"Grazie Marghe. This was a big help. Ah, you got the good muffin. That Vegan thing you bought last time was awful. Just awful. Thank you. What are your plans this evening? Isn't Benjamin in town?" he asked, putting the eggs in the fridge.

"I'm not sure," she said, internally shaking her head that her brother had not even mentioned his being in New York.

"Why don't you call him? Maybe you can go out together."

But Margherita felt like being alone. She didn't want to be with her brother that evening; his presence only reminded her of Francine. After all, it was the only thing that ever connected them.

She would go home, get dolled up, take herself for a drink at Frenchette. At the very least she would chat with Paul, the bartender, and she would feel a lift in proximity to fabulous New Yorkers in a buzzy restaurant. Maybe it would quell her anxiousness.

At the bar, as she sipped her Americano cocktail. She glanced around without seeming obvious, and found that for the foreseeable future, or at least until the two couples on either side of her finished their meals (and they were only on second courses) she would be drinking solo. Derek was at a conference in Chicago. She had spoken to him briefly that morning when he woke up, and he had suggested that she join him for the weekend.

"We could make a few days of it. You've never been to Chicago. Why not?" he had said. She was not excited at the prospect.

"I made lunch plans with a girl I met at yoga this weekend," she had said.

"Oh come on, you can move that," he had replied. This annoyed her. "No, why should I move it? Those are the plans I made. I have to run—my dad is calling me." Then she had hung up. Why should she alter her schedule for him? Why didn't he just come back and then she wouldn't have to go to an airport and through the whole ordeal of traveling just to walk around a bunch of tall buildings in a city she had no interest in visiting? Besides which, it was such a rarity for her to have plans with a female; she was more excited about that than she would have been to visit Derek in Chicago.

A middle-aged couple took two seats to her right. The man remained standing while his wife sat down. She felt his gaze. She tried to ignore the reflection of it in the mirror behind the bar. He was short, bald, unattractive. His wife was heavily painted, heavily jeweled, and heavily Long Island-accented.

Margherita glanced down at her phone.

Margherita: I am feeling very antsy today. Tried to shake it. Can't.

She waited for a response, her pinky at an angle between her teeth. A woman at the other end of the bar was talking about her to her date, she could sense it. They were likely trying to figure out Margherita's story. Was she waiting for someone?

No, I'm not, she thought.

Was she alone? Hoping to meet someone? Here? Everyone was in twos.

What happened to having a cocktail at the bar, she thought, defending herself in her imaginary conversation.

The middle-aged couple suddenly made a big scene about moving farther down the bar. Margherita felt the uncomfortable attention of the bald man's eyes as he passed behind her.

"My wife is intimidated by you," he said, loudly. She gave him an uncomfortable look of disbelief and shot her eyes up to Paul behind the bar. They exchanged a glance that said, *Whoa*. Paul turned around, shaking his head and laughing.

"Where is the fine gentleman you met here a little while ago?" Paul asked her when he turned back around.

"Ah, he's traveling this week."

"Ah. How's it going?" he asked.

Margherita shrugged with a coquettish smile. Paul gave a laugh that was part snuffle.

"You are impossible."

She looked down at her WhatsApp again.

Margherita: Confession. I am dating someone.

Alexandre: Oui? You? I don't believe it.

Margherita: Yup.

Alexandre: Is it love?

Margherita: What's love anyways

Alexandre: Are you quoting Prince Charles or being serious

Margherita: Ha. I suppose he made a good point

Alexandre: Well? Is it love?

Margherita: He is in Chicago for a work trip. And I am relieved. So you tell me.

Margherita: Do you believe love needs distance?

Alexandre: Interesting question. Interesting that you write to me about this.

Alexandre: Did you miss me? Is that why you are writing.

Alexandre: I miss you.

Margherita: ...don't....

Alexandre: Okay. To answer your question. I think it is natural to crave mystery. Some need it more than others. Some do not need it at all. You, my darling, need it constantly.

Margherita: That doesn't entirely answer the question.

Alexandre: I think your love needs distance. The love you want, too.

Margherita: You mean people need distance from me?

Alexandre: You are very intense. When you're in it. You know that.

Margherita: Humph. But if it's not intense it's not exciting.

Alexandre: I know my darling
Alexandre: But it's not sustainable.

She sat staring at her phone, rereading the message. Without distance, there was no mystery. Without mystery, there was no intrigue. Without intrigue, she lost interest.

Is that why people cheated? Is that why Nick cheated with her—to disappear into the seas of infidelity and let the current take over for a while, to feel that rush, the ecstasy of the unknown? Were they running from the constraints of the quotidian, which could be so hum drumly monotonous and borderline depressing—or was there something else at play?

Leave work, have barely enough time for the routine that you've carved out, with the person who you have fit into this routine...repeat, repeat, repeat. Where was the *living* in that? The same, the same, the same. That sounded awful to her, terrified her to no end. But people did it. Until, one day, a little flag appeared somewhere in their vision, or maybe a tiny thread came loose, and they became curious...and they might pull at it gently, testing its foundation. They might tug a little harder, just a little harder—and then suddenly it might pull at them instead.

> **Nick:** I am too, antsy.
> **Nick:** Where are you?
> **Nick:** Shall we be antsy together?

Rush of blood to the head. Rapid heartbeat in sharp bursts, from her thighs to her head. It never seemed to quit with him, that high.

> **Margherita:** Oui, oui monsieur. We shall.
> **Nick:** I am waiting for my roommate to flounce off. Would you like to come over in a half hour or so?
> **Margherita:** C'est bon.

She paid her bill and freshened up in the bathroom. Her heart beat loudly in her chest. It had been almost a year that she had been fooling around with Nicky, but still, every time she knew she would see him, she was positively aflutter. Would this disappear, though, if it were part of her quotidian, if *he* were part of her quotidian? She wondered if he wondered the same thing.

NEW YORK, NEW YORK

2019

AFTERWARDS, SHE LAY on her stomach and he on his back, side by side. He stroked the sway of her back, the curve from her lower spine to the top of her butt cheek.

"Do you believe in monogamy?" she asked, quite randomly.

He didn't flounder. "Um, I do. Yeah. Do you?"

She shrugged, scrunched her eyebrows together for a moment, pondering. "I do, in that I do not believe in open relationships. But I don't know; I don't think it's very natural. I find it hard to believe that there is one person that fulfills, or satisfies *everything* in another person. So when something intriguing comes along once in a while..." she trailed off, not entirely sure where she was going.

He watched her.

"Is that what this is? Something intriguing?"

"No," she rolled her eyes. "Well, maybe. I don't know."

"Are we now entering a heady conversation? Can you give me a reprieve? I only just ejaculated moments ago."

"Let's ask the Judge. Judge?" She looked upwards at the ceiling. "No, not granted. Our apologies from the court."

He rolled his eyes and pushed her away playfully.

"Do you think your girlfriend has ever cheated on you?"

He pushed himself upwards on the bed and leaned against the pillow. She pushed herself up on her elbows to look at him.

"Oh here she comes. The Overly Pensive Marghe."

She laughed. "Thanks! F- you."

"You can say the word. Fuck."

"Ladies don't swear." He eyed her. She met his stare with feigned innocence.

"I'm going to make a tea. Do you want?"

"Umm…oui. What kind?"

"I don't know. Let's look."

She followed him into the kitchen and watched him open a cabinet. He pulled a tray of tea bags down. It was one of the few real things she had seen him do, an everyday kind of a thing, pull tea down from the cabinet. She thought how little she actually knew him, how nonsensical it was that she had such strong feelings for a stranger.

"Peppermint, lemon verbena, something cinnamon, something *awful* that is supposed to taste like licorice—"

"Oh, sold," she said.

He looked up at her. That half smile, that overlapped front tooth. She smiled at him flirtatiously.

"Lemon verbena, per favore," she said.

"Me too." He put water on to boil and came around the island to stand in front of her. He took both of her cheeks in his hands and kissed her.

"What if someone cheated on you?" He returned to the subject. She looked up, a little laugh under her breath.

"What if? You love a hypothetical don't you. Is that how you make all your decisions, with hypothetical answers?" she asked, inspecting the tea box.

"It's a way of speaking." He went back to the kettle.

"Awfully careful of you," she mocked.

"Honey?"

"Depends. Let me see your honey," she said.

They brought their tea back to bed.

"So you didn't answer my question," he said.

"Which one?" She sipped her tea carefully, leaning against the pillows.

"If someone cheated on you. Hypothetically."

"What's the question?"

"Well, what would you do?" he asked.

"It all depends, doesn't it? Who is it, do I love this person, etc, etc," she said, apathetically.

"Okay. Assuming it is someone you love, someone you are very much in love with. Would you care?"

"Yeah, I think so." She seemed to decide. "How could I not? Would you?"

She thought about Derek. They hadn't been dating long enough for her to feel heartsick over him, and she doubted that she would feel shred to pieces if she found out he was still dating. By using that logic, though, she had spent not much more than an evening with Nick before she had fallen hard and fast for him.

"You *think* so?"

"Well, I don't know. Look what I'm doing. I'm hardly one to talk," she said.

"Kind of sad, isn't it," he said, stirring a small spoon around inside his mug.

"What?"

"Cheating."

One of their first conversations crept into her head. She had asked him if he thought he would always cheat, and he had replied, "Anything's possible."

Maybe it just means we're in the wrong relationships, she thought. *If we're always cheating. God, I hope that's what it means. I hope that's all it is.*

She rested her head on the back of her hand, facing him. He placed his tea on the bedside table and pushed himself back down to horizontal, laying next to her on his side, his head resting on the back of his hand, as she did.

"Do you think…" he started.

"What?" She widened her eyes at him.

"Do you think you'll ever be able to trust? Considering…"

She raised her eyebrows. "Ooofa. Do you trust her? Considering…" she asked slowly, hesitantly.

"I don't know," he said. "I'm not really sure, actually."

She pursed her lips and shifted onto her back, looking up at the ceiling.

Then she sat up abruptly. "What time is it?" She reached for her phone on the bedside table.

She lay back down, head against the pillow, looking at her phone above her face. She turned on her Spotify and played "Passing Trains" by George FitzGerald.

"Did you ever want to be with any of those guys in Italy? The married men?"

She put her phone face down on the table again and turned to face him, gently running her nails along the inside of his forearm.

"No."

He waited for her to say more.

She waited for him to say something else.

She looked down at her fingers, slightly melancholy.

"Do you miss it?"

"Italy?"

"Yes."

"Loads," she said. "I miss my friends, my routine, my weekend adventures, the food, the people at my places-my cafès, my shops, my dry cleaner...the walk from my apartment to my espresso...The interesting encounters. The open-endedness of it. The distance from everything at home." She paused and adjusted her hair underneath the pillow.

"I miss the person who I was there. It sounds silly," She suddenly stopped.

"It's not silly."

She turned her head to face the ceiling again.

He reached his hand out and placed it gently on her rib cage, but she was already sitting up.

"I have to wake up so early tomorrow." She checked her phone again. "I should go." She took another sip from her tea. "Where's my top?" Her eyes scanned the floor.

I wish he would convince me to stay, she thought.

"Do you want to see the short film I made for film school?" He sat up.

"Sure," she said.

NEW YORK, NEW YORK

2019

CALLIE: HEY…I'M COMING back to the city early. The show was so lame. Caroline and I are on the train…we left the rest of them there. Dinner your place tonight?

Nick read the text in a panic. Callie wasn't due back until the next day. He looked up at Margherita, who had wandered over to a trash can at the end of the block to throw out their ice cream cups. She was in a light mood.

Shit. He thought they'd had a great two days together, and he reviewed them while he sat there with his phone in his hand, thinking what to do. Margherita had cooked dinner the night before—had wanted to, had shooed him out of the kitchen when he tried to help. Grilled fish with grilled vegetables and a big salad with lettuce from the Tompkins Square farmers market. She was a natural in the kitchen and evidently preferred to be sans sous-chef. He so enjoyed watching her, as he took on the role of DJ and chose the tracks for the evening. When he went to the store to buy a bottle of white wine, he'd asked the clerk for advice.

"Something really excellent. I am quenching the thirst of someone who knows the cheap stuff from the good stuff," he had said.

After dinner, they sat on the roof with the remainder of the bottle and a bag full of grapes and jelly beans (mixed by Margherita), listening to Paul Simon and random 80s hits. They had laughed endlessly, compared freckles, and shared opinions on the greatest movies of all time. She had shown him her curved pinky fingers, and admitted to feeling lonely sometimes in New York. He had tried to make her feel better by offering his perspective—that people start to go their own direction in their thirties, pair off and get married and have babies, and pretty soon they only see each other once every few months anyways.

"Yeah, well, at least they are paired off. That's built-in company," she said.

He looked at her sideways. She was lying on her back, looking up at the dark sky, empty wine glasses behind their heads. He was lying on his side, his head propped up on his hand, looking at her profile.

He wanted to say, *But you don't want a relationship.* She had made it so clear that she was scared of relationships, that she preferred situations that were defined, with four walls and four windows, and plenty of escape routes. He did not want to ruin the mood of the evening, though, and so he said nothing.

The next morning he woke to complete calm within himself. It was the first time Margherita had slept over. He watched her, lying next to him in his bed, her hair on the pillow, her face tipped the other direction toward the wall, her body in a loose S on his mattress. He had put his hand on the side of her rib cage and pulled her closer to him. She moaned a little, almost a whine, and she let him nestle her into his warmth. He wrapped his arm around her, held her hand, and breathed into her neck, happy.

And then his mind drifted to Callie—Callie who would be home the next day. Callie, who laid in his bed days before. Callie, whose longer torso nearly competed with his, whose body he had gotten used to and no longer gave him the same feeling of sheer contentment. He suddenly felt a wave of guilt, of shame. What was he doing? He would have to wash the sheets. He wasn't sure if she would notice, but what if she smelled something? What if she saw a long dark brown hair somewhere? He would have to vacuum.

Margherita stirred then. She sat up slowly, rubbed her eyes for a moment, shuffled to the end of the bed and walked to the bathroom. When she returned, she was more awake. She had brushed her teeth. She climbed on top of him and kissed him on the mouth, on the clavicle, on his chest. He moaned, definitely not a whine. Definitely a moan.

He shook himself back to the present.

There they were, having just had a vegan Van Leeuwen ice cream—they were both lactose intolerant—enjoying a lovely, lazy afternoon. He looked at his phone again as Margherita began the stroll back from the garbage can.

Nick: What time? I was going to swim.

He tried to think on his feet. Swim. Fuck. That was a dumb excuse. That would only take an hour, two max.

Callie: The train gets in in half hour. I can pick up some food...what do you want?

"Such a nice day," Margherita said, turning her face toward the sun. He put his phone back in his pocket as nonchalantly as possible.

"Yeah," he said, his thoughts racing. Margherita had a few things at his place didn't she? Or did she? He couldn't remember. Was there evidence that two people had cooked there the night before? Did he have clean sheets to put on the bed…shoot. He couldn't remember.

"You still want to go to the 4:30?" she asked, sitting down next to him on the bench, her face turned toward him. They had decided to see the new Bradley Cooper movie at the East Village Cinema.

"I um, I'm not sure." He had no idea how to maneuver the moment. They hadn't made any plan to separate for the remainder of the day, the evening, and now he somehow had to get rid of her. God, that sounded awful. He didn't want to *get rid of her*, but how could he send her away without upsetting her?

"What?" she asked, head tilted, eyebrows furrowed.

"Oh, gosh. I really want to. But I just got an email from Max. He bumped up a big presentation for a potential investor and now I am stressed out I don't have enough time to fine tune the presentation."

Fuck, he was a horrible person. He felt like an absolute asshole in that moment. Margherita's face had disappointment strewn across it as if she had chucked her ice cream cup on the sidewalk.

"Okay…but it's only Saturday. You can work on it tomorrow, right?"

"I can't work on it tomorrow. I have plans," he said, as gently as possible.

She nodded in slow motion, churned her jaw slightly and looked out in front of her, then to the right towards the avenue, away from him. What was she thinking. She was mad. He could feel the whole energy of the day shift in that second.

"I'm really sorry," he said. He wished he could explain it to her.

"That's fine. My bag is upstairs though."

"Okay. Totally fine. We can go back and get it," he said, trying to be light, as if nothing were out of the norm. Her face was stone, and she was not going to let a word slip. He could tell.

They rose from the bench and began a silent and awkward walk up First Avenue, toward his block. She didn't say a word and busied her eyes on the sidewalk in front of her, or the stores across the street.

"What are you going to do tonight?" he asked, in a somewhat feeble attempt at conversation.

"Oh, I don't know," she said, passive-aggressively.

At the top of the stairs he couldn't bear her silence any longer. When he opened the door, she went straight to the bedroom to get her bag and he followed her there.

"Callie is coming back early. That's what it is. I'm sorry. I didn't know what to say. She just texted me when we were getting ice cream. I wasn't expecting her until tomorrow." He felt he could go on, but didn't want to muddy things any more than necessary. She looked at him with angry eyes. Her eyes, and her pursed lips and tight jaw that told him she was having a thousand thoughts, but not sharing them.

"I'm really sorry," he said, sheepishly.

She began shaking her head. She took a step forward as if to leave the room.

"Marghe, please don't be mad."

"I'm not mad. I'm not. I feel a little dismissed…that's for sure. But I guess this is what I signed up for right. My decision." She said, falsely calm.

He didn't want to dismiss her. He didn't want her to feel dismissed. He reached out his hand to hers but she pulled her whole body backwards and skirted around him.

"I can't lie to her. She wants to come here. I can't tell her no—she won't understand why."

"Right. You can lie to me. Presentation bumped up. That's fine. Because I'm not your girlfriend. But actually aren't you lying to her in totality? By not telling her what you do when she's not around?"

"I'm sorry that I said that. It was stupid. I didn't know what to do in that moment. But I'm telling you the truth now."

She shook her head again. "I thought I had said to you that I don't want to do this if you only call me when your girlfriend is out of town. I hate this feeling. I am something to keep you entertained when she isn't here. Nothing more."

"That's not true at all!" Nicky exclaimed. "You turn it into something it's not. It's not as flimsy as you make it sound. You're not here purely for entertainment. It is not that at all. You can't be mad, Marghe, if I suddenly have to pivot my schedule. I've been clear from the start. I am not as free as you want me to be. I don't have the flexibility you expect me to have."

"Right," she said, tightly and controlled. The silence vibrated.

"It's not an easy situation."

"It's far easier for you, Nicky. You get two scoops."

"That's not fair. This is hugely difficult for me. You always make me out to be this jerk who thinks he is getting the best of both worlds, who thinks he is playing a game. That's not so, not so at all. That's not what is going on here. You don't seem to get it," he said, growing frustrated.

"Get what?"

He didn't have time for an argument. He needed to run around the apartment and make sure nothing had been left out, that her scent had not lingered, that there was nothing detectable.

"I don't want to do this anymore. I never wanted this, actually. This." She motioned between the two of them, to the space around her head, as if the gesticulation explained the situation and exasperation. She felt her blood growing hot.

"You've said that before. It's meaningless."

"You don't know me. You've seen me in one situation, a little game we constructed in our heads. We've never seen each other outside of it. Those five blocks were the first time we actually walked down a street together. Usually, it's just straight here to hide. And you know what—I thought that was fine. I really tried to talk myself into it all being fine, tried to tell myself that's all I wanted anyways. Whatever. This is pointless." She had been looking beyond him, and when she looked him in the eye, his face expressed simultaneous impatience and fatigue.

"I don't know where to begin. But fine, Marghe. You want to make it stop. Go ahead. I've never stopped you. I've never forced you to be here. You are free to do as you choose."

"Exactly, Nicky. This is either the longest game you've ever played and you simply don't care enough to tip the bucket, or you are a total coward."

"Maybe I am a coward. But it's more complicated than you make it. It's not so black and white."

"But that's your choice! To make it complicated. You can make it simple, but that wouldn't appeal to you."

He brought his hands to his head in exasperation and rubbed his forehead with the tips of his fingers.

"This is exhausting." He didn't look up.

She stood with her bag dangling from her hand.

"You are the one who goes hot and cold. Who turns on me. Who can't make up their mind. I never know which Marghe I'm getting from day to day. Can we not do this right now?"

She left the apartment and slammed the door behind her.

He felt the high of the past two days drain from his body. She tended to have that effect on him, to either fill him up or drain him completely. He decided to take a cold shower before scouring the apartment in preparation for Callie. He would write to Margherita in a few days after she cooled down. It was not over, no matter what she said. He knew she knew that. It was a form of torture that gave them both feelings of ecstasy and tumult. They were both addicted to it.

Over dinner that night, Nick eyed his phone at least a dozen times. Not a peep from Margherita.

Callie sat on the sofa going through her purse, something she did about once a week to clean it out. She always made a mess—tiny little things fell to the floor and never got picked up—receipts, hair pins, stray almonds.

"Oh my god, I almost forgot to tell you. Derek is dating someone."

"Really?" Nick asked, not having thought about his friend in what felt like a while. He had given up apologizing to him months earlier.

"Yeah. Grace told me…their families always go to Aspen

together. And she said her mom told her that his mom said he might be bringing a girl this year. A new girl..."

"Oh?"

"Apparently no one has met her. I think she's Italian? Or lived there? Grace said she's some sort of architect or designer or something. She didn't get her name or anything else so I can't Google. Have you heard anything?"

Nick was suddenly very nervous and curious. An Italian girl who was some sort of architect...could that be a coincidence?

"Do you know where she works?" he asked.

"No. All I got was that she grew up in Manhattan, she moved back from Italy, and she does something with boutique design or something."

Nick's heart raced.

NEW YORK, NEW YORK

2019

Nick: Can I talk to you?
Nick: Maybe we can have lunch at the caffè?

She didn't want to respond. She assumed he was going to tell her that he wasn't interested in seeing her anymore, which she already felt was quite clear. She was not going to step into that trap, into a final sting that would pierce whatever pride she had left.

That evening, as she walked down her block, her bladder about to explode, she noticed a figure sitting on the stoop. She was so nearsighted that it wasn't until she was within ten feet that she realized it was Nicky.

"You haven't responded," he said.

"What are you doing here?" she asked, moving to the side to let two dogs and their owner pass.

"I told you, I'd like to speak to you."

"Well, I am about to pee in my pants," she said. She'd just come from another materials meeting in Dumbo and hadn't wanted to use the warehouse bathroom.

He motioned towards the door with his eyebrows raised.

"Fine, come in for a second. But just a second," she said, rushing to put the key in the door, one knee skewed towards the other.

"Fuck, fuck, fuck," she said under her breath as she struggled to unlock her front door.

"You really do have to go," he said quietly.

When she emerged from the bathroom, she found him standing with his arms crossed in the middle of the studio, facing the door.

"Tell me the truth," he said.

"About…." she said, wearily, pushing her shoes towards the door.

"Are you seeing someone?"

She scrunched her eyebrows and eyed him carefully.

"As in, seriously. Seeing someone, seriously."

She sat down at the small vintage caffè table she had taken from her parents' disregarded furniture. She didn't say anything.

"Someone who plans to take you to Aspen."

Confused, she wondered, *How did he know Derek?* Her heart beat faster. Had he spoken to Derek? Did Derek know about Nicky?

I don't owe him anything, she thought. Out loud, she said, "What is going on?"

"Answer the question." He demanded, with more force.

"How do you know about Aspen?"

"Answer the goddamn question, Marghe."

She moved her head back ever so slightly. She had never seen Nick angry; it was mildly enlightening, even exciting, to see a side of him she hadn't been privy to before.

"Okay may I assume we are talking about Derek?" she asked calmly.

He rolled his eyes with impatience.

"I think it is reasonable for me to ask how you know him."

"We used to be friends," he shrugged.

Her eyebrows scrunched up. "When?"

"Ages ago," he said, vaguely.

"Do you still speak to him?"

"If you are seeing someone, why didn't you just say so?" he said. "I didn't peg you for such a sneak. Although, I shouldn't be surprised."

"A sneak? Okay, first of all, F you. I'm not being sneaky at all. I just didn't think I had to tell you," she said, defensively. "Do you still speak to him?"

"No. But that's not the point. You were always so judgmental, but look at you—you're doing the same thing I am," he said, walking a few steps into the kitchen and retrieving a water for himself from the cabinet. She looked at the bottle, and at him, as he returned to stand in the middle of the room.

She was about to say something and stopped herself.

"What?" he asked, holding tight to the unopened bottle.

She shook her head and shrugged.

"What?" he asked again. "You don't think it's a little hypocritical? Actually, it's worse isn't it? I didn't enter a relationship—a new one—knowing I was already involved in something complex. And continuing it! That feels so twisted."

"That's not fair. It's no different from you. It doesn't matter who came first," she shot back. "Why don't you speak to him anymore?"

He looked at her, pushing his palms into the water bottle. "Just feels different to me. You came along. I didn't go looking for you. You went looking for him. You were and always have been, and hey—maybe you still are—looking for guys. Always picking up someone new."

"Is that how you think of me? Out there picking up guys?" she asked, her arm gesturing towards the world at large. "Why can't you answer me? Why aren't you guys friends anymore?"

"Well…isn't that what you told me? That you date guys for a few weeks at a time, that you're always dating someone?" he challenged her.

Amazing the things that they never forget, she thought. *Why is he avoiding this question, though?*

"So are you judging me for dating? For being single and dating?"

"No. No. Not at all." He put the water bottle down on the caffè table. He glanced at the pile of neatly folded linens on her bed. She looked at them too. She felt on display.

"So…what?" she asked.

He didn't say anything.

"Was I supposed to not date? Just wait around for the odd encounter with Nicholas? Once in a while? Stay at home and wait for her to go out of town?"

Fuck what am I doing, she thought. *Shut up now.*

"Look," he said, exasperated. "You…you…you—appeared. You just appeared out of nowhere," he said, gesticulating. "And this thing grew, whether we wanted it to or not. But you started something fresh already knowing you were being deceitful. You were selfish from the start, knowing full-well. And I don't know, I don't know you very well, do I—maybe you knew I used to be friends with him. Maybe you found Derek on purpose," he said, in a throwing-guesses-in-the-air sort of way.

"I hope that is a joke."

He rubbed his eyes and forehead and turned to look out the window. There was a little preschool across the street. It was a darling view.

"I can't always be the secret. I don't want to always be someone's secret," she said softly.

He turned and sat down at the caffé table.

"I was very honest," she said. "Your favorite word. I told you I wanted something real, with someone who wanted me. And Derek does."

He guffawed under his breath. His nostrils flared.

"What?" she demanded.

"Derek is proving a point," he said, angrily.

"What?"

He shook his head.

"What the hell, Nicky."

He leaned his elbows into his knees and stared at the floor.

"Derek is a really good guy. I don't know how you know him, or from when, but he treats me well, and he is wonderful, and we enjoy each other. I haven't been mining for a boyfriend, but he came along—just like you came along— and he wants to be with me."

He guffawed again.

"Decisively," she added.

Which you never are, she thought.

"And suddenly you're decisive?" he asked.

"That's so unfair. This—*this*—situation made me indecisive. You're indecisiveness made me indecisive."

"And you were not going to end it? You were just going to carry on with this as you begin a new relationship with someone who treats you so well and is so wonderful? And you think he deserves that?"

"Whoa. Whoa. Relationship advice, from you? Are you serious?"

"Who are you kidding? You've never had a relationship. You're probably dating him to get back at me. And he's dating you to get back at Callie. And me. You don't even know how to be in a relationship. You don't know the first thing. Are you as capricious with him as you are with me? How long do you think that will last, Marghe? How long until he grows tired of your chaos? Not everyone has the patience for your games, you know, and whatever stories you tell yourself—your drama."

Her face wilted for a split second, and then suddenly her eyes were fierce and her eyebrows furrowed together and her forehead creased.

"That's a shit thing to say."

He fumed silently.

"Fuck you, Nicky. I don't know what you are even talking about—that he's getting back at you. And I don't want to know. You are truly the most self-serving, egocentric person I've ever had the pleasure of—"

"—Of fucking?" he interrupted her, hostility boiling out of him.

She regarded him with hurt. It was salt in the wound.

"I never want to hear from you again. I really mean it. You should leave," she said calmly, and she stood, expectantly.

"Jesus, Marghe, didn't he tell you about his last relationship? He's Callie's ex boyfriend. They were together, and she cheated on him with me," he blasted this at her shoulder blades as she walked defiantly away from him towards the door.

She stopped. She tilted her head upwards, appearing to be looking at the wall where it met the ceiling. She turned to face him, eyes confused, angry.

"And you are saying he is dating me as some sort of filler—to show you both that he is over it? Or to get back at her? At your goddamned precious girlfriend?"

He looked at her, his breath audibly coming from his nose, his jaw firmly shut.

"So I guess what you're saying is, he could have chosen anyone. He just needed a figurehead. So you think he doesn't actually want *me*..."

"Possibly."

"You are a horribly selfish person, Nicky. You think only of your own feelings. No one else's. I would hate to be your girlfriend. I wouldn't wish it on anyone."

"Fuck off," he snapped back.

"What do you want with me, Nicky?"

He looked at her, and his face belied nothing.

"You accuse me of wavering, of being indecisive. Well here is an absolute: you are a jerk. That is finally, permanently ingrained in me," she said, and opened the door for him to leave.

"Marghe."

Nobody actually wants me. Nobody actually wants to be with me, she thought.

She felt her tongue grow thick in the back of her mouth. She knew if she said another word her voice would break. She risked it.

"You need to leave."

NEW YORK, NEW YORK

2019

THE NEXT DAY after work, she walked the twenty or so blocks to Derek's apartment, biting the inside of her cheek— simultaneously repeating Nick's dismissal of her ability to be in a relationship and trying to erase it from memory. Between the two of them, they had created an irreversible mess, and she was not sure who was more to blame.

Her phone beeped and she frantically grabbed it from her bag, but it was just a message from Chiara in Florence. Not a peep from Nick.

At Derek's building, she said her cordial hellos to the doorman and rode the elevator to the penthouse, her limp body leaning against the mirror. At the top floor, she turned right and then another right. Her pace slowed and her heartbeat quickened. What would she say to him? How should she act? Would he see Nicky's words emblazoned all over her?

She turned the key in the door, the key that Derek had given her with such sweet and straightforward intentions, that sinless smile of his.

"So you can sleep here and go to the six a.m. class with me, or if you just want to come snuggle after work," he had said.

With every act of supreme decency, with every confession of purity, Derek became more peculiar to her, more off-putting, and in turn she felt more corrupt. When did he show foolishness or disorder? Unpredictability? It wasn't meanness she was searching for, and besides which, she was capable of feeling slighted by him without his participation. She felt it when he went a whole day or two without contacting her. She felt it in his lack of enamoredness. She felt the absence of smitten. Here she was, a girl addicted to the chase, the pursuit, the games, faced with a man who inadvertently gave her all of that in his sheer demeanor.

She walked into the apartment slowly. It was quiet, the lights were off, and the floor to ceiling automatic shades were lowered. There were two envelopes on the marble countertop, staggered so both return addresses were visible. On the table next to the door, she noticed he had left his portable charger and his AirPods, lined up next to the dish where he kept his keys. Down the hall, she opened the door to the bedroom, to triple-check he wasn't home, but all that met her was his perfectly-made bed and the layers of variously-sized pillows in their rotating shades of grey and slate blue. She couldn't believe that he was, or had been, friends with Nick. They seemed so different. Nick was bursting with life, with energy—truly the centerpoint of the room. Derek was so controlled.

On the terrace, she lay in a chaise lounge and covered herself with a thick cashmere blanket that he had brought back from a recent work trip to Switzerland. It was seven p.m., and she still hadn't heard a peep from him.

She must have fallen asleep because when she woke, he was standing at her side, looking down at her.

"Hi sleeping beauty." He leaned towards her to kiss her forehead. "You're cold—how long have you been out here?" He put his hands on her upper arms, squeezing her. Oh, the relief she felt in his warmth. She couldn't help but smile at him, achingly. Then she remembered what Nick had said.

"What time is it?" she yawned.

He checked his watch. "Nine. Are you hungry? Come inside; it's cold."

She raised her heavy body and left the blanket behind as he put his arm around her and led her inside, where he had turned the lights on and there was a take-out sushi bag on the counter. "I ordered take-away—I didn't know you would be here. What do you want? This is a random mix of nigiri if you want it, and I can order more."

She wasn't hungry. "Oh no, amore, you have it. I'll eat later." She found a cozy spot on the sofa, facing the television, her feet under her, as he unpacked the nigiri, folding the paper bag and placing it in his recycling bin under the sink.

"How was your day?" he asked the back of her head.

"Oh, it was fine. Took a looksie at new job postings. Just in case."

He joined her in the living area and sat down on the chair kitty corner to her, his nigiri on the coffee table before them. "I thought you were going to wait it out? Try to talk to Alexandre next time he's here?"

"Yeah. Well, just in case. Just to see."

"Jobs in New York, right? I can ask around a little, if you want?"

She pursed her lips into a gracious smile and watched him take his first bite—medium fatty tuna it looked like—from her favourite underground sushi spot in Tribeca. For her, it was the kind of place that had been a special treat once in a while—its pricey fish flown in daily from Japan— but to Derek, it was a go-to at least once a week.

"Can I ask you something?" she asked timidly, spinning her serpent ring.

He looked at her, waiting, and took another bite. Scorched salmon.

She looked at the ceiling. God, she hated being that girl. She was about to say something and then stopped herself.

He huffed with a smile. "What is it?"

She clenched her jaw and bit the inside of her cheek. "Why do you want to be with me?"

He immediately looked confused, enveloped in the serious expression that she found so endearing. His head cocked to the side, his eyebrows furled, and his lips sort of pouted. She imagined that if he ever ran for political office, that would be the look his face took on when he faced a serious debate question, and needed a moment to prepare his diplomatic answer.

"What is it that makes you want to be with me? I just feel…I don't know. I'm having a day. Humor me."

His expression had not changed, and it was making her nervous. He put his dinner down on the table and the tips of his fingers rested at the edge.

"I mean, I'm not sure if I'm the natural 'choice' if one is looking for a straight-laced, country club, five kids and PTA meetings kind of gal. And sometimes I get the sense that that's what you want, and I just wonder, but then why is he with me? Does he think that's me?"

He rested his elbows on his knees and pushed his forefingers into his jaw bone ever so slightly. He looked at her inquisitively.

"Mar—"

She wiped an errant tear as it dashed from her eye to her jawline. She felt another one in the other eye and used the back of her hand to wipe it away. She didn't know where it was coming from. Maybe it was Nicky's words festering. Maybe it was the fact that Nick hadn't said anything since. Maybe it was the expression on Derek's face—how he didn't seem to have the answer she was looking for, at the speed in which she was looking for it. He probably didn't have it at all. He probably never would.

He pushed his dinner out of the way and sat on the coffee table in front of her, placing his hands on her legs and rubbing them as if she were a crying baby. "Marghe, hey. Hey. Look at me. What's going on?"

He showed concern and sympathy in his eyes, he wanted to help her with her wound, but she could not tell if he was able to. She didn't say a word.

"Hey. First of all, that's not the kind of person I want to be with. And second, I'd have to have never met you to think you are that kind of woman."

"I just—I just wonder if it has anything to do with your ex-girlfriend. I don't even know her name. But, I know you were really hurt by what she did. And I can't help but wonder if..." she trailed off as his expression changed from concern to hardness.

"I'm not sure where you're going with this, but one has nothing to do with the other. What happened sucked—it completely sucked. And I learned a lot from it. But it's behind me."

They had barely spoken about his break-up. She let the subject alone, and it meant that they didn't bring up her past either. She knew he wouldn't like the sound of her previous relationships and was thankful to not have to explain herself. If she *had* told him, she felt that she likely wouldn't be sitting there with him that evening.

He put his hand under her chin and tilted it towards him. "Hey- look at me. What's going on in that head?"

She pushed her chin downwards and held her hands over his hands while they held her face. Derek's ability to soothe her, the comfort she felt in his arms, was perhaps her favorite part of being with him.

Nicky's embrace was different: it was duplicitous. He held his girlfriend in that way; he couldn't have it twice. There was something sordid and charlatan about it. Yet it was all she wanted from him.

"I'm going to get some water." She pushed herself up. Derek watched her, holding on to her hand until the last second as she walked away. She stood at the counter as she filled her glass with purified water (she had told him a thousand times that the city water was very clean but he still didn't trust it), and she watched him stare at his abandoned dinner on the table. She had alarmed him, she could feel it.

He stood up and joined her at the kitchen island. He sat in a bar stool and she went to stand in front of him. He looked into her green eyes, searching.

She looked down at his lap. "I think I've always wondered—why me?"

He pressed her hair behind her ear. "I never thought of you as the kind of person who needed that reassurance, so it never occurred to me to give it to you. Maybe that's my fault."

She shook her head with vehemence and grasped his large hand in hers. "No, no...no. I'm not. I'm not the kind of person who needs it. But it's different with you, I guess. I don't know why. I don't know."

She didn't want to say what she was thinking. She didn't want to make him doubt his feelings for her, nor could she possibly say *Your ex-friend Nick who fucked your ex-girlfriend, and is now fucking me, suggested that maybe you have a hidden agenda.*

What she wanted to say was that she never felt like he was really smitten with her, he never exuded any passion towards her, he never expressed that he was head over heels for her. But she didn't want to highlight that, and she didn't want him in turn to wonder the same—that perhaps she wasn't head over heels for him either. Derek wasn't the type to play head games or to pursue. He was too pragmatic, unsentimental, rational. She was the opposite, wasn't she? But she was tired of being alone all the time.

"Marghe, I want to be with you for all kinds of reasons. For big reasons and for small reasons. And for some medium reasons too."

He held her face in his hands and looked into her eyes. She could see that he did not know what to say. She couldn't tell if he was smoothing over a pothole that was sure to resurface many times down the road, or if he was merely tired and hungry and wanted to return to his sushi. She let it go. He enveloped her in a hug, wrapping his arms around her tightly, and there, with her chin tucked into Derek's shoulder, hearing the sound of his murmur, and smelling the scent of his spring breeze laundry detergent, she thought of Nicky. Nicky who knew exactly what she wanted to hear but probably would never say it. Nicky would never be able to give her an unblemished sense of security. Derek, on the other hand, would never be able to say the right thing, even if she fed him the words, because they weren't coming from the person she wanted to hear them from.

She slept at her own apartment that night but couldn't relax her mind. At three a.m. she rose out of bed and wandered down to the promenade overlooking the Lower Manhattan skyline. There was the square building, at the tip, sitting at an angle, where her mom worked in her late twenties. She was just a river's width away from it, from a version of Francine she never knew. Some days, the wind was so strong on Lower Manhattan, the building set up ropes for people to hold onto while they walked. Her mom had told her that once.

In her mother's dressing room, there was a photo of Francine sitting on that plaza. She was about Margherita's age at the time, wearing a floral blazer and skirt and smiling at the camera. Margherita felt her breath catch in the back of her throat. She wished she could have known her mom then. She hoped she was like Francine—tough, independent, brave. Her mom had spent her twenties and thirties surrounded by men. Margherita always assumed this was why her mother was so hard, why she could not give her daughter the softness and sensitivity she sometimes needed. Maybe this was why Margherita had such a hard time knowing which feelings were meant to be shared and which were meant to be caged; she hadn't really ever learned.

In the silence of her apartment, she typed out an email in an effort to close the door on the mess she had gotten herself into. She thought if she was honest for once, she might feel relieved. Maybe it would feel good to share.

Margherita:

Here goes.

You probably think I am a lot colder than I am. Frigid or something. Maybe I am a little cagey, like you say, but it's not because I am heartless and unfeeling. It's not because I am only interested in having affairs and secret sex and nothing more. To be honest, I feel quite tortured by all of this. I wish to the sky that I had never met you. I feel hopelessly buried in this thing. Maybe I was cagey because your interest is permanently circumscribed. Maybe I've been cold because I was afraid I might misunderstand where you were coming from. You see, I thought I was really good at protecting myself. I thought of it like a talent. And then with you, it became a farce, and I didn't know if I should try to build it back up again or just let it crumble, and you never said anything decisive to guide me.

Here is something I never told you. I wrote a note to you once, but I never sent it. I was too embarrassed. Or nervous. Do you know when the last time was that someone made me actually nervous? It is such a rarity for me. I know when it happens though, it will be hard to shake. You always made me nervous. Always. Every Time.

Here is the email I never sent. I'm not sure why I'm bothering now. I guess I just want you to know I am more than the version you saw. You are always saying how you hate to be judged. I hate to be judged too. And I think you judged me based on this maelstrom. I hate to think that, but it's too late now, I suppose. So anyway, here is what I had once wanted to say to you, but didn't...

———————————

I don't know why, but you are stuck in my head. You got stuck there when we met, when I heard your voice, your accent, I think. And you looked me in the eye, diagonally from across the high-top table, and I knew that I needed to talk to you before you left but I didn't know how, without seeming strange. You had finished your chicken. There was nothing but remains in front of you, and you had already forgotten that it was ever there to begin with.

Maybe it's that you were, and always have been, a mystery. I don't know you at all- that's how you want it; I assume. I don't know how you are, what you act like with other people, in certain situations, what you've been through, who you've been through. Has anyone been through you? I don't think so. Maybe that's all it is. Chemistry + Nothing to tang it up= Chemistry. It's a 1 + 0 kind of equation. And not much else.

So here I am- knotted up in something. It's unknown territory for me, and I don't know how it happened. I feel submerged, and I am frustrated. I don't know how to act, because I don't know you, and I don't know what you're up to, what your angle is, and you never say what you mean, in classic English fashion, you imply things but never say them, and I am left guessing at your vagueness. I don't know what you think of me or of this or if you feel anything at all, because you've never actually said. Such an evil sickness, that wanting. That stuckness. So I am tangled in something opaque and I can't get out, and I so badly wish you had finished your chicken sooner, and that you had already been done and gone, and that I wouldn't have had to hear your voice and meet your penetrating eyes, looking at me diagonally across the high top table.

But, strangely enough, if you had asked me again, what do I want to feel... Well, I would have said this-this strange, foreign feeling that shakes me upside down. You see, the truth is, I actually love this feeling. And if you had asked me again, what do I want...I would have said... you. Because, in this moment of bravery, I might as well come out with it- Well, the truth of all truths, is that there isn't anyone else I want to be with. It's true I like a little bit of drama and a little bit of a story, but the only scene I've been waiting for since the very start is the one where you tell me you want to be with me too. It would have been enough to tie me over, forevermore.

Please don't think you have to respond to this. In fact, please don't.

She sent the email, took a Xanax, and tried to sleep.

NEW YORK, NEW YORK

2019

THE BAR AT Il Buco was one of her safe havens in the city. It was reliably cozy and convivial and the team knew her well. It reminded her of Italy with its worn wood and its eclectic mix of painted ceramics. She sipped her wine and tried not to look at her phone, to just *be*. She was excited to see Noah. He was a newly married man.

"And how was wedding week?" she asked him once they had clinked glasses to his new life as someone's husband.

"It was really nice! We rented a house for everyone in the wedding party. That got a little complicated. But it was fun."

"Complicated how?"

"The meals. Everyone had a thing. For breakfast I had to go to the store three different times for three different types of Malk."

"Malk?"

"Like fake milk." He rolled his eyes.

"Oh LA," she sighed.

"It's so gross. Have you ever had it? I hate everything milk related."

"Don't say hate. Such a strong word."

"What should I say?"

"I don't know. Dislike. Abhor."

"Oh this is good. Cleanse my soul," Noah said seriously.

"Example: 'I have an aversion to Malk.' Or, for LA, 'I feel hostility towards the valley.'"

"I feel like a better human being already," Noah said as he clinked her glass.

"Good. Anyway so you rented a house and bought Malk and then what."

"Well it rained all day on the actual day, but we didn't care. Kara's dress got pretty wet. So did my suit. But whatever. We ate weed gummies all night afterwards and then Kara and I drove to Montecito and had a few nights to ourselves, which was much needed."

"Aw lovely, and what did you do?"

"We stayed in our hotel room and made love and ate ice cream in bed. It was perfect," he said happily.

"Aw you two! I am so happy for you, Noah," she said, a big smile on her face. She rubbed his upper arm tenderly. "I can't believe you are married!"

Noah nodded, smiling. "I know. I'm in love. I couldn't be happier."

Margherita had never seen Noah so content, so full. He was her dry-humored, always sarcastic, usually cynical friend, and at that moment she barely recognized him.

Before long, as he often did, Noah turned the subject back to Margherita. He was one of the few people in her life who genuinely wanted to know what was going on with her.

"How is- what's his name- Derek?"

"He's fine?" Margherita said, squishing her face into something between guilt and boredom.

"Already?!" Noah exclaimed.

"I don't know. I'm not entirely sure why he's with me and not Diane Von Furstenburg's granddaughter or something. I am really, really, really trying," she said, her palms holding the edge of the wood bar. "Had a little nervous breakdown with him recently but we are gliding on, Wasp-style."

"So you stopped seeing what's-his-face?"

She looked to her wine glass and raised it for a sip.

"Uh huh," Noah said.

"Derek is—" she stopped herself and looked around the restaurant to be sure she didn't know anyone there. "Derek is really sweet. I just don't feel the zaza."

"Sweet guys don't have zaza, unless you yourself are dull."

"Exactly. I have a hard time with the sweet guys. I don't want someone who gives in to me so easily. Someone too sweet. It's so...." she struggled to articulate her thoughts.

"Normal?"

"Ugh, you know. It's like there is no middle ground. They are either sweet and 'normal' or they're selfish, arrogant jerks."

"Maybe give the shy guys more of a chance. Maybe they need a few dates to build their courage around you. You are kind of intimidating—you know that, right?"

She rolled her eyes. "That is such a load of crap. What is so intimidating about me?" she asked rhetorically.

"Marghe, you literally part subway crowds. I've walked with you on a crowded subway platform. People literally stare at you and move to the side," he said dryly.

"Oh that's bullshit. People stare because I'm always alone."

Noah gave her a look of disbelief.

Their entrees arrived and he swirled a few strands of spaghetti around his fork. She did not touch her octopus; she was still wrapped up in the chaos of her own making.

"So how is your little friend?" Noah asked, ordering another glass of wine.

"Which one?" Her eye was toward the bartender, trying to help get his attention.

"You know which one."

"The same. Wolf in sheep's clothing."

"And we still don't know why he stays with his girlfriend."

"Besides the fact that he is a selfish bastard, no, we have no conclusive explanation," she said.

"Well, yes, that."

"I just don't get it. Cheat on your wife—okay. Marriage is complicated and long. But thirty-two, thirty-three, thirty-four-year-old guys cheating on a girlfriend of less than two years? What for? Just break up!"

"I agree. It's immature."

"Anyway, I'm pretty sure it's over. Think I've successfully ruined it. Well done me. I kept trying to separate it. To convince myself that, *Oh whatever, he's a jerk, look what he's doing, I don't want that for myself, and the sex is fun so just enjoy it.* Because I can't have sex with just anyone, believe it or not. I don't understand how people do that. I have to really like the person, or it won't be good, and I'll feel horrible afterwards," she said. Noah was the only straight man with whom she had ever maintained a genuine friendship and could discuss these things with. She knew he never had other goals in mind.

"That's true for many people. Think about the physical act. Penetrating someone. It's not a particularly becoming thing. It's about the connection with a person. When there is a genuine connection, then suddenly it's fireworks and all that," Noah said, his hands in the air, miming the act of fireworks exploding.

"Yeah. I just wish I didn't like him so much. I never like anyone. Ever. Why him?"

"Because it's safer. You can't have him," Noah said, twirling more spaghetti.

"Right. So isn't that messier—more risky?"

"No. Not for you. For you, messy and risky would be a real relationship," he said, looking straight at her.

Her forehead creased and she pursed her lips. *Humph,* she thought.

"So what are you going to do?"

"Nothing. I think I went crazy enough to dissuade him from even taking advantage of the extra sex. I sent him a heartfelt message a few weeks ago. Crickets. I feel like such an idiot. I can't remember the last time I felt so embarrassed and foolish."

"That's mean. It's mean to not respond to someone."

"I agree. F-ing acknowledge it. This has been going on for a while. You can't just ignore me. He is such a jerk. I don't know why I can't wrap my brain around that."

"That is the struggle, my friend. The truth is we just want to be loved. And when you feel the chemical connection, it washes out the negatives. It's hell. I'm sorry."

"Yeah. Me too. I need to get over him. I need to get out of it." She looked into her empty wine glass.

"Hi—can I do another?" she asked the bartender with a smile. "Grazie."

"And work? Your Meryl Streep boss?"

"Disaster. Ugh. What am I doing here?" She bowed her forehead into her hands and Noah patted her on the back.

NEW YORK, NEW YORK

2019

MARGHERITA LEFT HER yoga studio two blocks below Canal Street and headed west on White Street. She checked her phone: a message from her father (*heading home now. Love you.*), one from Benjamin (*Two meetings Friday in NY- have lunch free if you'd like?*) and one from Derek (*did you decide about Aspen next week? I need to book your ticket!*).

She shuddered and put her phone away. The pressure she felt from Derek's question was enough to undo the temporary calm she had accumulated at her vinyasa class. No message from Nick. Not a peep since she sent the email. She texted Benjamin back:

Margherita: Ciao…. Lunch Friday sounds good.
Please let me know if you plan to cancel though so
I don't get in trouble again with my boss :)

She wondered what she should do with herself for the rest of the evening. What she wanted was to be dolled up at the bar at Frenchette, with a dashing man on her left, a toss of her hair behind her shoulder, a gin and soda in front of her, and a glimmer of excitement in her blood. She looked at her phone again, though she knew that if he had texted, she would have heard it. At White and Church, she crossed over to the Roxy Hotel and decided to sit down for a few minutes with a tea at the sidewalk caffè. The sky was looking a little dark, but she wasn't ready to go home and sit by herself. She would send a voice message or two to Chiara.

NEW YORK, NEW YORK

2019

NICK TOOK THE elevator downstairs after his meeting for a little fresh air. It was going to be a late evening at the office and he hadn't stepped outside all day. He walked west on Canal and dipped down Cortlandt Alley. Maybe he would get a tea at the Australian caffè on Church Street a few blocks south. It reminded him of trips to Perth, where his mother was from. He looked up at the sky when he felt a raindrop, and saw ominous-looking clouds overhead. *Fuck it*, he thought, and walked on, quickening his step.

At the caffè, he exchanged a few pleasantries with the two young Aussie guys behind the bar and ordered a black tea. He thought of Margherita, of the big pot of lemon verbena they had drunk together while huddled over his laptop watching his amateur directorial debut. She had seemed to like it, complimenting the camera direction, the editing, and even the plot itself. She had made intriguing comments, asked him questions, encouraged him to dip his toes into film again in New York.

"Why not take a directing course at the New School? Or NYU? Just to mix in it again, just to feel close to it," she had said. He had shrugged. He didn't have time for that. When he showed it to Callie, she was distracted by her Instagram halfway through it.

He took out his phone as he emerged onto Church Street with his tea and opened a WhatsApp chat with Margherita. She was online, he could see. He closed out of the app. Then he opened it again, and he looked down at her name. What would he say though? He closed it again, and put the phone back in his pocket.

NEW YORK, NEW YORK

2019

ON THE SOFA in Jane's office, she picked at the cuticle on her left thumb. She had a habit of picking at her fingers on that sofa. It was not until she left that she noticed she had ruined a manicure and one finger was bleeding.

She had been telling Jane about the unanswered email.

"Why do I need his acknowledgement?" she questioned rhetorically.

"You were honest. It was brave," Jane said.

"I feel like an idiot. Like a flimsy, inconsequential idiot."

"Have you thought about telling Derek?"

"No! No. There is no reason for that. And besides, when being described to a third person, all it is is a guy cashing in on side-sex, and a dumb girl who gives in."

"Why is the girl dumb?"

"Do you see *him* writing an emotional letter?" Margherita quizzed sarcastically.

"So what? It doesn't boil down to his interpretation. He has a story; you have a story. He has a perspective; you have a perspective. Don't minimize yours based on assumptions of his. You are worthy of your own perspective," Jane said evenly.

Worthy, ugh, Margherita internally rolled her eyes.

"Yes I used the word *worthy*," Jane said.

NEW YORK, NEW YORK

2019

Nick: Hello
Nick: How are you

She stared at her phone, her heart beating fast.

"Are you having the polpo?" Tommaso asked his daughter. They sat at the bar at Upland in Flatiron. Margherita tried to extract Tommaso from his Carnegie Hill safety net whenever she could. "Marghe? Hello?"

"Yes, please!" she said, looking up at the waiter. She immediately looked down at her phone again with furrowed brows.

"What is it? Yulia?" Tommaso asked.

"No…no, it's nothing," Margherita said, and she slid her phone in her bag. "I'm just going to run to the ladies room."

Downstairs, past the lemons, she locked herself in a bathroom and took out her phone.

Margherita: You're going to ignore what I wrote, aren't you

Nick: I'm sorry.

Nick: I didn't mean to. I meant to respond.

Nick: I read it.

Nick: I was away

Nick: And had to delete it.

Ouch, she thought.

Margherita: That's nice

Nick: It's honest

Margherita: I do have feelings, you know.

Nick: I know that.

Nick: How are you?

She washed her hands and returned to the bar seat next to her father.

NEW YORK, NEW YORK

2019

MARGHERITA SAT ON one side of the large table in the glass conference room. There were windows on two sides and the sun caused her to squint at Yulia and Amy from Human Resources across the table. It was so wide, if they had all outstretched their arms toward each other, they wouldn't have reached.

"This allegation is absurd. I am speechless. I have been working for you for long enough for you to be a good judge of my character, and I would never do something like that."

"I disagree. There was Beck..." Yulia was determined to break Margherita. Amy glanced at the two- one then the other.

"That is absurd! This is ridiculous. Alexandre and I have known each other for a long time. He has been a friend to me, outside of this job, as much as I know you don't like to hear that."

"Okay let's keep this conversation calm..." Amy interjected.

"I think it is fair, at this point, to know why Margherita got this job in the first place. Why she left Milan," Yulia directed herself toward Amy as if Margherita was no longer able to speak for herself.

"Because I was qualified!" Margherita interjected.

"Excuse me. I am speaking to Amy."

"I do not think Margherita was hired for any other reason besides her qualifications so perhaps we should stick to the discussion at hand here," Amy said.

"Well, in that case, I have to disagree again. I believe her to be under-qualified. She has made numerous mistakes on important proofs. She constantly fails to confirm my meetings and appointments—"

"It's not my job to confirm your cellulite reducing treatments!"

Yulia sucked back a waft of glassy conference room air and regarded her as if she just been slapped.

"That is extremely inappropriate. I simply cannot work with this level of immaturity. And I refuse to work with a subordinate who sleeps her way to my job. Hasn't your mother taught you anything? Manners? Grace? Self-restraint? Principles?"

Margherita swallowed. She placed her hands on the chair handles and rose to her feet.

"You are pathetic." She grabbed her purse from the floor and wished the door wasn't one of those soft, quiet doors as she stormed out.

NEW YORK, NEW YORK

2019

Nick: Hello
Nick: I am sorry for being an ass.
Nick: I would like to see you.
Nick: I assume you to be very busy.

LATER THAT DAY, he wrote:

Nick: I read the Rose Yallo book that you recommended ages ago. You were right- spot on enjoyable. What's next
Nick: Margherita
Nick: Are you going to ignore me forever

NEW YORK, NEW YORK

2020

"Margherita. I spoke to Yulia. I seem to have reached an agreement with her," Alexandre said over the phone.

Margherita's heart raced.

"Okay...?"

"This is horrible to have to say. But I'm just going to be straight with you."

Nick watched her from the corner of Broome and Crosby Streets. Her palm swatted at her eyes and she turned her back to the street. One of her arms flung up wildly a few times. Then she rubbed her forehead with one hand and held the phone to her ear with the other, periodically wiping her face. Her head nodded a few times and she sunk down onto a step. Max stood next to him, on his phone, unaware of what had caught Nick's concentration.

"Alright man, he's pulling up now. Ready?" Max gestured toward the front door of the building. Nick nodded without registering fully, his feet stuck in place as Margherita dug in her bag for something, still crying, still on the phone. Who was she speaking with? He had never seen her cry. Certainly not with so much angst, so much upset, so much release, right there in front of the back entrance to Bloomingdale's. He wondered what was going on in her life. She had been ignoring him for a month, and then this.

Max's bellow interrupted his thoughts. "John, nice to meet you. Max, and this is my partner Nick." Nick turned his attention to the real estate broker about to show them an office space.

"Nice to meet you," he said, and he followed them into the building, leaving Margherita on the street.

Nick: How are you?

Silence

Nick: I saw you today
Nick: On Crosby
Nick: You were on the phone
Nick: Crying

Missed call Nick

Nick: Maybe you don't want to talk about it
Nick: Whatever it is
Nick: But I want you to know
Nick: I am here
Nick: Whenever
Nick: If ever
Nick: You do

Margherita lay on her side facing the wall. Her pillow was damp. She had left her apartment only twice in the previous 72 hours; once to walk to the supermarket for bananas and once to push the box of water delivered every month through her front door. She had taken approximately one shower and had not shared the news of her sudden unemployment neither with her father nor with Derek.

Nick: Is everything ok?

Margherita: I'm fine

Nick: okay
Nick: I am not sure I believe you
Nick: I wish you would pick up

Margherita: I'm fine really.

Nick: I wanted to go over to you but I wasn't alone
Nick: It was very hard not to
Nick: I just didn't know how to walk away from my meeting

Margherita: okay. It's fine. Goodnight

Nick: wait
Nick: Don't
Nick: Do that

NEW YORK, NEW YORK

2020

NICK WALKED DOWN Crosby Street toward Howard for lunch. Every time he went to the caffè where they had first met, he hoped to run into Margherita.

Up ahead of him, he was positive he saw the waves of Margherita's long hair as she turned the corner onto Crosby. Yes, it was definitely her, with those long chocolate waves. They were approaching each other—she coming from Howard, he coming from Grand.

"Hi," he said. She was caught off-guard; she had been looking at her phone from beneath her sunglasses.

He placed his hands on his hips, taking on an ironic smile.

"Thought that was you."

She didn't respond; she stood there holding her phone in her right palm.

"Have you eaten by chance? I was on my way to the caffè. If you'd like to join me. I know you are heading the other direction, but…" he motioned back towards Howard Street.

"I, um, I can't. I'm heading to a meeting."

"Oh. Okay," he said, waiting for her to say more.

She pursed her lips and began to move around him.

"Marghe," He pleaded.

"I really do have to go. I'm already late."

He gently reached for her arm. She was wearing a soft sweater—cashmere it felt like—and it was casually pushed up her forearms. It was an unseasonably warm afternoon and he too had left his coat in his office. He could feel her arm bone as he squeezed through the fabric.

"If you're already late what's one more minute?"

She bit her lower lip and looked down the sidewalk, beyond him, allowing him to hold her arm.

"Can you look at me?" He searched for her eyes beneath her sunglasses and gently pulled them away from her face before she could stop him. There they were, those floating emeralds soaked in honey, and she immediately looked away.

"Hey—don't." She reached for her sunglasses.

She looked tired. Her eyes were red and the circles underneath were poorly concealed.

"Just stop for a second. I have been trying to talk to you for what feels like decades."

She shrugged.

"Who were you on the phone with that day? When I saw you crying?"

She reached for her sunglasses but he kept them behind his back.

"Look. I have known you for, well, a while now, and when I saw you crying, so upset about something, I realized I know so little about all the things you don't talk about. You don't talk about so much. And it feels kind of shit. I want to be there for you."

"You can't be."

"Why not?"

"Because that is not the relationship that we have. Or had."

"What does that mean?"

"We don't do that. I don't really know you, not really, and you don't really know me. I know some of the songs you like, and you know some of the books I read. And that's the way we are. You've never wanted it any differently. Remember in the beginning? How I wanted to be your friend? And you didn't. You wanted an affair. Pent up energy. Secrets. Hiding. Mystery and deceit. Give them back. I have to go." She grabbed for her sunglasses.

He regarded her with a hint of aggravation, of hurt and betrayal, as if she had brought their dirty laundry out to Soho for everyone to see.

"You were confusing. It was either sex and role playing or something I couldn't give you, and nothing in-between."

"There's no such thing as in-between. Grow up." She grabbed her sunglasses with venom and started walking away.

He stood there, pissed off. She was irreconcilable. He didn't know how to give her what she wanted, especially after the muck they made of everything. He didn't know how to fix it.

He caught up to her and stepped in front of her again. "Marghe."

The tip of her nose had reddened. A crease in her forehead had appeared that wasn't there before.

"No. If you suddenly feel ashamed or regretful or grow a conscience, I'm happy for you. But I don't need to be involved in that reckoning. You can do that on your own."

"Marghe that—"

"Leave me alone, Nicky. I'm serious." Her voice was layered with imminent tears.

She tried to push past him but he wouldn't let her.

"I am not going to do that." He held her upper arms in his hands and looked straight in her sunglass-covered eyes. He felt her tension ease slightly and he cautiously removed his grip and put his hand on the back of her head, his thumb on her jawline. He removed her sunglasses again and looked into her glassy eyes. The emeralds were more green than he'd ever seen them. She cast her glance to the side and wiped her hand under her eyes.

He gave her an empty beat and waited for her to say something.

"I quit. Or I got fired. There was some sort of coup d'etat," she said, letting out a small smile in an attempt to ward off tears.

"What happened?"

"My boss accused me of something so ludicrous, so insulting... and now I am going to meet the CEO to resign—if that's what you can call it. It's all so f-ed up. And I can't re-sign the lease to my apartment without a job. And Derek asked me to move in with him and I broke up with him instead, because I am some sort of masochist," she said more quietly, almost to herself. "And I can't move home, because it's too sad to see my dad alone every day, using the washing machine for the first time in his life. Having Christmas burgers from the Monkey Bar just us two. My thirtieth birthday just us two, no walk around the reservoir with her. And I just want to talk to her. And ask her what to do." Her voice broke and she stopped herself short.

He pulled her toward him and held the back of her head. He rubbed her hair with his thumb while his heart raced.

"Marghe, you can talk to me. I'm here."

She pushed him away with both hands and caught her breath, sniffling.

"No. No." She shook her head, growing angry again. "You're not my boyfriend. You're not my friend. You've never been there—there as in, *there*. For me. I sent you that note—I've never done anything like that—and you ignored it completely. You *deleted* it. You were there for sex and nothing more."

"That's not true at all. I am your friend. I am."

She started to walk away again. He followed her and walked along next to her as she sped up and tried to outpace him.

"Marghe, I didn't know what to say. You wrote not to respond. I thought I was doing what you wanted. And I haven't heard from you, and I assumed you wanted me to leave you alone, like you always asked me to. And then I saw you crying, and I felt this...this...this.... *Crack* run through me. I felt it just open." He gesticulated with arms wide. "But you always push me away."

She shook her head while walking. At the corner she stopped and turned abruptly toward him.

"You can't do this to me anymore. I can't deal with it. I don't want to participate in this...this...this *crack*." She waved her arm in the air.

His face was hurt and his brows furrowed together slightly. He looked so sweet and genuinely concerned, and she hated his guts for it.

2020

"To love and not be loved in return leads to terrible states. Anger, jealousy, sadness, desperation," Alexandre had said to her. They had been in Paris for the re-opening. He had approached it as essentially a lover's rendezvous, when really her days were filled with appointments for the company's unveiling of the newly refurbished Left Bank boutique. She had felt somewhat suffocated by him, by his messages, by his heaviness. She had wanted to enjoy his company as a friend, as a mentor maybe, but he ruined it with a deadweight of leaden philosophizing. He could not simply *be*. He needed to talk, to talk about her, about the possibilities they could have together (as if), to pontificate and indulge his thoughts. It had been exhausting.

He had pronounced that in a little sliver of a restaurant in the Marais, where he had drank nearly a bottle and a half of wine himself, and she had spent half the evening silently wondering what his wife was like; did they ever have fun? She had her elbows on the table and her legs crossed under the white cloth. Her hands were clasped and she rested her chin on top of her knuckles, listening to him, thoughts elsewhere.

It was that trip that had instigated Yulia's ludicrous accusations. It was that evening when Alexandre had walked Margherita back to the hotel and given her a tight, drunken, midnight hug on the cobblestones, and one of Yulia's seven dwarfs in the office had happened to be returning at the same time and snapped a photo of them in what appeared to be a very romantic pose. She had put Alexandre in an impossible position, had essentially blackmailed him and placed Margherita in a horrible rat trap. In his defense, Alexandre made an effort to clear the situation, but Yulia was a shark. He made the best maneuver he could to save face for them both, though neither had truly done anything wrong; he gave Yulia the Paris promotion she was after and accepted a resignation from Margherita.

IN FLIGHT

2020

SHE FELT A timid tap on her arm. She turned away from the small oval window, where she had been entranced in the white nothingness in the sky.

"Would you like a water?" The flight attendant asked. She shook her head politely and turned her attention back to the window. A tear slid down her cheek. Flying always had that effect on her. There was something about staring out into the vastness. She always thought deeply in the sky, which was interesting, because shouldn't the thinner atmosphere make her feel lighter?

The letter Benjamin had given her was in her lap. She had taken it out of the envelope but hadn't unfolded it yet. She wasn't quite ready.

"Mom was so proud of you, you know that, right? She talked about you all the time, to all her friends too. 'Margherita is doing XYZ in Milan, Margherita met with so-and-so yesterday; Margherita is in Paris this week... She really was. Proud," Benjamin had said to her on a park bench overlooking the Jacqueline Kennedy Onassis Reservoir in Central Park.

Margherita looked confused and shook her head in

quiet disbelief. "She certainly never acted like it to me. I thought she stopped liking me, in the end," she mumbled. She felt a catch in her throat and swallowed a few times.

"Marghe, how ridiculous. She was really struggling—more than any of us knew. But she loved you. I think you reminded her of herself at your age. Fierce, independent, smart. Sometimes wicked."

"I don't feel so fierce anymore," she said, a tear rolling down her cheek.

"I think that's okay sometimes. You don't always have to be on the offensive in life. You'll see," he said, watching a little boy ride past on a scooter.

A smile crept onto his face.

"What?" Margherita asked, swiping an errant tear.

"Alice is pregnant."

"Oh, wow! Benjamin, that's amazing. Congratulations."

When will I ever—she began a thought.

"Here," he pulled an envelope from his jacket pocket and handed it to her. She recognized her mother's handwriting. *To my bambina* it said.

She looked up at him with glassy eyes.

"There was one for each of us. I've had yours. I'm sorry. I tried to give it to your dad to give to you; I didn't think I should be the one to give it to you. But he was adamant. I think…I think they thought it would bind us somehow, if I gave it to you," he said, and his eyes were suddenly glassy too. "Marghe, I know I'm not always around. But I'll always be your brother. And your friend. You can always call me, or come to London and stay with me. I'll always take you somewhere where there is octopus on the menu. You know that, right?"

NEW YORK, NEW YORK

2018

To my bambina,

I know this will be a difficult year for you, my beautiful girl, but it will get better. I promise you that. You will make good and exciting things happen for yourself, and I am always here for you when you need me. I can't be next to you, but I am here. I will always be here for you.

You bring so much joy into this world, and you always know how to make someone smile. You know the things that make you smile too, and you will do them. You will find more ways to make yourself smile. And more wonderful friends who make you smile too. You are so loved. We all love you. So much.

Please do what your dad says and follow your heart. Follow the sparkle. You know what it is. Don't let anyone stand in your way. Don't worry too much. Everything always has a way of working out. And nothing is forever if you don't want it to be.

Isabetta Andolini

I know you will do great things. Italy is waiting for you. A new beginning. I love you with all my heart, my bambina.

Love forever and per sempre,
Mommy

MILANO, LOMBARDIA

2020

SHE LANDED IN Milan and made a beeline for the train. She had done the walk dozens of times and did not need to read signs in the terminal. She took the elevator down one flight, bought a ticket, and waited for the next train to Stazione Centrale. On the train with her were other foreign travelers—Americans, Germans, a few French…tired from their flight and anxious to know that they were going in the right direction…she could see their question marks and excitement at what was to come on their vacation. She watched them as an outsider, relieved that she was not with anyone, that she did not have to speak to anyone for a while, at least until she met Chiara that evening.

At Centrale, she purchased a ticket on her phone for a train to Venice. She walked up one track and down another, admiring the station that she had been in perhaps a hundred times. She loved its open center and extraordinary architecture. It left her in awe every time, no matter how stressed she was to catch a train, no matter how much second hand smoke she was forced to inhale. She was forever a little bit in love with that station. The first time she had seen it was with her mom. She felt her throat close.

Isabetta Andolini

On the train to Venice, she let herself fall asleep. They passed miles and miles of flat farmland, not all of it very pretty, and then they were suddenly crossing water—the unmistakable entry into Venice's Santa Lucia station.

She instructed her Google map to guide her to Chiara's apartment which was across the city. She dragged her suitcase along the stones, up the steps, over the steps, up the steps, and over more steps, during the six p.m. rush hour. She walked narrow sidewalks along canals, traversed through crowds, and stopped to take only a handful of photos. She had never been very enamored of Venice. She was there for one reason, and one reason only—to mend in the company of a friend.

Of course, she would have loved to have been home in Milan, but there was something reassuring about being somewhere where she didn't know anyone, other than Chiara. She would be isolated in her own world in Venice, and she would be allowed to be numb and maybe to cry, and she would not be concerned about it in the slightest.

That evening, after a quick change, she and Chiara walked back towards the center to the casual enoteca her friend had chosen. It was dark by then, and the Venetians were either rushing home to dinner, or on their way to meet friends. Margherita followed Chiara like a little girl; her friend knew the maze like the back of her hand. Over canals, through a few neighborhoods, past churches and pasticcerie and fruttivendoli that were closing for the evening, until they came upon the enoteca and squeezed in next to a group of friends. They ordered a plate of hot items from the counter, along with two glasses of red wine, and sat down at a small wooden table against the wall. Margherita was tired from the jet lag and not that hungry, but she gladly ate the simply prepared vegetables and the octopus. Nobody did octopus or vegetables like the Italians, and she would never turn them down.

She was too tired to talk about all the reasons she had purchased her ticket within two days of the flight. She only wanted to listen to Chiara tell her about her dissertation, her meetings with her advisor, and her previous weekend with her beau. The gentleman was fifteen years older than Chiara, recently divorced and positively smitten with her. Margherita felt the tears burn in the backs of her eyes, and she stared down at the cooked greens in front of her and the last piece of grilled radicchio, and she couldn't fathom how she managed to eat any of it.

That night, she and Chiara made up the pull-out sofa bed. She put on multiple layers of pajamas; the apartment was cold and it seeped in through the windows. As she lay in bed, she contemplated writing to Nicky. She had not given Chiara the full story; she knew her friend would tsst-tsst her, and she knew what her opinions would be. Margherita also knew that she would never have Chiara's self-discipline. She turned her phone off so that she did not feel tempted to write and stared at the ceiling instead.

Maybe it was worse from the jet lag, but she felt hopelessly at sea in the mess she had made for herself. She knew it had to be over, and that was the feeling she had been dreading since the moment it began. There was nothing but the insufferable absence where he had been; that familiar crater where the adrenaline and excitement and potential adventure had circulated. It had formed when she left Italy, and it was gaping and huge like a crevice in the road and she didn't know how to push it back together or how to fill it.

When Nicky appeared, the hole seemed to fill, and it had fogged the feelings of missing Italy and thinking about Francine. She replaced her sadness with lustfulness and nervous energy. She hadn't felt so alone. She hated to think that he was the reason she felt put back together again. She hated to give him that credit. She hated to think that she couldn't do it alone.

So she needed to fill the damn hole again, and she wasn't sure how to do it, or with what. Certainly not with just one person, because that was risky. She needed to find multiple elements, interchangeable elements, so that she could breathe and wiggle in case she needed to, and she could become attached to more than one thing in case something came loose. She wasn't sure how to do that, though.

She thought of her mom, Francine. God, how badly she missed her mom. How badly she wanted to text her at that moment. She would have written *Hi mommy*, and Francine would have known she was needed.

She turned her phone on.

With tears running down her face she typed out a message.

Margherita: I have something to say to you.
Margherita: I have many things to say to you actually.

He came online and read the messages.

Margherita: I'm not sure where to begin.
Nick: Begin at the beginning.
Margherita: Can I ask you something first

Nick: Yes

Margherita: Why didn't you ever respond to my letter

He typed and stopped a few times. She bit the edge of her thumb nail.

Nick: Marghe I am really sorry. I was a selfish jerk. It was never anything you did, I want you to know that. The way I acted, wasn't because of what you ever did or said.

She sat silent.

Nick: I tried to keep what we were doing in a vacuum, with as few emotions as possible. I made you out to be a certain type of girl because it made it easier. To act in a certain way, to treat you in a certain way, to sleep at night. But you were never that girl.

Margherita: I think I made myself out to be that girl too.

Margherita: I'm not sure at what point we really know what type of girl or boy we really are.

He typed and stopped. Typed and stopped.

Nick: You are amazing. That's what you are.

She felt a lunge in her throat and tears fell from her eyes once again. She turned off her phone and shoved it under the pillow.

She thought about the conversation she had had with Alexandre the week before, when she had arrived with eyes still red after running into Nicky, and she and Alexandre had finalized her resignation.

"I was hoping you would say something magically wise," she had said in a corner booth at La Mercerie in Soho.

"To the fact that you are in love and running away from it as fast as you ran into it?" he asked, signing the bill.

"Who said I'm in love? I'm leaving the job...this is about the job. And your evil, wack-job employee Yulia," she had said.

He smirked and rolled his eyes. "I know you. I know when you're emotionally agitated. I know those red eyes aren't about jewelry. But listen kid. There is no wisdom in love. And you are that way. You run from things. It's okay. You're either afraid of someone getting to know you and not wanting to be with you, or you're afraid it might actually work out. You might actually find yourself in a relationship if you let yourself. But then you won't have to look for it anymore. And that would be a great loss. Because the search is the fuel of things, not the finding..."

She swallowed and bit the inside of her lip. Alexandre placed his long slender fingers on her small hand and leaned towards her.

"There is, for everyone, a love they will never get over. It could happen in kindergarten. That smack in the heart. Maybe in one's late fifties. But it lives on, a gentle but painful ache in the back of one's mind, an invasion of one's major organs. Don't fret, mon chere. C'est la vie," he said, and rose from his seat as she unhooked her bag from the arm of the chair.

"So did you buy a one way ticket?"

A FEW OF THE GREATS

'Sparring Partner' - PAOLO CONTE

'Meraviglioso' - DOMENICO MODUGNO

'Stasera... Che Sera' - MATIA BAZAR

'Via Con Me' - PAOLO CONTE

'Sapore di Sale' - GINO PAOLI

'Senza Fine' - GINO PAOLI

'Il Cielo in una Stanza' - MINA

'Un anno d'amore - MINA

'Non piangere Maria' - DOMENICO MODUGNO

'Love in Portofino' - FRED BUSCAGLIONE

'Il Mondo' - JIMMY FONTANA

'Un bacio è troppo poco' - MINA

'Nessuno' - MINA

'Amore Disperato' - NADA

'Dio come ti amo' - DOMENICO MODUGNO

'Another Day of Sun' - MINA

'A far l'amore comincia tu' - RAFFAELLA CARRÀ

'Tintarella di Luna' - MINA

CPSIA information can be obtained
at www.ICGtesting.com
Printed in the USA
LVHW031057180821
695524LV00002B/65